Killer Books

Berkley Prime Crime Books

By Jean Swanson & Dean James

By a Woman's Hand
By A Woman's Hand, Second Edition
Killer Books

Jean Swanson and Dean James

Killer Books

A Reader's Guide to
Exploring the Popular World
of Mystery and Suspense

BERKLEY PRIME CRIME, NEW YORK

Killer Books
A Berkley Prime Crime Book / published by arrangement with the authors

Printing History
Berkley Prime Crime edition / April 1998

The Penguin Putnam Inc. World Wide Web site address is
http://www.penguinputnam.com

ISBN: 0-425-16218-4

Berkley Prime Crime Books are published
by The Berkley Publishing Group,
a member of Penguin Putnam Inc.,
375 Hudson Street, New York, New York 10014.

The name BERKLEY PRIME CRIME and the BERKLEY PRIME CRIME
design are trademarks belonging to Berkley Publishing Corporation.

PRINTED IN THE UNITED STATES OF AMERICA

10   9   8   7   6   5   4   3

For Martha Farrington,
sine qua non

Acknowledgments

From Jean: Thanks to my husband, Jim Thompson, for all his help with the entries, not to mention help with editing and computers and other items too numerous to mention. Thanks to David Thompson and Sandi Richey for help in getting books I needed.

Thank you to the University of Redlands and especially Dean Philip Glotzbach and Library Director Klaus Musmann, for supporting my request for a sabbatical leave. I planned, researched, and wrote a fair amount of this book while on leave from the university. It was a great help, and a wonderful experience as well.

And I'd like to thank Earlene Fowler, Terry West, Bruce Engelfried, and Megan Bladen-Blinkoff for helping me think through some of the ideas for organizing this book. And of course agent extraordinaire Nancy Yost and editor Natalee Rosenstein, who were, as always, patient, supportive, and understanding.

From Dean: I'd like to echo Jean's thanks to Nancy Yost and Natalee Rosenstein. Writers couldn't have two better advocates in their corner! Thanks for everything—and that's an understatement.

Thanks to my mother, Ruth, for all the things she does to help make the writing process go much more smoothly.

A special thanks to Edith Brown, for her help with information on certain authors and for many other favors that have made life easier during the writing of this book! Another special thanks to David Thompson (a.k.a. my little brother) for annoying the heck out of me for no good reason and putting his passion for movies and television to such good use.

Big hugs all around to my family at Murder by the Book, who make work such a pleasure: Megan Bladen-Blinkoff, David Thompson, Barbara Douglas, Angela Miller, Wick Rowland, Rabun Bistline, Cindy Patton, and Cathy Monholland.

Finally, thanks to Elizabeth Foxwell for lots of cheery E-mail, constant encouragement, and unfailing good humor. How could I start my mornings without you?

Contents

Private Eyes 131

Legal Thrillers 183

Romantic Suspense 209

Capers and Criminals 223

Reporters, Writers, and Filmmakers 241

Amateur Sleuths 257

Sci Fi/Horror/Fantasy Mysteries 323

Indexes 335

Foreword

Most of us enjoy a mystery. All of this century it has been one of the best-loved types of story. There are whole bookshops that sell nothing else and do it superbly, knowing their customers and their tastes so well they become like clubs, little islands from the bustle of everyday life where one can always find friends of like mind.

But there are "So many books, so little time!" What kind of mystery or thriller do you like best? Police procedurals? Private eyes? Hard-boiled or "soft-boiled" (i.e., "cosy")? Do you like your sleuths old or young? Male or female? Or do you even like them with fur, claws, feathers etc.? Do you want to laugh or cry, think about something serious, learn something new, travel in place or time? Do you want to laugh?

Or perhaps you haven't really decided what you want?

In any of these cases you could use the services of a guide who has wandered all these paths not only with expertise but also with love. Jean Swanson and Dean James are just such people. In *Killer Books* they have written about all the categories and given a thumbnail outline of the career and style of all the principal authors, and some of their most outstanding characters and works. In a very few words they have given an idea of the flavor captured, the setting, and that writer's best gifts, whether they be the art of creating suspense, the exploration of the darkest sides of known experience, the vividness of setting and atmosphere, the charm and reality of character, a sense of humor or wit, originality, expertise in some exotic skill or locality, or raising the questions of morality and compassion.

If you already know whose work you like, then this guide will offer you the names of other writers whose books possess similar qualities. If you are an explorer, then this will take you into *terra incognita,* to the places you will find fun and interesting while helping you to avoid wasting time, and possibly money, traveling where it is not your taste. And with so many books in the world, which of us wishes to waste precious reading time in an area that has not the treasures we seek?

Perhaps someone has recommended a book or an author to you, and you are not certain if you really wish to read it. *Killer Books* will help you to make a rapid assessment of their style, and perhaps liken them to others you may already know, without taking the time—and facing the temptation—of going out to a bookstore to find the actual book.

Or if you are in a generous mood, maybe you are looking for a gift for others. You know them and their tastes, and would like to learn who else writes in the vein of their favorite author, and therefore would be most likely to please them. There are comparative lists to help you. For example, if you are looking for African-American detectives, Scotland Yard detectives, or gardening mysteries, there's a list for you.

Every writer and all shades and colors of the great wealth of mystery, crime, and suspense novels are addressed and described with insight and appreciation.

Welcome to the world of exploration. "Beyond this place there be dragons"—believe me, wonderful, bright, exciting dragons, beasts of the imagination full of terror and excitement, color, drama, tragedy, compassion, and wit.

Take this map and enjoy yourself!

Anne Perry

Introduction

Mysteries have been a part of English and American literature since the 1840s, when Edgar Allan Poe first published his "tales of ratiocination." In these stories, Poe set down some of the conventions of detective fiction that are still followed by many writers more than one hundred and fifty years later. It was not until the 1860s, however, that novels of mystery and intrigue began appearing, from the pens of English writers such as Wilkie Collins and Mary Elizabeth Braddon. They were followed in the 1870s by a best-selling American writer, Anna Katharine Green, who is little known these days. Short stories flourished during the latter half of the nineteenth century, and without doubt, the most popular writer of mystery stories in that period and in the early twentieth century was Sir Arthur Conan Doyle, creator of Sherlock Holmes.

Sherlock Holmes was the first of the "great detectives" to seize the popular imagination. With the success of Holmes, naturally other writers began to create detectives, and the mystery short story flourished. But by the end of World War I, the popularity of the short story began to wane somewhat, and in the 1920s and 1930s, the mystery novel became very popular, thanks to writers such as Agatha Christie, Margery Allingham, and Dorothy L. Sayers in England and Dashiell Hammett, S. S. Van Dine, and Erle Stanley Gardner in America. The mystery story was a favorite form of escape literature in the English language and has been ever since, and mystery stories soon took their place in popular mythology. Who hasn't heard of Sherlock Holmes, for example?

This book is an attempt to offer a guidebook to the reader of mysteries and escape literature. Any reader who has come to the end of a favorite series of books and been left wondering "What do I read next?" will find this book useful. We have grouped the writers together in different categories, each one representing a particular genre of mystery novel. For example, those who have either read the best-selling novel *The Silence of the Lambs* or seen the Academy Award–winning movie can consult that section of the book to find other novels of suspense to keep them up late at night—after checking, of course, that all the doors and windows are secure!

Throughout the book we use various terms that might need some explanation for the casual reader of mystery fiction. *Cozy* or *traditional mystery* refers to the type of murder story that follows comfortably in the tradition of Agatha Christie: little explicit violence, an enclosed setting (like an English country house during a blizzard or a university English department), and a limited cast of characters, usually all known to one another. *Hard-boiled* refers to stories in which there might be explicit violence and lots of action, but chiefly the term indicates a mood, a connection to what Raymond Chandler called the "mean streets." *Psychological* suspense novels might be those in which the emphasis is more on *whydunit* than on *whodunit*, as in the novels of Ruth Rendell or Minette Walters. A *thriller* or *suspense* novel can be defined as a story that keeps the reader turning the pages to find out what's going to happen next, with the emphasis on how it's going to turn out, rather than simply on *whodunit*. The *police procedural* can follow the patterns of many of the previous types of mysteries, but generally procedurals rely on the routines of police activity to answer the vital questions of whodunit, whydunit, and howdunit.

Obviously a guidebook to mystery fiction has to be selective; otherwise it would be thousands of pages long and cost hundreds of dollars. Therefore we have had to leave out descriptions of the work of some fine writers in various categories who, had we the space and time, might have been included here. Each of the categories contains profiles of some classic writers in the genre, but the majority of the profiles are devoted to contemporary practitioners. In addition to the profiles, we have given suggestions for similar series or authors where appropriate, as we did in *By a Woman's Hand*, our guidebook to mystery fiction by contemporary women writers. We have also tried to supply lists of television series and movies in the style of the particular genre in each section, as well as lists of other authors readers might seek out for similar reading.

Finally, a note on the many awards we mention throughout the text. Here's a quick guide to the awards:

1. The Edgar—named for Edgar Allan Poe, this award is given in numerous categories by the members of Mystery Writers of America. It is a peer award, decided chiefly by committee. MWA also has named some eminent mystery writers Grand Masters.

2. The Daggers—these are awarded by the Crime Writers' Association in Great Britain in various categories; the Gold and

Silver Daggers are given to the top two mystery novels, and Gold Daggers are awarded in other categories as well. This is another peer award. The Crime Writers' Association also gives the John Creasey Award for Best First Novel.

3. The Agathas—these are fan awards, given in four categories, from the members of the Malice Domestic mystery convention, which is held every spring in the Washington, D.C. area. Malice Domestic is devoted to the traditional mystery, and books that win these awards fall into that genre.

4. The Anthonys—another fan award, the Anthony is given in numerous categories by attendees at the Bouchercon, the World Mystery Convention, held in the fall in a different location each year. Bouchercon celebrates all genres of the mystery novel.

5. The Macavity—a third fan award, the Macavity is given by the members of Mystery Readers International, and sponsored by the *Mystery Readers Journal*, edited by Janet Rudolph.

6. The Arthur Ellis Awards—these are peer awards, given by the Crime Writers of Canada, in numerous categories.

7. The Shamus Awards—another group of peer awards, given by the Private Eye Writers of America. Awards in this category of course are limited to novels and stories in the private eye genre.

Though we have said it before, it perhaps bears repeating: "So many books, so little time." There are hundreds of mysteries published every year, and hundreds of mystery writers working very hard to entertain us all. Perhaps this guidebook will help you find some of the writers who have eluded you up to this point, and you'll find some good books that will keep you up late into the night, take you back into the past, or off to a foreign country you've always wanted to visit. Enjoy the journey!

Jean Swanson and Dean James

List of Authors Included

Cops
Calling Scotland Yard

Jo Bannister

M. C. Beaton

W. J. Burley

Gwendoline Butler

Deborah Crombie

Clare Curzon

Colin Dexter

Peter Dickinson

Marjorie Eccles

Anthea Fraser

Elizabeth George

Caroline Graham

Ann Granger

Martha Grimes

Cynthia Harrod-Eagles

John Harvey

Reginald Hill

Michael Innes

Bill James

P. D. James

Peter Lovesey

Ngaio Marsh

Jill McGown

William McIlvanney

Jennie Melville

Patricia Moyes

Janet Neel

Ellis Peters

Joyce Porter

Sheila Radley

Ian Rankin

Ruth Rendell

Peter Robinson
Dorothy Simpson
Susannah Stacey
Jill Staynes
Margaret Storey
Josephine Tey
June Thomson
Peter Turnbull
R. D. Wingfield

Hill Street Blues

Thomas Adcock
Eleanor Taylor Bland
James Lee Burke
Michael Connelly
K. C. Constantine
Susan Rogers Cooper
Bill Crider
Susan Dunlap
Lesley Egan
Katherine V. Forrest
Paula Gosling
Jean Hager
Nancy Herndon
Lynn S. Hightower
Tony Hillerman
Chester Himes
J. A. Jance
Stuart M. Kaminsky

Faye Kellerman
Laurie R. King
M. D. Lake
David Lindsey
Elizabeth Linington
Margaret Maron
Francine Mathews
Archer Mayor
Ed McBain
Carol O'Connell
Lillian O'Donnell
Barbara Paul
Ridley Pearson
Dell Shannon
Julie Smith
Marilyn Wallace
Joseph Wambaugh
Charles Willeford
Mark Richard Zubro

From Foreign Shores

Jon Cleary
Michael Dibdin
Nicholas Freeling
Bartholomew Gill
Batya Gur
Stuart M. Kaminsky
H. R. F. Keating
Donna Leon
Paul Mann

William Marshall
James McClure
Magdalen Nabb
Medora Sale
Georges Simenon
Maj Sjowall and Per
    Wahloo
Arthur W. Upfield
Janwillem Van de Wetering
Eric Wright
L. R. Wright

Suspense/Psychological
The Silence of the Lambs

John Camp
Mary Higgins Clark
Thomas H. Cook
Patricia Cornwell
Dorothy Salisbury Davis
Jeffery Deaver
James Ellroy
Dick Francis
James W. Hall
Thomas Harris
Jack Harvey
Jonathan Kellerman
Judith Kelman
Margaret Millar
Abigail Padgett

James Patterson
Ridley Pearson
Ruth Rendell
Lawrence Sanders
John Sandford
Barbara Vine
Robert W. Walker
Marilyn Wallace
Minette Walters
Randy Wayne White
Stephen White
David Wiltse
Stuart Woods
Margaret Yorke

Historical Mysteries
Once Upon a Crime

Bruce Alexander
Stephanie Barron
Bernard Bastable
George Baxt
Emily Brightwell
John Dickson Carr
Michael Clynes
Max Allan Collins
Lindsey Davis
P. C. Doherty
Carole Nelson Douglas
Ann Dukthas

Carola Dunn

Elizabeth Eyre

Margaret Frazer

C. L. Grace

Robert Lee Hall

Paul Harding

Stuart M. Kaminsky

Philip Kerr

Laurie R. King

Kate Kingsbury

Peter Lovesey

Edward Marston

Maan Meyers

Miriam Grace Monfredo

Sharan Newman

Robin Paige

Michael Pearce

Anne Perry

Elizabeth Peters

Ellis Peters

Candace M. Robb

Lynda S. Robinson

Elliott Roosevelt

Kate Ross

Walter Satterthwait

Steven Saylor

Kate Sedley

Troy Soos

Leonard Tourney

Robert Van Gulik

Private Eyes

The Maltese Falcon

Linda Barnes

Lawrence Block

Rick Boyer

Robert Campbell

Raymond Chandler

Carol Higgins Clark

Liza Cody

Max Allan Collins

Peter Corris

Philip R. Craig

Robert Crais

Bill Crider

James Crumley

Janet Dawson

Marele Day

Jerome Doolittle

Arthur Conan Doyle

Sarah Dunant

John Dunning

Jack Early

Earl W. Emerson

Howard Engel

Loren D. Estleman

Janet Evanovich

Kinky Friedman

Joe Gores

Sue Grafton

Stephen Greenleaf

Parnell Hall

Dashiell Hammett

Joseph Hansen

Gar Anthony Haywood

Jeremiah Healy

Stuart M. Kaminsky

Jon Katz

Karen Kijewski

John Lutz

John D. MacDonald

Ross Macdonald

Val McDermid

Walter Mosley

Marcia Muller

Sara Paretsky

Robert B. Parker

Bill Pronzini

Les Roberts

Walter Satterthwait

Sandra Scoppettone

Roger L. Simon

Mickey Spillane

Dana Stabenow

Richard Stevenson

Rex Stout

Doug J. Swanson

Kathy Hogan Trocheck

Jonathan Valin

Valerie Wilson Wesley

Kate Wilhelm

Mary Wings

Don Winslow

Steven Womack

Legal Thrillers

Perry Mason for the Defense

Jay Brandon

Sarah Caudwell

Warwick Downing

Philip Friedman

Frances Fyfield

Erle Stanley Gardner

John Grisham

J. P. Hailey

Michael A. Kahn

John T. Lescroart

Margaret Maron

Steve Martini

Lia Matera

M. R. D. Meek

John Mortimer

Michael Nava

Perri O'Shaughnessy

Barbara Parker

Richard North Patterson

Manuel Ramos

Nancy Taylor Rosenberg

Lisa Scottoline

William G. Tapply

Scott Turow
Judith Van Gieson
Carolyn Wheat
Kate Wilhelm
Sara Woods

Romantic Suspense
The Road to Manderley

Eileen Dreyer
Daphne Du Maurier
Mignon G. Eberhart
Tami Hoag
Victoria Holt
Velda Johnston
Jayne Ann Krentz
Caroline Llewellyn
Barbara Michaels
Mary Roberts Rinehart
Nora Roberts
Mary Stewart
Phyllis A. Whitney
Sherryl Woods

Capers and Criminals
The Usual Suspects

Oliver Bleeck
Lawrence Block
Anthony Bruno
Liza Cody
James Ellroy

Carl Hiaasen
George V. Higgins
Patricia Highsmith
Elmore Leonard
A. E. Maxwell
Thomas Perry
Richard Stark
Ross Thomas
Jim Thompson
Andrew H. Vachss
Donald E. Westlake
Charles Willeford
Don Winslow

Reporters, Writers, and Filmmakers
The Front Page

Gerry Boyle
Edna Buchanan
Jan Burke
Susan Conant
Susan Rogers Cooper
Barbara D'Amato
David Handler
Carolyn G. Hart
Sparkle Hayter
Wendy Hornsby
Val McDermid
Gregory McDonald
John Riggs

Betty Rowlands
Sarah Shankman
Mary Willis Walker
R. D. Zimmerman

Amateur Sleuths
Nancy, Frank, and Joe Grow Up

Jeff Abbott
Deborah Adams
Susan Wittig Albert
Nevada Barr
Gail Bowen
Lilian Jackson Braun
Jill Churchill
Harlan Coben
Susan Rogers Cooper
Alisa Craig
Bill Crider
Amanda Cross
Mary Daheim
Diane Mott Davidson
R. B. Dominic
Carole Nelson Douglas
Aaron Elkins
Earlene Fowler
Jane Haddam
Jean Hager
Charlaine Harris
Carolyn G. Hart

Ellen Hart
Joan Hess
Susan Isaacs
Harry Kemelman
M. D. Lake
Jane Langton
Emma Lathen
Charlotte MacLeod
Sharyn McCrumb
Annette Meyers
B. J. Oliphant
Katherine Hall Page
Orania Papazoglou
Elizabeth Peters
Nancy Pickard
Craig Rice
Mary Roberts Rinehart
Lawrence Sanders
Phoebe Atwood Taylor
Alice Tilton
Margaret Truman
Mark Richard Zubro

Murder, She Wrote

Margot Arnold
M. C. Beaton
D. B. Borton
Heron Carvic
Hampton Charles
Agatha Christie

Joyce Christmas
Hamilton Crane
Anne George
Dorothy Gilman
Gallagher Gray
Carolyn G. Hart
Gar Anthony Haywood
Sherry Lewis
Stefanie Matteson
Ralph McInerny
Sister Carol Anne O'Marie
Monica Quill
Elliott Roosevelt
Corinne Holt Sawyer
Elizabeth Daniels Squire

The Butler Did It

Margery Allingham
Marian Babson
Robert Barnard
E. C. Bentley
Simon Brett
Dorothy Cannell
John Dickson Carr
Kate Charles
Agatha Christie
Edmund Crispin
Peter Dickinson
Carter Dickson
E. X. Ferrars

Jonathan Gash
Georgette Heyer
Susan Moody
C. F. Roe
Jennifer Rowe
Dorothy L. Sayers
John Sherwood
Patricia Wentworth

Sci-Fi/Horror/Fantasy Mysteries
The X-Files

Isaac Asimov
George C. Chesbro
Glen Cook
P. N. Elrod
Laurell K. Hamilton
Simon Hawke
Lynn S. Hightower
Barry Hughart
Katherine Kurtz and
    Deborah Turner Harris
Mercedes Lackey
Terry Pratchett
J. D. Robb
William Shatner

Cops

Television shows that have camera teams following around real cops as they track down criminals or stop speeding cars on the highways have their counterparts in mystery novels. Shows such as *Cops* and *Real Stories of the Highway Patrol* come from the tradition of what is known as the police procedural. The police procedural tells us how cops work every day, in the station house and on the streets, to solve crimes. It shows us the realities of daily stress, of teams working to investigate a major homicide, and of the toll that crime takes on the families of cops and of crime victims. *Hill Street Blues*, that celebration of the work of a whole station house, was one variation on a theme often used by mystery writers such as Ed McBain and Joseph Wambaugh. Several of Wambaugh's groundbreaking and best-selling novels were made into popular movies such as *The Onion Field* and *The New Centurions*. The police procedural has been popular since the 1950s, and its roots owe much to the comic book adventures of Dick Tracy, *noir* movie thrillers such as *He Walked by Night*, and perhaps most of all to the weekly exploits of Sergeant Joe Friday and the LAPD officers of *Dragnet*. Authors in other countries also have written powerfully realistic novels about their own police forces, including British writers such as Reginald Hill and John Harvey, Georges Simenon in France, and the Swedish team of Maj Sjowall and Per Wahloo.

Calling Scotland Yard: British Police Stories

Tales of the adventures of British bobbies and constables have been popular since Victorian times. They have traditionally been less hard-edged than American police stories, and have concentrated more on the exploits of an individual detective. There has been a long tradition of stories about the Scotland Yard detective called in to solve a murder in a country house. This stereotype found its way into numerous plays and movies in the 1930s and '40s (such as J. B. Priestley's *An Inspector Calls*), and it was satirized later by such films as *Sleuth* and *Deathtrap* and by quite a few Monty Python sketches.

It's only been in recent years that British writers have turned to writing hard-edged police dramas in their mysteries. The "new wave" of hard-boiled British writers includes such authors as John Harvey, Ian Rankin, and William McIlvanney. Increasingly, British authors have also branched out into the countryside, setting their mysteries in strongly evoked regional settings such as Scotland, Yorkshire, and the urban areas of Manchester, Nottingham, and Birmingham. Many of these books reflect the contemporary violence of Britain's inner cities and the often difficult economic and social realities of the postwar, post-Empire United Kingdom. But British writers also continue to write popular novels about such classic characters as the Scotland Yard inspector or the village bobby.

Bannister, Jo • A former journalist, Bannister is currently writing a series of police procedurals with a trio of major characters. Inspector Liz Graham has been brought in, by an old friend, to the Castlemere CID to help out an understaffed force. The old friend who has requested her aid is Detective Chief Inspector Frank Shapiro. He needs Liz Graham because of the recent death of his right-hand man. The third member of this intriguing trio is the Irish detective sergeant Cal Donovan, a bit of a rogue cop intent on going his own way most of the time. The three first appear together in *A Bleeding of Innocents* (St. Martin's Press, 1993). Each of the three is an outsider in her or his own way, but together they manage to work very effectively. Bannister writes tightly crafted plots and creates strong and interesting characters. She has also written thrillers, such as *The Mason Codex* (Doubleday, 1988), and an earlier series about amateur sleuth Clio Rees Marsh, who first appeared in *Striving with Gods* (Doubleday, 1984).

Beaton, M. C. • Marion Chesney, who has written many historical romances under her own name and several pseudonyms, also writes mysteries under the name of M. C. Beaton. Her first series of mysteries are unusual police procedurals: witty, light, and full of eccentric characters. The novels are

British cozies with an endearing Gaelic twist. The hero is Hamish Macbeth, constable of the small village of Lochdubh in northwestern Scotland. In his role as village bobby, Hamish sometimes acts deliberately stupid, and he uses the stereotype of the lazy Highlander to his advantage in dealing with suspects (especially snobbish English visitors). Hamish is also a crofter in the community, and so he knows the characters and the idiosyncracies of the villagers only too well. Some of the Hamish Macbeth novels were filmed for British television, and were shown later on American TV.

Beaton's second series features Agatha Raisin, a hard-hearted businesswoman who retires to a cottage in the Cotswolds and finds more than she had bargained for, what with bodies turning up regularly, not to mention the attractive but elusive gentleman next door. All of Beaton's novels combine gentle comedy and memorable rural settings with the traditional British mystery format.

Burley, W. J. • A former engineer and schoolmaster, Burley turned to writing crime fiction in 1966 and has done so full-time since 1974. Though he has written two series as well as some suspense novels, Burley is best known as the creator of Superintendent Charles Wycliffe of the West Country CID. A loving father and husband, Wycliffe is a quiet and compassionate man. Interested in people, Wycliffe does his best to learn as much as he can about anyone involved in the case on which he is working. In human behavior, usually, lies the chief clues to any case, he believes. The early books in the series often involve the murders of promiscuous young woman, though Burley avoids prurience, despite the subject matter. Later books in the series vary the approach and the type of murder victim, with great success. In all the books, the setting, chiefly Cornwall, is a lovely ingredient, and Burley makes good use of the area. First in the series is *Three-Toed Pussy* (Gollancz, 1968; later republished as *Wycliffe and Three-Toed Pussy*). One of the best in the series is the recent *Wycliffe and the Dead Flautist* (St. Martin's, 1992). The series has been televised in England but has not yet appeared in the United States.

Butler, **Gwendoline/Melville, Jennie** • Butler was a pioneer in the genre by being one of the first women to write a series about a woman police officer, under her pseudonym of Jennie Melville. She created policewoman Charmian Daniels, born and reared in Scotland but working in Deerham Hills, near London. Later she is promoted to a high position, working in London, but living in or near Windsor, as the series progresses. First in the series is *Come Home and Be Killed* (London House and Maxwell, 1964).

As Butler, she began writing mysteries, most of which featured Inspector Winter and his sergeant, John Coffin; the first is *Dead in a Row* (Geoffrey Bles, 1957). Then Coffin became the main character in a long series of novels, through the mid-1970s. Butler took a break from mystery writing during the late 1970s, then returned to both series in the 1980s.

Both Charmian Daniels and John Coffin are intelligent, intense, and curious about their fellow human beings. Whether writing as Butler or Melville, the author has a style quite different from any of her peers. She creates a chilling sense of unease unlike anyone else, except perhaps Ruth Rendell or Minette Walters. The murderer's presence is eerily tangible throughout each novel, like a goblin hovering on the periphery of vision. Readers looking for an unusual variation on the traditional English mystery will find Butler worth a visit. Readers should check the library and used bookstores for some of these books.

Crombie, Deborah • Though she is a native Texan, Crombie sets her mysteries in England, following somewhat in the footsteps of fellow Americans Elizabeth George, Martha Grimes, and Kate Charles. Crombie's main characters are Superintendent Duncan Kincaid and Detective Sergeant Gemma James of Scotland Yard. Kincaid, in his mid thirties, is a little younger than most men of his rank, but his intelligence and skill in his job have brought him early promotion. Gemma James is a young, divorced mother of a toddler, Toby; she is bright, sometimes impulsive, but altogether an appealing character. Kincaid is cast in the mold of the sensitive, thinking detective, like Adam Dalgliesh and Thomas Lynley, but Kincaid is not constantly riven by soul-wrenching angst, as are his peers. The first appearance of Kincaid and James is in *A Share in Death* (Scribner, 1993), which was nominated for the Agatha Award for Best First Novel. Subsequent books in the series show Crombie developing considerable skill in characterization and atmosphere, making her an ever more distinctive voice in the field of the contemporary English mystery.

Curzon, Clare • After writing a series of mysteries in the 1960s under the name of Rhona Petrie, Curzon turned away from crime for a while, until the publication of *A Leaven of Malice* (Collins Crime Club, 1979). Eight Curzon novels were published in England before the ninth, *Three-Core Lead* (Doubleday, 1990), was published in the United States. Most of the Curzon novels feature the Thames Valley Serious Crimes Squad under the direction of Detective Superintendent Mike Yeadings. Yeadings much of the time is the central character in this series, but in true police procedural fashion, Curzon aims her spotlight on various members of the team, such as Detective Inspector Angus Mott, Yeadings's right-hand man, throughout the books. Curzon weaves authentic details of ordinary police procedure into her tales, which feature solid plotting and engaging series characters as well. Curzon's world of the Thames Valley Serious Crimes Squad is very much contemporary England, but occasionally there are echoes of the England of the classic detective novel. Curzon's work is an effective and entertaining blend of both, as demonstrated in the recent *Close Quarters* (St. Martin's Press, 1997). Readers should check the library and used bookstores for some of these works.

Dexter, Colin • Thanks to the series *Mystery!* on PBS and to reruns on the Arts & Entertainment Channel, Dexter's creation Chief Inspector Morse, portrayed by actor John Thaw, has become one of the most popular of television's crime-solvers. The enigmatic Morse, fond of his beer, crossword puzzles, the poetry of A. E. Housman, and of music (chiefly Wagner), has intrigued readers for more than twenty years now. The setting for the series is the city of Oxford and its environs. Morse first appears in *Last Bus to Woodstock* (St. Martin's Press, 1975), where, aided by the long-suffering Sergeant Lewis, he solves the brutal murder of a schoolgirl. Dexter delights in creating puzzles that hark back to the

Golden Age of the mystery novel. He presents red herrings with all the aplomb of Agatha Christie, merrily misdirecting the reader. Morse, however, is not so easily misled, unlike poor Sergeant Lewis. Morse teases Lewis, though he listens to his subordinate's ideas. Morse can be testy with Lewis, but he is obviously fond of him, as the series progresses. Dexter has won numerous awards for these books, including the Gold Dagger for *The Wench Is Dead* (St. Martin's Press, 1990) and *The Way Through the Woods* (Crown, 1993). The most recent book in the series, rumored to be the last, is *Death Is Now My Neighbor* (Crown, 1997); here, for the very first time, Dexter reveals Morse's first name. Dexter's legions of fans, of course, hope that this is truly not Morse's swan song.

Dickinson, Peter • See the section "The Butler Did It."

Eccles, Marjorie • Eccles wrote a number of romance novels in her native England before turning to a life of crime, and the mystery lover's gain may well be the romance world's loss. Her series features Detective Chief Inspector Gil Mayo, a Yorkshireman now transplanted farther south. In the first of the series, *Cast a Cold Eye* (Doubleday, 1988), Mayo investigates the death of a prominent architect. Eccles demonstrates a quietly effective hand with both plot and character. The focus in each novel is the cast of characters whom the murder most directly affects; Mayo and his supporting cast from the police are developed slowly as the series progresses. Working within the classic traditions of the British mystery, Eccles takes an old form and makes it both contemporary and entertaining. A standout in the series is *More Deaths Than One* (Doubleday,

1991), which puts Eccles on a par with such favorites as Dorothy Simpson and June Thomson. Readers should check the library and used bookstores for some of these works.

Fraser, Anthea • She began her writing career with short stories and had her first novel published in 1970, going in turn from romantic fiction to paranormal fiction to crime fiction. With *A Necessary End* (Walker, 1986) and *A Shroud for Delilah* (Doubleday, 1986) Fraser commenced a series of police detective mysteries starring Inspector David Webb. The viewpoint of several of the early novels is a young woman character, different in each book, of course, but nevertheless similar in some respects. Often estranged from her husband or family, the young woman is in a vulnerable position in which murder threatens. In the more recent books, however, Fraser has shifted toward the telling of her stories mostly from the viewpoint of Webb, and this has added considerable strength and variety to her plotting. With *The Nine Bright Shiners* (Doubleday, 1988) Fraser began taking her titles from the old folk tune "Green Grow the Rushes-O." One of the strongest in the series is *Six Proud Walkers* (Doubleday, 1989). Fraser's work falls well within the conventions of the contemporary British police procedural—engaging characters, deftly constructed plots, and regional English setting. Readers should check the library and used bookstores for most of these books.

George, Elizabeth • Although Elizabeth George lives in Southern California, she writes classic mysteries set in Great Britain. Her first novel was *A Great Deliverance* (Bantam, 1988), which won both the Anthony and the Agatha Awards for Best First Novel. She has created an unforgettable group of continuing characters: Scotland Yard Inspector Thomas Lynley, the eighth earl of Asherton; his feisty working-class partner, Sergeant Barbara Havers; forensic pathologist Simon Allcourt-St. James and his wife Deborah, a photographer; and Lady Helen Clyde, St. James's laboratory assistant. The central characters, except Barbara, have all known each other for years, and the novels not only follow the dark and puzzling murder cases they investigate but also recount the ongoing dramas and conflicts of their personal lives. However, in *Deception on His Mind* (Bantam, 1997), Barbara Havers takes center stage. Although recovering from injuries, she helps to investigate a murder in a seaside town rife with bigotry, racism, and religious animosity. All of George's novels in this excellent series are complex and psychologically intense narratives, with vividly described backdrops.

Graham, Caroline • With her first novel published in the United States, the Agatha-nominated *The Killings at Badger's Drift* (Adler & Adler, 1988), Graham quickly became a favorite among English mystery fans. Her traditional style harks back to the Golden Age classics, but her subject matter and the frank treatment she gives it make her work thoroughly contemporary. Those who love the work of James and Rendell will appreciate the psychological acuity with which Graham delineates her characters and the flashes of wit with which she leavens the mixture. Her detective, Chief Inspector Barnaby, is a likable and intelligent figure. In *Death of a Hollow Man* (Morrow, 1990) the author uses her own experience with theater and television to construct a complex and engaging story. Graham's third novel, the funny *Murder at Madingley Grange* (Morrow, 1991), offers a contemporary twist on the classic country-house scenario. In the recent *Written in Blood* (Morrow, 1995), she is at the top of her witty and wonderful form. Powerful and compelling at her best, Graham is a fine voice in the English mystery tradition.

Granger, Ann • Like her heroine, Meredith Mitchell, Granger has worked in the British diplomatic service in various parts of the world. Mitchell is back in England, living and working in London, when she attends the wedding of a cousin's daughter in the first of the series, *Say It with Poison* (St. Martin's Press, 1991). The wedding proves a good occasion for murder, and Meredith finds herself involved in the case, along with an attractive Cotswolds policeman, Chief Inspector Alan Markby. In subsequent books Meredith is usually visiting in the Cotswolds when she finds her growing relationship with Markby continually strained by murder. Fans of the traditional English mystery will find an able practitioner in Granger, who handles characters, plots, and settings with skill.

Grimes, Martha • American fans of the traditional English mystery greeted Grimes's debut novel, *The Man with a Load of Mischief* (Little, Brown, 1981), with a warm reception. Grimes's next two novels, *The Old Fox Deceiv'd* (Little, Brown, 1982) and *The Anodyne Necklace* (Little, Brown, 1983), followed in much the same vein, Agatha Christie and Dorothy L. Sayers blended with the early P. D. James. Subsequent books began to take on something of a different flavor and demonstrated, perhaps, the cross-breeding of an American, albeit a devout Anglophile, writing the traditional British mystery. Grimes's moodiness and flair for the eccentric have made her chief characters, the policeman Richard Jury and the aristocrat Melrose Plant, an unusual and somewhat unlikely duo. Grimes is also possessed of a wicked sense of humor, which surfaces in many of the books, perhaps most notably in *I Am the Only Running Footman* (Little, Brown, 1986), with the creation of the Warboys family, a dangerously inept crew running a country pub. In *The Horse You Came In On* (Knopf, 1993), Grimes aims her guns at literary theft with humorously entertaining results. But the intensity of her plots and the emotional appeal of her characters have made Grimes a great favorite with the American reading public, who have put her onto the best-seller lists. The titles of all the Jury books are taken from the names of English pubs.

Harrod-Eagles, Cynthia • The prolific Harrod-Eagles penned more than thirty historical and fantasy novels before turning to the crime novel with *Orchestrated Death* (Scribner, 1992), which introduced London policeman Bill Slider. Slider is a detective inspector, and he is content with his rank, though his wife keeps nagging him to work for promotion. Promotion, however, would take Slider away from the work of detection into the world of administration, and he fights against it, though it could cost him his marriage. In *Orchestrated Death* Slider is investigating the case of a murdered female, left naked and unidentifiable, the only clues at the scene a priceless Stradivarius and a giant can of olive oil. From this Harrod-Eagles fashions a complex and engaging police procedural novel. Later books in the series build on this strong foundation, developing the relationships between Slider and other characters, and Harrod-Eagles's wicked wit stays rapier sharp throughout.

Harvey, John • Harvey's crime novels feature Nottingham detective inspector Charlie Resnick in a British version of the classic hard-boiled police procedural. Resnick is from a Polish family, but he was born and brought up in the industrial English Midlands. Resnick is divorced and owns four cats, and he loves to listen to classic jazz; drink strong coffee; and eat large, sloppy sandwiches, which inevitably drip onto his shabby clothing. He is a distinctly lonely man, and a thread of melancholy runs strongly through him. In the series, Resnick is the featured player surrounded by a continuing cast of detectives and police constables. Harvey creates strongly realized Nottingham settings, and Resnick's cases involve him with the modern urban ills of violence, unemployment, and racial hatred. There are usually at least two threads in each novel: the crime under investigation, and a crisis in the life of one of the detectives. Harvey creates well-realized secondary characters in the detectives and constables, and in the criminals they pursue. The books are infused with Resnick's love for jazz, and the local color is authentic and gripping. Harvey's depiction of urban ills conveys a longing for the days when cities were not so unlivable, and so full of violent youths, the hopeless unemployed, and decaying industrial buildings. First in the series is *Lonely Hearts* (Holt, 1989).

Hill, Reginald • Once a schoolmaster and college lecturer, Hill has since 1981 been a full-time writer. Though he has written various types of fiction, Hill is best known as the creator of a police procedural series, set in Yorkshire, featuring the duo of Dalziel and Pascoe. Superintendent Andrew Dalziel (pronounced Dee-*ell*), known as "Fat Andy" to friends and enemies alike, is coarse, ribald, and unpolitically correct before it was chic to be so. Sergeant (later Inspector) Peter Pascoe is university-educated and sensitive—some, including Dalziel, would say "too sensitive" on occasion for the job he has to do. Other important characters in the series are Ellie Soper, later Pascoe's wife, first introduced in *An Advancement of Learning* (Collins, 1971; Countryman Press, 1985), and Sergeant Wield in *A Pinch of Snuff* (Harper, 1978). Ellie Soper is a staunch feminist who often finds her politics in opposition to the necessities of her husband's job, and Wield is a closeted gay man who lives in fear that his secret will be discovered, at least in the early books in the series. Though at times Dalziel can seem like he has no redeeming qualities, he is complex and not easily categorized. Pascoe, too, seems to be typical of a "bleeding heart" liberal in a conservative-type job, but there are interesting nuances to his character as well. The strength and depth of Hill's characterizations, the intricate structure of his plots, and his never-failing sense of humor have made him one of the standouts of the English detective novel. He received the Gold Dagger for *Bones and Silence* (Delacorte, 1990) and the Diamond Dagger for Lifetime Achievement in 1995.

Innes, Michael • Innes is the pseudonym of J. I. M. Stewart, who was born in Scotland and became a noted Oxford professor of literature. He wrote many sophisticated academic and literary mysteries as Michael Innes, as well as some mainstream novels that were published under his own name. Innes's mysteries are sharply witty, bright, and amusing. Most of them feature John Appleby, a police inspector whose career flourishes throughout the series. Appleby rises through the ranks to end up as the Commissioner of the Metropolitan Police, and he receives a knighthood. He meets his wife, the aristocratic and eccentric sculptor Judith Raven, in *Appleby's End* (Dodd, 1945). She sometimes helps him in his detection and, when murder occurs among the rich and elite, she often provides an entrée for him to snoop about their country houses. Innes packs each book full of literary quotations and strange doings in the English countryside, and peoples his books with peculiar aristocrats, quixotic Oxford dons, and bohemian artists. Odd things happen in Innes's mysteries, but readers are having so much fun with the puns and allusions that it seems perfectly normal when the plot turns are whimsical and unorthodox in these very English mysteries. Innes creates a wonderfully eccentric world in which Appleby amuses the reader while solving intricate criminal puzzles.

Innes wrote several books with minor series characters, including Charles Honeybath, an elderly portrait painter, and Hildebert Braunkopf, an art dealer. Innes's books may often be found in used bookstores and in libraries.

James, Bill • James writes of a society rapidly breaking down, and the police who are the ostensible heroes of his books are just as prone to corruption as the criminals they chase. Unlike the policemen who are the heroes of writers such as Colin Dexter and P. D. James, the cops in Bill James's procedurals have been deeply affected by the world in which they live and work. The two chief characters in this series are Assistant Chief Constable

Desmond Iles and Chief Superintendent Colin Harpur. Their first appearance is in *You'd Better Believe It* (Countryman/Foul Play, 1985). The mood is bleak in this series, and the characters are pessimistic. Justice may prevail in some fashion, but it is not the notion of justice always familiar to the readers of more upbeat procedural series. Bill James is one of a group of contemporary British crime writers, such as Ian Rankin, John Harvey, and William McIlvanney, who have a far different view of contemporary society than do many of their peers in the field. In addition to the Harpur and Iles series, James has written under the names of David Craig and James Tucker (his real name).

James, P. D. • In private life, this renowned British mystery writer is Phyllis Dorothy White, but the queen has awarded her a life peerage as Baroness James of Holland Park, and she now sits in the House of Lords. James is considered by many critics and readers to be one of the top crime writers of her generation, and many of her best-selling books have been turned into successful television miniseries, with Roy Marsden in the lead role. In most of her mysteries, the hero is Commander Adam Dalgliesh of the Metropolitan Police. The usual trademarks of the Dalgliesh novels are acutely observed characters, a looming atmosphere of menace, accurate medical details, and a loving attention to architecture and design in the settings. Dalgliesh is known for his exactitude and objectivity, and for being a published poet as well as a Scotland Yard detective. He first appears in *Cover Her Face* (Scribner, 1966).

Well before the modern trend in female private eyes began, James wrote a mystery with a fascinating woman private eye character, Cordelia Gray. Cordelia has been trained as a private investigator by Bernie Pryde, who commits suicide at the beginning of *An Unsuitable Job for a Woman* (Scribner, 1972), leaving Cordelia his agency and his gun. In this and subsequent novels, Cordelia is less confident and controlled a detective than Dalgliesh, but she is a fine detective nonetheless.

James also has written nonseries books, including suspense and science fiction novels. She is known for her extensive use of literary quotations and symbolism as well as for her adroit plotting. Her elegant prose and psychological intensity make her works notable among crime novels.

Authors of Classics Featuring Scotland Yard Inspectors

Christianna Brand (the Inspector Cockrill series); Freeman Wills Crofts; Michael Gilbert (the Petrella series); Alan Hunter; J. J. Marric (the Gideon series).

Lovesey, Peter • After many years of writing historical mysteries, Lovesey turned to the contemporary crime novel with *The Last Detective* (Doubleday, 1991), which subsequently won the Anthony Award for Best Novel. This book introduced Bath police detective Peter Diamond. This Diamond is definitely a "diamond in the rough," for he finds it difficult to get along with his superiors, despite his abilities as a detective. Indeed, by the end of *The Last Detective* he is off the force, and in the second novel, *Diamond Solitaire* (Mysterious Press, 1992), he is working as a security guard in Harrods. When he fails to spot an intruder in the store—a mute Japanese child hiding in the furniture department—he loses even this job. To salvage the situation—and his own self-respect—Diamond goes to work to find out just who the little girl is. Will he ever get back his job in the CID? The answer lies in the third and fourth books in the series, *The Summons* (Mysterious Press, 1995) and *Bloodhounds* (Mysterious Press, 1996). These novels won consecutive Silver Dagger Awards. With this top-notch contemporary crime series, Lovesey is one of the outstanding writers in the genre.

For Lovesey's numerous historical mysteries, see the section "Once Upon a Crime."

Marsh, Ngaio • Though she was born and reared in New Zealand, Marsh came to be known as one of the great English mystery writers of the first Golden Age, thanks to her enduring creation, Inspector Roderick Alleyn of Scotland Yard. She was living in England, though, at the time she decided to pen her first detective story, which was subsequently published as *A Man Lay Dead* (Bles, 1934; Sheridan, 1942). Thus began a writing career that spanned nearly fifty years. Roderick Alleyn, with his upper-class background and education, offered a distinct difference from many of the Scotland Yard men featured in detective stories of the time, and his urbanity and quiet wit soon made him a favorite with readers in both England and America. Marsh had once intended to become a painter, not a writer, and this was perhaps the inspiration for the creation of Agatha Troy, the painter who becomes Alleyn's wife after their meeting in *Artists in Crime* (Furman, 1938). Marsh's love for, and experience in, the theater are also in evidence in some of her best work, such as *Killer Dolphin* (Little, Brown, 1966) and *Light Thickens* (Little, Brown, 1982), her last book. She featured her native New Zealand to great effect in such books as *Died in the Wool* (Little, Brown, 1945) and *Photo Finish* (Little, Brown, 1980). Sparkling dialogue, well-drawn characters, and ingenious plots are the hallmarks of Marsh's work, and at her best she was more than a match for her peers Christie, Sayers, and Allingham. In 1966 Marsh was awarded the D.B.E. (Dame Commander, Order of the British Empire) for her services to the theater, and was thereafter known as Dame Ngaio Marsh.

McGown, Jill • Thanks to her standout police procedurals McGown is fast earning an excellent critical reputation. Beginning with the enjoyable *A Perfect Match* (St. Martin's Press, 1983), McGown has written a number of novels featuring the police detectives Lloyd (who maddeningly refuses to divulge his first name) and Judy Hill, his partner and lover. The relationship of Lloyd and Hill serves in these novels as an interesting counterpoint to the mystery plots, and McGown handles the relationship with skill, avoiding the clichés that some writers fall into with their series characters. The mystery plots of McGown's novels, moreover, are a marvelous fusion of the intricately knitted classic English school and the fully fleshed character novels of contemporary mystery fiction. For example, *Gone to Her Death* (St. Martin's Press, 1990; *Death of a Dancer* in England) utilizes the setting of an English public school to great effect. McGown takes the conventions of the traditional English mystery and gives them a thoroughly modern interpretation. In addition to the Lloyd and Hill series, McGown has produced a number of suspense novels with memorable characters and settings, such as *The Stalking Horse* (St. Martin's Press, 1988). These works feature excellent puzzles as well. McGown has published a novel as Elizabeth Chaplin, titled *Hostage to Fortune* (Mysterious Press, 1993), which is much like her nonseries novels as Jill McGown.

McIlvanney, William • McIlvanney has written only a few mysteries, but his work has been influential and highly acclaimed. His novels are set in Glasgow, Scotland, and they feature police officer Jack Laidlaw. These police procedurals are hard-boiled in a uniquely Scottish way, with dual strains of kindness and toughness ever-present. Laidlaw is a melancholy figure, almost obsessive in his hunt for the truth behind violent crimes. In the first novel, *Laidlaw* (Pantheon, 1977), his marriage is coming apart under the strain of his constant intensity about work and life. Laidlaw is certainly prone to having dark nights of the soul, but he is also compassionate, and he despises cops who treat criminals as monsters of evil instead of human beings who have committed a crime. McIlvanney's mysteries are beautifully written, with a fine marriage of poetic imagery and action sequences. He tells us much about violence and the potential for violence in people, without needless gore and bloody scenes. Glasgow, with an atmosphere of seaminess and urban decay, permeates his novels. As Laidlaw walks about the city, looking for his murderer, and we see the diverse neighborhoods, and the average people whose lives are destroyed by violence, drink, intimidation, and despair, all the manifestations of "the soul in pain." It is clear that Laidlaw is not an easy man with whom to live or work, but he's a tour de force of a character. McIlvanney has also written several volumes of poetry, and is a well-regarded mainstream writer in Great Britain.

Melville, Jennie • See **Butler, Gwendoline**.

Moyes, Patricia • An accident while on a skiing holiday led Moyes to write her first mystery novel, and though Moyes may not have spent her holiday entirely as planned, this fortuitous accident witnessed the birth of a distinguished career in the mystery field. This first novel, titled, aptly enough, *Dead Men Don't Ski* (Rinehart, 1960), introduced Scotland Yard Inspector Henry Tibbett and his good-natured wife, Emmy, who are on a skiing holiday in the Italian Alps. For nearly four decades now Moyes has delighted fans of the traditional English mystery with her dazzling combination of razor-sharp wit, complex plots, and the knack for describing unusual settings vividly. Henry Tibbett is one of those who has a true "nose" for crime, and he has learned never to ignore his hunches, which have brought him success and recognition at Scotland Yard. Moyes also has a keen sense of humor, a talent for picking out the unusual, as evidenced by the engaging Manciple family, the centerpiece of two novels, *Murder Fantastical* (Holt, Rinehart, & Winston, 1987) and *A Six-Letter Word for Death* (Holt, Rinehart, & Winston, 1983). In *Johnny Under Ground* (Holt, Rinehart, & Winston, 1965), Moyes tells a poignant tale of Emmy's reunion with some of her World War II Air Force buddies, and the easygoing Emmy proves as engaging a character as her husband. The Moyes books also offer a variety of settings, from Switzerland, Holland, Washington, D.C., and the Caribbean, all places where Moyes has lived.

Neel, Janet • Neel's mysteries are an engrossing mixture of police procedural and the British psychological crime novel. They feature Detective Inspector John McLeish of the London Metropolitan Police and Francesca Wilson, a brilliant but erratic government analyst in the Department of Trade and Industry. In the first book in the series, *Death's Bright Angel* (St. Martin's Press, 1988), John and Francesca begin a difficult and entertaining relationship and a sleuthing partnership when a criminal case brings them together. Relationships are hard for Francesca, since she is an overworked, ambitious woman who also is trying to be a mother to her four younger brothers. There are brilliant singers among the brothers, including one pop star, and Neel's depiction of an eccentric English family and their musical obsessions is skillful and amusing. In her novels, Neel also gives readers an insider's view of the innermost workings of the British civil service system, and the shenanigans of international high finance and politics. It's a praiseworthy series all around, and the characters are especially memorable.

Authors of Mysteries With Musical Themes

Carole Nelson Douglas (the Irene Adler series); Kinky Friedman; Janet Neel; Barbara Paul (the opera series); Ellis Peters (the Felse family series); Audrey Peterson; Jesse Sublett.

Peters, Ellis • Novelist Edith Pargeter launched her mystery-writing career in the early 1950s with the novel *Fallen into the Pit* (Heinemann, 1951; Mysterious, 1994). But Pargeter fans, who were used to the author's historical novels and general fiction, were somewhat confused by the switch in genres, and thus the Peters pseudonym was born. For nearly thirty years Ellis Peters produced excellent novels of mystery and suspense with contemporary settings, many of them featuring the Felse family. The Felses, consisting of father George, a policeman, mother Bunty, a "retired" opera singer, and son Dominic, star in several outstanding novels, including the Edgar Award-winning *Death and the Joyful Woman* (Doubleday, 1962). In many of her contemporary novels Peters effectively uses her interest in music, such as in *Mourning Raga* (Morrow, 1970) or *The Horn of Roland* (Morrow, 1974). George Felse is most often the main detective in the series, although Bunty and Dominic play important roles in almost every book. Bunty is the main character in *The Grass-Widow's Tale* (Morrow, 1968) when she is kidnapped, and only her own strength of character and her intelligence save her from being murdered. *Mourning Raga* is the first of two novels set in India, with Dominic at the helm. One of Peters's best—and funniest— novels is the nonseries *Never Pick Up Hitch-Hikers!* (Morrow, 1976), in which a young man seeking to escape from an overprotective mother winds up in the hands of criminals. A delightful comedy of errors, this is more of a caper novel than a mystery, but it shows Peters's sense of humor at its best.

For Peters's best-selling series of historical mysteries, see the section "Once Upon a Crime."

Porter, Joyce • Readers may find any number of incompetent police officers in the pages of mystery fiction, but the late Joyce Porter raised incompetence to an art form in the person of her sleuth, Inspector Wilfred Dover. Dover is obese, crude, an embarrassment to Scotland Yard, but somehow he manages to get his cases solved—perhaps because the criminals he is after are just a bit more stupid than he is, to paraphrase the author herself. Dover's first case is reported in *Dover One* (Scribner, 1964). Dover is summoned to remote Creedshire to investigate the disappearance of a young housemaid who was a bit of a slut and a blackmailer besides. Has she been murdered? When the truth is revealed, the motive for the crime turns out to be one that is surely unique in all of crime fiction. Porter draws her characters in broad strokes, but Dover is revoltingly funny through the series, the last of which is *Dover Beats the Band* (Weidenfeld & Nicholson, 1980). In addition to the Dover books, Porter also wrote about Eddie Brown, inept international spy, and the Honorable Constance (a.k.a. the "Hon Con") Morrison-Burke, an amateur sleuth with more energy than tact. Humor is ever at the forefront of a novel by Joyce Porter, and readers looking for parody will find much to enjoy in these books.

Radley, Sheila • Her first novel, *Death in the Morning* (Scribner, 1979), marked Radley as a writer to watch develop. This novel, featuring English police detective Douglas Quantrill, set the tone for much of Radley's work to follow: a fairly traditional mystery in its framework, but with a blending of the psychological style in the vein of Rendell and James. Radley at some point worked for the postal service in a village, and her experience there has come through in her writing. Her keen eye for characters and their motivations never fails to make her novels interesting, and her ability with characterization has allowed her to experiment successfully with the traditional form of the English detective story. *A Talent for Destruction* (Scribner, 1982) is more a psychological study than a tale of detection, and *This Way Out* (Scribner, 1990), though it again features Inspector Quantrill, offers an intriguing variation on Patricia Highsmith's *Strangers on a Train* (Harper, 1950). The blend of psychology and detection that is such a prominent feature of contemporary English mystery fiction at its best is a staple with Sheila Radley. Readers should check the library and used bookstores for most of these works.

Rankin, Ian/Harvey, Jack • The ancient and beautiful city of Edinburgh has always had its fair share of bloody goings-on, and the capital city of Scotland seems a fitting place to set a stunningly dark, brooding series of crime novels. John Rebus is a police inspector in Edinburgh, and the hero in an excellent series of hard-boiled mysteries by Ian Rankin. The author depicts the dark side of a city that most people only know as tourists, and portrays the darkest side of its inhabitants. In the series, murder sometimes occurs on the crime-ridden housing estates, where violent youths and career criminals abuse alcohol and drugs, and where brawls can erupt at any moment. Or it might be found in the walled-up medieval streets that lie beneath the oldest section of the city, where plague victims were entombed and susceptible locals claim they still can see ghosts. Although he's a policeman, Rebus seems to be drawn toward the dark corners of the city. He wanders through the busy city on his dogged investigations, he makes terrible puns and sarcastic jokes to everyone he meets, and sometimes he even gets his mind off the job long enough to engage in a romantic relationship. He's a bit of a Calvinist in his morals, and he is naturally inclined toward melancholy. Rebus is an independently minded, obstinate detective with decided opinions, and he is not easy on himself or on his coworkers. One of the best books in the series, *Mortal Causes* (Simon & Schuster, 1995), is a fascinating story about the running of guns and money to violent extremist Protestant Loyalists in Northern Ireland. It's a rare depiction of the other side of the divide from the IRA terrorists more commonly found in fiction.

Rankin has also written some spy novels, and he publishes thrillers under the name of **Jack Harvey** (not to be confused with Nottingham writer John Harvey).

Rendell, Ruth • She has been hailed by some critics as the best mystery writer in the English language anywhere in the world, and she is generally mentioned in the same breath as her peer and countrywoman, P. D. James, as one of the leading lights of the modern crime novel. Rendell's career began in the mid-1960s. *From Doon with Death* (Doubleday, 1965) introduced Reginald Wexford, her popular policeman detective. The Wexford novels in the early years followed the fairly traditional pattern of the English police detective mystery, but Rendell's skill in characterization and puzzle-making has lifted the Wexford books far above the ordinary. Through the course of the series, Rendell reveals much about the life of her main characters: Wexford; his wife, Dora; their two daughters; and Wexford's dutiful "Watson," Mike Burden. With chilling intensity, Rendell limns character and devises plots that are as compelling for "whydunit" as for "whodunit." A recent book in the series, *Simisola* (Crown, 1995), explores race relations in contemporary England, as Rendell successfully blends sociology with crime fiction in her own incomparable way.

For Rendell's novels of psychological suspense, some of which are written under the name **Barbara Vine**, see the section "The Silence of the Lambs."

Robinson, Peter • Yorkshire-born and -bred, Robinson has lived in Canada for more than twenty years. It was Yorkshire, however, that he chose for the setting of his superb series featuring Chief Inspector Alan Banks. Reared in the South of England and having worked there, Banks has asked for a transfer to the North of England to get his family away from the big-city troubles of the South. They have ended up in the Yorkshire Dales, in Eastvale, where they are adjusting to the slower rhythms of life. In Banks's first recorded case, *Gallows View* (Scribner, 1990; published in England and Canada by Viking, 1987), a Peeping Tom is annoying women in Eastvale. The townspeople don't think the police are taking the case seriously enough, fearing that the Peeping Tom will turn violent. In the meantime, Banks is working on another case, which is violent, and the violence is escalating. As the series continues, Robinson creates complex and interesting stories, filling them with well-drawn characters, a picturesque setting, and the trials and travails of modern life. Various books in the series have been short-listed for a number of awards, and *Past Reason Hated* (Scribner, 1993; published in England and Canada by Viking, 1991) won the Arthur Ellis Award for Best Novel. *Wednesday's Child* (Scribner, 1994) was nominated for the Edgar for Best Novel. In addition to the Inspector Banks novels, Robinson has written two suspense novels, neither of which has yet been published in the United States.

Simpson, Dorothy • Her first novel, *Harbingers of Fear* (Macdonald, 1977), was suspense; her second, *The Night She Died* (Scribner, 1981), was an English police procedural in the traditional vein. With this series, starring policeman Luke Thanet, however, Simpson found a special place in contemporary mystery fiction. Her cop Thanet is an ordinary family man with a wife and two children. As the series begins, Thanet's wife, Joan, is at home with the two children, then young, and as the series progresses the reader watches the natural growth and evolution of the Thanet family. This core of "ordinariness," with a series character grappling with the common problems of daily life, offers a center to Simpson's fiction, which is rather unusual in contemporary mystery fiction. The Kent town of Sturrenden and its environs serve as the setting for the series. Simpson delineates her area with a loving eye and brings to her writing an excellent understanding of English urban life in the latter decades of the twentieth century. The excellent *Last Seen Alive* (Scribner, 1985) won the Silver Dagger from the British Crime Writers' Association. Readers should check the library and used bookstores for most of these works.

Stacey, Susannah/Staynes and Storey • Jill Staynes and Margaret Storey are the authors of a series of British police novels. In America their books are published under the Stacey name; in Britain the books appear under the names of Staynes and Storey. Their hero, Superintendent Robert Bone, is a quiet, intelligent detective. His personal life, however, has been molded by tragedy. His beloved wife has been killed in a car accident and he is struggling to bring up his teenage daughter, Charlotte, by himself. Charlotte has a speech impediment and other injuries from the accident, and she is a strong influence on her father. Bone works out of Tunbridge Wells, and the mysteries that he solves mostly take place in the Kent countryside. The people that he encounters in the course of his investigations are often eccentric folk whose personal oddities become an important part of the plot. The first Superintendent Bone mystery is *Goodbye Nanny Gray* (Summit, 1987). A nanny is murdered, and there are many suspects in this well-written English village mystery. *Grave Responsibility* (Summit, 1990) is a bleak and rather gory tale of multiple murders that occur within the very peculiar Clare family.

Also look for the **Elizabeth Eyre** entry in the section "Once Upon a Crime." Eyre is another pen name used by Staynes and Storey.

Tey, Josephine • Though she wrote only eight mystery novels, Tey is yet considered one of the primary figures of the first Golden Age of the English detective novel, along with Margery Allingham, Agatha Christie, Ngaio Marsh, and Dorothy L. Sayers. Six of Tey's novels feature the Scotland Yard detective Alan Grant, including the first, *The Man in the Queue* (Dutton, 1929; published under the pseudonym Gordon Daviot). Grant doesn't have to work for a living, having inherited enough money to live comfortably, but he chose police work because he likes to work out puzzles. Intelligent and well bred, he is very much like Ngaio Marsh's Roderick Alleyn. Grant is also severely claustrophobic, and thus he seeks the wide-open spaces whenever he can. Grant gets strong feelings about potential suspects from looking at their faces and eyes, and this unorthodox method proves very important in his most famous "case," recounted in *The Daughter* *of Time* (Macmillan, 1952). Laid up in the hospital, Grant takes up the famous puzzle of the Princes in the Tower, the two nephews whom Richard III supposedly murdered. Grant is determined to prove Richard innocent, because he doesn't look like a killer. Surely one of the most unusual mysteries ever written, *The Daughter of Time* is a compelling read. Thus it often appears near the top of lists of "the best mysteries ever written."

Thomson, June • Thomson has the distinction of being perhaps the only current mystery writer whose series detective has a different name on either side of the Atlantic. Known to British readers as Inspector Finch, the character had his name changed to Rudd in the United States, because Thomson's longtime American publisher, Doubleday, already had a detective named Finch on its list (the Inspector Finch of the novels by the late Margaret Erskine). Finch/Rudd first appeared in *Not One of Us* (Harper, 1971). From the beginning Thomson demonstrated a keen insight into the psychology of her characters, many of whom live in the smaller towns and villages of England. Her writing style is succinct, with no excess verbiage to trim, particularly when compared to that of P. D. James, but at her best, Thomson is no less compelling or less psychologically acute. Finch/Rudd is an intriguing and believable character, and Thomson gives him tantalizing puzzles to solve. Especially noteworthy are *The Long Revenge* (Doubleday, 1975) and *The Habit of Loving* (Doubleday, 1979). Readers should check the library and used bookstores for most of these works.

Turnbull, Peter • Glasgow, Scotland, is the vividly described setting of Peter Turnbull's police procedurals. Like the "Hill

Street Blues" type of police stories, these are station-house mysteries about the daily lives of the police officers of "P" division. Each book has a major crime to be investigated, usually murder, with many strands of evidence and plenty of suspects to follow. The stories follow each officer who works on the case, and we follow their professional and personal problems as well. In each book in the series, we meet the officers of the squad, such as Ray Sussock, who's trying to figure out how to be single again when he's in his fifties and exiled to a tiny flat; Detective Inspector Fabian Donoghue, who labors in charge of the division; Erika Willems, who fought sex discrimination to get assignments to cases; and Malcolm Montgomerie, the resident lady-killer. The first book in the series is *Deep and Crisp and Even* (St. Martin's Press, 1982), and it's set in the darkness of a northern winter, where the detectives are hunting a serial killer, Slow Tom, who is killing people with a stiletto. Turnbull has a good ear for the nuances of the Glaswegian accent, told so that Americans can easily understand it. The dialect is not broad, it's just enough, a word scattered here and there, to season the dish. The reader is pulled out of the ordinary by the unusual setting, into the city's dark side, into the common acceptance of widespread drunkenness, the dreadful tenement housing for poor folk, and the viciousness of life in the public housing projects. Reading these books is an uncommon experience indeed.

Wingfield, R. D. • He is inclined to be coarse, he dresses in clothes that make him look more like a derelict than a detective, and he constantly drives his superiors mad as they try to cope with his antics. Detective Inspector Jack Frost of the

Denton police, for all his faults, somehow seems to find his way right in the end. Though he takes a wrong turn now and again on his way to the solution of a case, Frost manages to make things turn out right. In his first appearance, *Frost at Christmas* (Bantam, 1995), he has to take charge of the search for a missing child; at the same time he has to break in a new detective constable—who just happens to be the Chief Constable's nephew. On top of that, he turns up a long-dead corpse, and now he has a murder on his hands as well. Subsequent cases have Frost seeing justice done in his own inimitable fashion. He has been portrayed on television by David Jason in a series that has run on A&E. Readers should check the library and used bookstores for some of these works.

For Further Reading • Jane Adams; Janie Bolitho; Christianna Brand; John Creasey/J. J. Marric; Freeman Wills Crofts; Michael Gilbert (the Patrick Petrella books); S. T. Haymon; John Buxton Hilton/John Greenwood; Alan Hunter; Quintin Jardine; Michael Kenyon; Bill Knox; Elizabeth Lemarchand; Emma Page; Maurice Procter; Jonathan Ross; Andrew Taylor; John Wainwright; Colin Watson; Pauline Glen Winslow.

Look for these movies • the Blake of Scotland Yard series; *Brannigan*; *Cribb*; *Deathtrap*; *Green for Danger*; *An Inspector Calls*; *Sleuth*; *The Wicker Man*.

TV shows • *Cracker*; *Dalziel and Pascoe*; the Adam Dalgliesh series; *Dempsey and Makepeace*; *Frost*; *Hamish Macbeth*; *Inspector Alleyn*; *Morse*; the *Prime Suspect* series; *The Ruth Rendell Mysteries* series; *The Sweeney*; *Taggart*.

Hill Street Blues: American Cops

American writers have been writing police stories for more than one hundred years, but most of the early novels were about one policeman and how he caught a wanted criminal. Then came *Dragnet*, in the early 1950s, and it changed the whole way we thought about how police work was done. Now the public could see how most crimes were solved: by methodical, detailed paperwork and questioning conducted by several investigators. From those first, innocent days came today's gritty, realistic tales of the roughest side of crime in America: the big-city police beat. And now we get a look at rural crime, too, and at mysteries in large and small towns all across the country. We ride along with the Navajo Tribal Police, with campus cops at our universities, with the law enforcement rangers of the National Park Service, and with the FBI agents who track down serial killers. America's a big country, and somebody's got to police it.

Adcock, Thomas • New York City policeman and Hell's Kitchen denizen Neil "Hock" Hockaday is the hero of Adcock's gritty and atmospheric series of police procedurals. Before making his first novel-length appearance in *Sea of Green* (Mysterious Press, 1989), Hock appeared in various short stories. In *Sea of Green* he is recovering from a divorce, having moved out of the suburbs back to the Hell's Kitchen neighborhood where he grew up. He is assigned to SCUM, otherwise known as "Street Crimes Unit Manhattan." He is assigned to investigate death threats against a popular minister in Harlem, and when murders begin occurring in Hell's

Kitchen, the cases are soon connected. In the third book in the series, *Drown All the Dogs* (Pocket Books, 1994), Hock and his lover, actress Ruby Flagg, go to Ireland to visit Hock's dying uncle Liam. Intrigued by the possibility of finding out more about his father, who vanished during World War II, Hock is eager to make the trip. But strange things start happening, threatening the lives of both Hock and Ruby, and Hock has to try to figure out what his father's disappearance has to do with the current situation. Adcock creates strongly realized characters and settings, infusing them all with warmth, color, and passion. The second book in the series, *Dark Maze* (Pocket Books, 1993), was awarded the Edgar for Best Paperback Original. Readers should check the library and used bookstores for some of these works.

Bland, Eleanor Taylor • Bland writes a series about African-American police officer Marti MacAlister, who left her job with the Chicago Police Department to get her family away from the tragedy of her husband's death. They now live in Lincoln Prairie, Illinois, where Marti soon discovers that suburbs and smaller towns have just as many problems, sometimes, as the big city. Marti is paired with a cop, Vik Jessenovik, with some old-fashioned attitudes about gender and race, but she manages to impress him with her aptitude for and dedication to the job. Marti is tall and imposing, tough and intelligent, and Bland writes with a quiet compassion about everyday people caught up in tragic events beyond their control. The first book in the series is *Dead Time* (St. Martin's Press, 1992). Readers should check the library and used bookstores for some of these works.

Burke, James Lee • Burke writes lyrical tough-guy tales of life and crime in New Orleans and southern Louisiana. *The Neon Rain* (Holt, 1987) is Burke's first book with Dave Robicheaux, a former homicide cop and recovering alcoholic. Dave lives in the bayou country near New Iberia and runs a bait shop and fishing business, and he sometimes works as a detective for the sheriff's office. Periodically violence erupts in his world, often because someone threatens his family or friends. In the classic tradition of the hard-boiled private eye, Dave must then solve crimes while keeping his principles intact. Burke intersperses strongly violent scenes with lyrical prose and superb descriptions of the natural world. Cajun culture, food, and especially Dave's friends, family, and neighbors come alive vividly for the reader. Dave goes through some dark nights of the soul in dealing with the many tragedies of his life, and he fights his alcoholism, his flashbacks to Vietnam, and his urge to commit violent acts. As part of his vigilance on behalf of the weak or vulnerable, he must deal with crimes that are rooted in the social and racial issues of the day. Dave's Catholic convictions that evil exists, and that good must constantly do battle with evil, also permeate these novels. Burke's mysteries are journeys into Dave Robicheaux's psyche and mind, as well as explorations of the corruption and evil that lurk in modern society.

Burke won an Edgar Award for Best Novel for *Black Cherry Blues* (Little, Brown, 1989).

Connelly, Michael • A Pulitzer Prize-winning crime reporter, Connelly has combined his long-term interest in crime fiction with his experience on the crime beat to pen a series of outstanding crime novels, most of which feature Los Angeles homicide cop Harry Bosch. Introduced in the Edgar-winning *The Black Echo* (Little, Brown, 1992), Bosch is an intense, dedicated cop. He's determined to see a case through, no matter what the cost might be, personally or professionally. In his first case, his own experience as a "tunnel rat" in Vietnam helps him crack a difficult case involving the murder of one of Harry's fellow tunnel rats. Harry often finds his personal life entwined with his professional life in unusual ways. His mother was a prostitute who was murdered when he was a child, and in *The Last Coyote* (Little, Brown, 1995), Harry investigates her death. She named her only child "Hieronymus," after the Dutch painter, because she had seen a painting of his and liked it. *The Concrete Blonde* (Little, Brown, 1994) finds Harry in court defending himself against a wrongful death charge in connection with one of his earlier, and most infamous cases, the "Dollmaker Case." The killer's family claims Harry killed an innocent man. When a new body, with the Dollmaker's trademarks, is found and the date of death is determined to be *after* Harry killed the Dollmaker, it looks like Harry is in deep trouble. Did he really kill an innocent man? Or is there something darker and more devious going on here? Connelly handles the intricate plot with a sure hand.

Recently, Connelly produced a nonseries thriller starring Jack McEvoy, an investigative reporter. In *The Poet* (Little, Brown, 1996), McEvoy investigates the supposed suicide of his twin brother, a homicide cop in Denver. As in the Harry Bosch books, *The Poet* offers a fast pace, a serpentine plot, and an interesting hero.

Constantine, K. C. • Rocksburg, a fictional town in western Pennsylvania, is the setting for Constantine's series about Chief of Police Mario Balzic. Constantine uses the small-town setting to great effect in these books, because it is Balzic's knowledge of the people of Rocksburg that makes him so effective at his job. He is very much attuned to nuances of behavior, and these can be significant in the books. Constantine writes with great attention to the foibles of human nature, and he portrays them well in the many characters who people this series. As the series progresses, the reader witnesses the many strains and problems in the life of Balzic and his family, and in this way Constantine makes his characters all the more believable. Like other writers who use the regional setting to advantage, such as Sharyn McCrumb and Loren D. Estleman, Constantine chronicles the story of his own slice of Americana. First in the series is *The Rocksburg Railroad Murders* (Saturday Review Press, 1972). The last novel in which Balzic takes the lead role is *Cranks and Shadows* (Mysterious Press, 1995); with *Good Sons* (Mysterious Press, 1996), he has retired, and Ruggiero "Rugs" Carlucci is filling in as police chief until a new one is hired. Readers should check the used bookstores and the library for some of these works.

Cooper, Susan Rogers • A versatile writer with three series to her credit, Cooper chose small-town Oklahoma as the setting for her series featuring Chief Deputy Milt Kovak of the Prophesy County Sheriff's Department. In his first recorded case, *The Man in the Green Chevy* (St. Martin's Press, 1988), Milt has to deal with a rapist and murderer of little old ladies, and the whole county is horrified. Cooper describes her territory well, and she conveys the atmosphere of rural and small-town Oklahoma with considerable skill. She also makes Milt Kovak sound like a completely believable, somewhat irascible middle-aged man. In a voice that is wry, reflective, and occasionally raunchy, Milt narrates these tales of murder and misbehavior with a definite southwestern inflection.

For Cooper's two series with amateur sleuths, see the "Nancy, Frank, and Joe Grow Up" section.

Crider, Bill • Crider uses his familiarity with small-town Texas life to good effect in his series of police procedural novels starring Sheriff Dan Rhodes of mythical Blacklin County. In his first appearance, *Too Late to Die* (Walker, 1986), Rhodes has been a widower for about a year and lives with his adult daughter. He is facing reelection, but he's not much of a politician. Confronted by a murder, he just wants to do his job, but politics get in the way. He is surrounded by an amusing cast of supporting characters, the types who make small-town life so much fun to read and write about. As the series continues, Crider portrays for the reader an engaging community with its share of problems, and a very likable man who must do his best to see justice done. *Too Late to Die* won the Anthony Award for Best First Novel. In addition to the Dan Rhodes books, Crider writes two other series: the Truman Smith books (see "The Maltese Falcon" section) and the Carl Burns books (see "Nancy, Frank, and Joe Grow Up").

Dunlap, Susan • Dunlap has written three sets of novels featuring female sleuths Vejay Haskell, Jill Smith, and Kiernan O'Shaughnessy. Her main series features Berkeley homicide detective Jill Smith. Smith is a good cop, smart and persistent, always determined to solve crimes in spite of discrimination against her as a woman detective. The uniquely strange nature of the populace of Berkeley makes for some truly oddball criminal events in Jill's patch, like the murder of a guru in the first book, *Karma* (Raven, 1981). *Death and Taxes* (Delacorte, 1992) is the witty and baffling story of the murder of an IRS agent and the hunt for a murderer among his innumerable enemies and financial victims.

Dunlap has also written three books about Vejay Haskell, an executive dropout turned meter-reader in Russian River, California. *The Last Annual Slugfest* (St. Martin's Press, 1986) is one of Dunlap's best, with its vivid descriptions of the small settlements among the redwoods in northern California.

Another series by Dunlap is about Kiernan O'Shaughnessy, a former medical examiner and gymnast who has become a private eye. She specializes in cases with medical oddities, charges enormous fees, has an attractive male housekeeper, and lives a guilt-free and affluent life in her beach house in La Jolla. First in the series is *Pious Deception* (Villard, 1989).

Dunlap's style is spare and humorous; her heroes are curious, bright women with a cynical eye for the absurdities of life and crime in trendy California.

Egan, Lesley • See **Linington, Elizabeth.**

Forrest, Katherine V. • Mysteries with lesbian characters are a popular trend now, and Katherine Forrest was one of the first authors to write them. Forrest's books are about Kate Delafield, a detective in the Los Angeles Police Department.

The most recent book in the series is *Apparition Alley* (Berkley, 1997). Kate works every day in an occupation notable for its homophobia, so she has kept her private life a secret from her coworkers, but she struggles all the time with the issue of being closeted vs. coming out. Kate is a good police officer: thoughtful, sensitive, and scrupulous about the details of her work. Above all, she has integrity. She deals fairly with suspects in interviews, and the scenes in which Kate questions suspects are especially effective. Forrest also writes knowledgeably about the forensic details of murder investigations. There usually is an explicit sex scene or two in each novel.

Gosling, Paula • A daughter of the American Midwest, Gosling has lived in England for more than three decades. She sets many of her mysteries in America, including her two interconnected series of police procedurals.

With *Monkey Puzzle* (Doubleday, 1985), which won the Gold Dagger for Best Novel, Gosling launched her first series. This combination academic mystery and police procedural is set in the midwestern city of Grantham, and the main characters are homicide cop Jack Stryker and English professor Kate Trevorne. They appear as supporting characters in the hilarious *Hoodwink* (Doubleday, 1988), which demonstrates Gosling's knack for writing deliciously funny physical comedy scenes. Two further novels have featured Stryker and Trevorne as main characters, including the first in Gosling's new Blackwater Bay series, titled appropriately *The Body in Blackwater Bay* (Mysterious Press, 1992). On vacation in the Great Lakes area, Stryker and Trevorne find their holiday interrupted by murder, and Stryker helps Sheriff Matt Gabriel find the killer.

Subsequent books in the series feature Matt Gabriel and other denizens of Blackwater Bay. Sharply drawn characters, witty dialogue, and neatly constructed puzzles are hallmarks of all of Gosling's work, and the Blackwater Bay series is an example of a master at her finest. Readers should check the library and used bookstores for some of these works.

Hager, Jean • Hager writes several series, including a set of police procedurals. These have a background of Cherokee lore and medicine, and they are set in Oklahoma. Police Chief Mitch Bushyhead is one-half Cherokee, but he is an outsider to the tribe since he was raised as a white man and married a white woman. His wife is dead, and now he is trying to raise a teenage daughter by himself. Bushyhead works hard to solve crimes and dispense the white man's justice, while Cherokee medicine man Crying Wolf uses his own medicine to work criminal and family problems out in the historic Cherokee way. The first novel in this unusual and effective series is *The Grandfather Medicine* (St. Martin's Press, 1989).

Herndon, Nancy • The fictional West Texas city of Los Santos is the setting for this series of mysteries starring Elena Jarvis of the Crimes Against Persons Division. In the first of the series, *Acid Bath* (Berkley, 1995), Elena investigates an odd case of attempted murder. An "erotic poet" at a local private university claims that his ex-wife has tried to kill him, using an exploding snail. When a corpse turns up floating in acid in the man's bathtub, Elena wonders whether the man was as nutty as she first thought him. Trying to solve the case before the killer can strike again, Elena is hampered by an interfering ex-husband, also a cop, and by her own growing friendship with the woman who should be the chief suspect in the case. Elena is attractive and intelligent, and she is supported by an engaging—and often amusing—cast of secondary characters. Herndon writes with a pleasant mix of humor and mystery. Readers who enjoy their police procedurals on the lighter side will find this series fun.

Authors of Southwestern Mysteries

Nevada Barr; Cecil Dawkins; James D. Doss; John Dunning; Micah Hackler; Nancy Herndon; Tony Hillerman; J. A. Jance (the Joanna Brady series); Kirk Mitchell; Richard Parrish; Walter Satterthwait; Jake Page; Aimee and David Thurlo; Judith Van Gieson.

Hightower, Lynn S. • With several futuristic police procedurals and one private eye novel to her credit, versatile novelist Hightower then turned her talents to a series featuring Cincinnati homicide detective Sonora Blair. First in the series is *Flashpoint* (HarperCollins, 1995), in which Sonora is on the trail of a vicious serial killer, a woman who likes to set her victims on fire—while they're still alive. Soon Sonora is engaged in a deadly duel with the killer, who seems to know more about Sonora's life than is safe for Sonora or her family. Sonora is a well-drawn character, intelligent, passionate, and all-too-human. Hightower creates high-octane suspense, and readers can feel the impact of each new entry in this series long after the book has been put away. In addition to the Sonora Blair books, Hightower has written one novel about Lena Padgett, a private eye in Lexington, Kentucky. *Satan's Lambs* (Walker, 1993) won the Shamus Award for Best First Private Eye Novel.

For Hightower's other series, see "The X-Files" section.

Hillerman, Tony • Hillerman is one of the most respected and acclaimed of contemporary mystery writers. Many critics and writers agree that he broke new ground for mysteries in his emphasis on setting and his creation of heroes who are far from traditional police officers. Most of Hillerman's atmospheric novels are set on the Navajo reservation, and his two detectives are Joe Leaphorn and Jim Chee, both Navajo tribal policemen. Each mystery teaches the reader about the Navajo way of life, and the stories often illustrate the ongoing conflict between a traditional way of life and the white man's values and materialism. The first novel, *The Blessing Way* (Harper, 1970), introduces Lieutenant Joe Leaphorn. Leaphorn is an older man, who uses his deductive ability and knowledge of Navajo culture to solve crimes. Officer Jim Chee is introduced in *People of Darkness* (Harper, 1980). Chee is younger than Leaphorn, and he follows a more traditional Navajo way of life. He wants to become a shaman and is learning the traditional ceremonies. In later books, the methodical Leaphorn and the intuitive Chee sometimes work together on cases.

Hillerman won an Edgar Award for Best Novel with *Dance Hall of the Dead* (Harper, 1973), and an Anthony Award for the short-story anthology *The Mysterious West* (Harper-Collins, 1994), which he edited.

Authors of Native American Sleuths in Mysteries

Margaret Coel; James D. Doss; Jean Hager; Tony Hillerman; Mercedes Lackey; Louis Owens; Thomas Perry; Aimee and David Thurlo; J. F. Trainor; M. K. Wren; Chelsea Quinn Yarbro.

Himes, Chester • Himes was once imprisoned for armed robbery and served time in Ohio State Penitentiary. Afterward he worked for the Works Progress Administration (WPA) Writers' Project in Ohio for several years and on the *Cleveland Daily News*. From 1941 onward he worked in shipyards in California, and after 1953 he lived in Paris and Spain. Himes began writing mystery stories at the proposal of a French editor and publisher of *noir* crime stories. His first book, *A Rage in Harlem* (first published as *For Love of Imabelle* by Fawcett, 1957; later published under the better-known title by Avon, 1965), was an instant success, winning him the French Grand Prix de Littérature Policière in 1958. In Europe, Himes was accepted as a serious novelist who wrote sociological crime novels, but American critics and readers were much more wary.

Himes's series characters are Grave Digger Jones and Coffin Ed Johnson, Harlem policemen who have to adapt their jobs as police officers to the necessities of surviving the tough streets of Harlem. They have to struggle against corruption on all sides to preserve the law, but as the series progresses, so does their shared disillusionment with the world around them. Violent, grotesquely humorous, the world of Chester Himes is dark and disturbing, but illuminating and evocative of place and time. Readers should check the library and used bookstores for some of these works.

Jance, J. A. • The author has established a large following for her series of novels featuring Seattle homicide cop J. P. Beaumont. Beau, as he is known to his friends, is a bit of a maverick, lover of junk food and the booze, in the best tradition of the free-wheeling cop of mystery fiction. In the first book of the series, *Until Proven Guilty* (Avon, 1985), Beau's on the trail of a child-killer with his new partner, Detective Ron Peters. During the course of the investigation Beau meets and falls for a mysterious, wealthy woman, whom he marries. Police procedurals by form, the series is fast-paced and generally full of action. Beau, though stubborn and irascible, demonstrates that he's capable of change as the series progresses. He's willing to rethink some of his prejudices and ideas, though he remains steadfast in others. The Seattle setting is an important component of the books, and Jance makes the city a living entity, much in the way Sara Paretsky makes Chicago integral to her work or Julie Smith makes New Orleans in her Skip Langdon books. Recently Jance has begun a new series with a female character in *Desert Heat* (Avon, 1993). Joanna Brady is the widow of a sheriff's deputy in Cochise County, Arizona. Like the Beaumont books, this series promises fast action and a tough, yet appealing, central character. Jance has, in addition, penned one novel of psychological suspense, *Hour of the Hunter* (Morrow, 1991).

Kaminsky, Stuart M. • Not content with two popular series, Kaminsky recently introduced his third, featuring Chicago policeman Abe Lieberman. His partner is William Hanrahan, and together the two are known, not always affectionately, as "the rabbi and the priest." Abe is an insomniac, and Hanrahan is an alcoholic, whose fondness for drink can complicate their cases. The duo first appear in *Lieberman's Folly* (St. Martin's Press, 1991). Details of Abe's family life are important in the books. Abe is an observant Jew, and his wife, Bess, is president of their synagogue. Their daughter Lisa leaves her husband and moves back in with them, along with her two children. Abe's brother, Maish, owns a deli, which is a spot frequented by Abe and some of his buddies. Abe is in his sixties, and his health causes him some concern as he nears retirement. As in his series of procedurals set in Russia, Kaminsky conveys a powerful sense of place, as readers see the Chicago neighborhoods undergoing constant change. Kaminsky writes with considerable insight into human behavior as well. Fans of the better-known Russian series (see the section "From Foreign Shores") should enjoy these books as well.

For Kaminsky's series of historical private eye novels see the section "The Maltese Falcon."

Kellerman, Faye • Kellerman writes supenseful police procedurals, with an emphasis on Jewish belief and culture. The hero is Peter Decker, an LAPD detective in the Foothill Division. In the acclaimed first novel in the series, *The Ritual Bath* (Arbor House, 1986), Peter meets Rina Lazarus, a widow with two young sons, as he investigates murder in an Orthodox community. Their relationship deepens throughout the series. Peter, who was an adopted child, discovers his own Jewish background and learns about his religion. Many of the books in the series, especially *The Ritual Bath* and *Day of Atonement* (Morrow, 1991), provide fascinating details of the customs and rites of the Orthodox community. When it comes to solving crimes, however, there is also quite a bit of graphic realism in these police stories, and it is contrasted with the security, faith, and love that Rina offers to her family. *Justice* (Morrow, 1995) may have been Kellerman's breakout book for a bigger audience. It's a mesmerizing story of murder, sex, loyalty, and betrayal among a group of teenagers. Kellerman's tales often concern the murder and abuse of children, and she has a distinct talent for reminding readers of what it's like to be a kid.

King, Laurie R. • The creator of two very distinctive series of mysteries with strong women characters, King made quite a splash in the mystery world by winning the Edgar for Best First Novel with *A Grave Talent* (St. Martin's Press, 1993). This book introduced San Francisco homicide detective Kate Martinelli, a woman with some secrets of her own to hide as she works hard with her new partner, Al Hawkin, to solve the sensational murders of two young girls. Suspicion quickly focuses on the inhabitants of an unusual artists' colony near San Francisco, and upon one artist in particular. Kate Martinelli has to adapt to working with a partner, the demands of her personal life, and the dangers of mixing her public and private lives in a very compelling debut novel. King, who has a master's degree in theology, examines the effects of a crime upon those involved, and her themes are among some of the most unusual and original in contemporary mystery fiction.

For King's other series of mysteries, featuring a young woman who is a protégé of Sherlock Holmes, see the section "Once Upon a Crime."

Lake, M. D. • See the section "Nancy, Frank, and Joe Grow Up."

Lindsey, David • Though he lives and writes in Austin, the state capital of Texas, Lindsey uses Houston, fourth-largest city in the United States, as the basic setting for his crime novels. He has written several novels about HPD homicide detective Stuart Haydon, the first of which is *A Cold Mind* (Harper & Row, 1983). Independently wealthy, Haydon drives an expensive car and thus seems a bit out of place among his peers at HPD. Lindsey uses the city of Houston to great effect, giving the reader a guided tour of the many neighborhoods, making the Bayou City as important a character as any of the people in the books. Lindsey also ranges farther afield in the books, as the stories sometimes encompass broader issues, such as Central American politics in *Body of Truth* (Doubleday, 1992). In addition to five Stuart Haydon novels, Lindsey has written one book featuring HPD homicide detective Carmen Palma, titled *Mercy* (Doubleday, 1990). One of Lindsey's best, this novel features a serial killer with a savage taste for marking victims. Dark, brooding, violent, and at times disturbing, Lindsey's work is compelling reading.

Linington, Elizabeth • With her various pseudonyms and numerous series of mysteries, the late Elizabeth Linington has legions of fans for her police procedurals. Under her own name, Linington, she began a series about policeman Ivor Maddox in *Greenmask!* (Harper & Row, 1964). The policemen in this series work out of the Hollywood section of the Los Angeles police force. As **Lesley Egan**, she created two series. The first Egan book, *A Case for Appeal* (Harper & Row, 1961) features policeman Vic Varallo and lawyer Jesse Falkenstein; both men went on to have their own separate series in subsequent books. Linington may be best known, though, under her pseudonym **Dell Shannon**, for the series featuring Lieutenant Luis Mendoza of the LAPD. Mendoza debuted in *Case Pending* (Harper & Row, 1960). Most of the books that Linington wrote share certain characteristics. She had rather an idealized view of the police; they were always the "good guys." Readers won't find corruption in the LAPD in her novels. Also, Linington's cops do not get divorced, nor do they suffer from alcoholism, two fates that seem to befall many cops in the grittier police procedurals now in fashion. Despite this, however, Linington created characters whom readers came to know and care about, so that each new Linington, Egan, or Shannon promised further revelations about the lives of old and dear friends. In addition to her mysteries, Linington published a Gothic suspense novel, *Nightmare* (Harper & Row, 1961), under the name **Anne Blaisdell**. A number of her books were published under the Blaisdell name in England. She also published several historical novels under various names. Look for these books in the library and used bookstores.

Maron, Margaret • Maron writes two series of mysteries, both of which are rich in character, setting, and dialogue. Sigrid Harald, Maron's first character, features in a series of police procedurals in the traditional vein set in New York City; her debut was in the novel *One Coffee With* (Raven House/Worldwide, 1981). Sigrid is a tightly sealed-up character, efficient and seemingly emotionless as the series opens, but as the books progress, Sigrid slowly becomes less uninvolved with those around her, largely thanks to a relationship with a character introduced in the first book of the series. This series is a textbook example of how a writer can use a series for a natural and interesting development of a character who continues to grow and change. The most recent book in the series, *Fugitive Colors* (Mysterious Press, 1995), shows Sigrid having come a long way in her personal relationships, as she deals with the death of a loved one. The sixth novel in the series, *Corpus Christmas* (Doubleday, 1989), was nominated for the Agatha Award for Best Novel.

For Maron's series about lawyer Deborah Knott, see the section "Perry Mason for the Defense."

Mathews, Francine • Nantucket Island is the setting for this series of police procedurals by Mathews, who also writes a series of historical mysteries as Stephanie Barron. The heroine in the contemporary series is Meredith "Merry" Folger, a detective on the Nantucket police force. Merry is having some difficulties in her job, because her boss doesn't always want to take her seriously or let her handle difficult assignments. Her father is the police chief, and he's just a tad overprotective. Merry's grandfather, who was once police chief, has more confidence in her abilities, however, and he supports her as she tackles her first murder investigation in the first of the series, *Death in the Off-Season* (Morrow, 1994). The black sheep of one of the island's wealthiest families turns up dead in a cranberry bog on his brother's land, and Merry follows a tenuous chain of evidence until the killer is finally unmasked. Merry Folger is a bright, capable, and appealing sleuth, and Mathews uses the setting to great effect in this series.

For Mathews's historical mysteries, written under the name **Stephanie Barron**, see the section "Once Upon a Crime."

Mayor, Archer • The police procedural comes alive in the experienced hands of Vermont's Archer Mayor. Mayor sets his impressive stories in Brattleboro, a decaying industrial town in Vermont. Police lieutenant Joe Gunther is a Korean war vet, and a thoroughly appealing character. He's a thoughtful, rather melancholy man who has been widowed for many years when he finally meets Gail Zigman, a local realtor and town select-man, and his personal life changes for the better. Mayor depicts Brattleboro as an old, gritty New England town that has seen better days when there was more employment for its workers. It's an old-fashioned town, not a cookie-cutter suburb, and it has a unique local atmosphere and the normal complement of good and bad citizens. Mayor creates exciting, challenging cases for Joe to investigate, and there are always plenty of twists and turns in the stories. *The Dark Root* (Mysterious Press, 1995), for example, concerns the fight against crimes committed by Asian gangs in Vermont and Montreal. There are fascinating details about how Chinese and Vietnamese gangs are organized, how their foot soldiers operate, and how they use legitimate businesses such as Chinese restaurants to launder drug money and provide way stations for illegal aliens. These are high-quality procedurals, and Joe is an interesting, growing character. Although Joe knows all about how to follow routine police procedure in setting up an investigation, sometimes he is likely to ignore the demands of the official hierarchy and charge straight ahead to get at the truth about a crime. He has good instincts and training, as well as an excellent investigative mind.

McBain, Ed • The man who practically invented the police procedural genre, McBain has also been writing longer than any of his peers in the procedural game. Though his *Cop Hater* (Permabooks, 1956) wasn't the first true police procedural, it was among the first, and McBain's popularity through four decades of writing about the 87th Precinct has assured him a prominent place among the genre's giants. The 87th is a precinct in the fictional city of Isola, which is modeled on New York in various ways. Chief among the characters in the series is Steve Carella, but he shares the stage in most books with other cops from the precinct, such as Lieutenant Barnes, chief of the detective squad; Meyer Meyer, a long-suffering Jewish detective; Bert Kling; and Cotton Hawes, among others. In true procedural fashion, the books contain more than one plot line, and McBain uses this to great effect to vary his approach, so that the series has not grown stale, even after forty years. Most of the principal characters grow and change as well. One of the best in the series is *Ice* (Arbor House, 1983). In addition to the 87th Precinct books, McBain has written a series of mysteries starring lawyer Matthew Hope, and a number of crime novels and thrillers under his real name, Evan Hunter. Perhaps his most famous novel as Hunter is *The Blackboard Jungle* (Simon & Schuster, 1954), which was made into the classic film.

O'Connell, Carol • Media attention and glowing reviews, as well as an Edgar nomination for Best First Novel, greeted O'Connell's debut, *Mallory's Oracle* (Putnam, 1994), and readers have responded in kind. Kathleen Mallory, the heroine of O'Connell's work, is one of the most original and compelling characters to come along in many a year. At age ten or eleven, street kid Kathy Mallory was trying to break into a Jaguar when homicide cop Louis Markowitz stopped her. Instead of turning her over to the juvenile authorites, Markowitz took Kathy home to his wife Helen, a gentle but fiercely protective woman who did her best to humanize this savage child of the streets. At the beginning of *Mallory's Oracle* Helen Markowitz has been dead of cancer for a year or so and Louis Markowitz has been found murdered at the scene of another murder, perpetrated by the serial killer known to the Big Apple as the "Invisible Man." Sergeant Kathy Mallory, though she is suspended from the force, works on the case with the aid of Charles Butler, who had been exhorted by Markowitz to look after her, and her father's friends in Homicide. Mallory's genius with computers and her skill in hacking into practically any database are integral parts of each investigation. Kathy Mallory is enigmatic, seemingly conscienceless, and ruthless. Having met her once, readers will find it difficult to forget her.

O'**Donnell, Lillian** • Long before female cops and private eyes became popular staples of fiction, Lillian O'Donnell was writing police procedurals with a strong woman character. Norah Mulcahaney is a policewoman who starts her career on the bottom rung of the New York City police force. She is a perceptive, honest cop who is devoted to what she calls The Job. Norah grows and changes in her personal life, as well as her career, over the years depicted in the books. Eventually she is promoted into homicide. Norah is one of the first strong policewomen who care deeply about their careers to be depicted in mystery fiction. The Norah Mulcahaney books are well written, methodical, detailed police procedurals. O'Donnell often uses contemporary news items, such as the stories of mugging victims who shoot their assailants, or a teacher who hires teenagers to kill her husband, to add verisimilitude to her books. She also creates realistic New York City settings for her crime novels.

O'Donnell also has written a few books about Mici Anhalt, a caseworker for the Crime Victims Compensation Board, and New York private eye Gwenn Ramadge. Readers should check the library and used bookstores for some of these works.

Paul, **Barbara** • Barbara Paul began her writing career with theatrical mysteries, including a series of three opera mysteries with the great Enrico Caruso and Geraldine Farrar as amateur sleuths. They are *A Cadenza for Caruso* (St. Martin's Press, 1984), *Prima Donna at Large* (St. Martin's Press, 1985), and *Chorus of Detectives* (St. Martin's Press, 1987). These mysteries all have superb historical backgrounds, and of course a fascinating view of backstage life with all its petty quarrels and crises.

Paul has also written some wonderful mysteries about oddball characters and manipulative scoundrels. She is excellent at characterizing the sort of fiendishly self-obsessed people among whom murder seems liable to brew. Sometimes she even writes mysteries with no good people at all, just different varieties of villains. *He Huffed and He Puffed* (Scribner, 1989) is one of the best. It's full of crafty connivers who love deceiving, blackmailing, and outwitting each other over truly vicious business intrigues. The novel is funny and wonderfully nasty, just like its characters. Paul has a distinct talent for creating Machiavellian schemes and vivid villains. Readers should check the library and used bookstores for some of these works.

The Renewable Virgin (Scribner, 1985) begins Paul's series about New York City policewoman Marian Larch. Larch is assigned to investigate a crime involving Kelly Ingram, a television actress. Throughout the series, many of Larch's cases seem to revolve around theatrical folk. As her career grows and changes, Marian learns her trade, gets promoted to detective, and meets unusual people (including some memorable rogues) along the way.

Pearson, Ridley • See the section "The Silence of the Lambs."

Shannon, Dell • See **Linington, Elizabeth**.

Smith, Julie • The first Edgar Award for Best Novel given to an American woman since 1956 was awarded to Smith for *New Orleans Mourning* (St. Martin's Press, 1990). Smith's first mystery series featured San Francisco lawyer Rebecca Schwartz. Rebecca, who identifies herself as a Jewish feminist lawyer, matures in her personal approach to life and in her career throughout the series. The Schwartz novels are generally light, amusing fare, although *Dead in the Water* (Ivy, 1991) is more harrowing and violent than the earlier books.

Smith then wrote two Paul McDonald mysteries, also set in the Bay Area. Paul is a freelance writer and former journalist; these are humorous, hard-boiled private eye novels. The first is *True-Life Adventure* (Mysterious Press, 1985); the second is *Huckleberry Fiend* (Mysterious Press, 1987).

Julie Smith's most recent crime series chronicles the adventures of Skip Langdon, a policewoman in New Orleans.

Smith hit her stride as a mature writer with these novels. The first, *New Orleans Mourning*, gives the reader an insider's view of Mardi Gras and particularly its high society participants. Skip Langdon is a fully rounded, believable character; readers learn about her neuroses, weaknesses, and insecurities, as well as her talent as an investigator. She is confident and skilled in her job, but she feels awkward about almost everything else. The Garden District social background that Skip grew up in has been of assistance in her crime-solving, even though she felt out of place there and has abandoned that life to become a cop. Smith brings a vivid, bawdy, drunken, and hedonistic New Orleans to life in her novels, but she also captures the inner lives and motives of the natives of the city.

Wallace, Marilyn • With her debut novel, *A Case of Loyalties* (St. Martin's Press, 1986), Wallace won the Macavity Award for Best First Novel. This book also introduced her series characters, Jay Goldstein and Carlos Cruz, who work out of the Oakland, California, Police Department's Homicide Division. Goldstein, who likes to spend his spare time reading philosophy, comes from a prominent Bay Area family; his father is an influential lawyer. Cruz is a family man with two sons and a working wife. Both men, despite their widely differing backgrounds, are dedicated to their work and their ideals of justice, and they balance each other's weaknesses with their strengths to make an effective team. Wallace tells her stories through multiple viewpoints, allowing the reader to have a wider view of the story than just through the eyes of the detectives. This is particularly effective in *Primary Target* (Bantam, 1988), in which a mysterious group named the "Brotherhood of Men" attacks the presidential campaign of Congresswoman Jean Talbot. Readers should check the library and used bookstores for these works.

For Wallace's suspense novels, see the section "The Silence of the Lambs."

Wambaugh, Joseph • Wambaugh can always be relied on for great cop stories, since he was a cop in Los Angeles who began to write to tell the public what life was really like for the average LAPD officer. His first book was *The New Centurions* (Little Brown, 1970), and in this and his next few best-selling novels, he broke new ground with his strongly realistic police procedurals. No more whitewashing and cleaning up the gritty and raunchy details of crime scenes; Wambaugh told it the way cops saw both life and death on the streets. He paved the way for the accurate depiction of cops by the current generation of crime writers. Wambaugh is especially good at cop talk, at showing the way cops think, and how cops go bad and start to beat up suspects. He writes street-smart dialogue and creates interesting, lively characters, and he's especially good at showing the ups and downs of an officer's life, with real incidents drawn from his own years of experience. Several of his later books are set in the Coachella Valley and Palm Springs, in inland Southern California. This is a very different area from his old territory of Los Angeles. It's populated by an odd mix of rich old people and abysmally poor Hispanic workers, the heat is brutal, and the land is barren and beautiful. The three oddly matched heroes in the riotous *Fugitive Nights* (Morrow, 1992) are all in pursuit of a middle-aged, bald foreigner, who may or may not be smuggling drugs into Palm

Springs. Or maybe he's a hired hit-man, or an Iranian terrorist bent on blowing up a golf tournament, or who knows? It's a funny, adroit, and always readable combination of police procedural and thriller. Wambaugh just seems to get better and wittier as he gets older, and his stories get even wilder.

Wambaugh has also written some notable nonfiction, which is often highly praised as realistic and gripping by reviewers. *The Onion Field* (Delacorte, 1973), which was made into a well-known movie, is about the wanton killing of a cop by a sociopath.

Many movies and television shows have been made from Wambaugh's books, and he has often served as a consultant on the adaptations, always insisting on authentic depictions of a cop's life.

Willeford, Charles • See the section "The Usual Suspects."

Zubro, **Mark Richard** • Illinois schoolteacher Zubro pens two series of mysteries, one of which features gay Chicago cop Paul Turner. Turner is a single father with two teenaged sons, the younger of whom was born with spina bifida. Aided by elderly neighbor Rose Talucci, Turner does his best to take care of his sons while he meets the demands of his job as a homicide detective. His partner is Buck Fenwick, a diamond in the rough with a foul mouth, but he is a staunch friend to Paul, and they work well together. Turner made a brief appearance in one of the early novels in Zubro's other series, the Tom and Scott books; his first full-length appearance comes in *Sorry Now?* (St. Martin's Press, 1991). Turner and Fenwick investigate the attack on noted right-wing evangelist Bruce Mucklewrath and his daughter. The daughter is murdered, but Mucklewrath escapes serious injury. Was the attack motivated by one of Mucklewrath's many enemies, or is there a nastier explanation, one closer to home? As Turner and Fenwick search for answers, they discover that other right-wing leaders around the city have been the objects of attack. Zubro mixes Chicago politics, civil rights, and everyday life in an entertaining mix in this series.

For Zubro's other series of mysteries, see the section "Nancy, Frank, and Joe Grow Up."

For Further Reading • John Armistead; Noreen Ayres; William Bayer; Earl Derr Biggers; P. M. Carlson (the Marty Hopkins series); William Caunitz; D. J. Donaldson; Noreen Gilpatrick; Leslie Glass; Ruby Horansky; Fred W. Hunter; Jon Jackson; Richard and Frances Lockridge; Christopher Newman; Susan Oleksiw; Dave Pedneau; Helen Reilly; April Smith; Aimee and David Thurlo; Lawrence Treat; Thomas Walsh; Hillary Waugh; Charlene Weir; Teri White (the Spaceman Kowalski & Blue Maguire series); Collin Wilcox.

Some cop films are • *Basic Instinct*; *Black Rain*; *Black Widow*; *The Blue Knight*; *Bullitt*; *Charlie Chan at Treasure Island*; *Charlie Chan in London*; *Dick Tracy*; the *Die Hard* series; the *Dirty Harry* series; *Fargo*; *The FBI Story*; *Fort Apache, the Bronx*; *48 Hours*; *The French Connection*; *The Glitter Dome*; *In the Heat of the Night*; *Jennifer 8*; *Kiss the Girls*; *Laura*; the *Lethal Weapon* series; *Lone Star*; *Miami Blues*; *Mulholland Falls*; *Murder at 1600*; *Night Falls on Manhattan*; *The Onion Field*; *Serpico*; *Seven*; *Tango & Cash*; *The Thin Blue Line*; *Tightrope*; *To Live and Die in L.A.*; *Turner & Hooch*; *The Untouchables*; *Vengeance*; *Witness*.

TV shows with cops • *Adam-12; The Andy Griffith Show; Baretta; Barney Miller; Brooklyn South; Burke's Law; Cagney & Lacey; Car 54, Where Are You?; Columbo; The Commish; Dragnet; The FBI; Gunsmoke; Hawaii Five-O; Hill Street Blues; Homicide; Hunter; Ironside; Kojak; Law & Order; McCloud; McMillan and Wife; Miami Vice; The Mod Squad; The Naked City; Nash Bridges; NYPD Blue; Police Story; Police Woman; Starsky & Hutch; TJ Hooker; The Untouchables; Walker, Texas Ranger; Wyatt Earp.*

From Foreign Shores: Police Stories from Other Lands

Readers of mysteries are probably very familiar with the way the police do business in American and English mysteries, but when it comes to police work in other countries, readers may observe some startling differences. Some of the foreign police-detective series are written by writers native to that particular culture—such as Georges Simenon's books about the French Inspector Maigret, or Janwillem van de Wetering's books about Amsterdam cops Grijpstra and de Geer. Other writers move to a distant land and end up writing about it, as the late Arthur W. Upfield did with his long-running series about Australia, and some write police stories with an intent to show the reader just how society operates in a particular corner of the world.

From Australia and Canada to Russia and South Africa, the writers in this section show us how it's done in those corners of the world. Reading authors such as James McClure and

Stuart Kaminsky can give you insights into some cultures strikingly different from our own. After you've finished their books, you can plan your travel accordingly!

Cleary, Jon • A full-time writer for more than half a century, Australian writer Cleary is perhaps best known for his long-running series of police procedurals featuring Scobie Malone. First introduced in *The High Commissioner* (Morrow, 1966), Scobie is a strongly principled man, devoted to his family, and dogged in his pursuit of justice. He is based in Sydney, where most of his cases occur, but occasionally Cleary takes his detective to various parts of Australia. Over the three decades that Cleary has been writing this series, he has chronicled the various changes in Australian culture and politics, with the ever-likable Scobie Malone as the centerpiece. A nonseries book, *Peter's Pence* (Morrow, 1974), received the Edgar Award for Best Novel.

Dibdin, Michael • He began his career with two Victorian mysteries, one featuring Sherlock Holmes (*The Last Sherlock Holmes Story* [Pantheon, 1978]) and the other the poet Robert Browning (*A Rich, Full Death* [Cape, 1986]). Since then Dibdin has concentrated chiefly on suspense novels set in the present, in England, Italy, and America. He has written several novels featuring Aurelio Zen, a policeman from Venice. The first novel in the Zen series, *Ratking* (Bantam, 1989), won the Gold Dagger for Best Novel. The plot involves kidnapping and civic corruption, and the Italian setting is rendered compellingly. There is an intensity to the style that is reminiscent of suspense writers such as Ruth Rendell and Minette Walters. With the Aurelio Zen novels, Dibdin combines a number of elements: a disturbing portrait of contemporary Italy, psychological suspense, police procedure, and a compelling central character.

Recently Dibdin has published his first novel set in the United States, *Dark Specter* (Pantheon, 1996), a serial killer thriller.

Freeling, Nicholas • Not every mystery writer decides to kill his hero; Sir Arthur Conan Doyle tried it with Sherlock Holmes but was eventually forced to bring Holmes back. Freeling killed off his creation, Inspector Piet Van der Valk, in *Auprès de Ma Blonde* (Harper, 1972; published as *A Long Silence* in England), then wrote a book in which his widow acted as sleuth (*The Widow* [Pantheon, 1979]), but finally gave in and brought Van der Valk back in a case set prior to his demise, *Sand Castles* (Mysterious Press, 1990). Amsterdam policeman Van der Valk is thoughtful, cynical, unorthodox. He has few illusions about human behavior, but he has an intense curiosity about people that makes him an effective sleuth. For example, in *Criminal Conversation* (Harper, 1966), he is approached obliquely by an influential businessman, who believes he knows of a murder that has gone unsuspected. Van der Valk's curiosity leads him to confront the chief suspect, a well-known doctor, in a most unusual way.

The first Van der Valk novel is *Love in Amsterdam* (Harper, 1964; reprinted as *Death in Amsterdam*). Another Van der Valk novel, *The King of the Rainy Country* (Harper, 1966), received the Edgar Award for Best Novel in 1967. In addition to the Van der Valk novels, Freeling has written numerous stories about French policeman Henri Castang, but Castang is not as interesting a character as Van der Valk. The first of the Castang books is *A Dressing of Diamond* (Harper, 1974). Readers should check the library and used bookstores for most of these works.

Gill, **Bartholomew** • If you can't get to Ireland to see its sights and meet its people, you can always read Bartholomew Gill's mysteries and absorb plenty of authentic Irish atmosphere. Gill is the name that American writer Mark McGarrity uses for his cultured and literate series of Irish mysteries. The hero is tough, short, redheaded Peter McGarr, the chief of homicide for the Garda Siochana (the Irish Police) in Dublin. McGarr is a highly idiosyncratic cop, in a way perhaps unique to Dubliners. He loves good food and Irish whiskey, and he can always take time out from an investigation to eat and drink well. McGarr loves a good gossipy scandal that turns into an exciting chase after a crafty villain. His beautiful and smart wife, Noreen, who runs an art gallery and sometimes helps him in his cases, comes from an old aristocratic Irish family, and she gives McGarr a touch of class. McGarr is assisted by a team of homicide investigators, including the tall and coolly competent Ruthie Bresnahan; ex-boxer and womanizer Hugh Ward; and Bernie McKeon, busy father of eleven children.

Recently some of Gill's books have made use of literary backdrops, with the writings of such Irishmen as James Joyce and Jonathan Swift a central element in the plots. The very fine Edgar-nominated novel *The Death of a Joyce Scholar* (Morrow, 1989), for example, finds parallels to Joyce's *Ulysses* when a Joycean is killed during a Bloomsday celebration.

Gur, **Batya** • A best-selling novelist in her native Israel, Gur is a teacher of literature in Jerusalem. Her series of police procedurals stars Moroccan-born Michael Ohayon, who has the rank of Chief Inspector in the first novel, *The Saturday Morning Murder* (HarperCollins, 1992). In his first appearance, subtitled *A Psychoanalytic Case*, Ohayon is investigating the death of a well-known psychoanalyst in Jerusalem. Gur creates richly detailed backgrounds for each of her tales of murder, examining a particular community in thorough fashion. In *The Saturday Morning Murder*, the setting is a psychoanalytic institute; in the second book, *Literary Murder* (HarperCollins, 1993), the setting is the Literature Department at Hebrew University. Ohayon is a well-educated, intense professional who has considerable gifts of sensitivity and intuition. Sculpted in the mold of detectives such as Adam Dalgliesh and Reginald Wexford, Ohayon is definitely a "cousin" of the main characters in the best of the English police procedural school. Gur has successfully taken the form of the "English" detective story and transposed it to Israel. The novels offer a fascinating look at a complex society, a blend of both East and West.

Kaminsky, Stuart M. • A prolific author of several series of mysteries, Kaminsky won the prestigious Edgar Award for *A Cold Red Sunrise* (Scribner, 1988), his fifth novel about Moscow policeman Porfiry Petrovich Rostnikov. Kaminsky takes a locale that must seem exotic to many readers and uses it for a fascinating series of procedurals. These books offer Western readers startling glimpses inside the society and the psyche of a very different culture, but Kaminsky also allows readers to see just how alike Easterner and Westerner can be. The linchpin of the series is Rostnikov himself, a principled man looking always to see justice done in a system that is troubled by conflicting ideals. He is aided by numerous repeating characters: Emil Karpo, a man nicknamed "the Tatar" and "the Vampire" by his fellow police officers; and Sasha Tkach, a young man who finds himself increasingly torn by the demands of job and family. The plots of these books always involve politics of some sort, but they are not, in the final assessment, merely political thrillers. They are compelling and rewarding stories of human nature and a portrait of a society in transition. First in the series is *Death of a Dissident* (Berkley, 1981). Kaminsky also writes the Toby Peters (see "The Maltese Falcon") and Abe Lieberman (see "Hill Street Blues") series.

Keating, H. R. F. (Henry Raymond Fitzwalter) • A distinguished critic of mystery fiction, former president of the august Detection Club, and a Fellow of the Royal Society of Literature, Keating has written a long series of police procedurals starring Inspector Ganesh Ghote (pronounced "Gotay") of the Bombay CID. Humble and humane, Ghote is a thoughtful, methodical policeman, who desperately fears failure but who refuses to rush a solution to a case. Always attuned to the moral implications of his actions, Ghote seems sometimes like a bumbler, but despite problems and moral dilemmas, he generally figures things out. Aside from the endearing central figure of Inspector Ghote, these books offer a fascinating look at a culture in transition. The upper and upper-middle classes in India are still very much influenced by the hangovers of the British Raj, and the conflicting ideals of the cultures provide Keating with many opportunities. First in the series is *The Perfect Murder* (Dutton, 1965), which was filmed by the team of Merchant and Ivory.

Leon, Donna • The setting of Leon's series of novels about policeman Guido Brunetti is the intriguing city of Venice, which Leon has woven so thoroughly into her novels that the city is as much a character in the books as are any of the people. Guido Brunetti is a principled, intelligent, and caring man who has to steer his way carefully through the maze of Italian politics to see justice done. His wife comes from a very wealthy and prestigious Venetian family, and her connections are sometimes a hindrance, sometimes a help. In the first novel, *Death at La Fenice* (HarperCollins, 1992), which won Japan's prestigious Suntory Prize for Best Suspense Novel of 1991, Brunetti is called to the renowned opera house Teatro la Fenice to investigate the death of world-famous conductor-director Helmut Wellauer. In the second novel, *Death in a Strange Country* (HarperCollins, 1993), Brunetti is in charge of the investigation of the seemingly random murder of a young American from the nearby U.S. Air Force base. Leon uses the American military installation near Venice to give readers a glimpse of a setting rarely ever seen in most fiction.

Mann, Paul • Born and educated in England, and once a globe-trotting journalist, Mann now lives in the United States and writes a series of mysteries set in India. The main character in the series is Oxford-educated Inspector George Sansi. The product of a mixed marriage (an English father and an Indian mother), Sansi is something of an outsider in India, a half-caste. In the series opener, *Season of the Monsoon* (Ballantine, 1993), Sansi investigates a murder connected to Film City, Bombay's answer to Hollywood. Sansi's investigation takes him into a strange underworld in Bombay, and the political implications of the case threaten to destroy his career. Assisting him is an attractive American journalist, Annie Ginnaro, who becomes his lover. In *The Ganja Coast* (Ballantine, 1995), Sansi has left the police force to begin his law practice. He and Annie investigate a murder along India's "Ganja" coast in the sleepy beach community of Goa. Mann paints India in all her colors: exotic, frightening, poverty-stricken, yet always fascinating. Readers looking for a ticket to an unusual destination will find much to entertain them in the company of George Sansi.

Marshall, William • Born in Australia, Marshall has chosen the Far East as the setting for much of his output. He is best known for his series of highly unusual police procedurals set in the mythical precinct of Yellowthread Street in the equally mythical Hong Bay district in Hong Kong. Head of the ensemble of cops is Chief Inspector Harry Feiffer, who tries to ride herd on his unusual crew. Also on board are half-Irish, half-Chinese Christopher O'Ycc, and detective inspectors Auden and Spencer, one belligerently lower-middle-class and the other reluctantly upper. From the opening of the series, *Yellowthread Street* (Holt, Rinehart & Winston, 1976), this eccentric crew find themselves fighting crimes that are just as bizarre as the environment in which they live. In Marshall's work, Hong Kong is an exciting, tantalizing, mysterious blend of East and West, where things happen at a dizzying pace, almost faster than one can understand. The situations in the books often seem impossible beyond solution, but Marshall usually winds things up with aplomb, having led the reader a merry dance all the way. In addition to the long-running Yellowthread Street series, Marshall has written a couple of police procedurals set in Manila and two set in New York City in the late nineteenth century. Readers should check the library and used bookstores for most of these works.

McClure, James • Born and brought up in South Africa, McClure moved to England in 1965. When he began to write crime fiction, however, he chose his native South Africa as the setting. In a series of stellar police procedurals, McClure gives a chilling portrait of a deeply divided, violent society. In *The Steam Pig* (Harper & Row, 1972) he introduced his series characters, the Afrikaaner Lieutenant Tromp Kramer and his Bantu sidekick, Sergeant Mickey Zondi, of the Trekkersburg Police. The two men work well together, with mutual respect for each other's abilities, though the barrier of race sometimes presents problems for them. This series ably demonstrates how an outstanding writer can use the framework of a mystery novel to deliver not only an entertaining story but a deeply thought-provoking one as well. In his most recent novel, *The Song Dog* (Mysterious Press, 1992), a "prequel" to the series, McClure tells the story of how Kramer and Zondi first met. In addition to the Kramer and Zondi novels, McClure has written espionage and nonfiction about various police departments. *The Steam Pig* won the Gold Dagger for Best Novel. Readers should check used bookstores or the library for most of these works.

Nabb, Magdalen • An Englishwoman long resident in Florence, Italy, Nabb as a neophyte mystery writer could hardly have asked for higher praise than that which greeted her first novel, *Death of an Englishman* (Scribner, 1982), and from no less a writer than the late Georges Simenon. Writing about her adopted city, Nabb has created a superb series of novels starring a humane and very human character, Marshal Salvatore Guarnaccia. Sicilian by birth, the Marshal finds himself posted to Florence, where he learns to cope with the often mysterious ways of northern Italy and its people. Florence itself is an important character in these novels, but it is the Marshal, working slowly and steadily in each case, persisting against the stultifying pace of Italian bureaucracy, persevering in the name of justice, who makes the series so appealing. *Death of a Dutchman* (Scribner, 1983) and *The Marshal and the Madwoman* (Scribner, 1988) are excellent examples of Nabb's skill with plotting and characterization. Look for most of these books in the library or used bookstores.

Sale, Medora • This Canadian author has a Ph.D. in medieval studies from the University of Toronto, but when she turned to a life of crime-writing, she chose as her setting contemporary Toronto. Her first novel, *Murder on the Run* (Paperjacks, 1986), won the Arthur Ellis Award for Best First Novel from the Crime Writers of Canada and introduced Inspector John Sanders of the Toronto police. In her second novel, *Murder in Focus* (Scribner, 1989), Sale introduced Sanders's companion in crime and detection, architectural photographer Harriet Jeffries. The slowly developing relationship between Sanders and Jeffries, both of whom are definitely wary of emotional entanglements, is one of the chief appeals of this series. Sale handles the emotional topography of the relationship with restraint and insight. Above this, however, Sale also provides entertaining plots and an intriguing cast of secondary characters, some of whom sometimes take the lead role in the novels. An excellent example of this is *Sleep of the Innocent* (Scribner, 1991), in which Sergeant Rob Lucas investigates a murder involving an attractive young rock singer, while John and Harriet are on a disastrous vacation. This is a good, solid series that builds on the author's various strengths with each new book. Readers should check the library or used bookstores for most of these works.

Simenon, Georges • Incredibly prolific during his lifetime, Simenon was one of France's most prominent and critically lauded writers. He also created one of the most enduring detectives in the history of mystery fiction, Inspector Jules Maigret. Simenon's novels about Maigret are nominally police procedurals, in that Maigret is a policeman. Maigret does not solve his cases in routine police procedural fashion, however. Maigret doesn't depend on sophisticated forensic evidence, lengthy questioning of suspects, or the tried-and-true methods of other policemen around the world. Instead he soaks up the ambience of the world in which a particular crime has taken place, noticing all the details of behavior, the lay of the land (literally and figuratively), and the sights, sounds, and smells of the setting. He immerses himself into the case to the extent that he becomes part of it, and thus he comes to an understanding of the solution. Maigret calls himself a "repairer of destinies" (in *Maigret's First Case*), and this is how he sees himself—not as an avenger for the sake of justice, but one who can restore some sort of balance to a place or a group of people disarranged by crime. Simenon is a master of atmosphere, creating a mood and limning character with a modicum of words.

The many novels and stories featuring Maigret have appeared in numerous translations from the original French. Michael Gambon portrayed Maigret in a series produced in England and that aired in the United States as well.

Readers looking for a good introduction to Maigret might try *Maigret and the Flemish Shop* (originally published in English as *The Flemish Shop* in *Maigret to the Rescue*, [Harcourt, 1940]; now available on its own) and *Maigret and the Spinster* (Harcourt, 1977). Simenon takes Maigret out of his usual environment, to excellent effect, in *Maigret in Holland* (originally published in English as *A Crime in Holland* in *Maigret Abroad*, [Harcourt, 1940]; now available on its own). In addition to the eighty or so Maigret novels and collections, Simenon wrote more than a hundred other novels, highly regarded as well. American readers have seemed on the whole, though, to prefer Maigret.

Sjöwall, Maj, and Wahloo, Per • Folks who love Ingmar Bergman movies shouldn't miss an excellent series of police procedurals written by the Swedish husband-and-wife team of Maj Sjowall and Per Wahloo. Wahloo wrote a few mysteries on his own as well, but they are not as memorable as the ones produced (until he died) with his wife. These novels are very much in the station house tradition, in which a team of detectives works together to solve murders. Sjowall and Wahloo show every step of an investigation, and how much routine work must be done to solve crimes. These austere, sometimes bleak novels are set in the Swedish welfare state of the 1960s and '70s, when the economy was in good shape, but when society and the police were going through rapid and substantial changes.

The series begins in 1965, when the Swedish police force was nationalized, and there were major changes in the country's policing. The hero is Martin Beck, who is at first just a homicide detective in Stockholm (in later books, he's been promoted to Chief of the National Homicide Squad). His sidekick is Lennart Kollberg, and the other clearly drawn members of the homicide squad are Gunvald Larsson, Fredrik Melander, and Einer Ronn. Martin Beck may be calm, assured, and distant, but he is obsessed with getting his cases solved. The books show us the dark underbelly of Swedish society: the drugs, murder, theft, and crime in all its variety. Sjowall and Wahloo vividly describe the change of seasons, the cold Swedish winters, and the landscape of Stockholm and the South of Sweden, and these elemental forces influence the plots strongly. These are landmark police procedurals, which, along with Ed McBain's 87th Precinct novels, helped to set a trend that has been much imitated in later years. *The Laughing Policeman* (Pantheon, 1970) won a Best Novel Edgar, and was turned into a movie set in San Francisco, with Walter Matthau. *The Abominable Man* (Pantheon, 1972) was also filmed with the title *Man on the Roof*.

Upfield, Arthur W. • Among the many mystery writers of the first Golden Age, Upfield stands out by virtue of his series character, surely one of the most unusual of the "great detectives" of the time. Though he was born in England, Upfield lived much of his life in Australia, and it was there he chose to set his long-running series of mysteries featuring Inspector Napoleon "Bony" Bonaparte. Half aboriginal, Bony as a detective combines the best of both sides of his heritage. He has incredible patience, not worrying how long it may take him to crack a case—an attitude that often has him in trouble with his superiors, who want fast results. Many of Bony's cases take him to small towns or to settlements in the outback, and Upfield describes the settings vividly. In many ways, Upfield was a precursor to Tony Hillerman in writing mysteries that make deliberate use of setting as an important "character" in the novels. The first in the series is *The Barrakee Mystery* (Hutchinson, 1929; published in 1965 by Doubleday under the title *The Lure of the Bush*). Some of Bony's best cases include *The Bone Is Pointed* (Doubleday, 1947) and *Murder Down Under* (Doubleday, 1943; published as *Mr. Jelly's Business* in Australia and England in 1937 and 1938). Though Upfield was not always as sensitive to matters of race and culture as more contemporary mystery writers, he nevertheless remains readable and entertaining. Readers should check used bookstores or the library for some of these works.

Van de Wetering, Janwillem • The author once served as a reserve policeman in Amsterdam, and he has long been interested in Zen Buddhism. He has blended experience and interests into one of the most unusual series in contemporary crime fiction. Set chiefly in Amsterdam, Van de Wetering's books feature two Dutch policemen, Adjutant Grijpstra and Sergeant de Gier. The elder Grijpstra is the more stolid of the two; de Gier is more idealistic. They have established an unusual harmony in their working lives, symbolized by the drum-and-flute duets they play on a regular basis. Another member of the team is the Commisaris, known only as Jan, to whom Grijpstra and de Gier report. Jan serves as the moral center of the series. Van de Wetering gives a guided tour of Amsterdam as he takes his policemen throughout Dutch society in solving their crimes. First in the series is *Outsider in Amsterdam* (Houghton Mifflin, 1975), in which the duo investigates the death of a man who ran the Hindist Society, a combination commune and café. Was it suicide, or murder? And why was a man who eschewed material possessions wearing an expensive gold watch? Perhaps the best in the series is *Hard Rain* (Pantheon, 1986), in which the blend of action, atmosphere, and philosophy is most perfectly achieved.

Wright, Eric • Canadian author Eric Wright has won awards and critical acclaim for his series of mysteries about Toronto police inspector Charlie Salter. The first book in the series is *The Night the Gods Smiled* (Scribner, 1983), which won the Creasey Award for Best First Mystery. It introduces Charlie, a middle-aged police inspector with a wife and two sons. Bored since he's been sidelined by office politics, he is given a new job of assisting a Montreal cop with an investigation into the murder of a professor who has been killed at a literary conference in Montreal. His boredom evaporates as Charlie gets interested in the case. The series is notable for its realistic characterizations of Charlie and his family and the impressive descriptions of the city of Toronto.

In 1996 Wright began two new series with different heroes. One is Mel Pickett, who had a minor role in an earlier novel about Salter. Pickett is a retired Toronto cop, now living in a rural log cabin. The other series features Lucy Trimble Brenner, a former librarian who receives an inheritance from a long-lost cousin, moves to Toronto from a northern Ontario town, and takes over the cousin's failing private eye business. In the city, she shakes off the last shackles of her failed marriage and discovers that she is competent after all, even though everyone keeps telling her that she can't possibly become a PI. She makes some mistakes, like asking naive questions of mobsters and loan sharks, but she is learning all the time on her voyage of self-discovery.

Wright, L. R. • The "L." stands for Laurali, who is a journalist and novelist. Canadian Wright struck gold the first time out with a crime novel; her first, *The Suspect* (Viking, 1985), won the Edgar for Best Novel. Two elderly men are having a conversation, and suddenly one of them strikes the other dead, then toddles off home. Called in to investigate is Staff Sergeant Karl Alberg of the Royal Canadian Mounted Police, stationed in the town of Sechelt on Canada's Sunshine Coast. In his late forties, divorced but delving into the dating game again, Alberg is a shrewd, laconic detective. He works slowly through the evidence to identify the killer and the motive in this absorbing, inverted murder study. Subsequent novels in the series demonstrate Wright's interest in the reasons ordinary persons commit crimes. Each novel is in some ways a character study, either of a victim or a perpetrator, and of the people involved in the situation. As the series progresses, Alberg develops a romantic relationship with Cassandra Mitchell, the town's librarian. Thoughtful and compassionate, Wright looks into the nastiness in the human heart and creates fascinating novels of suspense. The Sunshine Coast is a vital part of her tapestry of crime, and her evocative descriptions of the area lend a strong sense of place to her work.

For Further Reading • Matthew Head; Mark Hebden; Elspeth Huxley; A. E. W. Mason; James Melville; Martin Cruz Smith; Ted Wood.

Some movies to look for are • *Cop au Vin*; *The Day of the Jackal*; *Gorky Park*; *Hardboiled*; *Inspecteur Lavardin*; the Pink Panther series; *Red Heat*; *A Shot in the Dark*; *Supercop*; *Touch of Evil*.

TV shows • *Citizen X*; *Maigret*.

Suspense/Psychological Mysteries

The Silence of the Lambs: Novels of Suspense

These days we seem to be fascinated by serial killers. The notion that a homicidal maniac may be out there, just around the corner, waiting to strike, has fascinated readers and moviegoers alike. Over the past two or three decades we have watched in horrified fascination as a number of diabolical serial killers have been caught: Ted Bundy, Ed Gein, John Wayne Gacy, and Jeffrey Dahmer, to name but a few. These real-life horrors are enough to keep some of us awake all night, with the lights on all over the house, but as terrifying as the real killers can be, their fictional counterparts can scare us just as much. Thomas Harris may have given the trend a jump start with his best-selling novel *The Silence of the Lambs*, which in turn became a hugely successful movie, but there are quite a few writers whose fevered imaginations have given us many spooky serial killers to keep us reading late into the night. The villains in some of these thrilling novels of suspense, often called "thrillers" for short, don't always have to be serial killers, but they do have to be nasty enough—

and clever enough—to outwit the hero or heroine on their trail, at least until the last pages of the book!

Camp, John • See **Sandford, John**.

Clark, Mary Higgins • They call her the Queen of Suspense. Mary Higgins Clark's thrilling novels have been making the best-seller lists since the 1970s. She never seems to run out of ideas for stories that make readers' flesh creep and keep them up long into the night. The books generally have attractive heroines or children in danger from a killer who is stalking them. The good guys are the police officers, doctors, lawyers, or even detectives who help find the evil villain (and Clark's villains are really wicked) and protect the vulnerable. Clark's protagonists are mostly upscale, sophisticated, and articulate people. The settings are always vividly drawn, and wintry scenes of northeastern cities and their suburbs abound. Her first novel, *Where Are the Children?* (Simon & Schuster, 1975), is set on Cape Cod, with a criminal who kidnaps two small children to frame their mother, who had been accused earlier in her life of killing two other children. In all of her novels, Clark slowly builds suspense with her clear prose and measured evocation of daily life, as a killer hovers and events move out of the control of the innocent. Incidents move inexorably toward a terrifying crisis that must occur before order can be restored at the end of the story. Meanwhile, Clark has given the reader a strong sense of the danger that can lurk even in the most protected and affluent lives.

Cook, Thomas H. • Cook is a wonderful writer, at his best when showing how lives can twine together, how a coincidence may engender a violent act that destroys those lives, and how the shape of a town can be changed forever by tragedy.

Early Cook novels include a series featuring Frank Clemons, originally a homicide detective in Atlanta, later a PI in New York City. The first novel in the Clemons series was the Edgar-nominated *Sacrificial Ground* (Putnam, 1988).

But perhaps his best work begins with *Breakheart Hill* (Bantam, 1995). It opens with: "This is the darkest story that I ever heard. And all my life I have labored not to tell it." It's a beautifully written story of obsessive love, scandal, hate, and betrayal in a small Alabama town. The story is recounted by Ben Wade, the town doctor, in flashbacks to 1962, when he was a high school student. A terrible crime, which happens at the base of Breakheart Hill, affects many in the community for years. The sorrows of the world are encapsulated in a single small American town in this elegiac and lyrical novel. With his next novel, Cook went on to win the Edgar Award for Best Novel for *The Chatham School Affair* (Bantam, 1996). This lovely, haunting book tells of a disastrous love affair in 1920s Cape Cod, and the murders that follow in its wake. It's told in the present and the past, weaving time together into an unbreakable strand in which every utterance is meaningful, love is both illimitable and tragic, and the past haunts us all.

Cook's powerful novels are emotionally absorbing and intense—not to be missed by readers looking for fine writing and unforgettable stories.

Cornwell, Patricia D. • Some writers take years to achieve best-seller status, but Cornwell did it very quickly. Cornwell took her years of experience as a computer analyst in the office of the chief medical examiner of the Commonwealth of Virginia and created a dynamic, forceful detective, Dr. Kay Scarpetta. The C.M.E. of Virginia, Scarpetta is an intense, driven character, and Cornwell keeps her busy with exciting stories of serial killers. Most of the books are set in Richmond and its environs, and the action never lags as Scarpetta starts on the trail of a vicious killer. As the series progresses, she forms a strong working relationahip with Richmond homicide cop Pete Marino, and her niece Lucy becomes an important secondary character in later books. Cornwell has a knack for explaining the complexities of forensic pathology to the layperson, and this attention to detail is one of the hallmarks of the series. She includes details that the squeamish might want to skim over, but she generally treats matter-of-factly the types of details that some writers tend to sensationalize. The commonplace and ordinary are never what they seem in the world of Cornwell and her creation Kay Scarpetta. The first in the series, *Postmortem* (Scribner, 1990), won most of the awards in the mystery world, including the Edgar, the Anthony, the Creasey, and the Macavity. A later book, *Cruel and Unusual* (Scribner, 1993), won the Gold Dagger for Best Novel.

Authors of Books With Medical Themes or Detectives

Robin Cook; Patricia Cornwell; Michael Allen Dymmoch; Leonard Goldberg; Christine Green (the Kate Kinsella series); Jonathan Kellerman; Mary Kittredge (the Edwina Crusoe series); Michael Palmer; Kathy Reichs; Stephen White.

Davis, **Dorothy Salisbury** • Davis was awarded the Grand Master Award by the Mystery Writers of America in 1984, and she has received multiple Edgar nominations for her books. She is known for creating a mean-streets atmosphere in her psychological mysteries, many of which are set in a vividly described New York City. One of her most memorable and famous works is *A Gentle Murderer* (Scribner, 1951). A young priest, Father Duffy, and Detective Sergeant Goldsmith are each searching separately for the same murderer. The murderer has confessed anonymously to Duffy, and the priest wants to find him to save his soul. The background and psychology of the killer are slowly revealed as Goldsmith and Father Duffy talk to the people who know the killer. Many of Davis's mysteries have a decidedly Irish-American atmosphere, and she is often concerned with issues of religion and moral dilemmas.

The Julie Hayes series has allowed Davis to depict an ongoing character who grows and changes as she matures and gains confidence in her intelligence. As the series begins, Julie is married to an older man who travels a great deal, and she finds herself insecure and restless. Acting on impulse, she sets up a storefront fortune-telling establishment and bills herself as "Friend Julie." She encounters crime and hostility in the seedy neighborhood, but also discovers that she can investigate murder successfully. Julie is a delightful character study, and her curiosity and frankness as she moves through the different classes of New York society make for a notable series of mysteries. Readers should look for most of these books in libraries and used bookstores.

Deaver, **Jeffery** • Deaver writes taut, suspenseful thrillers, some of which have been published under the name Jeffery

Wilds Deaver. His first book, *Manhattan Is My Beat* (Bantam, 1989), begins a series about Rune, an unusual Generation X heroine. In this novel, Rune is twenty and is living in a squat in New York City. She is an eccentric romantic, and she is always making up stories about the people she meets. Rune works in a video store, and she notices one customer who always rents a video of an obscure 1940s thriller. When he is murdered, Rune finds out that his favorite film was based on a true story about a crooked cop who stole a million dollars. She can't resist investigating further; what if he was involved with the old crime? In later books in the series, Rune continues to work in various aspects of the movie business. The novels are intelligently written, in spare and evocative prose.

Deaver's later novels are exciting thrillers. *Praying for Sleep* (Viking, 1994) is the terrifying tale of a giant crazed killer who escapes from a hospital for the criminally insane and comes after a woman who testified against him at his trial. Many different people, all with their own agendas, set out to hunt him down before he gets to his quarry. An acclaimed later book, *A Maiden's Grave* (Viking, 1995), is the story of three psychotic escaped convicts who take a school bus full of deaf girls and their teacher hostage in an abandoned slaughterhouse. Most of the book is the story of the siege that ensues and the story of the FBI's hostage negotiator, Arthur Potter, who is a master at negotiating with kidnappers. There's a great twist in the plot at the end. The book was turned into a made-for-cable movie called *Dead Silence*.

Francis, Dick • Dick Francis is a master at the art of creating exciting and nerve-wracking suspense thrillers. The Welsh-born Francis himself is a former champion steeplechase jockey who rode the Queen Mother's horses, and each of his books has some relationship to horse racing. The early ones are very directly about racing, with heroes who are jockeys or trainers, and plots about skullduggery at the racetracks. The first of these was *Dead Cert* (Holt, 1962). Francis may take a more tangential approach to the sport in his later books, but all of them are imbued with the excitement, the split-second timing, and the tension of racing itself. He generally creates a new hero for each book (although he has repeated protagonists a few times), and each new hero is a decent, hardworking man in an interesting occupation. Francis has written memorable novels about the wine trade, computers, trains, flying, toymakers, artists, veterinarians, actors, bankers, and many other topics that become fascinating because of his matchless storytelling ability. One of the most memorable of Francis's heroes is Sid Halley, who has appeared in three novels so far. Sid is a jockey who retires after a bad injury and becomes an investigator. He is physically courageous in spite of, or perhaps because of, his disability. Francis has received three Edgar Awards for Best Novel, plus Silver, Gold, and Diamond Dagger Awards. He also has been named a Grand Master by the Mystery Writers of America, and his books are best-sellers in many countries. Francis's thrillers are written in clear, spare prose, with memorable characters and plot twists.

Hall, James W. • Besides writing poetry, James W. Hall pens poetic adventure thrillers set in a South Florida that is under siege from developers and too many tourists. His series is about Thorn, a fisherman and renegade who has lived on Key Largo all his life. The first Thorn book is *Under Cover of Daylight* (Norton, 1987). Thorn has little money, lives in an old stilt house on Key Largo, and spends his time tying flies for bonefishermen. For years, he has been racked with anger and guilt over the drunk-driving deaths of his parents. In a flashback to his teenage years, we learn how Thorn took revenge on their killer. Now his adoptive mother, trying to save an endangered species, has been killed by drug dealers. What fresh revenge does Thorn have in mind this time? In *Mean High Tide* (Delacorte, 1994), Hall does a fine job of evoking the peace of daily life on the small island of Key Largo. But Thorn's peace is destroyed by murder, and he goes in search of the killer. It's a complicated tale of insanity, family secrets, and ecological disaster, but it might also be seen as a huge, almost mythic, fish story. An especially nasty villain breeds tulapia, a hardy fish that can live in fresh or salt water and reproduces like crazy. Thorn is afraid he will release them and swamp the Gulf of Mexico with fish that will take over and destroy native species. *Hard Aground* (Delacorte, 1993) is a wild treasure hunt for the gold from a wrecked Spanish ship. It's set in Miami, and Hall is good at showing how great life could be in South Florida if only man hadn't paved it over.

Authors of Detectives Who Like To Fish

James Lee Burke; Philip R. Craig; James W. Hall; David Leitz; William G. Tapply; Randy Wayne White.

Harris, Thomas • While Harris has published only three novels in twenty-five years, his works have all been popular successes and influential beyond their numbers. After working as a police reporter in Texas and later for the Associated Press, Harris produced *Black Sunday* (Putnam, 1975), a thriller about an attempt by Middle Eastern terrorists to kill the president and 81,000 other football fans during the Super Bowl. While presenting the usual character stereotypes (crazed Vietnam vet, beautiful female terrorist, gruff but lovable Mossad agent), *Black Sunday* takes the established disaster-thriller genre to new heights. *Red Dragon* (Putnam, 1981) introduced the memorable serial killer Dr. Hannibal "The Cannibal" Lecter, a paragon of good taste among psychos and an occasional advisor to the FBI on the capture of others like himself. Its sequel, *The Silence of the Lambs* (St. Martin's Press, 1988) has become the standard for serial-killer novels. With *Red Dragon*, it both capitalized on and furthered the popular fascination with serial murderers, which, in its current incarnation, began with Ed Gein's crimes in the 1950s and their dramatization in Alfred Hitchcock's film of Robert Bloch's novel *Psycho*.

Harris is a gifted narrator and constructor of plots, with a keen eye for character development, so it's not surprising that all three books have been made into films (*Red Dragon* under the title *Manhunter*). The film of *The Silence of the Lambs* was a major hit, and left a large opening for a sequel.

Harvey, Jack • See **Rankin, Ian,** in the "Calling Scotland Yard" section.

Kellerman, Jonathan • Best-selling novelist Jonathan Kellerman knows the criminal brain like nobody else. Kellerman is a child psychologist as well as being a writer, and he is married to mystery novelist Faye Kellerman. He seems to have tapped into a popular outpouring of interest in stories of children in jeopardy. Kellerman's thrillers feature Alex Delaware, a child psychologist in Los Angeles. Alex is a caring, sensitive amateur sleuth who often solves crimes in tandem with his good friend, LAPD homicide detective Milo Sturgis. Alex burned out after working too hard for too many years, so he took a very early retirement. But he can't resist helping kids who need him, and he begins working again as a consulting psychologist on criminal cases. These thrillers are filled with fascinating details about how psychologists work. The first one in the series is *When the Bough Breaks* (Atheneum, 1985), which won the Edgar and Anthony Awards for Best First Novel and was made into a movie. There are echoes of a famous Los Angeles child-abuse scandal of the day in this story of nefarious goings-on at a child care facility in Malibu. *Over the Edge* (Atheneum, 1987) is particularly rich in the particulars of forensic psychology, as Alex tries to find out about the case of a child genius who has been diagnosed as schizophrenic, then accused of being a deranged serial killer. Readers learn all about the different kinds of mental illnesses and their treatment, while being entertained by a fast-paced story. *Devil's Waltz* (Bantam, 1993) finds Alex dealing with a case of Munchausen syndrome by proxy, and it's a fascinating look at this rare psychological illness.

Kellerman departed from the Alex Delaware series with the atmospheric *The Butcher's Theater* (Bantam, 1988), which is set in Israel.

Kelman, Judith • For many years, Kelman has been writing suspense in the classic mode, in which women and especially children are in jeopardy from sociopathic serial killers. With

Killer Books

impressive skill, she depicts the warped mind of the murderer as he stalks his unwary victims and makes his dreadful plans. The books are generally set in the suburbs, especially in Connecticut, and Kelman contrasts the graphic violence and horror of a madman pursuing innocent children with the serene middle-class environment. In *The House on the Hill* (Bantam, 1992), a homicidal maniac, a missing child, and an attractive woman parole officer are the key elements of a thrilling suspense story. In *Where Shadows Fall* (Berkley, 1987), Kelman tells the story of a mother investigating her son's alleged suicide while at college. As with her other books, it is notable for her effective scene-setting and an atmosphere of lurking evil.

Millar, Margaret • The Canadian-born Millar grew up to become half of one of the world's most famous husband-and-wife teams. The late Kenneth Millar, perhaps better known as Ross Macdonald, turned to writing crime fiction after seeing the success of his wife. Margaret Millar began her career with three novels in the conventional detective vein featuring psychiatrist Dr. Paul Prye (beginning with *The Invisible Worm*, [Doubleday, 1941]). Prye's whimsical name is evidence of his creator's sense of humor, which is an underlying element in even the most hair-raising of her novels. Soon, however, Millar abandoned the detective story and concentrated on the mystery novel, and with such tales she found her greatest success. A prime example is the Edgar-winning *Beast in View* (Random House, 1955), often imitated, but never with the level of skill Millar brings to her work. Millar starts with some unusual event, a disappearance, a murder, a crime of some sort, then weaves a subtle tale of menace and suspense. Often the reader is never quite certain "whodunit" or "whydunit" until the last line of the novel. *The Listening Walls* (Random House, 1959) demonstrates this powerful technique beautifully. Late in her career, Millar created a new series character, the young Chicano lawyer Tom Aragon, who debuted in *Ask for Me Tomorrow* (Random House, 1976). Intelligent, compassionate, with a strong streak of unconventional humor, Aragon is an appealing sleuth. Standouts among the Millar oeuvre are *The Murder of Miranda* (Random House, 1979), *Beyond This Point Are Monsters* (Random House, 1970), and *How Like an Angel* (Random House, 1962). For her continued excellence in the field, the late Millar was named a Grand Master by the Mystery Writers of America in 1983. Readers should check the library and used bookstores for most of these works.

Padgett, Abigail • Padgett is a former court investigator who writes mysteries about children in danger. The heroine of her series is also one of the most memorable in recent years. Bo Bradley is a child abuse investigator, and she suffers from a manic-depressive illness. The series begins with *Child of Silence* (Mysterious Press, 1993), an eerie story about child abuse. Killers who are after a deaf child come after Bo, who is trying to stave off her own manic attack until she can get the child to safety and find his attacker. This is a highly unusual story and heroine, and Padgett's tale is rendered lyrically and suspensefully. Bo is often joined in her investigations by Andrew LaMarche, a Cajun pediatric surgeon who treats abused children. Bo makes a good sleuth; her illness makes her so aware of the details of her surroundings that she picks up very quickly on small impressions and nonverbal cues. She is delicately poised and alert to people's nuances. The Bo Bradley novels are intense books, hard to read lightly, but well worth the effort.

Patterson, James • Patterson has written several hugely popular thrillers, including a series of books about Alex Cross, an African-American homicide detective in Washington, D.C. Cross is not only a cop, but a psychologist as well, which gives him special insight into the minds of killers and the families of victims. Cross is also a dedicated family man, and he treasures his time with his grandmother and his two small children, Janelle and Damon. In the riveting suspense thriller *Along Came a Spider* (Little, Brown, 1992), Gary Soneji is a murderous sociopath who has long fantasized about the Lindbergh baby kidnapping. His obsession leads him to masquerade as a teacher at a private school to kidnap the daughter of a famous actress and the son of a cabinet member. Cross and his partner John Sampson are assigned to investigate the kidnapping, and they are drawn unwillingly into Soneji's web of deception. In *Kiss the Girls* (Little, Brown, 1995), a serial killer styles himself "Casanova" because he believes that he truly loves the women he murders. Cross is called in when it seems that Casanova has abducted Cross's niece. As in Patterson's other books, the suspense never lets up in this grisly and nerve-wracking story, which was made into a recent movie with Morgan Freeman. Novels by this best-selling author are always absorbing, with interesting characters and satisfyingly evil villains.

Pearson, Ridley • The thrill of the chase is everything in a Ridley Pearson book. Whether his characters are police officers, FBI agents, or psychologists, they are all dedicated to chasing down sophisticated killers or terrorists in these grip-ping thrillers. Pearson's series characters are Lou Boldt, a homi-cide sergeant in the Seattle Police Department, and Daphne Matthews, a Police Department psychologist. Lou and Daphne are both well-rounded characters, much more so than most characters in the techno-thriller genre. Pearson is also good at describing the harsh effects cops' jobs often have on their fam-ilies and personal relationships. Among thriller writers, Pearson is one of the best at depicting the forensic details of crime scenes. His exciting *Hard Fall* (Delacorte, 1992) is about an FBI investigator in pursuit of a group of German ecoterrorists who build bombs that bring down airplanes. Pearson tells us all about how plane crashes are investigated, and how the FBI tracks down terrorists in the United States. (Warning: Don't read this book while you're on an airplane!) In his gripping, persuasive techno-thrillers, Pearson uses all the technical details that he's learned in his obviously extensive research to take readers step-by-step through an investigation, with all the details laid out clearly. For example, *No Witnesses* (Hyperion, 1994) is an exciting, fast-paced thriller about the search for a killer who is tampering with food products in grocery stores. The absorbing details in this one include how an ATM bank-ing network works, how criminal profiling is done, and the grisly particulars of food poisoning. And the accumulation of authentic technicalities helps add weight to the inevitable buildup of suspense as the chase quickens after a mad killer.

Rendell, Ruth/Vine, Barbara • In addition to her long-running series of police procedural novels featuring Reginald Wexford, Rendell has penned numerous novels of suspense, which might better be labeled "crime novels." The first of these was *To Fear a Painted Devil* (Doubleday, 1965), which introduced readers to the "psychological" Rendell, one for whom the abnormal and unusual exert a powerful fascination. Rendell's interest in the "why" of crime has made her psychological novels, such as *Judgment in Stone* (Doubleday, 1978), some of the most original in contemporary mystery fiction. These novels are uncomfortable reading for some crime fiction fans who don't wish to know so much about the abnormal psychology of the criminal mind.

Rendell has written several novels under the pseudonym of **Barbara Vine**. These works have also attracted their share of awards and critical praise, such as *A Dark-Adapted Eye* (Bantam, 1986), which won the Edgar for Best Novel, and *King Solomon's Carpet* (Harmony Books, 1992), which won the Gold Dagger, as did *A Fatal Inversion* (Bantam, 1987). Though darker and certainly more psychological than the Wexford books, the Vine novels are often more approachable for crime fiction fans than the psychological Rendell novels. Whatever the reader's choice, Rendell has much to offer crime fiction aficionados.

Sanders, Lawrence • A consistent best-selling author since 1970, Sanders was perhaps the first mystery writer to strike gold with the "serial killer thriller." Taking a minor character from his novel *The Anderson Tapes* (Putnam, 1970), Sanders put Edward X. "Iron Balls" Delaney on the trail of a clever killer in *The First Deadly Sin* (Putnam, 1973). Delaney, a retired chief of detectives, is married to a woman with two adolescent daughters, and he has a strong and loving relationship with them. Fond of large, sloppy sandwiches, Delaney makes a formidable sleuth. Insightful, determined, he is deadly once he's on the trail of a killer. The first two "Deadly Sins" books are among the best of their kind, and Sanders was well ahead of his time with the first in the series. In addition to the four "Deadly Sins" books, which all feature Edward X. Delaney, Sanders has written several "Commandment" books and other best-selling thrillers. For his series of books about Archy McNally, see the section "Nancy, Frank, and Joe Grow Up."

Sandford, John/Camp, John • Mad-dog serial killers stalk the pages of John Sandford's thrillers. The novels in his Lucas Davenport series all have the word "Prey" in their titles, and they recount the chase for horrifyingly evil and cunning serial murderers. Davenport is a top-notch Minneapolis police detective with a moneymaking sideline as a video game designer. He uses his skills at gaming and strategy to hunt down murderers, and the suspense should keep readers turning pages long into the night. These are gripping and very bloody thrillers, and Sandford does a great job of creating fascinating portraits of psychotic killers. He also is excellent at drawing vivid Minnesota and Wisconsin landscapes for the backdrops of his novels, and *Winter Prey* (Putnam, 1993) especially shows us the fury and the danger of winter storms (it might remind readers of the movie *Fargo*).

John Sandford's real name is John Camp, and he is also a Pulitzer Prize-winning former journalist. He wrote a few lively computer caper novels using his own name, and now these have been reprinted under the Sandford name. *The Fool's Run* (Holt, 1989) and *The Empress File* (Holt, 1991) are fast-moving page-turners featuring Kidd, a computer consultant, professional artist, and con man. His sidekicks are LuAnn, a thief, and Bobby, a hacker who appears only in the form of on-line messages but is probably a black teenager somewhere in the Midwest. These three antiheroes get together to hack into computers and commit elaborate scams to get their hands on a lot of money.

Vine, Barbara • See **Rendell, Ruth**.

Walker, Robert W. • With the quick rise to stardom of Patricia Cornwell and her sleuth, forensic pathologic Kay Scarpetta, and the popularity of serial-killer thrillers, other writers are mining that same territory to entertaining effect. In 1992 Walker launched his series of mysteries featuring pathologist Dr. Jessica Coran, who works for the FBI, in *Killer Instinct* (Berkley Diamond, 1992). In this first of the "Instinct" books, Dr. Coran faces a particularly heinous killer, one who becomes known to the public as the "Vampire Killer," because he likes to drain his victims of blood. It quickly becomes obvious that one of the killer's main objectives is to add Dr. Coran to his collection of murder victims, and he nearly succeeds. In a later book in the series, *Pure Instinct* (Jove, 1995), this killer has escaped and is once again menacing Jessica's life as she works on a case in New Orleans.

Since she works for the FBI, Jessica Coran travels to various locations to work on cases, unlike some other pathologist sleuths, who work in essentially one jurisdictional area. Walker provides lots of detail of both FBI procedures and the forensic information that have helped make Cornwell's series so popular. Thus readers looking for mysteries full of forensic pathology will find much to enjoy here.

Wallace, Marilyn • After having written three police procedurals and edited a number of short-story anthologies (the *Sisters in Crime* anthologies, published by Berkley), Wallace penned a suspense novel, *So Shall You Reap* (Doubleday, 1992), somewhat in the vein of Barbara Michaels. Sarah Hoving finds herself in the midst of mysterious events in the small upstate New York town of Taconic Hills. Secrets from her own past and that of the town seem linked, and Sarah must discover why in order to save her own life. In *The Seduction* (Doubleday, 1993), two sisters in Taconic Hills are terrorized by a mysterious man who leaves strange and threatening gifts for one of them. What is the real purpose behind the gifts? Is it as sinister as they fear? In the recent *Lost Angel* (Doubleday, 1996) Wallace explores the heart-wrenching anxiety experienced by a mother whose child has been abducted. Whether she is writing police procedurals or suspense novels, Wallace writes crisply, with intelligence, and her stories are suspenseful and absorbing.

For Wallace's series of police mysteries, see the section "Hill Street Blues."

Walters, Minette • With *The Ice House* (St. Martin's Press, 1992), Walters won the John Creasey Award for Best First Novel, bestowed by the British Crime Writers' Association. Upon first look, *The Ice House* appears to be a fairly conventional English mystery. A body has been discovered in the abandoned ice house on an estate in Hampshire. Could it be the body of the estate owner's husband, who disappeared ten years ago? Or does it belong to someone else? From this starting point, Walters takes the conventions of the traditional English mystery and turns them topsy-turvy, sideways, and any which way she pleases, and the result is a compelling and engrossing story that never takes the tack the reader expects. With her second novel, *The Sculptress* (St. Martin's Press, 1993), Walters explores our modern fascination with brutal murderers. Roz Leigh, a journalist whose life is in shambles, reluctantly agrees to write a book about Olive Martin, a monstrous young woman who murdered her mother and sister, then calmly dismembered their bodies before calling the police to confess the crime. Fascinated by Olive, Roz delves further and further into the background of the crime to understand why it happened, and she finds herself drawn deeper into Olive's disturbing world. *The Sculptress* has been shown as a TV movie. Walters's third novel, *The Scold's Bridle* (St. Martin's Press, 1994), won the Gold Dagger for Best Novel. An elderly woman is found naked in her bathtub, wearing a medieval device forced on women who nagged their husbands too much. Did she commit suicide, or was she murdered? Walters conjures up a dark and brooding atmosphere in her novels in which nothing—and no one—are ever quite what they seem. Since each of her first three novels has been awarded a major prize from her peers in the mystery world, Walters has obviously established herself as a major force in the field.

White, Randy Wayne • White is a fishing guide in Florida, and he writes mysteries set in the islands on the Gulf Coast of Florida. Marine biologist Doc Ford, who lives in a stilt house on the edge of Sanibel Island, makes a precarious living by catching and preparing specimens of sea life for biological supply houses. He is also trying to live an easy, emotionally disconnected life in a place as close to paradise as he can find. When he tries to help out some folks who come to him with problems, Doc Ford becomes an amateur sleuth in spite of his reluctance to get anywhere near violence again. It seems that he is a burned-out former agent for the National Security Agency. He has a gun left over from his days as a spy, but he hates to use it. Ford says he feels no emotions, but he wants justice, perhaps even revenge, for the deaths of people he knows and just maybe loves. Doc Ford's best buddy and sidekick, Tomlinson, is an old hippie who is naive, kind, and highly intelligent. Ford is rational; Tomlinson is mystical, and this duality makes for a great sleuthing partnership. The Doc Ford books are a fascinating mixture of science and spirituality. White evokes a strongly atmospheric Florida setting and provides exceptional details about deep-sea fishing and the environmental dilemmas of modern Florida. White's novels are beautifully written, with ingenious plots and a sense of high adventure. One of the best in the series is *Captiva* (Putnam, 1996).

White has also written thrillers under the pseudonyms of Carl Ramm and Randy Striker.

White, Stephen • Who better than a psychologist to analyze the motivation behind a crime, do a psychological profile, and find the murderer? Colorado psychologist Dr. Alan Gregory goes off in hot pursuit of disturbed killers in these thrillers. In *Private Practices* (Viking, 1993), the first book in the series, one of Alan's female clients is brutally killed in his office building. The police want to look at his files as part of their investigation, but he is concerned about client confidentiality. But, he wonders, is this ethical principle worth maintaining when the killer may strike again if they can't catch him first?

Meanwhile, Alan's career is in trouble because of all the bad publicity from the murder, and later he has trouble reestablishing his good reputation and wooing back his patients. But he has made a good friend of a homicide detective, and he gets more forensic psychology work as the series continues. Alan is a decent, sensitive guy, and an enthusiast for mountain biking, in these thought-provoking thrillers. His lover, Lauren Crowder, has multiple sclerosis, and she struggles to lead a normal life in spite of her disease. Lauren is a stubborn, prickly woman, a smart lawyer, and a fascinating character study. (White himself began to write mysteries after he was diagnosed with multiple sclerosis.)

One of the best books in the series, *Higher Authority* (Viking, 1994), is not only a mystery but also a rather savage expose of the Mormon Church. When the lesbian clerk of a Mormon Supreme Court justice is murdered, Lauren's sister becomes a suspect. Lauren and Alan help search for the killer, and they stumble across secret material that could hurt the church. (Warning: readers who are Mormons may be offended.)

Wiltse, David • Wiltse has created a chillingly effective series sleuth, John Becker. Becker was an FBI agent who specialized in tracking serial killers. He has the ability to think like one of them; he should—he's been a killer himself. When he finds himself enjoying his job too much—he likes hunting them down and finding some way of killing them—he leaves the FBI. But somehow Becker keeps getting lured back into the hunt. *Into the Fire* (Putnam, 1994) is one of Wiltse's best. Becker is forced into helping the FBI with a particularly nasty killer, and despite his dislike of the agency, he becomes involved. The scenes involving the killer and his latest victim are eerie and chilling. In *Bone Deep* (Putnam, 1995), Becker investigates a nasty discovery in a small Connecticut town. A flood has unearthed a number of garbage bags filled with human bones. These bones are the remains of young women who were supposed to have run away from home. But, as Becker knows, the answer to their deaths is far more twisted. Wiltse has created some of the spookiest killers since Thomas Harris, and his main character, John Becker, is just about as spooky as the killers. Readers looking for something chillingly different will want to give Wiltse a try. First in the series is *Prayer for the Dead* (Putnam, 1991).

Woods, Stuart • Woods writes fast-moving, sexy thrillers, often featuring police officers or former officers. The seductive call of the high life is ever present in his novels. Woods himself lives in Santa Fe and Key West, and he often sets books in these locations, along with New York and Hollywood settings. *L.A. Times* (HarperCollins, 1993) is both a thriller and a black comedy about a charming sociopath, Vinnie Callabrese, who wants to become a film producer in the worst way. He seduces, kills, and cons his way into the film business in New York, with some help from his colleagues in the Mafia. Without a blink, he kills anybody who gets in his way, and when he moves out to Hollywood he gets along very well there for quite a while...

New York Dead (HarperCollins, 1991) is the first of Woods's thrillers to feature New York lawyer Stone Barrington. Stone is a police officer who is invalided out of the force after he is shot in the knee. He has a law degree, so he opens his own practice and starts by doing investigative work for lawyers. A beautiful TV anchorwoman is pushed over a balcony and falls, perhaps to her death. Her body disappears on the way to the hospital, so no one knows for certain if she's dead. Stone happens to see the accident, and inevitably he gets involved in the mystery. Stone returns in *Dirt* (HarperCollins, 1996).

Some of Woods's books have been turned into TV miniseries, including *Grass Roots* (Simon & Schuster, 1989), and *Chiefs* (Norton, 1981), which is about several generations of the same family who were all chiefs of police in a Georgia town.

Yorke, Margaret • Yorke began her mystery-writing with a series of conventional detective novels featuring Oxford don Patrick Grant, whose first appearance was in *Dead in the Morning* (Geoffrey Bles, 1970). Handsome, learned, and incurably nosy, Grant is much in the mold of the gifted amateur detective, and in his five appearances he serves as an entertaining, if not compelling, sleuth. After her fourth novel about Grant, Yorke wrote a novel that was to signal the direction of her career in crime. *No Medals for the Major* (Geoffrey Bles, 1974) is set in a much more contemporary edition of the traditional English village of the crime novel. In this setting Yorke has full range for her considerable talent in observing the ordinary routines of life and how these routines, and the people who effect them, can be altered, even destroyed, by crime. Yorke's world is no St. Mary Mead, and she mines this ground time after time with quiet effect. She focuses on ordinary people, not the psychopaths so beloved of her peer Ruth Rendell, and demonstrates to the reader just how easily crime can upset the delicate balance of an ordinary person. Other excellent examples of Yorke's craft are *A Small Deceit* (Viking, 1991) and *Criminal Damage* (Mysterious Press, 1992).

For Further Reading • Charlotte Armstrong; Patricia Carlon; Ursula Curtiss; Stanley Ellin; Joy Fielding; Joan Fleming; Celia Fremlin; Michael Gilbert; Ed Gorman; Elizabeth Sanxay Holding; P. M. Hubbard; Dorothy B. Hughes; Nancy Baker Jacobs; John Katzenbach; Andrew Klavan; Ira Levin; Helen McCloy; Patricia McGerr; Edgar Allan Poe; Mabel Seeley; Kay Nolte Smith; Julian Symons; Andrew Taylor; Teri White; Cornell Woolrich.

Suspense films to look for include • *Absolute Power; The Bad Seed; Basic Instinct; Cape Fear; City Hall; The Collector; Con Air; Conspiracy Theory; Copycat; The Crying Game; Death Trap; Diabolique; Dial "M" for Murder; Face/Off; Fatal Attraction; Frenzy; F/X; Gaslight; Hush…Hush, Sweet Charlotte; The Jagged Edge; The Juror; The Lady Vanishes; The Letter; The Lodger; The Man Who Knew Too Much; The Manchurian Candidate; Manhunter; Marnie; Maximum Risk; Misery; Night of the Hunter; North by Northwest; Notorious; Play Misty for Me; Psycho; Ransom; Rear Window; Rope; Sabotage; Scream; Shadow of a Doubt; Shallow Grave; The Silence of the Lambs; Single White Female; Sleeping with the Enemy; Sliver; Smilla's Sense of Snow; Sorry, Wrong Number; Speed; Speed 2; Spellbound; The Spiral Staircase; Strangers on a Train; Suspicion; Taxi Driver; The 39 Steps; Ulee's Gold; Vertigo; Wait Until Dark; Where Are the Children?.*

TV suspense shows • *Alfred Hitchcock Presents; Profiler; The Twilight Zone.*

Historical Mysteries

Once Upon a Crime

"The good old days." Everyone talks about them, now and again, though without any exact certainty of just *when* those good old days actually happened. But readers who long to escape into some past time, whether the days were good or bad, a few decades or a few centuries—or even a millennium— ago, now have the services of a number of expert travel guides. These guides are many of today's mystery writers who combine mysteries with historical fiction. Since early in the twentieth century, when a writer named Melville Davisson Post wrote mystery short stories set in the years just prior to the American Civil War, there have been historical mysteries. But it wasn't until the late Ellis Peters created a very popular hero in her twelfth-century monk-detective, Brother Cadfael, that the popularity of historical mysteries began to surge. Nowadays, mystery readers wanting to vacation in the past can just about pick the century they want to visit—and there's a series of mysteries just waiting to be read. Anne Perry, with two series of mysteries set in Victorian England, is a consistently best-selling author, and Caleb Carr penned a hugely successful novel, *The Alienist*, that left readers clamoring for more. For many readers, the mysteries of the past are just as compelling as those of the present day.

Alexander, Bruce • Jeremy Proctor, a thirteen-year-old orphan, is the narrator in Alexander's series of mysteries about Sir John Fielding, the Bow Street magistrate known as the "Blind Beak" in eighteenth-century London. Though blind, Fielding was known to be able to recognize the voices of several hundred criminals, and with his half brother, the novelist (and also magistrate) Henry Fielding, he founded the Bow Street Runners, England's first attempt at a modern police force. In *Blind Justice* (Putnam, 1994), Jeremy Proctor is brought before Fielding on a false charge of theft, and Fielding soon sorts the situation out and takes Jeremy into his protection. Fielding must solve the strange death of a nobleman whose body is found in a locked room, a seemingly impossible crime. But the "Blind Beak" proves a match for even the cleverest of the sighted, and Jeremy Proctor narrates the tale with gusto. Alive with the sights and sounds and smells of Georgian London, this is an enjoyable series, with a milieu very similar to that of Robert Lee Hall's series featuring Benjamin Franklin, about a decade earlier.

Barron, Stephanie • One of nineteenth-century England's greatest novelists is the sleuth in this delightful series of historical mysteries. In Barron's portrayal, Jane Austen proves to be every bit as clever and resourceful as one would expect from her own novels, and Barron has interwoven the facts of Austen's life and the gaps in our knowledge of it into her imaginative stories. In the first of the series, *Jane and the Unpleasantness at Scargrave Manor* (Bantam, 1996), Jane is visiting a friend, the young Countess of Scargrave, in Hertfordshire in the spring of 1803. When the Earl dies under mysterious circumstances, Jane turns detective to help her friend, who has fallen under suspicion of having murdered her elderly husband. Writing with scrupulous attention to the details of the period and with an ear to the rhythm of Austen's prose, Barron has endowed the "Immortal Jane" with a believable and engaging personality. Readers who enjoy mysteries set in the early nineteenth century should also try Kate Ross's books about Regency sleuth Julian Kestrel.

For Barron's contemporary mysteries, written under the name of **Francine Mathews**, see the section "Hill Street Blues."

Bastable, Bernard • Well-known English mystery novelist Robert Barnard chose the pseudonym "Bernard Bastable" for his historical mysteries, some of which feature an aging person named Mozart as the sleuth. The first book under the Bastable name, *To Die Like a Gentleman* (St. Martin's Press, 1993), is a Victorian mystery told chiefly in epistolary form. With the second Bastable novel, *Dead, Mr. Mozart* (St. Martin's Press, 1994), the author introduced Wolfgang Gottlieb Mozart, who is living in London in the 1820s. This Mozart is the composer of numerous works, but they have not received the attention they should have. Thus, with his alternative Mozart, Bastable offers a distinctly unusual historical sleuth. Weaving in the political intrigues of the time, Bastable fashions entertaining plots for his detective to solve. Readers looking for other mysteries set in the early nineteenth century should try the works of Kate Ross.

For **Robert Barnard's** other mysteries, see the section "The Butler Did It."

Baxt, George • Baxt broke new ground in the mid-1960s with his first mystery, *A Queer Kind of Death* (Simon & Schuster, 1966). The hero of this novel, Pharoah (sic) Love, is a gay black policeman. Thus it is the first detective novel with a gay hero. This is not really a police procedural novel; the main character just happens to be a policeman. The milieu is the gay underworld of New York, which Baxt used to even better effect in the second of the series, *Swing Low, Sweet Harriet* (Simon & Schuster, 1967). After a long hiatus, Baxt recently published two more novels in the series.

Today Baxt is perhaps best known for his long series of celebrity detective novels, most of which are set against the past of Hollywood and all the glamour of show business. Baxt's first venture into historical detection is *The Dorothy Parker Murder Case* (St. Martin's Press, 1984). The witty and acerbic Parker makes a delightful detective, as she and other members of the Algonquin Round Table nose around in crime. Later books make extensive use of Baxt's experiences in Hollywood and his insider's knowledge. He has brought some of the great stars of the Golden Age of Hollywood to life in these stories; for example, in *The Tallulah Bankhead Murder Case* (St. Martin's Press, 1987), *The Greta Garbo Murder Case* (St. Martin's Press, 1992), and *The Humphrey Bogart Murder Case* (St. Martin's Press, 1995). Readers with a taste for nostalgia and the glory days of Hollywood will find much to enjoy with these books. Most of them will be more likely found at the library.

Brightwell, **Emily** • Brightwell pens a series of light and enjoyable mysteries set in late Victorian England. The main character is Mrs. Hepzibah Jeffries, widow of a Yorkshire policeman and now housekeeper to a Scotland Yard detective, Inspector Witherspoon. A nice man who has inherited money, a house, and servants from an aunt, Witherspoon is rather inept as a detective. Mrs. Jeffries, along with the rest of the household staff, works behind the scenes to help the inspector with his cases. The other servants bring their information to Mrs. Jeffries, who then manages to feed it to Witherspoon, so that he is none the wiser. Though these books do not have the emotional depth or the wealth of detail of Anne Perry's Victorian novels, they have their own light charm. First in the series is *The Inspector and Mrs. Jeffries* (Berkley, 1993).

Carr, **John Dickson** • An American with a strong interest in English history, Carr about midway in his career as a mystery writer began to write mysteries set in the past. These are among some of the first historical mysteries in the genre. Carr was definitely captivated by the "romance" of ages past, and his tales of historical murder were often full of swashbuckling and derring-do, combined with his usual "locked room" or "impossible crime" mystery. His first novel in this vein, *The Bride of Newgate* (Harper, 1950), is a good example. This is the story of an aristocratic Englishman, reprieved from the hangman's noose at the last moment, imprisoned for a crime he did not commit. He gets the chance to solve the murder for which he was almost executed, and along the way he wins the heart of a fair maiden as well. *The Devil in Velvet* (Harper, 1951), among Carr's best in this vein, involves time travel as well as history. A contemporary historian of the Restoration period travels back to his favorite time to try to prevent a murder. Carr ingeniously spins these tales, packing them with fascinating and colorful details of daily life of the period in which they are set, and combining them with his trademark complex plots. Readers looking for these books should check the libraries and used bookstores.

For Carr's two long-running series of classic English detective stories, see the section "The Butler Did It."

Clynes, Michael • See **Doherty, P. C.**

Collins, Max Allan • For Collins's series of historical private eye novels, see the section "The Maltese Falcon."

Davis, Lindsey • A former civil servant with no formal training in classics, history, or archaeology, Davis now writes full-time, chiefly about the world of Rome in the first century A.D. Her series character is Marcus Didius Falco, a public informer, the ancient Roman ancestor of Philip Marlowe and Sam Spade. Falco's voice makes the first novel in the series, *Silver Pigs* (Crown, 1990), seem almost anachronistic in the early pages, but then the reader watches the streets and the people of Rome come vividly alive and forgets about the modern world. The plebeian Falco is an ardent republican in the days of the Flavian emperors, and, to his own disgust, he often finds himself working for the emperor Vespasian, or his son Titus. In *Silver Pigs* Falco meets the patrician Helena Justina, and the sparks fly between them, for Helena Justina is just as strong-willed as Falco. These lovers' paths to each other are difficult, for the barriers of social class and wealth are difficult to breach, but Davis makes the struggle an enjoyable and involving one. Davis is a fine historical novelist who spins tales that both entertain and educate.

Doherty, P. C. • From the sheer volume of his output, Doherty has established his own corner of the market for the medieval mystery novel. A Ph.D. from Oxford University who is now headmaster of a public school in North London, Doherty manages to pen several novels a year under various pseudonyms. As Doherty he is best known as the author of the Hugh Corbett series. Corbett is a clerk at the court of Edward I when he first appears in *Satan in St. Mary's* (St. Martin's Press, 1987). As Corbett's success in solving problems for the king continues, his status improves; he becomes Sir Hugh, and with his advancement come more dangerous assignments from the king. The plots of the novels are intertwined with events of the times, the late thirteenth and early fourteenth centuries in England and France. Also as Doherty, he has recently begun a second series, in which Chaucer's Canterbury pilgrims each tell a dark tale of mystery and murder; the first of these is *An Ancient Evil* (St. Martin's Press, 1995). As **Michael Clynes**, Doherty writes about the adventures of Sir Roger Shallot, a rogue and adventurer in the service of Cardinal Wolsey and Henry VIII. The first of this series is *The White Rose Murders* (St. Martin's Press, 1992). Under the name of **Paul Harding**, Doherty pens the "sorrowful mysteries" of Brother Athelstan, a Dominican friar who serves as priest for a poor parish in the slums of Southwark. He acts also as clerk to the coroner of the City of London, Sir John Cranston, a larger-than-life character who is one of Doherty's most entertaining creations. The first of this series, set in late fourteenth-century London, is *The Nightingale Gallery* (Morrow, 1992). Writing as **C. L. Grace**, Doherty has created his sole female series character, Kathryn Swinbrooke, a physician and apothecary in late fifteenth-century Canterbury. The first in this series is *A Shrine of Murders* (St. Martin's Press, 1993). Finally, as **Ann Dukthas**, Doherty has begun a series with a time-traveling detective. Nicholas Segalla has been condemned to travel through time, solving the unsolved mysteries of the past. In the first, *A Time for the Death of a King* (St. Martin's Press, 1994), Segalla tackles the murder of Lord Darnley, the ill-fated second husband of Mary, Queen of Scots.

Whatever the name, Doherty pens tales of adventure and mystery that make history entertaining. Readers should check the library and used bookstores for many of Doherty's works.

Douglas, Carole Nelson • Science fiction, romance, and two quite different series of mysteries all can be found among the books written by Carole Nelson Douglas.

But Douglas is known for writing Sherlock Holmes novels with a difference. And what a charming difference it is! The chief character in these books is Irene Adler, who appeared in the story "A Scandal in Bohemia" and is generally thought to be the only woman Holmes ever loved. Not only does Douglas show us classic mysteries through Irene's eyes, but also the novels include beautifully re-created Victorian backgrounds. They are narrated by Penelope (Nell) Huxleigh, a typist and poverty-stricken parson's daughter, who is Irene's best friend and perhaps the equivalent of Dr. Watson in these tales. In each book, Irene, Nell, and Irene's husband, Godfrey Norton, match wits with Sherlock Holmes himself in their investigations. First in the series is *Good Night, Mr. Holmes* (Tor, 1990).

Dukthas, Ann • See **Doherty, P. C.**

Dunn, Carola • The author of numerous historical novels, Dunn recently began writing a series of historical mysteries, set in England in the 1920s. The heroine of the series is the Honourable Daisy Dalrymple. A cousin has succeeded to her father's estate and his wealth, and rather than live on the charity of her family, Daisy has decided to work for a living, though it is not the thing done by a young woman of her class in 1923! In the first book of the series, *Death at Wentwater Court* (St. Martin's Press, 1994), Daisy has landed an assignment with *Town & County* magazine to do an article on Wentwater Court, the estate of the Earl of Wentwater. Little does Daisy know, however, that Murder will be a guest as well. Scotland Yard turns up to investigate the crime, in the person of a handsome chief inspector, Alec Fletcher. Daisy proves an able, though not always welcome, assistant to the Scotland Yard crew. Subsequent books in the series take Daisy on further assignments, where she continues to encounter murder and the handsome policeman. A relationship develops slowly between the two, hampered a bit by the differences in their social class. Readers nostalgic for the bygone days of the classic English mystery of the first Golden Age will find much to enjoy in these books.

Eyre, Elizabeth • The writing team of Jill Staynes and Margaret Storey (who also have written mysteries published under the name of Susannah Stacey) produces a successful series of historical mysteries set in Renaissance Italy. Sigismondo, the Duke of Rocca's agent, is an enigmatic and crafty sleuth in these atmospheric novels. The authors' complicated and intricate plots accurately reflect an ambience of conspiracies and constant Machiavellian scheming, along with finely detailed historical settings. The series begins with *Death of the Duchess* (Harcourt Brace Jovanovich, 1992). Readers should check the library and used bookstores for most of these works.

For the Inspector Bone mysteries by **Susannah Stacey**, consult the section "Calling Scotland Yard."

Frazer, Margaret • Margaret Frazer is a pseudonym for two American writers with a strong interest in the Middle Ages. Mary Monica Pulver is the author of a contemporary American mystery series, and her partner as "Margaret Frazer" is Gail Frazer. For their detective, the authors chose Sister Frevisse, a Benedictine nun at St. Frideswide's in fifteenth-century England. Frevisse is connected to the Chaucer family, and Sir Thomas Chaucer (son of the medieval poet) appears in several of the early books in the series. The first book is *The Novice's Tale* (Berkley, 1992), wherein Sister Frevisse (often called Dame Frevisse, in deference to her status both in the cloister and without) investigates the murder of an obnoxious noblewoman whose niece, the eponymous novice, is the chief suspect. The authors have an obvious love for their period, and they handle the details of the background nicely. Readers looking for engaging tales of historical murder will have a pleasant time in the company of Sister Frevisse. Beginning with *The Prioress' Tale* (Berkley, 1997), Gail Frazer is the sole author of the series.

Grace, C. L. • See **Doherty, P. C.**

Hall, Robert Lee • Many authors writing historical mysteries use historical personages in their stories, but not all writers use such figures as their sleuths. Hall has taken one of the great figures of American history, Benjamin Franklin, and turned him into a detective. Hall writes about Franklin during the period, beginning in 1757, when Franklin lived in London and served as agent for the Pennsylvania colony. *Benjamin Franklin Takes the Case* (St. Martin's Press, 1988) brings Franklin into contact with one Nicholas Handy, apprentice to a printer who has been brutally murdered. The dead printer was a friend of Franklin's, and Nick Handy, who narrates the tales, aids Franklin in solving the murder, of which Nick is at first suspected. Thereafter Franklin takes Nick on as his assistant, and Nick has a surprise in store, as he discovers the truth of his relationship to Franklin. Hall creates a vivid portrait of Georgian London, and his interpretation of Franklin's character is lively and engaging. The narrative voice of Nick Handy is appealing, never childish or coy.

Harding, Paul • See **Doherty, P. C.**

Kaminsky, Stuart M. • For Kaminsky's series of historical private eye novels, see the section "The Maltese Falcon."

Kerr, Philip • Philip Kerr has created a very distinctive world: the Third Reich as seen from the inside. Kerr is a Scottish writer who has been critically acclaimed for the historical mysteries known as the Berlin trilogy. *March Violets* (Viking,

1989) is set in 1936, as the Nazis are consolidating their power. *The Pale Criminal* (Viking, 1990) is set in 1938, and *A German Requiem* (Viking, 1991) takes place in the dark and despairing postwar Berlin of 1947. Kerr has done outstanding research on what daily life in Berlin was like before and after World War II. Every detail is carefully chronicled, and there is a strongly conveyed sense of place and elaborate descriptions of the setting and of architecture. The accumulation of details is built into a fascinating backdrop for the complex and dark plots. The series focuses on Bernie Gunther, a civil policeman and sometime private eye in Berlin. Bernie hates the Nazis and their terrifying bureaucracy, and he often gets into trouble with the Gestapo over his investigations. Bernie's cases tell us much about the intrigues of power groups and bureaucrats in Germany, especially the military versus the civil authorities in the Nazi hierarchy.

Kerr also wrote *Dead Meat* (Mysterious Press, 1994), which features Detective Yevgeni Grushko, and is set in St. Petersburg, Russia. Kerr depicts the realities of daily life in Russia as the Soviet Union disintegrates. A British television series was made from it, and it was republished under the title of the series: *Grushko* (London: Arrow, 1994). Another widely praised novel is *A Philosophical Investigation* (Farrar, Straus, & Giroux, 1993), which is set in the future, in the year 2013. Serial killers have proliferated over the years and now roam Europe, killing regularly. Kerr's main character is Jake, a female detective and head of the Gynocide Department at Scotland Yard (homicide now deals only with male victims). Jake is up against a killer code-named "Wittgenstein," who learns that his brain lacks a chemical that controls violence in men. He is sent over the edge by this news, and manages to find the computer files on other men who might turn into violent criminals. "Wittgenstein" decides he is saving society by killing these men. As usual, Kerr tells an exciting story full of intelligent musings on our moral and ethical dilemmas.

King, Laurie R. • In 1915 on the Sussex Downs, young Mary Russell stumbles over the legendary detective Sherlock Holmes, supposedly retired. Thus is born one of the most memorable partnerships in recent mystery fiction, in *The Beekeeper's Apprentice* (St. Martin's Press, 1994), an Agatha nominee for Best Novel. Mary is fifteen years old when she meets Holmes, but she proves more than a match for the great detective, however. Mary proves to be every bit as intelligent, resourceful, and dogged as Holmes himself. Their relationship continues in *A Monstrous Regiment of Women* (St. Martin's Press, 1995), as Mary nears graduation from Oxford University. In *A Letter of Mary* (St. Martin's Press, 1997), their relationship has taken on a new dimension. King has endowed Mary Russell with her own chief academic interest, theology, and the author makes fascinating use of her knowledge in this series, one of the most unusual and original in contemporary mystery fiction.

For King's series of contemporary mysteries, see the "Hill Street Blues" section.

Kingsbury, Kate • Kingsbury has assembled an engaging cast of characters for her series set in Edwardian England. The main character, Cecily Sinclair, is a widow who is running a resort hotel in the seaside town of Badgers End, ably aided by the hotel manager, Baxter. Two of Mrs. Sinclair's friends, the vicar's mother and the local herbalist, occasionally lend a hand with entertainments and floral arrangements to make the Pennyfoot Hotel a highly desirable vacation spot for England's upper crust. Working behind the scenes are the servants, like Mrs. Chubb, the housekeeper, and Gertie Brown, one of the housemaids. No matter how smoothly the Pennyfoot runs, murder keeps turning up as an uninvited guest, but Cecily Sinclair quietly perseveres to restore order and protect the reputation of her hotel. Baxter, the manager, often protests what he sees as Madam's unladylike interests in matters of crime, but he comes up to scratch when he has to help. Over the course of the series, the relationship between Cecily and Baxter grows warmer, and events in the lives of the servants become just as interesting as the mystery plots that Kingsbury devises. The charm of the ensemble and its two leading players make this a delightful series for the dedicated reader of cozies. First in the series is *Do Not Disturb* (Berkley, 1993).

Lovesey, Peter • A schoolteacher, Lovesey responded to the lure of a contest for the best crime novel by a new author; the prize was a thousand pounds. Lovesey won the contest with his first novel, *Wobble to Death* (Dodd, Mead, 1970), and introduced Victorian policemen Sergeant Cribb and Constable Thackeray to the mystery world. Each of the eight novels in the series has a particular facet of Victorian life as the backdrop: an athletic contest in *Wobble to Death*, music halls in *Abracadaver* (Dodd, Mead, 1972), and so on. This series was televised in England and shown in America as well, with Alan Dobie portraying Cribb. After the Cribb-Thackeray series, Lovesey penned several other period mysteries, most notably *The False*

Inspector Dew (Pantheon, 1982), for which he won the Gold Dagger Award for Best Novel. A shipboard mystery, this shows Lovesey at his best with both plotting and characterization. Recently, Lovesey has written several novels about Albert, Prince of Wales, known as "Bertie" to his intimates. This son of Queen Victoria, who later became Edward VII, is an engagingly bumbling sleuth, and with whimsy often to the forefront, Lovesey gives Bertie a good time as he does his best to prove his worth as a detective. First in the series is *Bertie and the Tin Man* (Mysterious Press, 1988). Another notable historical mystery by Lovesey is *Rough Cider* (Mysterious Press, 1987), which was nominated for the Edgar for Best Novel. Readers should check the library and used bookstores for most of these works.

For Lovesey's series of contemporary police procedurals, see the section "Calling Scotland Yard."

Marston, Edward • Marston is a pseudonym for English mystery writer Keith Miles, but it is under the Marston name that much of his work has been published in the United States. Marston's first series is set in the late sixteenth century and features a troupe of actors, Lord Westfield's Men. The "sleuth" in the group is the bookholder, or stage manager, Nicholas Bracewell. They first appear in *The Queen's Head* (St. Martin's Press, 1989). This series is full of fascinating detail about Elizabethan life, and is especially informative on the history of the theater. Readers who know their English literature will recognize witty parodies of famous real works of the period in the repertoire of Lord Westfield's Men and that of their rivals, the Earl of Banbury's Men. With *The Wolves of Savernake* (St. Martin's Press, 1993), Marston began a second series of historical mysteries. These are set in late eleventh-century England, after William the Conqueror has claimed the crown of England. In the years after his magisterial survey of England, the *Domesday Book*, William sends out commissioners to investigate discrepancies in the survey. Marston uses this historical fact to give his characters, the soldier Ralph Delchard and the lawyer Gervase Bret, the authority to investigate the strange puzzles of murder and malfeasance they encounter. In addition to these historical mysteries, Marston has, under his real name, published a number of sports-related mysteries. Readers should check the library and used bookstores for some of the earlier books in the series.

Meyers, Maan • Martin and Annette Meyers, a husband-and-wife team of writers, are writing a series of historical mysteries under the name of Maan Meyers. The books are set in New York City during various periods of the city's long and colorful history. The main characters are members of the Tonneman family, beginning with the first Tonneman, who emigrated from Holland to the New World, and continuing with his descendants. The series begins with *The Dutchman* (Doubleday, 1992), which features Pieter Tonneman, the *schout* or sheriff, for the community of New Amsterdam in 1664. In *The Kingsbridge Plot* (Doubleday, 1993), Pieter's descendant John Tonneman is a London-trained physician who returns to New York City just in time to witness the political upheavals of the colonies in 1775, and who manages to help solve a series of murders as well. Readers should check the library and used bookstores for most of these works.

Look for an entry on **Annette Meyers** in the section "Nancy, Frank, and Joe Grow Up."

Monfredo, Miriam Grace • A writer and former librarian who lives in western New York State, Monfredo has utilized her interest in the history of her area to produce an unusual series set in nineteenth-century New York State. The central character of the series is Glynis Tryon, librarian in the city of Seneca Falls. Determining early on that she wasn't too keen for the yoke of marriage, Glynis sets her sights on having a career at a time when very few women had such ideas. Her budding feminist ideas get her involved with Elizabeth Cady Stanton and the meeting on women's rights that was held in Seneca Falls in 1848. Around this historic occasion, Monfredo has fashioned an entertaining murder mystery with *Seneca Falls Inheritance* (St. Martin's Press, 1992), which was an Agatha and Macavity nominee for Best First Novel. By the time of the second novel in the series, *North Star Conspiracy* (St. Martin's Press, 1993), the time is 1854, and Monfredo wraps her tale around the story of the Underground Railroad. Though Glynis is determined to remain independent, the town constable, Cullen Stuart, has set his sights on making Glynis his wife, and their relationship adds emotional depth to an intriguing series. Readers looking for a satisfying blend of historical fiction and mystery novel will find Monfredo a welcome discovery.

Newman, Sharan • Newman has turned her scholarly interest in the Middle Ages to a series of mysteries set in twelfth-century France. The first in the series, *Death Comes as Epiphany* (Tor, 1993), introduces Catherine LeVendeur, a young novice in the Convent of the Paraclete, presided over by the famous Abbess Heloise. Catherine is an outstanding scholar, a young woman with a keen intellect and an inquiring mind. When a dangerous situation threatens the safety of the convent, Heloise sends Catherine on a desperate mission to the great abbey of St. Denis, near Paris. In the course of this mission, Catherine meets a mysterious young stonemason, a Saxon named Edgar, and soon she thinks that she may not be destined for the cloistered life after all. In the course of this investigation, Catherine also uncovers some long-buried secrets about her own family; her father is a wealthy merchant in Paris, but there are many things about his life that Catherine has never known. As the series progresses, readers are treated to a fascinating portrait of medieval life, with strongly drawn characters and entertaining plots. The third and fourth books in the series, *The Wandering Arm* (Forge, 1995) and *Strong as Death* (Forge, 1996), were both nominated for the Agatha Award for Best Novel.

P aige, Robin • Paige is a pseudonym for Susan Wittig Albert and William Albert, who collaborate on a series of mysteries set in Victorian England. The first book in the series is *Death at Bishop's Keep* (Avon, 1994). The main character is a young American woman, half English and half Irish in heritage, named Kathryn Ardleigh. Making her own way in the world in 1894, Kathryn secretly writes thrillers, or "penny dreadfuls." Summoned to England to meet an aunt she never knew existed, Kathryn finds herself embroiled in a plot just as lurid as one of her own concoctions. Here she meets Sir Charles Sheridan, an amateur scientist and a renowned photographer, whose interest in mysteries parallels her own. They become increasingly close as the series progresses. In a recent outing, *Death at Daisy's Folly* (Berkley, 1997), they work together to solve the mysterious deaths taking place at the estate of the eccentric Countess of Warwick. Much lighter in tone than the Victorian novels of Anne Perry, this series by Robin Paige offers an enjoyable visit to the England of the nineteenth century.

For **Susan Wittig Albert's** series of contemporary mysteries, see the section "Nancy, Frank, and Joe Grow Up."

Pearce, Michael • Cairo late in the first decade after the turn of the twentieth century is the setting for Pearce's series of seriocomic mystery stories. Captain Cadwallader Owen is the mamur zapt, the British head of the Political CID, in Cairo, and it is his job to keep the peace in a city torn by strife, both political and religious. Cairo is a city of three official languages and four competing legal systems, and Captain Owen has quite a task on his hands. The first book in the series, *The Mamur Zapt and the Return of the Carpet* (Doubleday, 1990), finds Owen working on the case of the attempted assassination of a politician. In *The Mamur Zapt and the Donkey-Vous* (Mysterious Press, 1992), Owen is troubled by the disappearances of tourists from Cairo's famed Shepheard's Hotel. Are these just ordinary kidnappings? Or are they politically motivated? Once again, the mamur zapt has to find the answers before the city erupts. Pearce writes with wit and considerable humor, deftly demonstrating that a clash of cultures can provide great entertainment for the reader while being educational at the same time. Readers should check the library and used bookstores for these works.

Perry, Anne • The Victorian era offers a rich vein of subject matter for the writer, and Perry brings her novelist's imagination and sensitivity to two series of novels set in this fascinating and complex period of English history. The longer-running series, set during the mid- to late 1880s, features Inspector Thomas Pitt and his wife, Charlotte, who has come down in the world by marrying a humble policeman. Having forsaken her comfortable upper-middle-class lifestyle after the first novel in the series, *The Cater Street Hangman* (St. Martin's Press, 1979), the intelligent and socially conscious Charlotte aids her educated and sensitive husband in all his cases. Using her own family connections to gain entrée to the homes of the wealthy and powerful, Charlotte, often assisted by her sister Emily (who married as far up the social scale as Charlotte married down), pokes her nose into the secrets of the Victorian upper crust. In the second series, set in the mid-1850s after the end of the Crimean War, the main characters are Inspector William Monk and nurse Hester Latterly. In the brilliant debut of this series, the Agatha-nominated *The Face of a Stranger* (Fawcett Columbine, 1990), Monk awakes in a hospital, having no memory of who he is. Confronted by a brutal murder case and a superior who would enjoy his disgrace, Monk struggles to solve the mystery of his own identity along with the murder. In both series Perry takes a keen sense of social justice and unsparingly lays bare all the hypocrisy and injustice of Victorian England, when a minute percentage of the population literally held the power of life and death over the vast majority. Perry's later works, such as *Belgrave Square* (Fawcett Columbine, 1992) and *A Dangerous*

Mourning (Fawcett Columbine, 1992), are particularly compelling. In Perry's hands the joining of social commentary, mystery plot, and historical novel means compelling reading.

Peters, Elizabeth • Peters, who writes several series of mysteries, is the *nom de plume* of Barbara Mertz. In addition to her mysteries, she writes suspense novels under the name **Barbara Michaels**. Peters uses her own scholarly background in Egyptology for a renowned series of historical mysteries featuring Amelia Peabody Emerson.

The first appearance of Amelia Peabody is in *Crocodile on the Sandbank* (Dodd, Mead, 1975). Amelia is a Victorian spinster who has inherited a fortune from her late father. Now free to fulfill her dreams, she has come to Egypt to indulge her passion for Egyptian archaeology. Here she encounters the archaeologist Radcliffe Emerson, and these two strong personalities at first clash and eventually unite. In these vivid and humorous adventure novels, Peabody is intelligent and adventurous, Radcliffe is memorably irascible and devoted to his sleuthing wife, and their hideously precocious son Ramses plays his part with verve as well. One of the strongest books in the series is *The Last Camel Died at Noon* (Warner, 1991), Peters's affectionate tribute to H. Rider Haggard's adventure tales.

For Elizabeth Peters's two series with contemporary amateur sleuths see the section "Nancy, Frank, and Joe Grow Up." For the suspense novels of Barbara Michaels see the section "The Road to Manderley."

Peters, Ellis • After writing a long series of mysteries with contemporary settings, Peters wrote what was to be a single excursion into the historical mystery with *A Morbid Taste for Bones* (Morrow, 1978). The plot of the novel was based on the story of St. Winifred and the Abbey of St. Peter and St. Paul in Shrewsbury, near where Peters had lived for many years. Once the story was finished, however, the main character, the Welsh Benedictine monk Cadfael, refused to let go of his creator, and thus was born one of the most beloved of all historical mystery series. Weaving the actual historical events of the period, beginning in the late 1130s, through the plots of the mystery novels, Peters gives her readers a tantalizing glimpse of the medieval past. Peters does not, however, impose modern characters and modern psychology upon the period; her characters are distinctly medieval. Her long experience as a historical novelist (with many books written under her real name, Edith Pargeter) has given Peters an unusual understanding of the complexities of medieval life, and her people are medieval to the core. The novels in the series often revolve, for example, around concepts that are peculiarly medieval, such as *The Sanctuary Sparrow* (Morrow, 1983), *The Pilgrim of Hate* (Morrow, 1984), and *The Potter's Field* (Mysterious Press, 1990). Peters's vivid prose, like that of Anne Perry and Lindsey Davis, conjures up the past and makes it almost tangible.

For Peters's series of contemporary mysteries see the section "Calling Scotland Yard."

Robb, **Candace M.** • Fourteenth-century York is the setting for this fine series of historical mysteries from the pen of Seattle medievalist Robb. The main character in the series is the Welsh Owen Archer, once captain of the king's archers. A wartime injury left Owen blind in one eye, and he chose to retire from his post, believing he could no longer perform his duties to the best of his abilities. For a while, he served as a spy for the wily Duke of Lancaster, John of Gaunt, but Owen transfers into the service of the Lord Chancellor and Archbishop of York, John Thoresby, an ally of the Duke. In Thoresby's service, Owen goes to York to discover the truth behind the death of one of the Archbishop's wards. The hapless victim died from a potion made by the apothecary Nicholas Wilton, and Owen goes undercover as an apprentice to Wilton to ferret out the truth. Wilton's lovely young wife, Lucie, herself an apothecary, soon presents Owen with a dilemma. Could he be falling in love with a murderess?

The first novel in the series is *The Apothecary Rose* (St. Martin's Press, 1993). Robb offers a richly detailed background with her portrait of late medieval York, and her portrayal of Owen Archer as a passionate, intelligent, and honorable man will likely win her many fans. Throughout the series, Robb demonstrates an acute awareness of the labyrinth of English politics of the period, and she often uses the political shenanigans to good effect, as did Ellis Peters in the Brother Cadfael series, set a little more than two hundred years earlier.

Robinson, Lynda S. • She writes award-winning historical romances as Suzanne Robinson, but for her series of historical mysteries set in ancient Egypt, she chose to write as Lynda. Robinson earned a Ph.D. in anthropology, with a concentration in archaeology, from the University of Texas at Austin. The first novel in the series is *Murder in the Place of Anubis* (Walker, 1994), and the main character is the Lord Meren, an adviser to young Pharaoh Tutankhamen in the Egypt of the

Eighteenth Dynasty. Lord Meren holds the title "The Eyes and Ears of the King," and, as such, he serves as a "chief of intelligence," rooting out palace conspiracies that could topple the reign of the young king. In the first novel, the murder of a scribe offers Lord Meren a complicated puzzle to solve. Not only does he have to find out "whodunit," Lord Meren also has to keep his job, for there are many who would like to see him disgraced. The series is full of the color and panoply of ancient Egypt, and readers looking for enjoyable historical mysteries will find much to entertain them here.

Roosevelt, Elliott • For the series of historical mysteries featuring Eleanor Roosevelt as the sleuth, see the section "Murder, She Wrote."

Ross, Kate • Regency dandy Julian Kestrel is the hero in this series of historical mysteries by Boston trial lawyer Ross. A genteel, impoverished man-about-town in London society in the early nineteenth century, Kestrel is a young man of keen intelligence and mysterious background. In his first appearance, *Cut to the Quick* (Viking, 1993), Kestrel rescues young Hugh Fontclair from a sticky situation in a gaming house, and Fontclair asks him to be best man at his wedding. The families of bride and groom, however, are at loggerheads, and soon murder disrupts the festivities. Aided by his Cockney manservant, Dipper, a reformed pickpocket, Kestrel solves the mystery. In *A Broken Vessel* (Viking, 1994), Dipper's sister Sally, a prostitute, is the link among suspects in a very puzzling case, and Kestrel finds Sally an intriguing riddle in herself. Ross has a keen sense of the period, both in her exquisitely wrought backgrounds and in her well-drawn characters. The rough-and-tumble world of Regency society, in all its glamour and its squalor, provides Ross a delightful canvas for her work. Readers of historical fiction who lament the passing of the late, great Georgette Heyer need look no farther than Kate Ross for a worthy successor.

Satterthwait, Walter • In addition to a series of private eye novels about Santa Fe investigator Joshua Croft, Satterthwait has written several historical mysteries, each very distinctive. The first of them is *Miss Lizzie* (St. Martin's Press, 1988). Satterthwait takes a look at the infamous Miss Borden some years after her supposed "forty whacks." It's 1921, and Lizzie Borden is living quietly in a town on the Massachusetts shore. Young Amanda Burton finds her stepmother brutally murdered—with an ax—and Miss Lizzie seems the prime suspect. But is she?

In *Wilde West* (St. Martin's Press, 1991), Satterthwait takes a real event, Oscar Wilde's lecture tour of America, and adds to it a mystery involving serial murders in the Old West. In his inimitable way, Satterthwait brings Wilde very believably to life. With *Escapade* (St. Martin's Press, 1995), nominated for an Agatha Award for Best Novel, Satterthwait introduces Pinkerton detective Phil Beaumont. It's 1921, and Beaumont is assigned to protect the legendary Harry Houdini. They're visiting an English country estate to attend a séance, and among the guests is the noted writer and spiritualism enthusiast Sir Arthur Conan Doyle. When their host is murdered, Beaumont joins forces with one of the guests, Jane Turner, to solve the case. Satterthwait evokes the classic English country house murder with the greatest of ease. A sequel detailing the further adventures of Beaumont and Turner is eagerly awaited.

For Satterthwait's series of private eye novels, see the section "The Maltese Falcon."

Saylor, Steven • A writer and editor with many short stories and essays to his credit, Saylor in 1991 published his first novel, *Roman Blood* (St. Martin's Press). This book introduced Gordianus the Finder, a "private detective" operating in Rome in the first century B.C. The well-known orator and advocate Cicero has asked Gordianus for help in the case of Sextus Roscius, a wealthy farmer from Ameria, who has been accused of one of the worst crimes in Roman society, patricide, the murder of one's father. A man of intelligence, warmth, and compassion, Gordianus sets about unraveling the knot of truth in the case of Sextus Roscius, and in Gordianus's company the reader gets to see the Rome of the period come alive. The second novel in the series, *Arms of Nemesis* (St. Martin's Press, 1992), takes place some eight years later, at the time of the slave revolts. Gordianus is called to the resort town Baiae by Marcus Crassus to solve a murder with horrifying implications. The overseer of a great villa has been murdered, seemingly by two slaves; if this is the case, Roman law demands that all slaves in the household may be killed in retribution. Gordianus literally races against time to discover the culprit in a fascinating case. Perhaps Saylor's finest book in the series is *Catilina's Riddle* (St. Martin's Press, 1993), in which Saylor offers his interpretation of the Catiline Conspiracy. This novel has the emotional depth, the richness of style and texture, and the attention to detail of the finest historical fiction.

Sedley, Kate • Sedley's series takes as its time frame a particularly turbulent era of English history, the Wars of the Roses. This period of political strife affords the author excellent opportunity to weave tales of murder into the fabric of history, as Ellis Peters does with her series set just over three centuries earlier. Sedley's detective is Roger the Chapman, a young man who had been sent as a novice to the Benedictine monastery at Glastonbury by his widowed mother. But Roger felt the call of the world outside the abbey, so he left the cloisters and eventually ended up as a "chapman," or peddler. Following this trade, Roger can travel around England as he pleases. In the first of the series, *Death and the Chapman* (St. Martin's Press, 1992), the year is 1471. While the York-Lancaster war rages on, Roger agrees to look for a wealthy young man who disappeared in London. Along the way, Roger becomes acquainted with Richard, Duke of Gloucester, the future Richard III, and does the duke a service. The duke calls upon Roger for help in the second book, *The Plymouth Cloak* (St. Martin's Press, 1993), and thus Sedley is establishing a strong link for her detective with the troubled figure of Richard III. Sedley handles the period detail with ease, and her sleuth, Roger, is an amiable and intelligent protagonist.

Soos, Troy • Take some of the great moments in the history of baseball, mix with the grand old tradition of an amateur sleuth who can solve a puzzling mystery, and put them together in a charming series, and you've got a recipe for success in the novels of Troy Soos. Soos tells riveting tales of murder and mayhem on the historic ball fields of the early twentieth century. He even brings real baseball figures such as Ty Cobb and

Casey Stengel into each book as important characters. The amiable, if a trifle bumbling, hero of these adventures is Mickey Rawlings, a utility ballplayer early in this century. Mickey describes himself as not too smart and not educated, but somehow he can manage to solve crimes. The first book in the series is *Murder at Fenway Park* (Kensington, 1994), where Mickey is playing for the Boston Red Sox. In *Murder at Ebbets Field* (Kensington, 1995), Mickey has been hired by the New York Giants, and is playing well in August 1914. The Giants are having a tough season, fighting off their archenemies, the Brooklyn Dodgers, and trying to stay in the race for the pennant. Unfortunately, murder intervenes and Mickey finds himself hunting a killer between home games. Mickey is still growing into his role as a professional baseball player and now he is learning the craft of sleuthing as well by interviewing suspects and making deductions. Baseball may be his first love, but detecting is an avocation that Mickey and his readers can relish in these amusing novels.

Other Writers of Sports Mysteries

Harlan Coben; L. L. Enger; Crabbe Evers; Alison Gordon; Dick Francis; John Francome; Shannon OCork; Julie Robitaille.

Tourney, Leonard • A professor of English literature, Tourney has made use of his academic specialties to provide the background for a series of mysteries set in late Elizabethan England. The main character in the series is Matthew Stock, a respected businessman—a clothier—who is also town constable in the Essex village of Chelmsford. Unlike the merry, dimwitted town constables beloved of Shakespeare, Matthew Stock is clever, industrious, and forthright. He is aided in all matters by his loving wife, Joan, who matches her husband well in every respect. They first encounter mayhem in *The Players' Boy Is Dead* (Harper, 1980), wherein a seemingly local crime turns out to have more far-reaching implications. The Stocks come to the attention of Robert Cecil, Lord Burghley, one of the Queen's most important advisers, and they are sometimes caught up in the intrigue surrounding him, as in *Witness of Bones* (St. Martin's Press, 1992). Tourney creates a vivid and interesting picture of his particular time in history—the reign of Gloriana herself, Elizabeth Tudor, in her later years, when England had achieved the status of an important political power in world events. Readers should check the library and used bookstores for most of these works.

Van Gulik, Robert • A diplomat from the Netherlands, Van Gulik was a noted expert on the culture and history of China, and he is responsible for introducing to the Western world the classical Chinese detective story. He translated an eighteenth-century Chinese novel about a historical figure from the seventh century, a magistrate who solved crimes, in *Dee Goong An* (published in 1976 by Dover as *Celebrated Cases of Judge Dee*). Then Van Gulik tried his hand at creating his own cases for Judge Dee to solve. The first of these is *The Chinese Bell Murders* (Harper, 1959). Van Gulik uses various Chinese motifs in these stories, thereby giving his readers glimpses of life and culture in medieval China. Van Gulik drew pictures to illustrate many of the stories, much in the way that Jane Langton illustrates her series of mysteries starring Homer Kelly. In addition, Van Gulik usually offers notes to the reader to explain some of the particularly Chinese elements of the stories that might be a bit obscure for Western readers. One of the finest of all historical mystery series, the Judge Dee books are a landmark in the history of detective fiction itself.

For Further Reading • Harold Adams; P. F. Chisholm/Patricia Finney; Dianne Day; Kathy Lynn Emerson; Anton Gill; Ray Harrison; Michael Jecks; Mary Kruger; Deryn Lake; Margaret Lawrence; Amy Myers; William Palmer; Barbara Paul (the opera series); Sharon Kay Penman; John Madox Roberts; Laura Joh Rowland; Francis Selwyn; Diane K. Shah (the Paris Chandler books); Sarah Smith; Charles Todd; Peter Tremayne; Ann Woodward; Deborah Woodworth.

Films to watch out for • *Doctor Zhivago; Gaslight; Madeleine; A Man for All Seasons; Mississippi Burning; The Name of the Rose; Sergeant Rutledge; Time Bandits.*

TV shows • *Cadfael; Gunsmoke; Have Gun, Will Travel; The Moonstone; The Rifleman; Sherlock Holmes Mysteries; Wanted: Dead or Alive; Wild, Wild West; Wyatt Earp.*

Private Eyes

The Maltese Falcon

Private eyes fascinate us. The lone operative, looking for a missing child or inquiring into a murder, finding information that the police missed, struggling on with a case even after a beating or a gunfight—it's an irresistible combination of courage, brains, and stubbornness that shows up in some of our favorite movies and books.

We tend to forget that even Sherlock Holmes was a private eye, although the phrase hadn't been invented yet. He was a "consulting detective," and he helped people who didn't want to go to the police or had been disappointed by their encounters with the official forces. And fictional detectives were all the rage after the Holmes stories became overwhelmingly popular.

But it was Dashiell Hammett and Raymond Chandler, two American writers, who radically changed the fictional private eye and created the modern, hard-boiled operative we know from countless movies, television shows, and books. Hammett had been an operative for the Pinkerton Detective

Agency, and he brought a new kind of realism to his stories about Sam Spade and the detective known only as the Continental Op. Chandler had never worked as a detective, but he was determined to bring crime stories back to the reality of the streets and end the proliferation of upper-class, drawing-room mysteries. These two writers told their stories so vividly that their private eyes are still the models for the PIs we see so often in popular culture. Of course, it helped to have Humphrey Bogart along to play Sam Spade and Philip Marlowe so memorably that *The Maltese Falcon* and *The Big Sleep* are still the classic private eye movies.

Now we have private eyes of all shapes and sizes. Marcia Muller, Maxine O'Callaghan, and P. D. James inaugurated the dazzling trend in women private eyes that began in the 1970s (although there had been a few female PIs back as far as Victorian novels). There are black, Native American, Hispanic, and gay private eyes, and they exist because they reflect all of us. After all, who wouldn't love to put on a trench coat and go adventuring?

Barnes, Linda • Carlotta Carlyle, feisty Boston private eye and part-time cabdriver, is a truly memorable character. Carlotta is six feet tall, half Irish and half Jewish, and a former policewoman. Readers may enjoy Carlotta's personality as much as the lively and thought-provoking plots, especially since Barnes has endowed Carlotta with an active sense of humor and a wry outlook on life. Barnes has created a notable group of secondary characters in the books as well. Carlotta's tenant and cleaning lady, Roz, is an eccentric artist who collects T-shirts with outrageously funny slogans. The suavely

attractive Sam Gianelli is a son (supposedly honest) of the local Mafia don; he and Carlotta have an occasional fling. Through the Little Sisters organization, Carlotta has found a young sister, Paolina, with whom she has a strong and fond connection. And, of course, a good private eye sometimes needs a friend in the police department; Carlotta has Mooney, an old buddy from her days as a cop. First in the series is the Edgar-nominated *A Trouble of Fools* (St. Martin's Press, 1987).

The first series Linda Barnes wrote featured Michael Spraggue, an independently wealthy actor and detective. These stories are located in Boston, Napa Valley, and New Orleans, and the first, *Blood Will Have Blood* (Avon, 1982), has a theatrical setting.

Block, Lawrence • Lawrence Block is one of the most admired and popular mystery writers of our time. He was named a Grand Master by the Mystery Writers of America in 1994. Block has written three series, as well as numerous non-series novels and nonfiction.

Block tells his stories in a clear, deceptively simple style. He loves to play with language, to repeat phrases and tie small details together to make a smooth, professional whole that is immensely satisfying. Block has a brilliant command of the English language and an acute ear for crisp urban dialogue.

The best-known and most critically acclaimed series by Block is the Matt Scudder series. The first novel is *The Sins of the Father* (Dell, 1976). Scudder is a former New York City police officer who left after accidentally shooting an innocent bystander. Now he does favors for people, but he doesn't have a formal private eye license, and sometimes he tithes whatever pay he gets to any church that's close by. In the early novels in the series, Matt is drinking heavily, his family life is in ruins, and he is still consumed by guilt. Living by himself in a residential hotel, he is deeply lonely, and he solaces himself with drink. These are classic private eye tales, pared down to the essentials and set on the violent, seedy streets of New York. *A Dance at the Slaughterhouse* (Morrow, 1991) won the Edgar Award for Best Novel. By this time Scudder has given up drinking and now has a fairly strong and loving relationship with his girlfriend Elaine. The cases Scudder takes on are still liable to be violent and disturbing; this one is about pedophilia and snuff films. It is gorgeously written, as usual, in Block's minimalist, elegant style, but it's also imbued with the darkness and nihilism of the *fin-de-siècle.* Living in a city with so much random violence is tough for Block's characters, but the stories they tell are so compelling that the reader wants to come back again and again.

See another **Lawrence Block** entry in the section "The Usual Suspects."

Boyer, Rick • His first novel was a Sherlock Holmes pastiche, *The Giant Rat of Sumatra* (Warner, 1976), but after that Boyer turned to a series starring Dr. Charles Adams, known as "Doc." Doc Adams is an oral surgeon in the affluent suburb of Concord, Massachusetts. He is not a licensed private eye, but the tone and style of the books fit comfortably into the private eye genre. Doc's real profession brings him monetary security. He and his wife, Mary, have a very comfortable home, plus a house on the Cape. But Doc isn't always satisfied with his material success; he longs for excitement as well. He gets it in spades, starting with the Edgar-winning *Billingsgate Shoal* (Houghton Mifflin, 1982). From his house on Cape Cod, Doc spots a ship in distress, and he calls the Coast Guard. Later he spots the ship in port, and he asks an acquaintance, a young scuba diver, to check it out. When the diver turns up dead, Doc feels impelled to investigate, certain that the death was no accident. Despite great personal danger, in this and in his subsequent cases, Doc hangs on until the truth is out. Perhaps the best book in the series is the second, *The Penny Ferry* (Houghton Mifflin, 1984), in which Boyer writes compellingly about the lingering legacy of the infamous Sacco and Vanzetti trial and execution. Doc Adams is a warm and appealing character, a man who will go to any lengths to aid a friend or family member in need of help, and the books are fast-paced and full of action. A note of trivia: Doc occasionally mentions his friend Brady Coyne, the Boston attorney who is the sleuth in a series by William G. Tapply.

Campbell, Robert • One of the more unusual heroes of detective fiction is Campbell's Jimmy Flannery. Flannery is a sewer inspector and Democratic Party precinct captain in Chicago, and he is also a most engaging sleuth. Flannery speaks in an urban slang rather like that of Damon Runyon's characters. Aside from inspecting the sewers, Jimmy's job is to keep the people in his precinct happy so they will vote for his party at election time. Jimmy takes this job seriously, not only for his and the party's sake but mainly because he loves to help people. And so, in a series of mysteries that all have animals in their titles, Jimmy doggedly goes after the truth in some pretty strange murder cases. There's the man who's found in the sewer, chewed in half by an alligator, in the charming and rib-tickling *Hip-Deep in Alligators* (New American Library, 1987). Or the case of the missing girlfriend of Janet Canarias, who is the first lesbian to be elected an alderman in the city of Chicago, in *Thinning the Turkey Herd* (New American Library, 1988). Jimmy's grammar is atrocious and he may smell a bit ripe after a day walking the sewers, but he's sweet-natured, compassionate, and an irresistibly charming detective. The first book in the series, *The Junkyard Dog* (1986), won an Edgar Award for Best Paperback Original.

Campbell also writes a popular series of very hard-boiled private eye novels, all set in what he calls "La-La Land" (Los Angeles). The series begins with *In La-La Land We Trust* (Mysterious Press, 1986), and it features Whistler, a down-at-the-heels PI who solves some bloody and complex murders for his varied clients. Campbell's grim vision of L.A. in these books is that of a sprawling metropolis with little hope of redemption or visible morality. The dialogue is, as in the Jimmy Flannery books, brilliantly conveyed, and the street-smart hustlers are vivid and memorable characters.

Campbell also writes mainstream novels under the name R. Wright Campbell.

Chandler, Raymond • Along with Dashiell Hammett, Raymond Chandler radically changed the nature of the mystery genre and inaugurated a new American art form. Chandler first articulated the "mean streets" theory of crime writing, saying that murder takes place in the streets, not in the artificial drawing room atmosphere so often found in traditional English mysteries of the Golden Age. Any man who

investigates murders, Chandler thought, must understand the criminals and the streets they prowl, but must himself be an honest man, a man of principle. Chandler's hero, Philip Marlowe, is all of that. Marlowe has strong ethical principles and despises corruption and crime of any sort. Marlowe gets beat up and lied to often enough, but he always struggles onward with his quest for truth and justice. Since the cops in these books are usually either crooks or sadistic bullies, Marlowe is deeply cynical about the American system of police and criminal justice. The stories are set in Los Angeles or in Bay City, which is a thinly veiled version of Santa Monica. The settings are highly atmospheric, with vivid details of life in Southern California from the 1930s to the 1950s. Chandler's writing is romantic, and sometimes it's lush with simile and metaphor. Chandler used a uniquely crafted spirit of place and mood to create darkly brooding prose poems in his *noir* mysteries. His plots can be so complex that the reader is challenged to keep up with what's going on. *The Big Sleep* (Knopf, 1939) is a good example: When it was made into a movie (with Humphrey Bogart), Chandler said even he still didn't know who had committed one of the murders in the story. A lot of good movies have been made from Chandler's books, and Chandler himself wrote some famous screenplays.

Clark, Carol Higgins • Actress and best-selling writer Carol Higgins Clark is also the daughter of famous novelist Mary Higgins Clark. Before she began writing herself, Carol learned her trade by doing research for her mother's novels. Carol's series heroine is Regan Reilly, a private eye who finds murder even on her vacations away from the office. Regan's father, a funeral director, and her mother, a renowned suspense writer, are continuing characters in these amusing and puzzling novels. The Agatha Award nominee *Decked* (Warner, 1992) is set on an ocean liner crossing the Atlantic. Just before sailing, Regan is hired as a replacement for a companion to a rich, elderly woman. Unbeknownst to her, the echoes of a murder committed ten years ago have followed her and her charge onto the boat. Clark moves her action to Miami in *Snagged* (Warner, 1993). Her parents are present for a funeral home convention, and Regan has come for a friend's wedding. Much of the action is set at a panty-hose convention, and it proves to be a clever idea and setting for murder. *Iced* (Warner, 1995) is set in Aspen, Colorado, where Regan has gone for a skiing vacation. Art thieves have been stealing paintings from the rich and trendy, and Regan and her parents naturally get involved in the search for the miscreants. Clark shows what happens when average middle-class people inadvertently get caught up in violence, and she is particularly good at portraying elderly characters sympathetically. She also has a brisk sense of humor that counterpoints the gripping suspense of her stories.

Cody, Liza • Cody has written two series of mysteries, but her main character so far is Anna Lee, one of the first female PIs created by a British writer. Anna is a gutsy, persevering sleuth, a former policewoman who works for Brierly Security in London. Unfortunately, her difficult boss doesn't exactly like women becoming investigators, so he gives her "female" cases, such as hunting for a missing daughter or providing security for a department store. Unlike some of her colleagues, Anna gets involved with the people she encounters in her cases, even when they're not the most pleasant people she's met. Otherwise, she tends to be a self-reliant lone wolf like so many fictional private eyes, although she gets constant hassles from her neighbors Bea and Selwyn. In Cody's later novels that feature Eva Wylie, it seems that Anna has started her own agency in partnership with her old colleague Bernie Schiller. First in the series is *Dupe* (Scribner, 1983), which won the John Creasey Award for Best First Novel from the Crime Writers' Association. *Backhand* (Doubleday, 1992) was nominated for the Edgar. A miniseries called *Anna Lee*, based on the novels, has been shown on British and American TV.

Look for another entry on Cody in "The Usual Suspects" section.

Collins, Max Allan • A prolific mystery writer, Collins has also been a musician and songwriter, a journalist, an English instructor at a community college, and a comic-strip writer, for *Dick Tracy*, since 1977, and several others. Collins has penned several series of mysteries, featuring three different one-named protagonists: Nolan, Quarry, and Mallory. The first two of these are very much in the hard-boiled tradition, with the Mallory books being slightly softer-boiled. Collins's major contribution to the mystery field, however, has been his series of historical private eye novels featuring Nathan Heller, set in the 1930s. In his debut, *True Detective* (St. Martin's Press, 1983), Heller has left the Chicago Police Department to go solo. Real people make appearances in these books, men such as Eliot Ness, Al Capone, Frank Nitti, and even Ian Fleming and Erle Stanley Gardner. Early books in the series tended to focus on a gangster theme, but later books have ranged more broadly, putting Heller into some of the twentieth century's most famous real crimes, such as the murder of Sir Harry Oakes in *Carnal Hours* (Dutton, 1994), or the Lindbergh kidnapping in *Stolen Away* (Bantam, 1991). The latter, along with *Blood and Thunder* (Dutton, 1995), about the assassination of Huey Long, are some of Collins's best work. Thoroughly researched, with an appealing hard-boiled hero, the Heller series combines historical fiction, true crime, and the private eye novel in an entertaining fashion.

Corris, Peter • Corris is probably the most famous Australian mystery writer, and his books deserve to be better known in other countries as well. Corris's series hero is Cliff Hardy, a hard-boiled Sydney private eye. Sydney clearly has its share of mean streets, and Corris does a good job of conveying a grittily authentic atmosphere. Cliff Hardy runs into both petty criminals and some very nasty ones in the course of his long career as a PI. He is such a hard-boiled investigator, though, that in some books he keeps getting beat up by the villains and yet still keeps coming back for more. He's a very world-weary, cynical gumshoe. *The Empty Beach* (Gold Medal, 1986) has a labyrinthine plot in which a woman hires Hardy after hearing rumors that her husband, assumed drowned years ago, has been seen alive again. Hardy promptly runs afoul of two rival criminal overlords and a couple of murderous thugs. Hardy is middle-aged by the time of *Wet Graves* (Dell, 1995), and he seems more calm and settled. His neighborhood in Sydney is being gentrified, he now lives alone except for a cat, and he is trying to drink less and eat less so he can stay fit to do his job right. His peace is threatened, however, when he learns that the government is considering lifting his license because a gambler has linked Hardy to an alleged criminal act. He goes off in his ancient Falcon in search of both the crooked gambler who set him up and a client's missing father. After many years, Cliff Hardy is still getting beat up, but he's still on the job.

Readers should check the library and used bookstores for most of these works.

Craig, **Philip R**. • Boston cop J. W. (Jeff) Jackson has to take early retirement after being shot. He's lucky enough to have inherited a cottage and a few acres on the island of Martha's Vineyard, off the coast of Massachusetts. Now he lives quietly, grows a bountiful garden, and does a lot of sea angling, especially for bluefish. J. W. doesn't have much money, but he can eat well from his garden and the sea, and he's creative about picking up bits and pieces of work on the island. Jackson's lover is Zee Madieras, a nurse at the island hospital. She is a feisty, somewhat sardonic lady who likes her independence. Sometimes J. W. is deputized by the local police chief to help out on a crime or a security detail, and so he and Zee get involved in murder. In his simple, clean prose, Craig gives us a sense of the serenity and happiness of island life, somewhat disrupted by the inevitable crimes and by "the August people" who throng the island in the summertime. These mysteries are memorable as well for their loving descriptions of the peace and fulfillment to be found in the fine art of fishing, especially sea angling. The Vineyard, too, is charmingly described, and as J. W. drives about it in his ancient Land Cruiser, we discover the fascination of its topography, history, and diverse neighborhoods. Readers should check the library and used bookstores for some of these books.

Crais, Robert • With his wisecracking private eye, Elvis Cole, Crais demonstrated that it was possible to take what looked like a moribund genre in the late 1980s, the male PI novel, and add new life to it. Nominated for the Edgar and winner of the Anthony for Best Paperback Original, *The Monkey's Raincoat* (Bantam, 1987), first in the series, gave readers a distinctive voice. Elvis Cole (born Philip James Cole, but legally renamed Elvis after his mother saw The King in concert) has a fresh mouth and a slightly eccentric sense of humor. His office in West Hollywood is decorated with Disney memorabilia, not something one expects from the hard-boiled kind of detective guy. A Vietnam veteran, Cole doesn't hesitate to use firepower when the occasion demands. His partner in the agency is an ex-LAPD officer, Joe Pike, who also served in Vietnam. Taciturn, difficult to know, Pike is nevertheless a staunch friend to Elvis, and in recent books Crais is allowing the relationship between the men to develop and deepen, with Pike becoming more human and humane. Like every other straight PI, Cole has his ups and downs in his relationships with women, but Lucy Chenier, introduced in *Voodoo River* (Hyperion, 1995), may turn out to be a more permanent fixture in his life. Long a successful writer for television, Crais creates vivid and believable action scenes for his novels. In addition to the action, though, Crais provides memorable characters and provocative situations that resonate beyond the limits of a simple thriller.

Crider, Bill • The island city of Galveston, Texas, hasn't figured very often in mystery novels, but Crider has made it the central setting for much of the action in his series of private eye novels starring Truman Smith. Smith is only reluctantly a private eye; a specialist in looking for missing persons, he has tried to find his own missing sister, but having no luck, has decided to retire. Then a friend needs help to find his missing daughter, and Smith is once again in action in the first of the series, *Dead on the Island* (Walker, 1991). In perhaps his most unusual case, Smith is hired to find out who murdered an alligator, in *Gator Kill* (Walker, 1992). As in most of Crider's books, the hero is likable, the humor is natural and understated, and the action is entertaining. In addition to the Truman Smith books, Crider also writes the Carl Burns books (see the section "Nancy, Frank, and Joe Grow Up") and the Sheriff Dan Rhodes books (see the "Hill Street Blues" section).

Crumley, James • Crumley writes some of the most strikingly original and strange mysteries of our time. He has two recurring characters: Milo Milodragovitch and C. W. Sughrue. Milodragovitch is a melancholy, drunken, and failure-prone PI in Meriwether, Montana. He loves women, liquor, drugs, and violence far too much to live a comfortable life. In *The Wrong Case* (Random House, 1975), Milo is asked by a beautiful blonde to look for her missing brother, just as in a typical PI plot by Chandler or Hammett. But this is a dark, post-Vietnam world, where a private eye is liable to get lost in his private hell of drugs and alcohol-altered reality, and Milo's case is anything but conventional. Crumley's talent for creating surrealistic plots continues in *The Mexican Tree Duck* (Mysterious Press, 1993). C. W. "Sonny" Sughrue is barely making a living as a PI in Montana by doing the most routine investigative jobs and working part-time as a bartender. As the book begins, C. W. is so angry that the bar's jukebox no longer plays songs by his favorite singer, that he snorts cocaine and drags the jukebox onto the railroad tracks, where it gets destroyed spectacularly by a train. C. W. then embarks on a loony mission to find a local biker's mother, who seems to have been kidnapped by the FBI or Mexican drug smugglers or both. He is helped out by two of his burned-out old Vietnam buddies, plus a pair of enormously fat tropical fish and weapons dealers, and other assorted weirdos. This is late Twentieth-century crazy America, as seen through the eyes of a master chronicler of adventures at the edge of the envelope. Crumley writes like a dream, but the situations that his characters find themselves in are more like a Kafkaesque nightmare. Both of his heroes are gonzo speed-demon private eyes, whose cases often involve looking for lost family members or taking violent and elaborate revenge for past crimes. Crumley sets his books in Montana and Texas, and he portrays a wild, bawdy, limitless West.

Dawson, Janet • Dawson's books are among the most impressive of the recent crop of mysteries featuring female private eyes. She writes thoughtful narratives with interesting plots and a somewhat off-beat location in the tough and historic city of Oakland, California. Her first mystery, *Kindred Crimes* (St. Martin's Press, 1990), introduces Jeri Howard, an Oakland PI. Jeri is hired to find a woman who has abandoned her child and disappeared. As she works for different clients in the same family, Jeri finds that her case really hinges on the story of an old crime. In *Till the Old Men Die* (Fawcett, 1993), a Filipino history professor has been murdered, and Jeri's father asks her to look into the circumstances behind his friend's death. As Jeri follows her leads in the Filipino-American community of Oakland and at the local naval base, she discovers the intricacies of Filipino politics and history. In *Don't Turn Your Back on the Ocean* (Fawcett, 1994), Jeri becomes involved with a complicated case that takes her, somewhat unwillingly, down the coast to Monterey. As with the books set in Oakland, Dawson draws a fascinating urban backdrop for her story, while establishing Jeri Howard as a memorably smart and interesting private eye.

Day, Marele • Day writes an award-winning Australian crime series featuring an off-beat female private eye. The protagonist is private investigator Claudia Valentine, who lives in a flat above a bar in a seedy area of Sydney. Claudia is divorced, with two young children; her mom is a former chorus dancer, and her father abandoned them when she was a child. These are fast-paced mysteries, with eccentric characters and snappy dialogue. Day won the Shamus Award for Best Paperback Original for *The Last Tango of Dolores Delgado* (Allen & Unwin, 1992). Claudia takes a job as a bodyguard to a professional tango dancer, Dolores Delgado. When Dolores dies onstage, Claudia digs into the many layers of secrets in her past. In *The Disappearances of Madalena Grimaldi* (Walker, 1996), she learns that her father has died some years before, and she goes on a journey of exploration into her father's life and death. She also is looking into the disappearance of a teenager in this moving, thoughtful story. Day creates memorable characters, and the feisty, rather melancholy Claudia is an unusual private eye. There is some Aussie slang, but it's not too overwhelming for American readers. These are well-written mysteries, hard to put down once you've managed to get hold of one (they can be hard to find in American bookstores).

Doolittle, Jerome • Tom Bethany, Doolittle's series hero, is a former Olympic wrestler, and all of the books use wrestling terms in the titles. Bethany is a private eye in Boston, a locale that seems to inspire some of the best American PI stories. He works hard to keep his real identity a secret from lethal enemies who might still be chasing him down. Bethany rents a place to live under the name of Tom Carpenter, and he deliberately has no phone, no credit cards, or any other records by which he could be traced under his real name. Even his romance is a secret and beleaguered one; the love of his life is Hope, a married woman who lives in Washington, D.C. Since Hope and Tom can only see each other for a couple of days at a time, he never has to face the possibility of commitment in his life (perhaps an advantage for a footloose shamus). Tom once worked for Teddy Kennedy's presidential campaign, and there is an atmosphere of liberal politics here, along with a vibrant urban ambience. Tom is a likable, easygoing guy in these satisfying private eye novels.

Doyle, **Arthur Conan** • What can we say about Sherlock Holmes, the greatest detective of them all? That he's famous, he's eccentric, and he's fascinating? Dozens of movies, television shows, imitations, and satires have been made about him. Legions of fans still read the stories a hundred years after their first publication. They are still worth reading, these gripping short stories, and like Agatha Christie they are still a great introduction to the world of mysteries. People feel like they "ought" to read the Sherlock Holmes stories; but the important thing to know is that they are still fun to read. Conan Doyle created not only a unique character but also suffused his stories with a hauntingly effective atmosphere of dreadful family secrets, lonely moors, outlandish villains, and exotic poisons. This is a backdrop to Holmes's odd friendship with Watson, Holmes's brilliant deductive ability, his dislike of women, his strange personal habits, and his restless mind. The language and topics are a bit dated sometimes, but the twists and turns of the puzzles are still fresh and intriguing. And the puzzle of Holmes's personality endures.

Dunant, Sarah • Former journalist and British television personality Sarah Dunant writes engrossing mysteries that not only tell diverting stories but also illuminate current social issues. After writing two thrillers with a coauthor, she wrote her own thriller, *Snowstorms in a Hot Climate* (Random House, 1988). A fine novel that deserves to be better known, it tells the story of two friends who get caught up in the seductive and dangerous world of cocaine smuggling. British academic Marla Masterson comes to America in response to a message from her friend Elly, only to find Elly mentally and physically dependent on her slick drug-dealer lover. The novel centers around the cocaine culture and trade and follows the addicts and their drugs from Colombia to New York to California to Scotland.

With *Birth Marks* (Doubleday, 1992), Dunant begins a series of mysteries featuring Hannah Wolfe, who does contract work for a London private eye agency. Parenthood, the relationship between children and their parents, and a woman's choice about whether to have children are all issues woven into the sharply told story of a missing ballet dancer. *Fatlands* (Otto Penzler, 1994), which won the Silver Dagger Award, takes Hannah into an investigation centered around scientific experimentation on animals. During the course of her investigation, Hannah must face a difficult personal issue: how devastated she is by the emotional and physical aftermath of violence she encounters on her job. In *Under My Skin* (Scribner, 1995), Dunant tells a strong story set in a cosmetic surgery clinic and examines why women feel the need to alter their bodies. The author is particularly good at showing both sides of difficult and controversial issues, perhaps a legacy of her days as a journalist.

Dunning, John • Mysteries about the world of books, often called bibliomysteries, tend to be very popular with readers. One of the most successful series of rare-book mysteries is written by John Dunning. He is a former journalist and rare-book dealer, and it's clear from his novels that he knows and loves the book trade. In *Booked to Die* (Scribner, 1992), the hero is Cliff Janeway, a former Denver homicide detective and now a rare-book dealer. The setting is Denver, where Janeway is investigating the death of a book scout (a person who searches for valuable books in garage sales and the like). Janeway is passionate about this constant hunt for rare books in unlikely places, and the author is matchless at conveying this bookish passion to his readers. The novel has become a cult favorite, especially with book collectors and bibliophiles, and it won a Nero Wolfe Award and an independent booksellers award for the book they most enjoyed selling. Its sequel, *The Bookman's Wake* (Scribner, 1995), was an Edgar and Anthony nominee for Best Novel. Janeway is back in this mixture of book lore and hard-boiled detective novel, but the backdrop here is the world of fine art printing of limited edition books. The plot concerns the search for a legendary small-press edition of Poe's *The Raven*, which may or may not have been printed by a famous Seattle printer and book designer in 1969. Cliff tries to help a young woman whose parents worked with the brilliant printer and who is accused of stealing books from a house in New Mexico.

Dunning's earlier mysteries include *Looking for Ginger North* (Fawcett, 1980), a racetrack mystery, which was nominated for an Edgar Award.

Early, Jack • See **Scoppettone, Sandra**.

Emerson, Earl W. • Emerson may well be the only firefighter currently writing mysteries. For his first series, Emerson created Seattle private eye Thomas Black. Like most of his peers in the business, Black was once a cop, but after killing a young man, Black decides to leave the force. His police pension brings him enough money so he can be choosy about the cases he takes. In the early books of the series, he rents out the basement apartment in his house to law student Kathy Birchfield. Early on, they have a platonic but close relationship. Later, they become lovers. First in the series is *The Rainy City* (Avon, 1985). Emerson offers complex plots, a laconic but engaging narrator, and lots of local color for those who would like to visit Seattle on the cheap.

Emerson's second series makes extensive use of his own years of experience as a firefighter. The main character is Mac Fontana, who has left a job in the East and moved to a small town near Seattle, named Staircase. Unlike Thomas Black, Mac Fontana is a widower with a son and no ongoing relationship with a woman. First in the series is *Black Hearts and Slow Dancing* (Morrow, 1988). This series is gritty, full of details about the daily life of firefighters, and Emerson writes with a quiet intensity that makes them compelling reading.

Engel, Howard • Canadian writer Howard Engel has a long-running series of mysteries featuring Benny Cooperman, a shambling, appealing private eye. The books are set in the fictional town of Grantham, Ontario, near Niagara Falls. Benny grew up in Grantham, and he has never moved away from his hometown. After all, his parents, Manny and Sophie, still live nearby, and it's easy for him to drop by their condo for a Friday night Sabbath dinner. Otherwise, this nice-guy shamus seems to live on milk and chopped egg sandwiches, eaten at a shabby neighborhood place. Benny may be a good private eye, but he doesn't make much money, and he's always anxious for more cases to solve. Engel has created a funny, unusual character in Benny, and he conveys the cold and dreary streets of Grantham very well indeed. Benny has two good friends on the Niagara Regional Police force, Sergeants Pete Staziak and Chris Savas, and he sometimes needs them when events go awry on the unusual cases he solves. For example, in *Getting Away with Murder* (Toronto: Viking, 1995), Benny is forcibly recruited by an organized crime kingpin to hunt for an attacker who is making attempts on the kingpin's life. After threats have been made against his parents and girlfriend, Benny has no choice but to work for the mobster. How can Benny find a killer when the victim has so many personal and business enemies who are in the killing business themselves? It's a suitably puzzling conundrum for this always entertaining series hero.

Engel has also written a first book in the projected Mike Ward series, *Murder in Montparnasse* (Toronto: Viking, 1992). It's set in Paris in 1925 and concerns the fate of some lost manuscripts by Ernest Hemingway.

Estleman, Loren D. • The Motor City, Detroit, is the setting for much of Estleman's crime fiction, and the city itself is as important a character as the series hero, Amos Walker. Blending urban sociology with crime fiction, Estleman portrays a city facing horrendous problems, with no easy solutions in sight. Amos Walker is, in many ways, cut from the same cloth as his predecessors in the genre. A loner, an introvert, Walker makes his way through the "mean streets" of Detroit, looking to see justice done. First in the series is *Motor City Blue* (Houghton Mifflin, 1980). In recent years Estleman has turned to writing historical crime novels about Detroit, the first of which is *Whiskey River* (Bantam, 1990). Each book in this series looks at Detroit during a specific decade and provides a historical portrait of the city at a moment in time.

Evanovich, Janet • Lingerie executive Stephanie Plum lost her job six months ago, and things are beginning to look grim. Then she gets the bright idea of blackmailing her sleazy cousin, the bounty hunter, into giving her a job. Now, Stephanie has no idea exactly what she's doing as a bounty hunter, but she understands the essential part: If she lands her man, she'll get a *lot* of money. Her target on her first assignment is a man she most definitely wants to corral. Joe Morelli, sexy, untrustworthy, but undeniably attractive, is a cop on the lam, and the bounty on his head is steep. To settle an old score with Morelli—and to inject a healthy sum into her expiring bank account—Stephanie goes after him. Though she makes just about every mistake possible, Stephanie sasses her way through everything. It's going to take a lot to keep this Jersey girl down in her debut, *One for the Money* (Scribner, 1994). Nominated for all the major awards, and winner of the Dilys, this was one of the top first mysteries of the year. In subsequent outings, *Two for the Dough* (Scribner, 1996) and *Three to Get Deadly* (Scribner, 1997), Stephanie Plum shows no signs of slowing down.

Friedman, Kinky • What's the closest equivalent in mysteries to a Marx Brothers movie? We'd nominate Kinky Friedman. Kinky (a.k.a. the Kinkster), the former leader of the country and western band Kinky Friedman and the Texas Jewboys, writes mysteries about Kinky Friedman, an amateur sleuth and country and western singer. Like his creator, the detective Kinky lives in Greenwich Village in New York City. He is smart-mouthed and brash, maybe even the epitome of a wiseass detective. Although Kinky is indubitably the central character in all of his novels, he drags in his real-life friends, family members, and associates to appear as characters, too. His buddies Ratso, Rambam, and McGovern all get involved in strange ways in Kinky's crime-solving activities. Even Kinky's cat plays a suitably mysterious part in his real and his fictional lives. Sometimes he solves crimes in Texas, too, while he stays on his father's ranch near Kerrville, in a dilapidated watermelon-green trailer home. But in the midst of all his sleuthing, the one-liners still come fast and furiously. Kinky brings the tradition of the eccentric detective to new heights—or depths, depending on your opinion of him. He is an equal-opportunity offender, not at all politically correct in his rambunctious adventures. He says of himself, "It takes a not quite normal mind to solve a case like this." For all his eccentricity, the Kinkster writes mysteries in the traditional format, with an edge of outrageous country *noir*. And they are a lot of fun to read.

Gores, Joe • Most of Gores's novels are hard-boiled private eye stories, but he has also written some suspense thrillers, as well as *Hammett* (Putnam, 1975), a critically acclaimed novel about PI writer Dashiell Hammett. Gores is probably best known for his tales of the DKA (Daniel Kearny Associates) private eye agency in San Francisco. The DKA men and women mostly do skip tracing and repo work—and what repo work! The DKA agents get cars back any way they can from their deadbeat owners, and in doing so they run into some of the craziest characters this side of a Carl Hiaasen novel. In particular, *32 Cadillacs* (Mysterious Press, 1992) is a hilarious tour de force about an elaborate confidence trick in which a band of Gypsies manages to steal thirty-two Cadillacs in just one day. Gores refuses to bow to political correctness in this tale of confidence tricks, Gypsies, and a wild cross-country chase. Supposedly it's based on a real scam, just as DKA is based on a real San Francisco private eye agency for which Gores once worked. Perhaps that accounts for the realistic details that Gores sprinkles through his unflinching depictions of the daily grind of a typical private investigator. Each book in the series highlights new professional and personal events in the lives of the DKA agents. Dan Kearny, Giselle Marc, Patrick O'Bannon, Bart Heslip, Larry Ballard, and Ken Warren are all firmly established individuals who appear throughout the series. Gores is a remarkable storyteller, and his tales are often uproarious and always engaging. One of his greatest strengths is in his plotting skills—he's wonderful at building elaborate plots with all of the intricate details pulled together into a big, exciting finale.

Grafton, Sue • She may be known as "the alphabet lady" to some of her more absentminded fans, but millions of readers know Grafton as the creator of Kinsey Millhone, one of America's favorite female gumshoes. In her early thirties, Kinsey is something of a loner. Twice divorced, she lives in a small apartment with few possessions and even fewer emotional attachments. One of Kinsey's most important emotional ties, however, is to her octogenarian landlord, Henry Pitts, a retired baker who supplements his income by devising crossword puzzles. Henry serves as something of a father figure and emotional anchor for Kinsey. Tough, stubborn, but with a healthy sense of humor as a saving grace, Kinsey is definitely a descendant of wisecracking, hard-boiled male private eyes such as Spade and Marlowe. The fictional California town of Santa Teresa, where Kinsey lives and works, is a thinly veiled Santa Barbara, home to one of Grafton's important influences, the late Ross Macdonald. Though she is part of an established tradition, Kinsey nevertheless remains an individual. Grafton's style, which moves easily between action and introspection, from grim reality to humorous aside, demonstrates the range of an author well in command of her voice. Kinsey debuted in *"A" is for Alibi* (Holt, Rinehart, & Winston, 1982), and her yearly progress toward the end of the alphabet is a much-anticipated event for mystery fans.

Greenleaf, Stephen • Thought-provoking novels that interweave discussion of contemporary social issues with action sequences are the specialty of San Francisco author Stephen Greenleaf. Usually the hero is John Marshall Tanner, a private eye in San Francisco. Marsh is always interested in politics and current events, and he is unabashedly liberal in his ideas. Some

Killer Books

plots in these books take their impetus from controversial issues of the time, like the resurgence of racism and hate crimes in the South that is depicted in *Southern Cross* (Morrow, 1993). This is a fascinating study, from a Westerner's point of view, of what life is like in the New South. Marsh is feeling a bit insecure and gloomily reflective when he goes to his twenty-fifth college reunion, but he is reinvigorated by getting together with his old roommate. He agrees to accompany his friend, a liberal Jewish lawyer, to his South Carolina home. Marsh helps his friend face down death threats from a neo-Nazi group, and he learns about the sometimes difficult realities of daily life for blacks and whites in Charleston. The mysteries in the John Marshall Tanner series are well written, socially aware, and always enlightening.

Greenleaf also has written some legal thrillers. *Impact* (Morrow, 1989) is about the crash of an airplane near San Francisco and the lawsuits that ensue. Old law school friends Alec Hawthorne, now a famous hotshot aviation attorney, and Keith Tollison, an unpretentious small-town lawyer, are brought together as competing attorneys for families of crash victims. Greenleaf has clearly done extensive research into aviation law, and he takes the reader through the lawsuit process step by step in this dramatic thriller.

Hall, Parnell/Hailey, J. P. • Creator of one of the most unusual private eyes in contemporary mystery fiction, Parnell Hall has worked as a private eye and actor. His creation, Stanley Hastings, is not the kind of private eye one usually sees on television and in the movies. Hastings is happily married, with one young son, and his main occupation is working as a field interviewer for a lawyer, Richard Rosenberg, who advertises on television for personal injury cases. Hastings has more experience toting a camera than he does wielding a gun, and he uses his nimble wit and quick-firing tongue to get him out of trouble whenever possible. Hall writes some of the best dialogue in the business, and the opening line to each new novel in the series quickly lets the reader know what type of case it's going to be. First in the series is the aptly named *Detective* (Fine, 1987), which was nominated for the Edgar for Best First Novel. One of the best in the series is *Juror* (Fine, 1990), in which Hall pays homage to one of his favorite authors, Erle Stanley Gardner.

In a second series, written under the name **J. P. Hailey**, Hall recounts the adventures of attorney Steve Winslow. The first in the series is *The Baxter Trust* (Fine, 1988). These books are even more affectionately modeled on the work of Gardner.

Hammett, Dashiell • Hammett is one of the founders (along with Raymond Chandler) of the hard-boiled American private eye genre. He wrote only a few novels, but his work has been a major influence on American fiction and film. In early novels and short stories, Hammett wrote about a nameless PI, the Continental Op, who works out of the San Francisco office of the Continental Detective Agency. (Hammett himself worked as a detective at the Pinkerton Detective Agency, and he knew the gumshoe business well.) The Op is cool, hard, a nearly imperturbable loner who likes to stir things up to find out the truth. He doesn't really care if people get hurt, as long as his case is solved. The Op takes graft and corruption matter-of-factly, and he doesn't mind lying to one gangster to get him to kill another gangster.

The character in Hammett's fiction that most people know about, though, is Sam Spade, in *The Maltese Falcon* (Knopf, 1930). Spade, in both the novel and the movie (as played by Humphrey Bogart), was a major influence in the way modern fiction portrays private eyes. Spade is an amoral womanizer, but he feels compelled to do something about it when his partner, Miles Archer, is killed. The cast of highly dubious characters is unforgettable. There's Effie, Spade's loyal secretary; Joel Cairo, the ineffectual but determined petty criminal; Casper Gutman, who's been chasing after a dream for long years; and Bridget O'Shaughnessy, whom Spade might even love. Everybody involved in the incredibly labyrinthine plot lies to each other constantly. Spade watches everyone and laughs, but he is caught up in the con game, too; he is an observer in this story as well as an actor.

Hammett's books have been made into very successful movies. There is much in them still of the pulp style of earlier short stories, and Hammett uses vivid dialogue and scene-setting to capture a dark and dangerous mood in Prohibition America.

In the 1930s, a series of successful and much-loved movies starring Myrna Loy and William Powell were based on Hammett's last novel, *The Thin Man* (Knopf, 1934). Nick and Nora Charles (and their little dog, Asta) are the charming, tipsy heroes.

Hansen, Joseph • Hansen took a conventional form and gave it an unusual new twist. His series character, Dave Brandstetter, is an investigator for an insurance company, much like a private eye, and the tone of the novels evokes memories of Raymond

Chandler and Ross Macdonald. Unlike Philip Marlowe and Lew Archer, however, Dave Brandstetter is gay. When he first appears, in *Fadeout* (Harper, 1970), he is still grieving over the death of his lover from cancer. Over the course of the series, Dave eventually establishes another long-term relationship. The Southern California setting is also in many ways reminiscent of the classics of the private eye genre, but Hansen with his spare style makes the territory his own. The final book in the series is *A Country of Old Men* (Viking, 1991). Most recently, Hansen has begun a series of semi-autobiographical novels about Nathan Reed, a young man who has fled his midwestern home for California in the 1940s. Nathan is looking to enlarge his experiences of life, both sexually and otherwise, for he wants to be a writer. First in the series is *Living Upstairs* (Dutton, 1993), though the second book published, *Jack of Hearts* (Dutton, 1995), is set two years prior to the first one.

Haywood, Gar Anthony • Haywood writes two very different series, one hard-boiled and the other light comedy. He also has written for the television show *New York Undercover*. Haywood, an African-American writer from Los Angeles, began writing mysteries with *Fear of the Dark* (St. Martin's Press, 1988), which won the Shamus Award for Best First Private Eye Novel. His hero is Aaron Gunner, a hard-boiled, African-American private eye. The series is set in the mean streets of South Central Los Angeles, and the mood is dark and ominous. Gunner has burned out on the sordid routine of divorce work, and trained to become an electrician. He is drawn reluctantly back into crime-solving and discovers that, in spite of the violence and despair that he encounters, he can make a difference. Haywood accurately captures the talk and the feel of urban America in this unusual series. Readers should check the library and used bookstores for some of these works.

Healy, Jeremiah • A professor at the New England School of Law in Boston, Healy is the author of a long-running series of mysteries about a Vietnam vet-turned-private eye, John Francis Cuddy. The series is set chiefly in Boston and environs. Cuddy saw violent action in Vietnam, and he was marked by it like so many of his fellow soldiers. Despite this, or perhaps because of it, he is capable of great sensitivity in his personal relationships, unlike many of his fictional peers. As the series begins, with *Blunt Darts* (Walker, 1984), Cuddy is still grieving for his recently deceased wife. In most of the books, Cuddy visits his wife's grave and often talks about his cases with her. As the series progresses, Cuddy meets a woman who eventually becomes a romantic interest, Assistant District Attorney Nancy Meagher. Healy follows many of the conventions of the private eye novel in this series, but he has changed the stereotypical tough loner for the better in John Francis Cuddy.

Kaminsky, Stuart M. • A professor of film studies, Kaminsky has used his knowledge of movie history to create one of the more unusual private eye series in the American canon. His hero, Toby Peters, makes his living, more or less, in Hollywood just before and during World War II. In each of his cases, Toby ends up rubbing shoulders with a veritable Who's Who of Hollywood history, like Judy Garland in *Murder on the Yellow Brick Road* (St. Martin's Press, 1978), the Marx Brothers in *You Bet Your Life* (St. Martin's Press, 1979), or Bela Lugosi in *Never*

Cross a Vampire (St. Martin's Press, 1980). First in the series is *Bullet for a Star* (St. Martin's Press, 1977). Like the classic private eye, Toby Peters is mostly a loner, though he does have a good friend in Sheldon Minck, the dentist with whom he shares an office. Toby has a troubled relationship with his older brother, a Los Angeles homicide detective. Much of the appeal in this series is the Hollywood lore and history on nearly every page. The movie buff will find much to enjoy here.

Katz, Jon • A journalist and contributing editor to *Rolling Stone*, Katz has begun a series of mysteries with an unusual private eye. Having escaped a former life on Wall Street, Kit Deleeuw is now a private eye, working in affluent Rochambeau, New Jersey. With a wife, two kids, a mortgage, and an office in the local mall, he is a bit on the soft-boiled side. His "mean streets" are the streets of suburban America. In his first case, *Death by Station Wagon* (Doubleday, 1993), he investigates the death of two popular high schoolers. The police have ruled it a murder-suicide, but the dead boy's friends believe that something more sinister happened. They hire Kit—with their parents' permission, of course—to find out the truth. The more Kit investigates, the more he sees that suburbia is not the safe haven for the family that everyone would like to think. Further cases allow the "suburban detective" even more scope for uncovering the nastiness of modern life.

Kijewski, Karen • A former bartender herself, Kijewski (pronounced Kee-yov-ski) writes about a smart and tough sleuth called Kat Colorado, a former bartender who runs her own PI business in Sacramento. Her old skill often comes in handy, especially when she goes undercover, as in *Copy Kat* (Doubleday, 1992). Each chapter in the books begins with an excerpt from the advice columns written by Kat's friend Charity, and these set the tone for the stories. All of Kat's friends and family, like her adopted grandmother, her best friend, Charity, and her lover, Hank, are strongly formed characters. Kat may be a hard-nosed PI but she still has plenty of room in her heart and mind for clients in need, especially kids and the elderly. Like many of the female private eyes who have appeared in recent years, Kat brings a female perspective to the practices and stereotypes of the hard-boiled PI, and the genre is all the richer for it. Kat takes her own risks, gets herself out of dangerous situations, and resents it when men automatically try to protect her. The first book in the series is *Katwalk* (St. Martin's Press, 1989), which won the Shamus Award for Best First Novel from the Private Eye Writers of America.

Lutz, John • A past president of the Mystery Writers of America and the Private Eye Writers of America, Lutz has won both the Edgar and Shamus Awards for Best Short Story, and he is the 1995 recipient of the Private Eye Writers of America Life Achievement Award. Once a prolific writer of short stories, Lutz now concentrates chiefly on private eye and suspense novels. His first private eye series sleuth, Alo Nudger, debuted in *Buyer Beware* (Putnam, 1976), set in St. Louis. Nudger is the kind of guy who just can't seem to win. He ends up with clients who won't pay him, his ex-wife won't leave him alone, and he's always short of money. He's also too compassionate for his own good, taking the knight-errant ethos of the American PI to an extreme level. Lutz's other series PI, Fred Carver, first appeared in *Tropical Heat* (Holt, 1986). A former cop drummed out of the department after being kneecapped by a street punk, Carver is tougher and harder-edged than Nudger. Carver's beat is central Florida, and Lutz uses the steamy heat of Florida to add atmosphere to this dark and compelling series.

In addition to his private eye novels, Lutz also pens suspense novels, such as *SWF Seeks Same* (St. Martin's Press, 1990), which became the hit movie *Single White Female*. Readers should check the library and used bookstores for some of these books.

MacDonald, John D. • MacDonald was creator of one of the truly classic American mystery series, the Travis McGee novels. MacDonald got his start in the pulp magazines, as did a number of the genre's greats, such as Dashiell Hammett, Erle Stanley Gardner, and Raymond Chandler. His creation, Travis McGee, is something of an updated version of the knight-errant of the Middle Ages. Travis seeks to right wrongs, and he gets paid extremely well to do it, but he gets great satisfaction in seeing justice, as he sees it, done. He does "salvage work," as he calls it. He is not a private eye, because he doesn't have a license. He lives on his boat, the *Busted Flush*, moored at the Bahia Mar in Fort Lauderdale. His first appearance is in *The Deep Blue Good-by* (Fawcett, 1964). Eventually Travis's friend Meyer, a retired economist, assumes an important role in the books. Each book also generally features a woman with a difficult problem, whom Travis aids in a number of ways. In addition to fast-moving stories, MacDonald includes a deep interest in the environment, specifically his native Florida, and like Carl Hiaasen today, MacDonald deeply resented the depredations of "progress" in Florida.

Macdonald, Ross • Macdonald is the pseudonym used by the American-born and Canadian-educated Kenneth Millar (his wife was the mystery writer Margaret Millar; see her entry in the section "The Silence of the Lambs"). Macdonald was one of the triumvirate of classic California private eye writers, along with Dashiell Hammett and Raymond Chandler. His protagonist is private eye Lew Archer, who has been played memorably (as Lew "Harper") by Paul Newman on the screen. Macdonald wrote clean, simple, elegant prose that is a joy to read. His private eye stories have plots and scenes that are pared down to the time-honored essentials. Lew Archer is a lonely man, with no family, and he often investigates cases that grow out of family troubles. Indeed, his characters are often in search of a missing father, whose absence has ruined them emotionally. These are dark stories that seem to reach straight down into the evil inside people. The mysteries are splendidly written, with memorable characters and settings. Most of them are set in Santa Teresa, which is modeled on Santa Barbara, where Macdonald and Millar lived. (In honor of Macdonald, best-selling mystery writer Sue Grafton named Kinsey Millhone's fictional hometown Santa Teresa as well.) Macdonald provides vivid depictions of what Southern California was like in the 1950s and '60s. His descriptions of the brushfire in the foothills in *The Underground Man* (Knopf, 1971), for example, are so good that he makes the reader feel the hot breath of the fire licking ever closer to the expensive houses that should never have been built on the rugged, dry terrain. The fire is a powerful metaphor, but Macdonald also depicts it as a part of the tough reality of everyday life in Southern California.

Macdonald brought the psychological aspect of crime into

the world of the hard-boiled private eye and thus affected the development of mysteries significantly. He was named a Grand Master by the Mystery Writers of America in 1973.

McDermid, Val • Scots journalist McDermid has created two separate series of mysteries. With *Dead Beat* (St. Martin's Press, 1993), McDermid introduces Manchester-based private eye Kate Brannigan. Kate lives next door to her lover, rock music journalist Richard Barclay. When a rock star, an old friend of Richard's, asks Kate to find an important person from his past, Kate has little idea that murder will be the result. In *Kick Back* (St. Martin's Press, 1993), Kate takes on two puzzling cases at once. Kate is intelligent, resourceful, and independent. A kick-boxer, Kate is well able to defend herself when the occasion demands.

McDermid is also the author of *The Mermaids Singing* (HarperCollins, 1996), a harrowing suspense novel that won the Gold Dagger for Best Novel.

For McDermid's series of mysteries featuring lesbian reporter Lindsay Gordon, see the section "The Front Page."

Mosley, Walter • Easy Rawlins is a rare and unforgettable character, and these are his stories. Walter Mosley first introduces us to Easy in the postwar Los Angeles of *Devil in a Blue Dress* (Norton, 1990). Easy is a black war veteran who is trying to make enough money to live decently and to pay the mortgage on his small house. He's proud of being able to buy a house, and sees the ownership of real estate as his personal and financial security against the racism and oppression of the time. Aside from his real estate investments, he helps people in the community who can't go to the police with their problems. And so he eases into a career as an informal private eye, solving cases in spite of suspicion and persecution by the LAPD. Throughout the series we follow the cases he investigates, and we follow the ups and downs of Easy's personal life as well. Easy's best friend is Raymond "Mouse" Alexander, who is completely unpredictable and a sociopathic killer, but who helps Easy out sometimes with his sleuthing. Over the course of the series, Easy grows and matures; he learns to deal better with the violent impulses in himself caused by racism and oppression. He learns that he loves children and is great with them, and they change his life. But perhaps Mosley's greatest achievement in these novels is the superb depiction of a vital black community in postwar Los Angeles, in and near Watts. He shows us the vitality of that community, and how the people in it take care of each other, kill each other over quarrels, and deal with racism, unemployment, and poverty. Reading these novels is like taking a long, loving look into the life of Watts from the late 1940s to the 1960s.

Devil in a Blue Dress was made into a fine, atmospheric movie with Denzel Washington.

Writers with African-American/Black Detectives

Nikki Baker; Robert Barnard; George Baxt (the Pharoah Love series); Eleanor Taylor Bland; Nora DeLoach; Grace Edwards; Terris McMahan Grimes; Gar Anthony Haywood; Chester Himes; Susan Moody (the Penny Wanawake series); BarbaraNeely; James Patterson; Gary Phillips; Robert Skinner; Valerie Wilson Wesley; Chassie West.

Muller, Marcia • Her female private eye Sharon McCone debuted in *Edwin of the Iron Shoes* (McKay Washburn, 1977) five years before her best-selling peers Sue Grafton and Sara Paretsky published the first novels in their private eye series. Muller has been called, by Grafton, the "founding 'mother' of the contemporary female hard-boiled private eye." Based in San Francisco and working chiefly for a legal cooperative, All Souls, McCone is tough and independent, certainly an engaging epitome for the characters who have come after her. The early McCone novels have a more soft-boiled feel to them, but with more recent works, such as *The Shape of Dread* (Mysterious Press, 1989) and *Wolf in the Shadows* (Mysterious Press, 1993), which won an Anthony for Best Novel, Muller displays a strong reflective and hard-edged voice that makes her work equal the best of Grafton and Paretsky. Muller has also written two other enjoyable but short-lived series. One featured Chicana museum curator Elena Oliverez, beginning with *The Tree of Death* (Walker, 1983); and the other starred art security expert Joanna Stark, who first appeared in *The Cavalier in White* (St. Martin's Press, 1986).

Paretsky, Sara • Along with Sue Grafton and Patricia Cornwell, Paretsky has been one of the few American women mystery writers who consistently receive serious critical attention and acclaim for their novels. She transformed the mystery genre with her thought-provoking stories about the tough, female private eye V. I. Warshawski. The first Warshawski book is *Indemnity Only* (Dial Press, 1982). Paretsky worked in the insurance industry for many years, and she began her series of mysteries by telling a strong story of insurance fraud. Although Paretsky uses many of the classic PI traditions in her novels, she adapts them to her new model of a private eye novel, with a feminist hero and stories that often center on contemporary social issues. The crimes that V. I. solves usually are not individual antisocial acts; they are murders committed against a backdrop of a larger social problem. V. I. might uncover a murderer, but order and justice may not always prevail in Paretsky's gritty urban tales. Especially memorable is her powerful evocation of a corrupt and grimy industrial Chicago.

Blood Shot (Delacorte, 1988), published in Great Britain as *Toxic Shock* (Gollancz, 1988), won the Silver Dagger Award in 1988. Paretsky has edited short-story anthologies, including *A Woman's Eye* (Delacorte, 1991), which won an Anthony Award. Paretsky also founded and was the first president of the influential Sisters in Crime organization.

The movie *V. I. Warshawski*, with Kathleen Turner, was based on books by Paretsky.

Parker, Robert B. • One of the most famous private eyes in fiction is Spenser, Robert B. Parker's hero in a long series of bestselling hard-boiled mysteries. Spenser is a private eye in the knight-errant mode, who searches for justice and tries to right the wrongs suffered by his innocent clients. Apparently he has no first name, but over the course of the series he acquires a long-term lover, Susan Silverman, and a sardonic and violent sidekick, Hawk. Hawk is an amoral black enforcer who watches Spenser's back in tough situations and has no problem with simply blowing away the bad guys in a gunfight. Spenser, Susan, and Hawk are all immensely clever at wordplay; they are as likely to be found exchanging wisecracks over dinner as they are to be hunting down killers. Parker conveys the atmosphere of

Boston with great success; he paints a vivid portrait of the city in his novels. Like many gumshoes, Spenser has his little eccentricities: He loves to cook and eat gourmet food and drink specialty beers, and his preparation of each meal is lovingly described. We see more of Spenser's private life than we did with most of the detectives in earlier PI novels, and his personal relationships change and grow throughout the series. The ex-boxer Spenser becomes less violent and more sensitive over time, but he never loses his street smarts and his concern for his clients. Since Robert B. Parker's books have been hugely popular for years, Spenser probably has been the model for the more caring and compassionate private eye that we have seen in many recent mysteries. Parker has moved away somewhat from the hard-boiled tradition and thus has altered the genre forever.

Pronzini, Bill • A prolific and well-liked mystery writer, Pronzini is best known for his series of private eye novels featuring the "Nameless Detective." These are good, solid mysteries, with an interesting San Francisco setting and an accurate recounting of the details of a PI's life. "Nameless" is an ex-police officer who loves to collect old pulp magazines (as does Pronzini himself). His sidekick is Lieutenant "Eb" Eberhardt of the SFPD; Eberhardt later quits the force to become a partner in the agency owned by the "Nameless Detective." Unlike most fictional private eyes, "Nameless" ages throughout the series, and Pronzini chronicles his illnesses and physical changes realistically. For example, in 1991 he's fifty-eight, and he looks and feels his age in the story. Another characteristic that differentiates "Nameless" from many PIs is that he genuinely cares about people, more than he cares about abstract ideas of justice and the American way. He just wants people whose cases he takes on to survive, to live to see another day. "Nameless" is basically a nice, decent guy. He's not promiscuous, or very hard-drinking, and he has only two long-term relationships with women throughout the series. Readers should check the library or used bookstores for most of these works.

Pronzini is married to mystery writer Marcia Muller, and they have written one book featuring "Nameless" and her series detective, Sharon McCone, working together on a case. Pronzini also has written mysteries under the pseudonyms Jack Foxx, William Jeffrey, and Alex Saxon.

Roberts, Les • Les Roberts writes two very different series of hard-boiled private eye mysteries. He began with the Saxon series. Saxon is a Los Angeles private eye, apparently possessing no first name, and an actor who works as a PI between his acting jobs. The first Saxon mystery, *An Infinite Number of Monkeys* (St. Martin's Press, 1987), was the winner of the Shamus Award for Best First Novel. In the novel, Buck Weldon, a writer of hard-boiled and violent novels, is the victim of a series of murder attempts. Buck has a beautiful daughter, and it's easy for Saxon to fall in love with her while he's trying to help her father stay alive. Wisecracks abound, and Saxon gets off some good one-liners. The Saxon mysteries are sexy, violent tales of the Southern California way of life and death.

Roberts also writes a series with Milan Jacovich, set in Cleveland. Milan's ethnic background is Slovenian, and a running joke in the books is about how everyone he meets mispronounces his name in a different way. Cleveland has thriving East European ethnic communities, and Roberts clearly knows the territory well. The Slovenian atmosphere adds a welcome diversity to these well-crafted PI novels. *Pepper Pike* (St. Martin's Press, 1988) is a story about a rich woman who hires Milan to find her missing husband. The husband had already called and asked for protection, but Milan got there too late. The Mafia, the local cops, rich businessmen, and some advertising agency folks all get involved in the case and become suspects in Milan's thorough and professional investigation.

S**atterthwait, Walter** • After penning two action-adventure novels (now out of print), Satterthwait turned to writing two distinctive types of mysteries, private eye novels and historical mysteries. His private eye novels feature Santa Fe investigator Joshua Croft. Croft's partner in his work is Rita Mondragon, who has been confined to a wheelchair by an accident before the series begins. Croft has much in common with the traditional private eye, including the ability to toss off wiseass remarks with no encouragement whatsoever. Satterthwait's dialogue is crisp, and his descriptions of setting are just like his dialogue. Satterthwait also knows how to pace a story; each of the books in the series moves along briskly, drawing the reader quickly into the plot and keeping her or him there until the end. First in the series is *Wall of Glass* (St. Martin's Press, 1988), in which Croft is asked to fence a stolen diamond necklace. When the cowboy who offered him the job is murdered, Croft figures it's in his best interests to know who killed him. One of the best in the series is *The Hanged Man* (St. Martin's Press, 1993; published in England as *The Death Card* by Collins, 1994).

For Satterthwait's historical mysteries see the section "Once Upon a Crime."

Scoppettone, **Sandra/Early, Jack** • Early on in her writing career, Sandra Scoppettone published three hard-boiled mysteries under the name **Jack Early**. The first was the Edgar nominee *A Creative Kind of Killer* (Franklin Watts, 1984). It features Fortune Fanelli, a private eye who lives in the SoHo area of New York City. Fortune is a single father of two teenagers, and a charming character. As in most of her novels, Scoppettone has created a vivid Italian-American family. *Donato & Daughter* (Dutton, 1988) is a darkly dramatic suspense novel about a series of killings of nuns. Police lieutenant Dina Donato heads a crime team set up for these cases, and her father, Sergeant Michael Donato, assists her. A television movie starring Charles Bronson was made from the novel. The Jack Early novels have now been reprinted under the author's own name.

Scoppettone also has written a series of mysteries with lesbian private eye Lauren Laurano. The first in the series is *Everything You Have Is Mine* (Little, Brown, 1991). Lauren is a bright and observant character, and she shares her life with her long-term lover Kip, a psychotherapist. These novels are fairly hard-boiled mysteries, and Lauren is a witty and observant sleuth. Lauren is fond of comparing herself to fictional female detectives. When she's caught up in an interesting case, she might ask herself, "What would Kinsey Millhone [or another fictional PI] do?" Scoppettone's New York City settings are gritty and realistic backdrops to her stories of urban crime.

Simon, **Roger L.** • Simon stood the often conservative private eye genre on its head in the 1960s and '70s with his depiction of a counterculture PI, Moses Wine. The stories are set in Southern California, and they are very much of their time. Wine is a hip,

Jewish, counterculture investigator. In *Wild Turkey* (Straight Arrow, 1975) he is working with a gonzo journalist on a case in which a controversial writer has died. Maybe it's suicide, or just maybe it's murder. Wine's investigation leads him straight into a zany potpourri involving Cuban mobsters, TV journalists, corrupt politicians, and sexual liberation freaks. It's all wild and weird, but still structured very much in the classic private eye mode, with Wine as the wisecracking, self-aware gumshoe. In *California Roll* (Villard, 1985), Wine has sold out his radical principles to work for a Silicon Valley computer company as their first head of security. In the later novels, Wine is an old '60s hippie still looking for himself in Reagan's America. In *Raising the Dead* (Villard, 1988) he is hired by an Arab antidiscrimination group and goes to Israel in search of a possible suspect in the bombing death of an Arab-American leader. He rather enjoys searching for his roots, even though he's always been an agnostic. This is a more serious novel than the usual wacky, sexy Moses Wine capers. Wine deals with his personal issues of faith and heritage while entertaining readers with a tour of Israel and discussions of Arab-Israeli relations. Moses starts out as a radical and gets less radical as the series goes on, but he remains a savvy, persistent shamus. Readers should check the library or used bookstores for most of these works.

Spillane, Mickey • Spillane is the creator of perhaps the hardest of the hard-boiled private eyes, Mike Hammer. Tough, brutal Hammer is well-named. In his heyday, Spillane was an enormously best-selling author, but in recent years he has not written very often. Though later incarnations of the private detective have softened some of Mike Hammer's roughest edges, Spillane was influential in shaping the ethos of the American private eye. *I, the Jury* (Dutton, 1947) is Hammer's first case, and in some ways, still his most famous. Hammer is back from serving his country in World War II, and his best friend, who lost an arm saving his life during the war, is murdered. Hammer hunts down the killer, and in the end acts as judge, jury, and executioner. Though many critics have castigated Hammer and his creator for just such behavior, readers don't seem to have minded. Check the library or used bookstores for most of these works.

Stabenow, Dana • Alaska is a new frontier for mysteries, and Dana Stabenow guides readers around it in her highly atmospheric mysteries. The series features Kate Shugak, an Aleutian Indian who is a former investigator for the district attorney's office in Anchorage. Kate has retreated to live in the bush after being seriously injured, but she is still curious and vital. Often the books in the series are set in a fictional national park that covers thousands of acres of mountains, glaciers, and forests. During her investigations, Kate discovers a lot about the illicit life of the bush country, where average citizens might grow marijuana or poach protected animals. In the first book, the Edgar Award-winning *A Cold Day for Murder* (Berkley, 1992), Kate needs to find out what has happened to a missing park ranger and an investigator sent in after him. In *Dead in the Water* (Berkley, 1993), Kate goes on a tough undercover job on a fishing boat to find the killers of two crewmen. Kate's not always alone on her investigations: She gets help from Mutt, her half-wolf, half-husky dog; her on-again, off-again lover, Jack Morgan; and her friend Bobby Clark, a raucous, intelligent Vietnam vet. Stabenow's books are memorable, with their vivid descriptions of the Alaskan wilderness, the Aleut towns, and the fiercely independent bush dwellers.

Stevenson, Richard • The state capital of New York is the setting for Stevenson's series featuring Donald Strachey, one of the few gay private investigators in contemporary mystery fiction. In the opener to the series, *Death Trick* (St. Martin's Press, 1981), Strachey investigates a murder in the gay community. A gay activist, the son of a wealthy businessman, is the chief suspect in a murder, and he has disappeared. Strachey is hired to find him. In this novel, as in others in the series, Stevenson blends mystery, politics, and activism in an interesting mix. Strachey is similar in many ways to his peers in the private eye profession, with one singular exception. An important part of the series is Strachey's longtime lover, Timothy Callahan. Through Strachey and Callahan, Stevenson shows that not every private eye is a loner with difficulty maintaining personal relationships, and the difference is refreshing.

Stout, Rex • Rex Stout is one of the great masters of the mystery genre. Stout's many Nero Wolfe books are classic puzzle yarns, much beloved by mystery readers. Wolfe is a plump and eccentric private detective, famous for almost never leaving his West 35th Street house in New York City on a case. Archie Goodwin, who tells each story in his own sardonic voice, is Wolfe's loyal and eternally wisecracking sidekick. Stout created vivid New York City settings; Wolfe's brownstone (one of the most famous of fictional addresses) is so memorably described that readers often can remember every detail years later. Wolfe, a deductive genius, is an inheritor of the Great Detective tradition, very much in the Sherlock Holmes mode. Stout has endowed Wolfe lavishly with eccentric habits, such as growing orchids and eating lavish gourmet meals cooked by a resident chef. Indeed, Stout is a master at noting the small details of Wolfe's life, his household, and his unvarying daily routine in order to draw the reader into Wolfe's world and make it seem real. Against this highly formalized and unchanging backdrop, the cases that Nero Wolfe and Archie Goodwin solve change with each book. Wolfe solves mysteries by "cerebration," as do Holmes and Dupin, and not by action. Action, when needed, is Archie's business. Archie and Wolfe are a classic team, even though they annoy each other mightily and often, and their verbal sparring still sparkles after forty years of Nero Wolfe mysteries. The series began with *Fer-de-Lance* (Farrar, Rinehart, 1934).

In the 1930s and '40s, Stout also wrote several mysteries with the characters Tecumseh Fox, Dol Bonner, Alphabet Hicks, and Delia Brand.

Swanson, Doug J. • Reporter Doug Swanson mines a rich vein of down-home, raunchy humor for his Texas mysteries. His hero is Jack Flippo, a former assistant district attorney who lost his job in a sex scandal. Jack's life has gone into a tailspin, and now he's reduced to being a seedy private eye in Dallas. He ekes out a precarious living as a wedding photographer and part-time "keyhole man," who tails straying spouses to cheap motel rooms and photographs them in the flesh for divorce evidence. Along the way Jack gets himself involved in some bizarre and hilarious cases. Swanson is great at creating memorable wackos as secondary characters and villains, and at setting up complex plots and traps into which his criminals inevitably fall. Perhaps his most unforgettable villain so far is Teddy Deuce, a low-life enforcer consigned by his New York Mob bosses to the boondocks of Dallas owing to Teddy's total incompetence. Teddy's thought processes are not at all bright, and he messes up every criminal plan he makes. He's a sociopath and narcissist who can think only about the drape of his 100 percent silk sports jacket while he runs over an innocent bystander with a stolen car. Teddy has a cleanliness fetish, and he is liable to interrupt his robberies and assaults to brush his teeth and spot-clean his clothes. Swanson's first novel, *Big Town* (HarperCollins, 1994), was nominated for an Edgar Award, and it earned Swanson an enviable reputation as a hot new writer. Swanson has a gift for street talk, and his dim-bulb criminals are recorded in all the glory of their extreme stupidity. The stories are fast-paced, and the Dallas settings are sleazily appropriate for this fresh brand of country *noir*.

Trocheck, Kathy Hogan • Formerly a reporter for the *Atlanta Journal-Constitution*, Trocheck has turned a sharply observant eye on life in the modern South in a new series about former cop and not-quite-former private eye Julia Callahan Garrity, "Callahan" to her friends. Burned out by the male-dominated worlds of the police and the private eye game, Callahan has gone into business with her mother, Edna Mae Garrity. As owners of House Mouse, Callahan and her mother, along with a deliciously funny staff of "mice," clean houses in some of the best sections of Atlanta. In the first book of the series, *Every Crooked Nanny* (HarperCollins, 1992), Callahan takes on a cleaning job for an old sorority sister, Lilah Rose Beemish, who soon turns to Callahan for help with more than just overgrown dust bunnies. Her family's Mormon nanny has absconded with jewelry, furs, and files of a secret business deal that could land Lilah Rose's husband deep in trouble. Callahan dusts off her private eye license and tries her best to help the obnoxious Beemish family. Callahan Garrity is smart, funny, and tenacious, whether she's tracking down a murder suspect or trying to get that noisome stain out of the living room carpet. With helpers such as Neva Jean, one of her cheerfully "white trash" House Mouse employees; the elderly black sisters Sister and Baby Easterbrook; and the irrepressible Edna Mae Garrity, Callahan has her hands full solving crimes in Atlanta. Trocheck's trenchant humor takes no prisoners when it comes to the idiosyncracies of modern American society or of southern culture. The second novel in the series, *To Live and Die in Dixie* (HarperCollins, 1993), was nominated for an Agatha Award for Best Novel. Recently Trocheck has begun a second series, set in Florida, starring retired journalist Truman Kicklighter. First in this series is *Lickety-Split* (HarperCollins, 1996).

Valin, Jonathan • Private eye Harry Stoner of Cincinnati is the hero in a series of very hard-boiled stories by Valin. In *Natural Causes* (Congdon, 1983), Stoner is hired to investigate the possibility that a recently dead soap opera writer was playing a con game on the corporation for which he worked before his death. The company sponsors the television show, and it wants to be sure that no hanky-panky by the stars or writers is going to ruin the company's moral image with Americans. *Fire Lake* (Delacorte, 1987) is the story of how Harry tries to help an old college friend who returns to Cincinnati after many years. Lonnie Jack began taking drugs in the '60s, when he and

Harry were roommates, but he's gotten worse over the years and has turned into a junkie. Lonnie has given his name as Harry Stoner in a fleabag motel. When they call Harry, Lonnie has overdosed, and everyone thinks it's a suicide attempt. Harry is aided in his quest by Lonnie's ex-wife, and it's a bittersweet task, constantly evoking memories of his own past. Valin writes complex plots, very much in the classic tradition of the tough American PI novel. Readers should check the library and used bookstores for many of these works.

Wesley, Valerie Wilson • An editor-at-large at *Essence* magazine and the author of several books of fiction and nonfiction for younger readers, Wesley also pens a series of novels starring African-American private eye Tamara Hayle. Based in Newark, New Jersey, Tamara is a divorced mother trying to make a living for herself and her teenaged son Jamal in *When Death Comes Stealing* (Putnam, 1994), the series opener. Jamal's father, DeWayne Curtis, comes calling on Tamara for help. He is convinced someone is murdering all his sons from previous marriages and liaisons, and he wants Tamara to find out who's doing it before Jamal becomes the next target. In *Devil's Gonna Get Him* (Putnam, 1995), Tamara is hired by Newark's wealthiest black businessman, Lincoln Storey, to get the scoop on the relationship between his stepdaughter and a documentary filmmaker, who just happens to be an old flame of Tamara's. When Storey drops dead at a political fundraiser, Tamara keeps digging to protect the young sister of a good friend accused of the murder. Wesley brings a trenchant voice to the private eye novel, with Tamara's observations on being black and female in today's world, and she also offers a stark portrait of contemporary

Newark and its environs. *When Death Comes Stealing* was a Shamus Award nominee for Best First Private Eye Novel.

Wilhelm, Kate • Winner of the two most prestigious prizes in science fiction, the Hugo and the Nebula Awards, Wilhelm is perhaps better known as a science fiction writer. In recent years she has written in both genres. In her mysteries there is a strong sense of place, underscored by the belief that environment plays a significant role in the shaping of character. Wilhelm pays much attention to the development of her characters, creating her people through disciplined, descriptive language. First introduced in a short story, the husband-and-wife team of Charlie Meiklejohn and Constance Leidl has been featured in several novels, beginning with *The Hamlet Trap* (St. Martin's Press, 1987). Charlie, a former New York City arson investigator, now works as a private investigator, and Constance is a professional psychologist, a Ph.D. with impressive credentials. In combination these two make a very effective team, and their relationship provides a strong emotional core to the novels. Wilhelm is not afraid to experiment, as with *The Dark Door* (St. Martin's Press, 1988), a Charlie and Constance novel that blends science fiction and mystery. Other books, such as *Seven Kinds of Death* (St. Martin's Press, 1992), are more traditional, though Wilhelm remains strongly individual, whatever she writes. Readers should check the library and used bookstores for most of these works.

For Wilhelm's legal mysteries see the section "Perry Mason for the Defense."

Wings, Mary • Lesbian sleuth Emma Victor is the main character in Wings's memorable series of mysteries. Although she is really an amateur detective, Emma is also a strong-willed investigator in the classic hard-boiled mode. In *She Came Too Late* (Crossing Press, 1987), Emma is working at the women's hot line in Boston. Emma finds out that a woman who has called her for help has been murdered, and her death leads Emma into a highly dangerous world of biological engineering and illicit drugs. By the time of *She Came in a Flash* (New American Library, 1988), she has moved to California and is helping out an old friend by handling her publicity. Emma looks into the death of a religious cult member as a favor to her friend, and becomes involved with the activities of a selfish and arrogant rock star, Nebraska Storm, as part of her investigation. The claustrophobic atmosphere of the cult is conveyed forcefully in this well-written novel. The Emma Victor series continues in *She Came by the Book* (Berkley, 1996).

A nameless woman tells a bizarre and tragic story in the award-winning *Divine Victim* (Dutton, 1992). The woman has traveled with her new lover, Marya, to clean out an old house in Montana that Marya has inherited from an aunt. As they clean, they discover countless images of the Virgin Mary in and around the house, and they begin to uncover the dark story behind the aunt's obsession with Mary and other female saints. Meanwhile, the nameless woman knows that danger is not far away.

Winslow, Don • See the section "The Usual Suspects."

Womack, Steven • Former journalist Steven Womack writes a series of country *noir* mysteries set in Nashville, with private eye Harry James Denton. These are very atmospheric novels, somewhere between hard-boiled and cozy. Of course, country music is the big industry in Nashville, and readers learn plenty about it in these hip, funny stories. Harry is perpetually short of money, and he drives around Nashville in a broken-down old car. He is a former reporter who lost his job and his wife and ended up as a small-time PI. In *Way Past Dead* (Ballantine, 1995), an up-and-coming country singer is murdered, and a songwriter friend of Harry's is suspected in the murder. While Harry tries to prove his buddy's innocence, he is also worried about his girlfriend Marsha, the medical examiner, who has been caught in a hostage drama down at the morgue. Some crazed cult members want the body of their founder's wife back from the coroner, as they believe she can be resurrected only if her body is whole and has not been autopsied. Besides his facility with plot and southern idioms, Womack is great at writing natural-sounding dialogue. These southern urban mysteries capture not only the ambience of Nashville but also the ironies and absurdities of contemporary life.

Earlier, Womack wrote a few novels about Jack Lynch, a public relations director for a New Orleans bank. Jack is the personal troubleshooter for the president of the bank, a big local wheeler-dealer. A rich New Orleans atmosphere and an air of municipal corruption pervade these well-written and memorable novels.

Womack is a successful screenwriter as well as an award-winning novelist. *Dead Folks' Blues* (Ballantine, 1993) won the Edgar Award for Best Paperback Original, *Torch Town Boogie* (Ballantine, 1993) was nominated for a Shamus Award, and *Murphy's Fault* (St. Martin's Press, 1990) was a *New York Times* Notable Book of 1990.

For Further Reading • Michael Allegretto; Rudolfo Anaya; Richard Barre; Steve Brewer; Rex Burns; Stan Cutler; Catherine Dain; Thomas B. Dewey; Stephen Dobyns; A. A. Fair; G. M. Ford; Ruthe Furie; William Campbell Gault; Brett Halliday; David Housewright; Richard Hoyt; Robert Irvine; Phyllis Knight; Jonathan Latimer; Martha Lawrence; Wendi Lee; Dennis Lehane; John Leslie; Dick Lochte; Randye Lordon; Arthur Lyons; William P. McGivern; Wade Miller; Katy Munger; William F. Nolan; Gary Phillips; Sandra West Prowell; Robert J. Randisi; William J. Reynolds; S. J. Rozan; Alan Russell; James Sallis; Mark Schorr; Randall Silvis; Gillian Slovo; Cath Staincliffe; Ronald Tierney; Mark Timlin; Sharon Zukowski.

Some private eye movies are • *The Big Fix*; *The Big Sleep*; *The Blue Dahlia*; *The Cheap Detective*; *Chinatown*; *Dead Men Don't Wear Plaid*; *The Drowning Pool*; *Farewell My Lovely*; *The Glass Key*; *The Hound of the Baskervilles*; *I, the Jury*; *Lady in the Lake*; *The Late Show*; *The Long Good-bye*; *The Maltese Falcon*; *Marlowe*; the Michael Shayne series; *The Moving Target* (also called *Harper*); *Murder, My Sweet*; *Satan Met a Lady*; *Shaft*.

Television series • *Anna Lee*; *Banacek*; *Barnaby Jones*; *Cannon*; *Crazy Like a Fox*; *Honey West*; *Magnum P.I.*; *Mannix*; *Martin Kane, Private Eye*; *Matt Houston*; *Mike Hammer*; *Moonlighting*; *Peter Gunn*; *Remington Steele*; *Riptide*; *The Rockford Files*; *Sherlock Holmes Mysteries*; *Simon & Simon*; *Spenser: For Hire*; *Tenspeed and Brownshoe*.

Legal Thrillers

Perry Mason for the Defense

Lawyers have been a staple of television fare, almost from the beginning. Perry Mason used to solve his cases, almost at the last minute, with some dazzling revelation in the courtroom that took everyone by surprise. Ben Matlock used southern charm and a deceptive small-town-hick demeanor to fool many a clever murderer into thinking he or she had gotten away with it. And that slick ensemble cast on *L.A. Law* gave us several seasons' worth of entertaining legal shenanigans. Lawyer jokes aside, the profession of the law and the mystery novel make good partners, for the stakes are rarely higher in the courtroom than when a jury has to make a decision in a murder trial, literally a life-or-death decision. In recent years John Grisham has taken the "legal thriller" and made it virtually his own, becoming a household name. His books and the movies they have spawned have made Grisham probably the most recognizable writer of legal mysteries in the world. Readers eager for other mysteries with a legal connection have plenty of suspects to investigate.

Brandon, Jay • Texas attorney Jay Brandon's first few novels were gripping suspense thrillers. *Tripwire* (Bantam, 1987) is a riveting novel about the lingering aftereffects of murder and the Vietnam War. A woman who has witnessed a murder is hidden away from the wrath of the killers. Meanwhile, her son, who was declared dead in Vietnam, has suddenly turned up alive. Is he the real son, or is he an impostor planted by the murderers who are looking for her? Brandon clearly knows how to write exciting suspense novels. In recent years he has proved himself to be adept at penning legal thrillers, too. Several of his courtroom mysteries feature San Antonio District Attorney Mark Blackwell, including the Edgar-nominated *Fade the Heat* (Pocket Books, 1990) and *Loose among the Lambs* (Pocket Books, 1993). Brandon is expert at advancing his plots with absorbing legal details, and the suspense in these novels never falters. At first, *Loose Among the Lambs* seems to be a simple story about a child abuse case, but as Mark Blackwell prepares the case for trial, he keeps discovering new problems and new depths to the case. He finds that abusers tend to be adults who were once abused children themselves, and are now perpetuating the dreadful cycle of abuse into the next generation. In *Local Rules* (Pocket Books, 1995), a former prosecutor, now a criminal defense attorney, is asked to defend a teenager who killed his best friend and is suspected in the death of the most popular girl in town. Judicial and municipal corruption seem to be rife in the small town where the murder occurred. But perhaps things are not what they seem to a big-city attorney from San Antonio. The contrast of rural versus urban Texas customs and attitudes toward law and order makes for a thought-provoking and entertaining novel.

Caudwell, Sarah • Though she has only three books thus far to her credit, Caudwell has achieved a wide following for her mirthful tales of murder and malfeasance. With an erudition and precision of language reminiscent of the late Dorothy L. Sayers and Margery Allingham, surely her spiritual ancestors in the genre, Caudwell does what she does quite unlike anyone else writing contemporary mystery novels. The narrator of Caudwell's work is an androgynous Oxford professor of law, Hilary Tamar. Though readers may claim to know whether Hilary is male or female, Caudwell smilingly refuses ever to settle the debate. The affairs that Hilary so amusingly relates concern young London barristers, each of whom has her or his own particular talent for running into trouble. In the brilliantly funny *Thus Was Adonis Murdered* (Scribner, 1981), Julia Larwood, who knows the Finance Act inside out but who can't quite remember where she left her passport, becomes embroiled in murder while she's on holiday in Venice. Hilary, of course, must come to the rescue. The combination of wit, humor, and intelligence makes Caudwell's work a rare vintage. Caudwell's third novel, *The Sirens Sang of Murder* (Delacorte, 1989), won the Anthony Award for Best Novel.

Downing, Warwick • Downing is a fine writer who can keep his readers absorbed and happy. He is skilled at leaving much to the reader's imagination; he slowly develops his characters throughout the story by telling you a bit here and a bit there about their backgrounds and personalities, until he's built up a picture of an individual that makes sense to the reader. Downing has written only a few mysteries, but they're well worth seeking out. His series tells the stories of lawyers who are part of the National Association of Special Prosecutors, and about their opponents, the defense lawyers. *A Lingering Doubt* (Pocket Books, 1993) is about Jack Bard, a savvy, experienced defense lawyer, and an old liberal with strong principles. He is defending Drusus Church, a young black man who has been trying to turn his life around when he is accused in the murder of a vicious neighborhood drug dealer. Church's past life as a gang member comes back to haunt him, and the case against him seems to be so strong that there is little hope. Jack believes in his innocence, but can he convince a jury—and is his client really innocent anyway? In this and his other books, Downing creates fascinating novels, well above the ordinary legal thrillers. Readers should check for these books in the library and used bookstores.

Friedman, Philip • Friedman sets up dramatic personal circumstances for his characters, adds in a strong dose of courtroom tension, and thus produces some of the most absorbing legal thrillers being written today. *Reasonable Doubt* (Fine, 1990) is about Michael Ryan, a lawyer whose only son, Ned, has been murdered. Michael has never been close to Ned, but he is still devastated. Ned's wife, Jennifer Kneeland Ryan, is arrested for the murder. She is unhappy with her lawyers, and she asks Michael to defend her. He assumes she is guilty and hates her for it—until she tells him she is pregnant with Ned's child. Amazingly enough, Michael takes her case, in the interest of his grandchild's welfare. The book concentrates not just on the trial itself, but also on the pretrial preparation and the research that Ryan and his associate do to try to find another possible killer and thus get Jennifer off the hook. With *Inadmissible Evidence* (Fine, 1992), Friedman has gained assurance in his writing, and he produces a fine tale of a murder trial that turns into a media circus because of allegations of racism. His hero is Joe Estrada, an ambitious assistant district attorney charged with prosecuting local hero and minority group leader Roberto Morales for the brutal rape and murder of a beautiful young woman. Friedman is especially good at providing details of how legal work and research are done, and explaining them reasonably and clearly for the reader.

Friedman also wrote *Rage* (Atheneum, 1972), which was made into a movie with Martin Sheen and George C. Scott.

Fyfield, Frances • A solicitor for the Crown Prosecution Service in London since 1975, Fyfield uses her experience in criminal law to lend authenticity to her writing. Fyfield's series characters, Crown Prosecutor Helen West and Detective Super-intendent Geoffrey Bailey, demonstrate with quiet effect the often opposing goals of the law courts and the police. Fyfield's great strength as a writer comes from the assurance with which she delineates character. Her plots are always meticulous in their construction, but her ability to conjure fully fleshed and compelling characters makes for powerful reading. Her first novel, nominated for the both the Edgar and Agatha Awards, is *A Question of Guilt* (Pocket Books, 1989). The third novel in the series, *Deep Sleep* (Pocket Books, 1991), won the Silver Dagger.

Fyfield has also written, thus far, two books about solicitor Sarah Fortune, the first of which is *Shadows on the Mirror* (Pocket Books, 1990). After the death of her unfaithful husband, Sarah chooses to share her affections with men who appear to warrant her special gifts. In her first appearance, she encounters two men with very different needs, and one of them just might be a psychopath. In the sequel, *Perfectly Pure and Good* (Pantheon, 1994), Sarah finds her past coming back to haunt her in a terrifying way while she tries to sort out the legal problems of an eccentric but compelling family.

Gardner, **Erle Stanley** • It is difficult to imagine that most people would not recognize the name "Perry Mason," thanks to the long-running (and perpetually syndicated) television series starring the late Raymond Burr in the title role. Perry Mason, the lawyer with the dazzling courtroom style, was the creation of Gardner, himself a lawyer, but one who (like many lawyers today) seemed more interested in writing than in lawyering. Gardner got his start by writing stories for the pulp magazines in the 1920s, and in 1933 he sold his first novel, Perry Mason's debut, *The Case of the Velvet Claws* (Morrow, 1933). Eighty-one more adventures followed, with the last being the posthumously published *The Case of the Postponed Murder* (Morrow, 1973). For forty years Gardner was one of the most popular and best-selling mystery novelists in the United States. Ably assisted by his secretary, Della Street (played by Barbara Hale in the series), and backed up by private detective Paul Drake, Perry Mason seemed invincible. Readers looking for cleverly constructed plots will find Gardner still entertaining.

In addition to the Perry Mason novels, Gardner wrote twenty-nine books about private detectives Donald Lam and Bertha Cool under the pseudonym A. A. Fair, and nine books about small-town district attorney Doug Selby under his own name. But it is the character of Perry Mason who has forever etched himself into the popular consciousness as the epitome of the "legal eagle."

Grisham, John • John Grisham has been a publishing and film phenomenon of the 1990s. Is there anybody out there who hasn't heard of him? His legal thrillers have been wildly successful best-sellers, and most of them have been made into blockbuster films. Grisham's first book was *A Time to Kill* (Wynwood, 1989), and it's the only one so far that was not an instant megaseller. The plot centers on the mayhem that ensues when an outraged black father kills two rednecks after they have raped and beaten his daughter. An idealistic young lawyer defends the father, the Ku Klux Klan appears, and the trial becomes a publicity circus in a sleepy southern town. Everyone wonders if a black man who has killed two white men can get a fair trial. Grisham's next book, *The Firm* (Doubleday, 1991), was his first big best-seller. An innocent but ambitious and materialistic young lawyer comes to Memphis as a promising recruit for a law firm. They offer him money, a sports car, everything he could want. The new associate begins to wonder what is going on when the FBI asks him to spy on his coworkers. The firm is suspiciously affluent, and no lawyer ever seems to have left it—not alive, anyway. It is, of course, a melodramatic plot, but Grisham certainly knows how to write gripping page-turners, and his characterizations are strong. *The Pelican Brief* (Doubleday, 1992) has another of Grisham's typically complicated, dramatic plots, this time about the assassinations of two U. S. Supreme Court justices, one a liberal icon and the other a young conservative. Grisham's view of the legal establishment is pretty cynical, as is his view of the American criminal justice system. He is from Oxford, Mississippi, and his books tend to be strongly southern tales of legal mayhem.

The popular movies that have been based on the books feature such major Hollywood stars as Julia Roberts, Sandra Bullock, Denzel Washington, Gene Hackman, and Tom Cruise. A television series was based on *The Client* (Doubleday, 1993). Along with Scott Turow, Grisham has repopularized the legal thriller in film, television, and fiction much as it was in the days of Erle Stanley Gardner and the enormously popular *Perry Mason* TV show.

Hailey, J. P. • See **Hall, Parnell**, in the section "The Maltese Falcon."

Kahn, Michael A. • Rachel Gold has left the prestigious Chicago law firm of Abbott & Windsor, where she started her career, to strike out on her own. But when her former boss, the firm's managing partner, asks her help with a delicate case, Rachel is intrigued enough to help. A senior partner in the firm has died in the arms of a prostitute, and his will leaves forty thousand dollars to maintain a grave in a pet cemetery. But the dead man had never owned a pet. Rachel starts searching for what was really buried in the grave. Thus begins the first in the series, *Grave Designs* (Signet, 1992; originally published under the title *The Canaan Legacy* by Lynx Books, 1988). Rachel's best friend is Benny Goldberg, who had been at Abbott & Windsor during her time there, but he left to become a professor at De Paul University's law school. In the second book in the series, Benny is sharing office space, thanks to overcrowding on the De Paul campus. Benny can be crude and sometimes irritating, but he is devoted to Rachel, and he is a very shrewd lawyer. By the third book in the series, *Firm Ambitions* (Dutton, 1995), Rachel has moved home to St. Louis. Her father has died suddenly, and her mother needs her there. Rachel takes on a divorce case with some quirks, never suspecting that once again she'll be solving another murder.

Rachel Gold is an intelligent, forceful character with a strong narrative voice. Each of the stories combines legal detail, a complex plot, understated humor, and quirky characters.

Lescroart, John T. • Lescroart (pronounced "Les-cwa") produces some of the best thrillers around. They could be considered legal thrillers, since his main series character, Dismas Hardy, is a lawyer, but there are elements of the police procedural about them as well. It doesn't really matter; they grace whatever category they are placed in. One thing that unites his novels is that they are steeped in the culture of the Irish-Catholic enclave in San Francisco. The excellent novel *Dead Irish* (Fine, 1989) is the story of the apparent suicide of a promising young man in the local Irish-American community. Eddie Cochran leaves behind a beautiful pregnant wife and a loving family, so why would he want to kill himself? A friend asks Dismas Hardy, a former police officer and former lawyer, to look into the matter, and Dismas rouses himself from his downward slide into alcoholism long enough to begin his quest. Another recurring character in Lescroart's books is Abe Glitsky, a half-Jewish, half-black San Francisco homicide cop who is featured in *A Certain Justice* (Fine, 1995) and *Guilt* (Delacorte, 1997). In the suspenseful *A Certain Justice*, an outbreak of racial riots and violence occurs in San Francisco when a black man is set free by the police after allegedly killing a young white man. The white man's friends hold a wake in an Irish bar and get drunk, a black man's car breaks down in front of the bar, the drunks lynch him, and riots break out all over the city. A news photographer has captured the lynching in a graphic photo, and everyone thinks it shows clearly that one man led the lynching. The entire city is looking for that man, who is actually innocent but is running for his life. Readers may find Lescroart's exciting plots unforgettable.

Maron, Margaret • For her second series of mysteries, Maron left the New York setting of her Sigrid Harald books and returned to her native North Carolina for stories about lawyer Deborah Knott. Deborah's first novel-length appearance is in *Bootlegger's Daughter* (Mysterious Press, 1992), which made history in the mystery world by sweeping all four of the major mystery awards for Best Novel: the Edgar, the Agatha, the Macavity, and the Anthony. Surrounded by a large and loving family, Deborah sometimes feels a bit suffocated while trying to live her life on her own terms. But she has the wit, the intelligence, and the strength it takes for a professional woman to survive in an atmosphere that sometimes subtly undermines women like her. Rich in character, this southern series seems effortlessly realized, and the dialogue is pitch-perfect. Maron won an Agatha Award for the story "Deborah's Judgment" in the collection *A Woman's Eye* (Delacorte, 1991), Deborah's debut.

For Maron's series of police procedurals, see the section "Hill Street Blues."

Martini, Steve • Martini has worked as a journalist and a trial lawyer, and he brings an insider's knowledge of these fields to his exciting legal thrillers. He started out writing something a bit different, however. His first book was *The Simeon Chamber* (Fine, 1988). Pages from explorer Sir Francis Drake's diary turn up in modern San Francisco, and lawyer

Sam Bogardus finds them as he searches for a client's biological father. Sam's search also leads him back into the mystery of a World War II "ghost blimp" that came down over the city with no crew on board. This exciting novel is a combination of treasure hunt, historical research, pirate story, and mystery.

Martini is now writing a series of courtroom thrillers starring defense lawyer Paul Madriani. Family relationships figure heavily in these books, and Paul certainly has his share of family troubles, as well as concerns about the health of his law practice. In *Compelling Evidence* (Putnam, 1992) he is estranged from his wife and has been having a wild affair with his boss's wife. In *Undue Influence* (Putnam, 1994), which was made into a television movie, Paul must defend his wife's sister Laurel on charges that she murdered her ex-husband's new young wife and her unborn child. It all starts out as a hotly contested child custody case, but Paul gets more than he bargained for when his client is accused of murder. Martini builds twisting, labyrinthine plots in his thrillers, and all the legal maneuverings and ploys of a brilliant defense counsel are shown to full advantage.

Matera, Lia • Matera writes two series: one featuring Willa Jansson and one with Laura Di Palma, both of whom are San Francisco attorneys.

Willa Jansson's odyssey begins in law school, where she gets involved in her first murder investigation in *Where Lawyers Fear to Tread* (Bantam, 1987). Over the years, as she goes to work in the cutthroat legal world, she encounters her full share of crime. Along the way she grows up a bit, worries about her parents (a pair of old hippies who have never changed), fails at some jobs and relationships, and yet succeeds at her sleuthing. Willa is one of the most personally confused legal sleuths in crime fiction, and her failings and sardonic outlook on life endear her to readers. Matera pulls off a tricky combination of humor and legal thrills in these splendid books.

Laura Di Palma is a very different sleuth. In the early books in this series, she is a high-powered, tough defense attorney who has become notorious for defending a crazed bomber. She's close to being an unlikable character, since she seems so materialistic and blindly ambitious. But as the series progresses, she grows and changes radically. Matera constructs tight plots that interweave character development with fast-moving action, balanced against thought-provoking analysis of difficult social issues such as assisted suicide, or pornography and computers. The first book in the series is *The Smart Money* (Bantam, 1988).

Meek, **M. R. D.** • A retired solicitor, Meek brings her knowledge of the law and the legal life to a series featuring lawyer Lennox Kemp. In his American debut, *Hang the Consequences* (Scribner, 1985), Kemp is disbarred and working for McCready's Detective Agency. (An earlier novel, *With Flowers That Fell* [Hale, 1983] not published in the United States, apparently tells the story behind Kemp's disbarment.) In the next book in the series, however, Kemp has been reinstated at the bar, and the murders with which he becomes involved thereafter generally begin somehow with one of his legal cases. Meek, though British, displays an obvious affection for American detective fiction in her work, for the wry and cynical Kemp often has more in common with Archie Goodwin or Lew Archer than with Peter Wimsey or Hercule Poriot. Meek's prose is spare, yet often elegant, and her observations of the human character are penetrating and compassionate. This is a series rich in character, a special treat for those who value characterization, as well as clever puzzles, which Meek also handles with dexterity.

Mortimer, John • Mortimer's popular tales of aged barrister Horace Rumpole started out as television plays, with the series *Rumpole of the Bailey*, which first aired in England in 1975. The actor Leo McKern has portrayed Rumpole in this series and in all the subsequent ones. Eventually Mortimer turned these teleplays into short stories, and they are appealing in their print versions as well, though they lack McKern's zestful and inimitable portrayal of Rumpole. Rumpole is dowdy, sometimes downright shabby, forever strewing cigar ash and bits of his latest meal about him. He takes any case that comes his way, which means he will never be Head of Chambers. This to the great dismay of his wife, Hilda (a.k.a. "She Who Must Be Obeyed"), who never fails to let Rumpole know how far short of the ideal (her own father, once Rumpole's Head of Chambers) he has fallen. The stories are richly peopled with eccentric characters, and Mortimer comments with mordant wit upon the state of the legal system in Britain. With his courtroom theatrics, larger-than-life personality, and buoyant air, Rumpole remains a thorough original. *Rumpole of the Bailey* (Penguin, 1980) is the first collection of Rumpole stories published in the United States. In addition to these tales, Mortimer has published numerous novels and plays, a number of which have been successfully televised in both England and the United States.

Nava, Michael • Gay Mexican-American lawyer Henry Rios is the sleuth in Nava's multi-award-winning series of mysteries set in California. When the series opens, in *The Little Death* (Alyson, 1986), Henry works for the public defender's office, and it is in this capacity that he works on the case of Hugh Paris, who has been arrested on charges of drug possession, resisting arrest, and assaulting a cop. Rios discovers that Paris comes from a troubled family, and he becomes intimately involved with Paris and his problems, against his better judgment. In the second book, *Goldenboy* (Alyson, 1988), Rios meets Josh Mandel, who becomes his lover, though later their relationship falls apart because of Josh's HIV-positive status. In *How Town* (Harper & Row, 1990), Rios takes on the case of a man who is a known child molester; he must fight his own repugnance for his client in order to find the truth in this case. At the same time, he must confront ghosts from his own past. Nava writes with unflinching honesty, but with intensity and compassion, about what it is like to be gay and Mexican-American in contemporary society.

Authors of Other Gay and Lesbian Detectives

Nikki Baker; George Baxt (the Pharoah Love series); Lauren Wright Douglas; Sarah Dreher; Katherine V. Forrest; Joseph Hansen; Ellen Hart (the Jane Lawless series); Fred W. Hunter (the Alex Reynolds series); Laurie R. King (the Kate Martinelli series); Jaye Maiman; Val McDermid (the Lindsay Gordon series); Claire McNab; Elizabeth Pincus; Deborah Powell; J. M. Redmann; Sandra Scoppettone; Richard Stevenson; Jean Taylor; Barbara Wilson; John Morgan Wilson; Mary Wings; Eve Zaremba; R. D. Zimmerman (the Todd Mills series); Mark Richard Zubro.

O'Shaughnessy, Perri • Sisters Mary and Pamela O'Shaughnessy collaborate under this pseudonym to write a series of legal mysteries featuring attorney Nina Reilly. In the first of the series, *Motion to Suppress* (Delacorte, 1995), Nina finds her second marriage suddenly in flames. Fleeing San Francisco and her old life, Nina takes her young son to Lake Tahoe and sets up her practice. Her first case turns out to be a humdinger. Young Misty Patterson comes to Nina's office, seeking help in getting a divorce after a fight with her husband. She remembers hitting her husband over the head, then falling into a comatose sleep. When her husband turns up at the bottom of Lake Tahoe, Misty is in deep trouble, and Nina ends up practicing criminal law, instead of civil. Determined to do her best, Nina fights every step of the way, despite the obstacles put in her path by her client's family and others eager to see her fail. Nina returns in *Invasion of Privacy* (Delacorte, 1996), thinking that she's had her fill of criminal law. But her routine civil case has some unexpected twists, and Nina is facing yet another dangerous situation. The O'Shaughnessy sisters have created an intriguing heroine in Nina Reilly; she's scrappy when she has to be, fighting for what she thinks is right. The plots are complex and well crafted, and the resolutions are full of excitement, a combination of mystery puzzle and thriller.

Parker, Barbara • The hot, glitzy Miami scene is a stirring backdrop for Parker's legal thrillers. The first book in her series is the Edgar nominee *Suspicion of Innocence* (Dutton, 1994). Gail Connor is a defense attorney who works for a big Miami law firm. She has a failing marriage, a tricky financial situation, a young daughter, and far too much work. Then her sister Renee is found dead in the Everglades, and Gail realizes that her jealousy and anger at her sister kept her from knowing anything about Renee's private life. Perhaps inevitably, Gail becomes a suspect in Renee's death. She turns for help to Anthony Quintana, a very attractive Cuban lawyer. But is he really trustworthy, or is he involved in Renee's death? Parker brings more irony and concern for family relationships to her books than is generally found in legal thrillers. She concentrates not on courtroom scenes but on the personal lives of lawyers. In *Blood Relations* (Dutton, 1996) most of her characters' lives are badly tangled together, and no one is a completely sympathetic character. Several members of the same family play their parts in the multiple rape case of a teenage model, along with a Eurotrash designer, a sinister developer, a drug dealer, and a crooked lawyer. Parker depicts the materialism and shallowness of the club scene in South Beach, and details the empty lives of fashion industry riffraff. It all seems an inevitable part of the craziness of Miami and its escalating violence. Barbara Parker knows all about how to keep readers turning the pages in her stories of troubled families whose lives are blown apart by crime.

Patterson, Richard North • A recent resident on the bestseller lists, Patterson has been writing mysteries for nearly twenty years while he practiced law. His years of experience as a trial lawyer are evident in the finely crafted courtroom scenes in his novels. But he does not rely on courtroom theatrics alone for suspense. His characters are well drawn and believable, and the emotions are real and convincing. He has written several novels about attorney Christopher Paget. The first of these is *The Lasko Tangent* (Norton, 1979). Paget is an assistant U.S. attorney in Washington, D.C., and his job is to bring down a seemingly unassailable target, a self-made multimillionaire named William Lasko, who is a close friend of the president. Paget reappears in *Degree of Guilt* (Knopf, 1992). Investigative TV journalist Mary Carelli, the mother of Paget's teenage son, Carlo, asks Paget to defend her on a murder charge. Mary was to interview a famous American literary lion, Mark Ransom, in his hotel room. When Ransom attempted to rape her, Mary shot and killed him. The prosecution casts grave doubts on the accusation of rape, however. Patterson delivers a stinging criticism of the legal system and the way it treats women who bring accusations of rape, while at the same time delivering a powerhouse story.

Several of Patterson's novels have been adapted for television, including *Degree of Guilt* and its sequel, *Eyes of a Child* (Knopf, 1994).

Ramos, Manuel • Chicano attorney Luis Montez is the narrator of an unusual and highly atmospheric series of mysteries. The first book in the series is *The Ballad of Rocky Ruiz* (St. Martin's Press, 1993), which was nominated for an Edgar Award for Best First Novel. The novels are set in Denver, not the Denver that most tourists see, but the Chicano and the working-class neighborhoods. Luis Montez grew up in the North Side of Denver, a location that is often used in the series. He was an activist in the Chicano Movement of the sixties; now he is a middle-aged lawyer who is scrambling to make ends meet. Unfortunately, both his law practice and his family relationships have always been close to failure. Luis gets involved in his first murder case when he meets Teresa Fuentes, the attractive daughter of an old friend who was martyred in the Movement. His attempts to help her and investigate a murder take him on a wild ride through Colorado and Texas. Along the way, the reader learns a great deal about Chicano history, politics, and culture, and about the discrimination and racism that Chicanos still face. The novels are told in a flowing narrative style, like that of a ballad, and they recount many small details of Chicano life. Some of Luis's idealism has worn off over the decades, but he is still ready to come to the aid of old friends and worthy Chicano causes.

Rosenberg, Nancy Taylor • Best-selling legal thrillers with plenty of sex and violence flow from the pen of former probation officer Rosenberg. Her heroines are judges, lawyers, and probation officers, and all share a fear of the breakdown of the criminal justice system and a sense of impending peril. For example, in *Mitigating Circumstances* (Dutton, 1993), Lily Forrester, a workaholic prosecutor in Southern California, is attacked on the first night she and her young daughter stay in their new house. Violence can happen to anyone, we learn, even innocent children and strong advocates of law and order. This sense of the escalation of violence in society also permeates her second suspense novel, *Interest of Justice* (Dutton, 1993). The life of Judge Lara Sanderstone changes completely when her sister and brother-in-law are brutally killed. She takes in her nephew and tries to find out who killed her sister and why violence has destroyed her family. Rosenberg is especially good at showing how taking care of a child can revolutionize the life of a rather self-obsessed single woman. Rosenberg's *First Offense* (Dutton, 1994) tells the story of Ann Carlisle, a tough probation officer and former police officer who is attacked one day on the street for no apparent reason. Again, her family life is in disarray and she must find the strength to discover why she is in jeopardy. Rosenberg's talent lies in creating an atmosphere of menace lying in wait for the average person.

Scottoline, Lisa • Like the feisty, smart heroines in her legal thrillers, Scottoline is a lawyer who lives in the Philadelphia area. Her first novel, *Everywhere That Mary Went* (Harper, 1993), was nominated for an Edgar Award for Best Paperback Original. The heroine is Mary DiNunzio, a widowed lawyer. She is working hard to become a partner in her law firm when she realizes that someone is harassing and stalking her. She cannot call the police and have them investigate her colleagues or she will lose her job. Scottoline's expert version of the woman-in-jeopardy novel is professional, funny, and yet emotionally complex. The Edgar Award-winning *Final Appeal* (Harper, 1994) features Grace Rossi, a part-time assistant to a judge, who is murdered early on in the novel. This suspenseful, well-written novel has a smart, appealing protagonist and crisp, amusing details of the working lives of legal assistants. Scottoline's gift for vivid characterizations appears again in *Running from the Law* (HarperCollins, 1995). Rita Morrone is an assertive, tough lawyer who will do practically anything to win. Her father and his friends have taught her to play poker avidly, and Rita has played her legal games like a champion, until someone sets her up for a fall. Scottoline creates marvelous secondary characters in the old men who are her poker buddies and who are anxious to help Rita play the ultimate game of outwitting a murderer.

Tapply, William G. • Brady Coyne, the Yale-educated Boston lawyer who is the sleuth in Tapply's series, is selective about his clients. He prefers older, wealthy clients, because the fees he gets from them allow him to work as he chooses and indulge the true love of his life, fishing. The cases often get complicated, however, and Brady is as much detective as legal expert in this series. For example, in *The Vulgar Boatman* (Scribner, 1987), a Massachusetts gubernatorial candidate asks Brady to look for his missing son. The boy has disappeared after his girlfriend was murdered; the father needs someone with Coyne's discretion to nose around and uncover the truth. Coyne is an easygoing character, with a wry narrative voice. Readers will enjoy the combination of legal mystery-private eye novel that Tapply proffers. First in the series is *Death at Charity's Point* (Scribner, 1984). Readers should check the library and used bookstores for most of these works. One note of trivia: Coyne makes mention in many of the books of his good friend Doc Adams—who is the star of Rick Boyer's series of mystery novels. In addition to the Brady Coyne novels, Tapply has written several nonfiction books about fishing.

Turow, Scott • Legal mysteries are very different now because of the immense influence of one writer, Scott Turow. He revolutionized the form with his emphasis on character development, courtroom pyrotechnics, and exciting twists and turns in his plots. Turow's *Presumed Innocent* (Farrar, 1987) was one of the most famous first novels in recent years, and it went on to become a blockbuster movie with Harrison Ford in the leading role. It was a landmark legal thriller; many legal mysteries written since then have been modeled on it, especially in terms of the realistic depiction of courtroom procedures. The main character in *Presumed Innocent* is Rusty Sabich, a lawyer with a great job in the district attorney's office in Kindle County. Besides working with Assistant District Attorney Carolyn Polhemus, he is also having a passionate affair with her. Carolyn is murdered, and Rusty is the victim of an elaborately planned frame-up by the unknown murderer. Politics, sex, violence, a great surprise ending—this novel has them all. Turow's books are set in the fictional Kindle County, and it's a detailed, vividly lifelike depiction of an average midwestern county. His second novel, *The Burden of Proof* (Farrar, 1990), is about Alejandro (Sandy) Stern, who appeared as Rusty's superb defense lawyer in *Presumed Innocent*. Stern's wife, Clara, is presumed a suicide when she is found dead one day. As he mourns over the succeeding months, Stern discovers surprising new aspects of himself and his beloved wife, and the reader learns more about Clara's story. *Pleading Guilty* (Farrar, Straus & Giroux, 1993) is a literate, thoughtful novel about Mack Malloy, who is an over-the-hill lawyer in Kindle County. It's a detailed, loving characterization of a man whose personality has largely been formed by his Catholicism and by his parents' congenital meanness. Mack works for a big law firm, but his life is in a tailspin when the head partner asks him to look into the disappearance of one of the more eccentric and clever partners. As usual, Turow creates complex characters and plot developments, with surprises right up to the last page.

Van Gieson, Judith • Vivid New Mexico settings and an unusual lawyer set Judith Van Gieson's series of mysteries apart from the usual legal thrillers. Van Gieson's heroine is Neil Hamel, a lawyer with a small and languishing practice in Albuquerque. Her partner is Brink, who is lazy and ineffectual at his lawyering. Neil mostly handles run-of-the-mill divorces and real estate closings. It's no wonder that she has the time and energy to get caught up in current social issues and worthy causes, such as reintroducing an endangered species of wolf to its former habitat in *The Wolf Path* (HarperCollins, 1992), or opposing urban redevelopment in *The Other Side of Death* (HarperCollins, 1991). Aside from her casework, Neil has a lover and car mechanic known only as "The Kid," who may be the only person in her life able to see through her many defenses down to the real person underneath. Van Gieson's descriptive powers bring home to the reader the heat and the austere beauty of the desert Southwest, although most of *Raptor* (Harper & Row, 1990) is set in Montana. Throughout the series, Van Gieson's writing is spare, economical, and often sardonic.

The first Neil Hamel novel is *North of the Border* (Walker, 1988). *The Lies That Bind* (HarperCollins, 1993) was nominated for a Shamus award for Best Private Eye Novel.

Wheat, Carolyn • A former defense attorney with the Legal Aid Society in Brooklyn, New York, Wheat uses her extensive knowledge of the law and of the court system to lend a sometimes harrowing authenticity to her novels about Cass Jameson. When the series begins, with *Dead Man's Thoughts*

(St. Martin's Press, 1983), Cass, like her creator, is a lawyer with Legal Aid. One day Cass finds her lover and colleague, Nathan Wasserstein, murdered in his apartment in an apparent gay killing by a young Puerto Rican hustler. Cass refuses to believe what looks like a setup to her, and she turns detective to clear Nathan's name. By the second book, *Where Nobody Dies* (St. Martin's Press, 1986), Cass has left Legal Aid and set up her own practice, but she finds herself visiting all the familiar places of the system from her days as a Legal Aid attorney. In *Fresh Kills* (Berkley, 1994) Cass, against her better judgment, helps out an old acquaintance in what looks to be a routine adoption case, but it proves anything but. Cass is tough, principled, compassionate, and committed to seeing that justice is done to the best of her ability. The plots of the novels are neatly and tightly constructed, an excellent blend of the traditional mystery plot with contemporary, well-rounded characters. *Dead Man's Thoughts* was nominated for an Edgar Award for Best First Novel.

Wilhelm, Kate • In addition to her series of mysteries featuring a husband-and-wife investigative team (see the section "The Maltese Falcon"), Wilhelm has recently begun writing legal mysteries. The first of these, *Death Qualified* (St. Martin's Press, 1991), was a *New York Times* Notable Book of the Year. In this novel Wilhelm introduced attorney Barbara Holloway, who had given up practicing law five years before the events of story occur. Her father, a retired judge, summons Barbara home to Oregon to help with the defense of one of his neighbors, Nell Kendricks, who's been indicted for the murder of her estranged husband, Lucas Kendricks. Though reluctant at first, Barbara becomes intrigued by the case and its unusual aspects. Where had Lucas Kendricks been for seven years? The answer lies in some rather strange research being conducted into the perception of reality. Wilhelm blends fascinating elements of science fiction with a legal mystery to produce a compelling and provocative story. Barbara Holloway reappears in *The Best Defense* (St. Martin's Press, 1994) and *Malice Prepense* (St. Martin's Press, 1996; retitled *For the Defense* for the paperback edition published by Fawcett, 1997).

Wilhelm introduced Judge Sarah Drexler in *Justice for Some* (St. Martin's Press, 1993). Still mourning the loss of her husband, a prominent judge whose term she has been serving out, Sarah goes home to visit her father in Oregon and to see her children, who have been working for their grandfather. When Sarah's father dies in a seeming accident not long after Sarah's arrival, she is puzzled but accepting. Then a private detective hired by her father is murdered, and Sarah realizes her father's death could have been murder. Sarah investigates, digging into the past of her own family, and the result is a powerful study of family dysfunction. When Sarah decides to take justice into her own hands, Wilhelm explores the morality of law and justice in America in thought-provoking fashion.

Woods, Sara • The late Sara Woods wrote some forty-eight novels featuring barrister Antony Maitland; his wife, Jenny; and Antony's uncle, Sir Nicholas Harding. Using her own experience of having worked in a solicitor's office, Woods made the English legal mystery particularly her own, and Antony Maitland is perhaps the character in English mystery fiction closest to Erle Stanley Gardner's Perry Mason.

Maitland has a definite nose for crime, for he has hunches that nearly infallibly tell him when something is odd about a seemingly straightforward case. Courtroom scenes are often a part of the action in these novels, and Wood handles them with considerable aplomb, building tension in a manner worthy of Gardner himself. Through the course of the series, readers find out tidbits of the lives of the Maitlands; one book, *They Love Not Poison* (Holt, Rinehart, & Winston, 1972), takes the reader back to a period before Antony has qualified as a barrister and is thus a "prequel" to the rest of the series. Wood's literate style, attention to detail, and generally complex puzzles will appeal to readers who like their mysteries English and traditional. *Bloody Instructions* (Harper & Row, 1962) is the first in the series. Woods also wrote as Anne Burton, Mary Challis, and Margaret Leek. Reader should look for Woods's books in used bookstores and libraries.

For Further Reading • William Bernhardt; D. W. Buffa; Henry Cecil; William Diehl; Linda Fairstein; Anthony Gilbert; A. W. Gray; Sarah Gregory; Cyril Hare; Gini Hartzmark; Joyce Holms; Jonnie Jacobs (the Kali O'Brien series); Paul Levine; Harold Q. Masur; Robert K. Tanenbaum.

Some legal thrillers on film are • *Adam's Rib*; *Anatomy of a Murder*; *And Justice for All*; *Body of Evidence*; *The Chamber*; *The Client*; *The Devil's Advocate*; *A Few Good Men*; *The Firm*; *Inherit the Wind*; *Jagged Edge*; *The Juror*; *Legal Eagles*; *Murder in the First*; *My Cousin Vinny*; *Night Falls on Manhattan*; *The Pelican Brief*; the Perry Mason movies; *Presumed Innocent*; *Primal Fear*; *Red Corner*; *Reversal of Fortune*; *The Star Chamber*; *Suspect*; *A*

Time to Kill; To Kill a Mockingbird; Twelve Angry Men; The Verdict; Witness for the Prosecution; The Wrong Man.

Legal TV shows include • *Ally McBeal; Court TV; The Defenders; JAG; L.A. Law; Law & Order; Matlock; Perry Mason; The Practice; Rumpole of the Bailey; Michael Hayes; Night Court; The People's Court; Petrocelli; The Wright Verdicts.*

Romantic Suspense

The Road to Manderley

Romantic suspense novels have a long and honorable tradition as part of the mystery field. Many of the earliest mysteries included a romantic relationship as an integral part of the plot, like that in Mrs. Henry Wood's *East Lynne*. Two of the great classics of Victorian literature, *Jane Eyre* by Charlotte Brontë, and *Wuthering Heights* by Emily Brontë, are perhaps the most direct precursors of the twentieth-century mystery novels that combine a romantic theme with a suspense-filled plot. In 1938 Daphne Du Maurier published *Rebecca*, a novel that became both a classic of the genre and an Oscar-winning movie. This tale of a frightened young woman, very much in love with a mysterious, troubled husband haunted by his past, was the most obviously influential novel in what became a boom in publishing in the 1960s and '70s, led by such writers as Phyllis A. Whitney, Mary Stewart, and Victoria Holt. These thrillers, often called "gothic romances," in which romance was just as important as the suspense, sold extremely well and became a staple of the mystery genre. With the renewed popularity of the mystery novel in the 1980s and '90s, writers of romantic suspense are once again finding their way onto the best-seller lists. Some of the classic practitioners are still writing, but there are a number of striking new voices in the group. The way that writers depict romantic relationships in fiction may change over the years, but romance itself remains a popular feature of many a mysterious plot.

At their worst, in some of the excesses of the early gothics, women ran around helplessly, screaming for some strong man to save them, just as Doris Day does so annoyingly in the film *Midnight Lace*. But in the hands of writers such as Barbara Michaels, Jayne Ann Krentz, and others writing today, the heroine of the romantic suspense novel is made of much sterner stuff.

Dreyer, Eileen • Her own years of experience as a trauma nurse provide Dreyer with the background for her suspenseful medical thrillers, most of which feature trauma or critical care nurses as heroines. In *A Man to Die For* (HarperPaperbacks, 1991), Casey McDonough is working in the trauma unit of a large St. Louis hospital when she becomes convinced that the new obstetrician on staff is a dangerous psychopath. He's the darling of the hospital, and almost everyone thinks Casey is the one who's crazy—everyone, that is, except a perceptive, attractive homicide detective. Though the odds seem stacked against her, Casey refuses to give up. Wisecracking, feisty Casey is a likable heroine. In *Bad Medicine* (HarperPaperbacks, 1995) trauma nurse and death investigator Molly Burke starts to wonder why so many lawyers are turning up dead in the emergency room in St. Louis's Grace Hospital. Increasingly in danger from powerful folk who will stop at nothing to keep her quiet, Molly fights for her life, and for justice, in this suspenseful tale. Appealing heroines, well-realized medical backgrounds, nail-biting plots, and tension-relieving humor are hallmarks of Dreyer's work. Dreyer also writes romance novels under the name Kathleen Korbel.

Du **Maurier, Daphne** • Du Maurier is one of the great classic writers of sweeping romantic and historical novels. Her books often have a strongly mysterious element. Alfred Hitchcock turned Du Maurier's most famous novel, *Rebecca* (Doubleday, 1938), into a wonderful movie starring Laurence Olivier and Joan Fontaine. The plot is a masterpiece of suspense: Aristocratic widower Max de Winter marries a timid and unpretentious woman. He brings her to Manderley, his mansion in Cornwall. The young wife has a hard time adjusting, and she suspects that everyone sees her as inferior to Max's first wife, Rebecca, who died mysteriously. Bit by bit she learns more about her dead rival, until the mystery of Rebecca's death is finally and dramatically revealed. *Rebecca* begins with one of the most famous first lines in modern fiction: "Last night I dreamt I went to Manderley again...."

Du Maurier also wrote other absorbing suspense novels. *My Cousin Rachel* (Doubleday, 1952) is also set in a great house in Cornwall, and it's a lovely, old-fashioned story about the power and blindness of love and its slow turn into devastating suspicion. *The Scapegoat* (Doubleday, 1957) has a complex plot about two men who look exactly alike and who exchange lives, only to encounter more trouble than they can imagine.

Many of Du Maurier's short stories were made into

movies, such as *Don't Look Now* and *The Birds*, while her swashbuckling novel *Jamaica Inn* (Doubleday, 1936) was also made into a film directed by Hitchcock.

Eberhart, **Mignon G.** • For seventy years the late Mignon Eberhart wrote classic romantic suspense stories. Eberhart's mysteries often had much in common with the ever-popular Gothic romances. Usually the featured players are fairly affluent, the setting is exotic, and the suspense is taut in these entertaining tales. Eberhart's long career spanned many decades, and she wrote dozens of books, but she began by writing nursing mysteries, such as her first novel, *The Patient in Room 18* (Doubleday, 1929). In several of these early books, a sensible middle-aged nurse, Sarah Keate, and a dedicated young policeman, Lance O'Leary, worked together to solve criminal cases. Keate solved crimes on her own in a few later novels. She often worked as a private nurse in stately homes where evil might well lurk, and she prowled the great houses at night, looking for clues to baffling mysteries. Several of the Sarah Keate novels were turned into successful films (with a character called Sally Keating) in the 1930s. Eberhart also wrote short stories about Susan Dare, a mystery writer who was also an amateur sleuth. In her later romantic mysteries, Eberhart invested her stories with a lurking air of menace. Generally there is a young woman in danger, often from a man who should have been trustworthy and loyal to her. In the traditional fashion, there is an enclosed group of suspects, a creepy atmosphere, and an engrossing murder puzzle.

Eberhart was named a Grand Master by the Mystery Writers of America, and she won the Scotland Yard Prize in

1930 and the Lifetime Achievement Award from the Malice Domestic Mystery Convention in 1995.

Hoag, Tami • Like many of her peers now writing romantic suspense, Hoag got her start writing romance novels. With *Cry Wolf* (Bantam, 1993), Hoag entered the suspense sweepstakes. This novel features attorney Laurel Chandler, who has returned to the Louisiana bayou country to seek justice for past wrongs—wrongs that almost destroyed her life. She once again puts her life on the line, when a brutal killer makes her a target, but with a new man in her life, she has something important to live for. *Night Sins* (Bantam, 1995) is the first of two linked stories, set in a small Minnesota town; the second is *Cry Guilty* (Bantam, 1996). A sadistic kidnapper is playing a twisted game with the folk of Deer Lake, preying on children, and law enforcement personnel are doing their best to end the torment. In *Night Sins* Police Chief Mitch Holt and Megan O'Malley, an officer with the state criminal investigative unit, do their best to identify the kidnapper. In *Guilty as Sin* prosecutor Ellen North does her best to bring him—and his accomplices—to justice. Hoag writes compelling and convincing stories about the evil that can prey on the innocent, stories that have regularly put her on the best-seller lists.

Holt, Victoria • The late Eleanor Hibbert was a prolific and successful, though somewhat reclusive, writer, known to millions of fans around the world variously as Victoria Holt, Jean Plaidy, and Philippa Carr, among other pseudonyms. It was as Holt, though, that she achieved her greatest success. With a long interest in history, as evinced by more than sixty historical novels under the Plaidy byline, Holt combined her feel for times past with an interest in suspense and romance for a series of more than thirty best-selling novels of romantic suspense. Her first novel under the Holt name was *Mistress of Mellyn* (Doubleday, 1960). At the time of the book's publication, many thought that Daphne du Maurier or Mary Stewart might be hiding behind this pseudonym, for the book was well within the tradition of the work of these two writers. The tale of a governess who falls in love with her employer, despite hints about the sinister end that befell the man's first wife, *Mistress of Mellyn* is, in its way, a classic of the genre that became enormously popular in the 1960s and '70s. Holt had a knack for creating sympathetic heroines who found themselves in difficult situations, much like Charlotte Brontë's Jane Eyre had done more than a century before. Some Holt heroines were distinctly unconventional, such as the ambitious Kerensa Carlee of *The Legend of the Seventh Virgin* (Doubleday, 1965), a girl of humble beginnings who married her way into the upper classes and discovered that wealth and class were not always the avenues for true happiness. Holt also enjoyed exotic settings for her novels, setting several in Australia, such as *The Shadow of the Lynx* (Doubleday, 1971) and *The Pride of the Peacock* (Doubleday, 1976), Hong Kong in *The House of a Thousand Lanterns* (Doubleday, 1974), and India in *The India Fan* (Doubleday, 1988). Under the pseudonym Philippa Carr, Holt wrote a long series of historical romantic suspense novels known as the "Daughters of England" series; each book in the series featured the daughter or granddaughter of the heroine in the previous book. The series began with *The Miracle at St. Bruno's* (Putnam, 1972), set during the reign of Henry VIII.

Along with her peers Phyllis A. Whitney and Mary

Stewart, Victoria Holt was one of the mistresses of romance and suspense. Readers should check the library and used bookstores for most of the works under the Carr and Plaidy names.

Johnston, Velda • A veteran suspense novelist, with more than thirty novels to her credit, Johnston began her work in the heyday of romantic suspense with *Along a Dark Path* (Dodd, Mead, 1968). Though Johnston's work features most of the characteristics of the gothic novel, she is so skilled at the suspense half of the recipe that many readers quite often forget that they are reading a "gothic." The heroines of Johnston's fiction, whether contemporary or nineteenth-century, are independent, often stubborn, resourceful, and intelligent. Two of Johnston's early period settings, *The Late Mrs. Fonsell* (Dodd, Mead, 1972) and *Masquerade in Venice* (Dodd, Mead, 1973), rank alongside the best work of Victoria Holt and Phyllis A. Whitney. A more recent work, *The House on Bostwick Square* (Dodd, Mead, 1987), shows Johnston's skill at blending unusual and suspenseful elements into a not-so-traditional romantic suspense novel. *The Etruscan Smile* (Dodd, Mead, 1977), with its vividly etched foreign setting and intriguing plot, is one of the author's best contemporary suspense novels. Readers should check the library and used bookstores for most of these works.

Krentz, Jayne Ann • A prolific and best-selling writer of romance and romantic suspense novels, Krentz lives in Seattle, and she sets many of her contemporary novels in the Pacific Northwest. Krentz writes witty, sparkling dialogue, and she creates vivid and interesting characters, many of them with unusual backgrounds. Her heroines are vital, intelligent, and capable. A good example is Molly Abberwick in *Absolutely, Positively* (Pocket Books, 1996). Molly is descended from a long line of eccentric inventors, but she has inherited none of the family's scientific creativeness. Instead she's got a good head for business, and as trustee of her father's foundation to encourage inventors who don't have the money to develop their products, she is trying her best to find a good project. She has hired as a consultant Dr. Harry Trevelyan, a historian and philosopher of science, not knowing that he comes from a rather unusual background, one that is going to interfere with her current plans. The sparks fly between Molly and Harry, but when Molly becomes the prey of a stalker, she has more than just romance and business on her mind. Other recent romantic suspense titles by Krentz include *Trust Me* (Pocket Books, 1995), *Hidden Talents* (Pocket Books, 1993), and *Deep Waters* (Pocket Books, 1997). Under the pseudonym Amanda Quick, Krentz writes best-selling historical romances.

Llewellyn, Caroline • Following somewhat in the footsteps of her "ancestors" in the romantic suspense genre, Llewellyn demonstrates a knack for suspense and an eye for setting that are reminiscent of Mary Stewart and Phyllis A. Whitney. Llewellyn's heroines are intelligent professional women who find themselves in dangerous circumstances through no fault of their own. Though they may have the assistance of an attractive male in extricating themselves from danger, they do so with courage, wit, and resourcefulness. *The Masks of Rome* (Scribner, 1988) is set in Rome during Carnival time, and *The Lady of the Labyrinth* (Scribner, 1990) is set in Sicily. A more recent novel, *Life Blood* (Scribner, 1993), is set in England, while *False Light* (Scribner, 1996) is set in Cornwall, a setting often used by the late Victoria Holt. In all her work, Llewellyn makes effective use of setting. Readers should check the library and used bookstores for most of these works.

Michaels, Barbara • Barbara Michaels is the pseudonym used by Barbara Mertz (also known as Elizabeth Peters) for her many best-selling novels of suspense. The first novel that appeared under this name was *The Master of Blacktower* (Appleton Century Crofts, 1966). This and some of the other early books are unusual and memorable tales that reflect the "gothic" novels so popular in the 1960s, but they are of much higher quality than the average gothic romance of the time. Sometimes there is a tinge of the occult in these, and sometimes they are full-blooded ghost stories. Especially notable are *Ammie, Come Home* (Meredith, 1968), *Shattered Silk* (Atheneum, 1986), and *Stitches in Time* (HarperCollins, 1995), which feature recurring characters and a historic house in Georgetown. These very different stories reflect the mood of their times, but all are accomplished and suspenseful novels, with intriguing characters and vivid settings. The author's heroines in these novels are as unconventional as are the heroines in three different mystery series written under the name **Elizabeth Peters**.

For the contemporary amateur detective series published under the Peters name see the section "Nancy, Frank, and Joe Grow Up." For the series of historical mysteries see the Peters entry in the section "Once Upon a Crime."

Rinehart, Mary Roberts • Rinehart was one of the founding mothers of the traditional American mystery story. She has been called the originator of the "Had-I-But-Known" school of mysteries, in which an attractive young heroine tells the story with repeated references to ominous developments in the future. Early on in her long career as a writer, Rinehart wrote a short series with nurse Hilda Adams, nicknamed "Miss Pinkerton" by Detective Inspector Patton, who gives her assignments as an amateur sleuth. Since Rinehart trained to be a nurse, she was able to give her stories authentic nursing backgrounds. Rinehart also wrote a charming series of stories about Tish, a middle-aged woman who gets embroiled in wild adventures at the drop of a hat. Tish is a prototypical feminist (Rinehart herself was a suffragette). She drives fast cars and repairs them herself; she goes on hiking holidays and foils bank robbers; she is an ambulance driver in World War I. One of the earliest best-selling American mysteries was Rinehart's *The Circular Staircase* (Bobbs, 1908). It was turned into a long-running play, repeatedly revived, and then made into several movies, all called *The Bat*. By the 1920s Rinehart had several successful plays running on Broadway and was a famous writer of thrillers. In Rinehart's later mysteries, the heroine is generally a young woman in danger in a large old house, and often there is a romance. The mysteries are somewhat dated now, but they are still interesting, especially for their place in the historical development of crime fiction.

Roberts, Nora • The legendary Roberts has won millions of fans around the world with her tales of romance and suspense. The first writer to be inducted into the Romance Writers of America's Hall of Fame, Roberts has published more than a hundred novels, some of them category romance, others romantic suspense, and has recently begun a series of futuristic police procedural mysteries under the pseudonym **J. D. Robb**. (See the section titled "The X-Files" for more on this series.) In her romantic suspense novels Roberts paints lush backgrounds, as in *Carnal Innocence* (Bantam, 1991). The small town of Innocence, Mississippi, is the setting, and the heroine is a well-known concert violinist named Caroline Waverly. Returning to her family's home to recuperate from the rigors of her tour and the emotional fallout from the breakup with her lover, Caroline discovers that small towns have their share of deadly secrets and romantic possibilities. In the recent *Sanctuary* (Putnam, 1997) a successful photographer returns to her family's home to delve into painful family secrets, trying once and for all for resolution. But some secrets are better left buried, and it could be deadly trying to bring them to light, as the heroine soon discovers.

Roberts creates strong-minded women and puts them in challenging situations. The men are attractive, sometimes dangerously so, but just as strong-minded as the women. Together hero and heroine forge a new relationship that offers them a chance to put past shadows behind them. Readers looking for escape will find no better tour guide than Nora Roberts.

Stewart, Mary • Perhaps the foremost writer of classic romantic suspense novels, Mary Stewart has been writing since the 1950s. Generations of writers in the field have been influenced by her masterly use of the English language and her sure sense of timing and suspense. Stewart is known especially for her use of locations that were considered exotic for their time (such as the Greek islands and Lebanon) and for her poetic evocation of scenery. In many of her books Stewart uses the common gothic-novel plot about a young woman caught in a dangerous situation, from which she must use her own agile wits and strength to escape. But she brings to this familiar format her own touch of magic. A fine example is *Nine Coaches Waiting* (Mill & Morrow, 1959), set in the French Alps, which tells of a young boy protected by his teacher from the ill will of his evil relatives and a series of potentially fatal "accidents." Only the teacher suspects that too many accidents spell murder. *My Brother Michael* (Mill & Morrow, 1960), one of her best, combines brooding, austere Greek backgrounds with a twentieth-century revenge tragedy. The plot is shaped by both a wartime murder and a postwar search for justice and vengeance. Most recently Stewart has turned her attention to several different formats: She has been writing historical novels set in King Arthur's Britain, fantasy novels, children's fables, and impressionistic mysteries.

Whitney, Phyllis A. • Named Grand Master by the Mystery Writers of America in 1988 and given an Agatha Award for Lifetime Achievement by Malice Domestic in 1989, Whitney has been producing entertaining mystery fiction for adults and young adults for more than five decades. Her first novel was *Red Is for Murder* (Ziff Davis, 1943). Along with Mary Stewart and the late Victoria Holt, Whitney was a regular on the bestseller lists of the late 1960s and '70s. One of the hallmarks of Whitney's fiction is its strong sense of place. Born to American missionaries in Japan, Whitney was a world traveler at an early age, and this taste for unusual and interesting places makes a distinctive contribution to her work. Her novels vary in setting, from Turkey, South Africa, Greece, and Japan to various parts of the United States. Along with an expertly sketched setting, Whitney gives her readers entertaining stories with a masterful sense of pace and suspense. Whitney's heroines are generally young, sometimes a bit inexperienced, but always with a sense of self-responsibility and the courage to carry those responsibilities through often life-threatening situations. Among Whitney's best mysteries are *Emerald* (Doubleday, 1983) and *The Glass Flame* (Doubleday, 1978).

Woods, Sherryl • Woods writes two series of romantic mysteries, one set in Atlanta, and the other in South Florida.

The Amanda Roberts mysteries feature the ambitious and smart journalist Amanda Roberts, who moves South from New York City with her husband. The husband promptly dumps her, and she is stuck in small-town Georgia by herself, with her career on hold. She meets retired homicide detective Joe Donelli when both become involved in a murder case. Joe wants nothing more than to live a relaxed life; Amanda wants excitement and a rewarding career. Subsequent books chart a colorful personal and sleuthing relationship that develops between Roberts and Donelli.

In *Hot Property* (Dell, 1992), the first of the Molly DeWitt mysteries, Molly is a single mother who finds a man dead one morning in her condominium card room. She can't resist snooping about, which puts her in direct conflict with sexy Cuban-American homicide detective Michael O'Hara. O'Hara may be an official investigator on murder cases, but Molly is a sharp and persistent amateur sleuth in these romantic comedies.

For Further Reading • Joan Aiken; Evelyn Anthony; Mignon Ballard; Madeleine Brent; Catherine Coulter; Robert Goddard; Jane Aiken Hodge; Isabelle Holland; Kay Hooper; Mary McMullen; Carla Neggers; Karen Robards; Patricia Veryan.

Films • *American Dreamer*; *The Cat and the Canary*; *Charade*; *Dead Again*; *Desire*; *Gambit*; *Jamaica Inn*; *Jane Eyre*; *The Jewel of the Nile*; *The Lady Vanishes*; *Midnight Lace*; *The Moon-spinners*; *Notorious*; *The Perils of Pauline* (two series); *Rebecca*; *Romancing the Stone*; *Suspicion*; *The Talk of the Town*; *Time After Time*; *Wuthering Heights*.

TV shows • *Hart to Hart*; *Moonlighting*; *Oliver's Travels*; *Remington Steele*.

Capers and Criminals

The Usual Suspects

Caper movies have recently become very popular again. Caper books have been popular all along. A caper is a criminal undertaking, often a robbery or a confidence game, told in terms sympathetic to the criminals. The writer makes the bad guys so appealing, so *good*, that the audience wants them to succeed even though we know they're doing something illegal. It's a neat trick and a difficult one to pull off successfully.

Along with caper novels, crime writers have often written superb fiction in which even the cops and the PIs are crooked, maybe just a little, maybe a lot. Sometimes they just get tired of seeing bad guys go free and start meting out their own form of justice. Sometimes their job, especially in the case of police officers, gives them power over people, and they learn to like the power and then abuse it. And sometimes it seems that everybody—the cops, the criminals, the guy down the block—is just plain crooked. Welcome to the dark, explosive, and at times bizarre side of the mean streets.

Bleeck, Oliver • See **Thomas, Ross**.

Block, Lawrence • Besides his private eye novels, Block has written two series of caper novels. The best known one features Bernie Rhodenbarr, a charming burglar. Bernie sometimes gets involved in murder as a result of his burglarious ploys. In *The Burglar in the Closet* (Random House, 1978), for example, he is hired to burgle his dentist's ex-wife's apartment, to get back the jewels he gave her during their marriage. The ex-wife returns, Bernie hides in the closet, and she is murdered. There's some fine plotting here, and a gripping story, but also it's just great fun to read. The *Burglar* series is always amusing, since Bernie is an engaging burglar who loves *objets d'art*, good books, coffee and food, and sexy women. He's a memorable antihero who has an endearing ability to laugh at himself. In the later books, Bernie owns a bookstore, but he still burgles and enjoys both his skill at it and, of course, the thrill of it all. His best friend and confidante is Carolyn Kaiser, a lesbian dog-groomer. The New York City depicted in the Rhodenbarr books is much more civilized and livable than that of Block's Scudder series, but it's clear that Block loves the city in all its guises.

Block also wrote a series of diverting novels about Evan Tanner. *The Thief Who Couldn't Sleep* (Gold Medal, 1966) is the first in the series. Evan Tanner is a man who, because of an injury, can no longer sleep at all. He gets through all the long hours in each day by cultivating odd hobbies and by joining clubs and organizations of people with unusual political opinions. Some of these memberships end up leading him into adventures in spying, which gets him into hot water with other secret organizations, such as the CIA. These entertaining tales are some of the best Cold War adventures around.

Block has also written novels under the names Chip Harrison and Paul Kavanagh.

See another **Lawrence Block** entry in the section "The Maltese Falcon."

Bruno, Anthony • The grimy, corrupt, suburban New Jersey of Anthony Bruno's "Bad" series of novels is a claustrophobic amalgam of unpleasant towns, all the more desolate because nearby New York is so unattainable for the poor souls doomed to life on the wrong side of the river. Into this Mob-ridden, violent world Bruno injects two FBI agents, Cuthbert "Gib" Gibbons and Michael Tozzi, Gib's brother-in-law. Tozzi is brash, independent, and given to working outside of FBI standard procedures, while Gibbons is older, more cynical, and more patient. Tozzi practices the martial art *aikido,* often on the mobsters, and usually while working beyond his charge from the FBI brass, while Gibbons works to bail him out with the suits. Tozzi and Gibbons first appeared in Bruno's lead-off novel, *Bad Guys* (Putnam, 1988), followed by a consistently exciting string of books such as *Bad Blood* (Putnam, 1989) and *Bad Moon* (Delacorte, 1992). The "Bad" books, with their basement murders and junkyard shoot-outs, present a bleak (and probably a bit exaggerated) picture of the area in which the author grew up.

Bruno, a proficient *aikido* instructor in real life, has also written *Seven* (St. Martin's Press, 1995), a psycho-killer thriller that was made into a hit movie with Brad Pitt, and *The Iceman* (Delacorte, 1993), the true story of a killer for hire with more than a hundred victims.

Cody, Liza • After writing several novels about London PI Anna Lee, Cody has created a series around a very different protagonist. Her latest series, the Eva Wylie books, might be considered female caper novels (a very unusual thing). The series begins with *Bucket Nut* (Doubleday, 1993), the superb story of Eva Wylie, a female wrestler, petty criminal, and somewhat bent security guard. Eva is profane, gutsy, semiliterate, and street smart, very different indeed from the usual heroine in crime novels. She takes no abuse or disrespect from anyone and never wavers in her single-minded desire for fame as a wrestler. Anna Lee appears briefly in these books, but the focus is on the coarse and uncouth Eva, a.k.a. the "London Lassassin." In *Musclebound* (Mysterious Press, 1997), Eva's long-held dream comes true as her adored sister Simone reappears in her life. The scenario doesn't go as Eva planned, however, since Eva is down and out, struggling with a serious glitch in her wrestling career and a carload of cash stolen from some very annoyed guys.

Another entry on Cody appears in "The Maltese Falcon" section.

Ellroy, James • "Mad Dog" Ellroy, as he is known (in some cases affectionately) among mystery fans, has developed an unmistakable style that mixes a cynicism about every social institution, tabloid-style narration, corrupt characters, and the use of historical individuals mixed in among the fictional so seamlessly that they're sometimes hard to tell apart. *The Black Dahlia* (Mysterious Press, 1987) incorporates a real 1949 Los Angeles murder, and reflects the author's distress at the somewhat parallel murder of his own mother in 1958. It was followed by a trio of similar police novels set in L.A.: *The Big Nowhere* (Mysterious Press, 1988),

L.A. Confidential (Mysterious Press, 1990), and *White Jazz* (Knopf, 1992). In these, Ellroy interconnects the worlds of cops, murderers, politicians, the Mob, Hollywood moguls, and big money, all sharing an unrelenting corruptibility. This rank and dangerous landscape continues in *American Tabloid* (Knopf, 1995), which follows the rise and fall of the Kennedys from the mid-'50s through JFK's assassination and much more. The novel has hundreds of characters, many historical, but only one with even a shred of integrity, which doesn't last. Ellroy has stated that *American Tabloid* is to be the first of a trilogy; together with the L.A. novels, these will carry his dark vision of American society, and the ugly truth he sees beneath its myths and pretenses, from the late 1940s through to current times.

Ellroy has received critical acclaim for his autobiographical *My Dark Places* (Knopf, 1996), which relates his troubled past and his attempt to solve and understand the killing of his mother. *L.A. Confidential* was made into a critically-acclaimed movie which echoes the best of the film *noir* style.

Hiaasen, Carl • Hiaasen's books are wild and zany capers among some of the weirder denizens of South Florida. Besides providing the reader with raucous entertainment in his hilarious black comedies, Hiaasen shows us how the relentless advance of development into the Everglades and the flood of tourist dollars have resulted in the environmental devastation of South Florida. *Tourist Season* (Putnam, 1986) has a demented and unforgettable opening in which a tourist dies by having a rubber alligator souvenir crammed down his throat. In an ingeniously lunatic plot in *Native Tongue* (Knopf, 1991), some Florida blue-tongued mango voles, an endangered species, are missing from a theme park in

Key Largo. The park is trying to compete with Disney World for tourist dollars, and they need the voles back for their publicity value. Hiaasen does his best work with over-the-top crazy characters, con men, hookers with hearts of gold, gangsters, crooked politicians, and burned-out reporters. In the early books there's always one good guy who finally understands just how crooked everything around him is during the course of the novel. But perhaps Hiaasen's cynicism has increased over the years, for in the later novels, outrageous levels of personal, business, and governmental depravity are just taken for granted. *Stormy Weather* (Knopf, 1995), for example, is a great story about the corruption, scams, and brutality that flourished in the wake of Hurricane Andrew in South Florida. Hiaasen takes on crooked building inspectors and builders here, and the weirdness never stops. A wise fool often found in the novels is Clinton Tyree, known as Skink, who was the only governor of Florida to try to discourage tourism and development. Needless to say, he went almost crazy from stress and disappointment, and now he's a homeless swamp dweller who commits the occasional act of ecological terrorism, sabotages development projects, eats roadkill, and smokes toad poison. *Strip Tease* (Knopf, 1993), which was made into a movie with Demi Moore, is at least partially about a young mother who works as a stripper to make money to support her child. But of course there's an incredibly labyrinthine and hilarious plot with a corrupt congressman, a biker-bouncer, and the usual cast of Hiaasen weirdos. All in all, Hiaasen's Floridian tall tales are as strange and uproarious as mysteries get nowadays.

Higgins, George V. • Justly famous for his matchless tales of petty criminals and politicians, Higgins's many novels are classics of the modern hard-boiled style. He became famous with his first book, the acclaimed *The Friends of Eddie Coyle* (Knopf, 1971). Eddie is a small-time criminal whose friends run to gun-running, theft, and bank robbery. As with many of Higgins's other books, the story is told almost entirely through dialogue. Indeed, Higgins is a genius at capturing the street talk of thugs, con men, cops, thieves, lawyers, and politicians alike. Like Elmore Leonard, he knows exactly how to illuminate a man's character simply by letting him talk. Higgins is a former journalist and U. S. Attorney in Massachusetts, and most of his books are set in Boston. He's written some fascinating legal thrillers, such as *Outlaws* (Holt, 1987), which follows the arrest and trial of a group of left-wing radicals in the 1970s and updates their story years later. The dark and masterful *The Rat on Fire* (Knopf, 1981) is the story of a crumbling tenement building; its inhabitants; and a nasty, complicated arson scheme. Higgins's plots are deftly constructed with twists and turns aplenty. He has also written well-regarded novels about Massachusetts politics, graft, and corruption.

Perhaps the best known of the films and TV movies made from Higgins's books is *The Friends of Eddie Coyle*, a very good film starring Robert Mitchum.

Highsmith, Patricia • The late Patricia Highsmith gained acclaim for her first work, *Strangers on a Train* (Harper, 1950). It became a famous movie directed by Alfred Hitchcock, although by altering the ending he deprived the story of much of its punch. Two people meet accidentally on a train; one is quickly revealed to be corrupt, and the other is eventually caught up in his new friend's criminality in spite of himself. Highsmith's leading characters are often the criminals, but even their victims can be frightening and villainous people. Highsmith's stories usually include a strong dose of paranoia, intricate relationships, and sexual ambiguity.

Highsmith's best-known crime novels are the Tom Ripley series, beginning with *The Talented Mr. Ripley* (Coward, 1955) and continuing through to *Ripley Under Water* (Knopf, 1992). Tom Ripley is a young man, fired from his job and supporting himself through minor forgery, who's asked by a concerned father to go to Europe and persuade his son to return to America and the family business. Tom goes to Italy, looks up the son, and makes himself a part of his life. Eventually he assumes the son's identity, his income, even his clothing. When the man's friends start to question events, he can think of no solution other than to murder them. Through the Ripley series, Tom forges, impersonates, murders, and yet lives an increasingly luxurious life, free of guilt and penalty. The police are always suspicious of his lengthening list of dead associates, and yet they are never quite smart enough to pin anything on him. One of the Ripley novels was filmed by director Wim Wenders as *The American Friend*, starring Dennis Hopper.

Comedy and killing are inextricably mixed, the mood darkens from an initial everyday calm into terror, and crime is an accepted way to make a living in Highsmith's complex and shadowy novels.

Leonard, Elmore • Elmore Leonard is the master of street-smart dialogue. His convincing tales of life among the criminal classes take place in vividly described locales such as Detroit, Miami, and Hollywood. The multitalented Leonard's novels are masterpieces of black comedy, with plenty of violence and gritty realism. He is great at depicting sleazy characters, drunks, petty criminals, crooked politicians, and mobsters. Leonard doesn't create cardboard characters; even his career criminals are complicated people. He is also highly skilled at creating action sequences (perhaps this derives from a long stint at writing Westerns).

In his early crime novels, Leonard told stories about the criminal element in Detroit. Later the Detroit hoods in his books moved to Florida, and Leonard chronicled their adventures in an even crazier milieu. Then he began to tell great stories about the local malefactors in Florida. And then some of the Florida hoods moved to Hollywood and mixed with the not quite normal folks from the movie business. In all of these stories, Leonard catches the nuances of life among the down-and-outs and the criminal crazies. In some of the books, nominally respectable people get involved with hoods, and everything changes in their lives. Many of his books are about the interface between a criminal life and a respectable life, and how sometimes the line between the two lifestyles is not that visible. But regardless of his subject matter, Leonard tells his entertaining stories superbly well.

Leonard has also written many Westerns, and he writes screenplays, including some based on his own books. Some of Leonard's books have been made into very fine movies, such as *Get Shorty* (Delacorte, 1990), and some have been turned into unremarkable films, like *52 Pick-up* (Delacorte, 1974). *La Brava* (Arbor, 1983) won an Edgar Award for Best Novel, and Leonard was named a Grand Master by the Mystery Writers of America in 1992.

Maxwell, A. E. (Ann and Evan) • The husband-and-wife team of Ann and Evan Maxwell have written some witty, suspenseful caper novels together. They set their books largely in Southern California, often in coastal Orange County. The heroes are the mysterious and idiosyncratic Fiddler and his brilliant ex-wife, Fiora Flynn, an investment banker. Fiddler and Fiora may be divorced, but they often still live together and they can still out-wit some pretty tough criminals together. They are assisted by Benny Speidel, the former ice cream king of Saigon and Fiddler's buddy from his Vietnam days, a wheelchair-bound electronics genius who loves to set fiendish traps for bad guys. Fiddler is independently wealthy, so he is able to help people in trouble for free—but mostly for the excitement of the hunt and the violence. Fiora, on the other hand, knows all the money angles and con games used by confidence tricksters and white-collar criminals. The authors write fast, gripping action scenes to complement the intricate plots of these entertaining novels. Readers should check the library and used bookstores for most of these works.

Ann Maxwell has published science fiction and romantic suspense novels under her own name and is now producing a series of very popular romance novels under the pseudonym Elizabeth Lowell.

Perry, Thomas • Perry won the Edgar Award for Best First Novel for *The Butcher's Boy* (Scribner, 1982), a thriller about a professional killer and the Justice Department investigator assigned to one of his hits—one that backfires when his employers turn on him.

Over the next ten years, Perry wrote a number of exceptional caper novels, including *Big Fish* (Scribner, 1985), *Island* (Putnam, 1987), and *Sleeping Dogs* (Random House, 1992). Some of these have continuing characters, of whom the most memorable is Chinese Gordon, a young soldier of fortune who plans intricate and improbable scams and heists. The masterpiece of this series is *Metzger's Dog* (Scribner, 1983), the violent and amoral story of Gordon's attempt to extort millions from the city of Los Angeles by showing that his small gang can paralyze the city with simultaneous traffic blockages at seventeen carefully selected freeway intersections. Perry's description of this event is a classic of crime humor narration.

In his subsequent novels, Perry has broken new ground with his protagonist Jane Whitefield, an Indian of Seneca and Iroquois ancestry from western New York State. Whitefield's specialty is making people disappear—voluntarily, that is—and Perry's books *Vanishing Act* (Random House, 1995), *Dance for the Dead* (Random House, 1996) and *Shadow Woman* (Random House, 1997) explain the tradecraft of her business in great detail. The books have a strong sense of history and convey the geography of their scenes exceptionally well; they may remind the reader of the best of Dean Koontz or Charles McCarry, and Perry's skill at painting a scene compares well with that of Conan Doyle, one of his favorite authors. Jane Whitefield is an unusual female character in being sympathetic yet willing to kill, when necessary, without a second thought. She is fully aware of her tribal heritage and makes use of her family connections and local knowledge to outwit her clients' pursuers.

Stark, Richard • See **Westlake, Donald E.**

Thomas, Ross/Bleeck, Oliver • For thirty years the late Ross Thomas wrote some of the wittiest and most entertaining crime thrillers around. Writing in the 1970s as Oliver Bleeck, he created the character Philip St. Ives, "professional troubleshooter," a Bond-like sophisticate called in by the rich or the government to recover exotic stolen property or arrange a kidnap exchange. Titles in this series include *No Questions Asked* (Morrow, 1976) and *Protocol for a Kidnapping* (Morrow, 1971). As Thomas he produced Cold War intrigue and espionage with the memorable characters Mac McCorkle and Mike Padillo, a bar owner and a spy using the bar as cover and rendezvous. They become unintended partners in various dangerous exploits in the Edgar Award-winning *The Cold War Swap* (Morrow, 1966) and *The Backup Men* (Morrow, 1971), both novels that have become classics of their kind. McCorkle and Padillo return much later in *Twilight at Mac's Place* (Mysterious Press, 1990) as older and wiser men, with family and other complications in their lives.

Besides these two series, Thomas authored numerous works of capers and other crimes, each with an inventive and often outrageous twist. *The Fourth Durango* (Myterious Press, 1989) tells of events in Durango, California (the Durango no one's ever heard of, unlike the other three), where an entire town subsists on income from people who need a place to disappear. (For a different slant on a similar livelihood, see the Jane Whitefield novels of Thomas Perry.) Some of Ross Thomas's earlier books, such as *The Porkchoppers* (Morrow, 1972) and *The Yellow-Dog Contract* (Morrow, 1976) are gritty and cynical; his final works, like *Out on the Rim* (Mysterious Press, 1987), tended toward wistful amusement at the foibles of the crooked and would-be crooked.

Thompson, Jim • Now recognized as one of the century's great authors of psychological thrillers, Jim Thompson worked during his abbreviated lifetime as an underpaid writer of bus-station page-turners, a WPA Writers' Project administrator, a reporter, an oil rig roughneck, and in a variety of other dead-end jobs in the seamier avenues of Depression and post-World War II America. His failures, poverty, and numerous jinxed enterprises are reflected in the hapless, self-deluding characters who people his novels of murder and betrayal. Many incidents from his life are retold in such works as *Bad Boy* (Lion, 1953) and *Roughneck* (Lion, 1954). He wrote screenplays for two of Stanley Kubrick's movies, *Paths of Glory* and *The Killing*, and wrote a novelization of the TV show *Ironside* (Popular Library, 1967). A number of his best novels have been filmed, more or less faithfully, including his best-known work, *The Killer Inside Me* (Lion, 1952). *Pop. 1280* (Fawcett, 1964) and *The Grifters* (Regency, 1963) have also been made into movies. Donald Westlake's masterly screenplay for *The Grifters* is justly famed. (See an entry below for Westlake.)

Thompson's protagonist, such as Lou Ford of *The Killer Inside Me*, is likely to be amoral, crafty, crooked, and capable of fooling himself about his chances as easily as he fools others about his nature. His end will be horrific and violent, but he will take others down with him. Thompson's psychological insights, together with his exceptional skill with dialogue and first-person narration, enable him to construct so bleak a landscape of desperation and despair that the reader finishes each novel gasping for air, relieved that it's over like some brief but disturbing nightmare; happier at the thought that the story is merely fiction, but uneasy with the suspicion that for some, including its author, it's been all too real.

Vachss, Andrew H. • An attorney and crusader against child abuse, Vachss has channeled his passions into a series of crime novels that have a consistent theme. Burke, the main character of the series, functions in many ways like a private eye, but he is an ex-con and a scam artist who lives by his wits in the seedy under-belly of New York City. He takes cases for hire, usually those that involve the sexual abuse of children. Burke has several associates who assist him in his work: Max the Silent, a deaf-mute Tibetan who is an efficient killing machine; the Mole, a Jewish electron-ics whiz; Michelle, a preoperative transsexual prostitute who feeds him information from the street and assists in some of his scams; the Prophet, an elderly black ex-con who knows every-thing there is to know about running scams and mining the streets for information; and Mama Wong, who runs what looks like a restaurant but is really a front for more nefarious activities and is also a convenient "home away from home" for Burke and his associates. First in the series is *Flood* (Fine, 1985), in which Burke helps a woman track down the man who abused and mur-dered her best friend's daughter. Dark, disturbing, and violent, the world of Vachss and his creation Burke makes the mean streets into a one-way ticket to hell. For Burke and his associates there is no coming back, only a never-ending battle to survive.

Westlake, Donald E./Stark, Richard • One of America's finest and most prolific mystery and thriller writers, Westlake has been producing both serious and humorous crime novels since the early 1960s. He was named a Grand Master by the Mystery Writers of America in 1993. Using the name Richard Stark, he created the memorable crook Parker, a professional armed robber, in a series of realistic and matter-of-fact stories of violent yet pedestrian holdups and killings. Parker, fascinat-ing as a character with no personality whatever, works with various other professionals as the planner and strong-arm man, and as often as not ends up broke and bloody because another member of the team weakened or betrayed him. The Parker novels, including *The Man with the Getaway Face* (Pocket Books, 1963), are sequential, and follow Parker as he robs and shoots his way around the country—outsmarting the Outfit, having his face changed, and dispatching numerous lowlifes who richly deserve it. Parker returned after a gap of twenty-three years, in *Comeback* (Mysterious Press, 1997).

As Westlake, the author gives us the comic Dortmunder novels. Unlike Parker, Dortmunder is a pussycat, harming no one except himself, failing amusingly at every crime because of his hapless cohorts and his tendency to give away the loot. Yet he continues to contrive excessively intricate crime plans chock full of opportunities to go wrong.

In another series, Andy Grofield works in the off-season (often with Parker) to support his summer stock theater, in which he acts and produces. In *The Score* (Pocket Books, 1964) he's assisted by his wife, Mary, who fell for him as he held her at gunpoint while Parker's gang robbed every safe in an entire town.

Westlake has also written numerous nonseries mysteries and novels of intrigue, notably the Edgar-nominated *Kahawa* (Viking, 1982), an epic story of a train highjacking in Idi Amin's Uganda, and *Baby, Would I Lie?* (Mysterious Press, 1994), a criminal foray into the world of country music. Recently, his superb novel *The Ax* (Mysterious Press, 1997) has been hailed as a masterpiece. Burke Devore has been out of work for two years, downsized out of his middle management job. In his desperation, he decides to kill the other candidates for the job he must have to restore his life. Seldom has the personal and social destruction wreaked by corporate downsizing been explored more powerfully.

Westlake won an Edgar Award for Best Novel for *God Save the Mark* (Random House, 1967), and his Edgar-nominated book *The Hot Rock* (Simon & Schuster, 1970) was made into a movie.

Willeford, Charles • Willeford was an acclaimed writer of tough, extremely hard-boiled novels, often told from the criminal's point of view. He also produced a series of excellent books about Hoke Moseley, a homicide cop in Miami. Willeford's South Florida stew is impeccably rendered and possesses great verve. The books are noted for their realistic dialogue and their depiction of a dark and violent world. Willeford was not very well known until about the time he died in the late 1980s; now he's a cult figure, much admired by fans of the hardest of the hard-boiled, and by other mystery writers such as Elmore Leonard and Lawrence Block. *Sideswipe* (St. Martin's Press, 1987), a Hoke Moseley novel, weaves together a story about Hoke's burnout after too many cases are dumped in his lap together with the evolution of a major robbery plan masterminded by Troy Loudon. Troy is a criminal who meets Stanley, an innocent old man, in jail by mistake, and involves him in a big robbery plan that is the climax of the book. Troy tells Stanley right at the beginning that he's a psychopathic career criminal, but Stanley's needs for a friend and for some excitement in his dull life are so great that he goes along with the increasingly wild schemes Troy cooks up. The suspense and the violence are unrelenting. At the end, the reader and Stanley find out Troy's real plan, and the true nature of his craziness and viciousness.

Winslow, Don • Winslow writes a series of private eye novels, the Neal Carey series, that has become a cult hit. Neal does undercover jobs for a secret organization called "The Friends of the Family." He is the illegitimate son of a drug-addicted prostitute in New York when he picks the pocket of a Friends of the Family operative in the early 1960s. That operative, Joe Graham, takes the young boy under his wing and teaches him the tricks of the private eye's trade, like how to follow someone, how to search an apartment, and how to disappear so you can't be found. The Friends of the Family send Neal to school and on to Columbia, where he's a graduate student in English literature when the first novel, *A Cool Breeze on the Underground* (St. Martin's Press, 1991), begins. It's 1976, and Neal has been wrested from his exams and sent to London to track down the drugged-out daughter of a U.S. senator. She has fallen into the arms of some small-time but violent criminals who are part of Britain's punk scene. In *Way Down on the High Lonely* (St. Martin's Press, 1993), Neal poses as a ranch hand in Nevada to infiltrate the military training unit of a religious group and rescue a kidnapped child.

Since the Neal Carey series, Winslow has also written *The Death and Life of Bobby Z* (Knopf, 1997), a tour de force caper novel, with slam-bang action that never lets up. Tim Kearney is a three-time loser who is facing a messy death after he kills a Hell's Angel named Stinkdog in the prison yard. So when a couple of DEA agents propose a deal to him, he grabs it. Unfortunately, the deal involves posing as the legendary surfer and drug dealer Bobby Z, who is in deep trouble with a ruthless Mexican drug lord. And Tim can't even swim, much less (he thinks) hold his own among the rich, the jaded, and the terminally cool druggies of Southern California. Winslow creates a set of wild characters with amorally hip attitudes, spaced-out dialogue, and easy violence in their souls. We're not likely to forget them, especially if the movie made from this deranged trip to the Hotel California is as good as the book.

Winslow also has published *A Winter Spy* (Signet, 1997) under the pseudonym MacDonald Lloyd.

For Further Reading • W. R. Burnett; James M. Cain; Leslie Charteris; Nick Gaitano; David Goodis; Eugene Izzi; Nicholas Pileggi; Mario Puzo; Laurence Shames.

Look for these caper films • *Blood Simple*; *Blue Velvet*; *Body Heat*; *Bonnie and Clyde*; *Bound*; *Bugsy*; *Casino*; *Donnie Brasco*; *Double Indemnity*; the *Falcon* series; *La Femme Nikita*; *The Friends of Eddie Coyle*; *Get Shorty*; *The Getaway*; *The Godfather* series; *Goodfellas*; *The Great Train Robbery*; *The Grifters*; *Grosse Pointe Blank*; *High Sierra*; *The Hot Rock*; *I Love You to Death*; *The Italian Job*; *The Killer Inside Me*; *The Killing*; *Kind Hearts and Coronets*; *The Krays*; *The Ladykillers*; *The League of Gentlemen*; *Little Caesar*; *Married to the Mob*; *Miller's Crossing*; *Murder by Death*; *Natural Born Killers*; *North by Northwest*; *Ocean's Eleven*; *Payback*; *The Postman Always Rings Twice*; *Prizzi's Honor*; *Public Enemy*; *Pulp Fiction*; *Raffles*; *Repo Man*; *Reservoir Dogs*; *Rififi*; *The Roaring Twenties*; *Ruthless People*; *The Saint* series; *Scarface*; the *Shadow* series; *Sneakers*; *Strangers on a Train*; *Thelma and Louise*; *The Third Man*; *To Catch a Thief*; *Topkapi*; *The Trouble with Harry*; *The Usual Suspects*.

TV • *The A-Team*; *The Equalizer*; *La Femme Nikita*; *The Fugitive*; *It Takes a Thief*; *Knight Rider*; *Mission: Impossible*; *Players*; the various incarnations of *The Saint*; *Scarecrow and Mrs. King*.

Reporters, Writers, and Filmmakers

The Front Page

Stories are what fiction is all about. And who is better at finding out about a story, a strange and baffling story, where action and imagery, life and death come together in explosive circumstances than a writer? So writers, journalists, and filmmakers, too, make excellent sleuths in mysteries. They already know how to dig for the facts, organize their information, make intuitive leaps of logic, and imagine scenarios with plenty of drama. They understand (or think they understand) people's motivations for their activities. And besides knowing all this, writers just plain love to snoop into people's lives. They call it doing research. We think it makes for great mystery fiction.

Boyle, Gerry • An award-winning journalist himself, Boyle has shared his profession with his protagonist, Jack McMorrow, in a series of mysteries set in Maine. Boyle's Maine is not the cozy coastal village of Jessica Fletcher's Cabot Cove, but the town of Androscoggin, where the economy depends on the success of the local paper mill. Jack McMorrow, a former reporter for the *New York Times*, has taken over the local weekly newspaper in Androscoggin as the series begins in *Deadline* (North Country Press, 1993). A staff photographer, Arthur Bertin, a man with few friends, is discovered dead in the river, and McMorrow is curious why the police aren't more interested in the case. He turns amateur sleuth to get at the truth, and the answers lead him to a deadly confrontation and an unusual physical cost to being nosy. In *Lifeline* (Putnam, 1996), McMorrow once again tangles in small-town business. A young woman complaining of spousal abuse gets no help from the authorities, and when she's murdered, McMorrow finds himself under suspicion. Boyle writes with quiet intensity about the dangers of small-town life and the deadly effects of corruption. His Maine is sharply drawn and evocatively portrayed, not cozily picturesque but all too ruggedly real.

Buchanan, Edna • Buchanan is a Pulitzer Prize winner for her journalism; her first crime novel was *Nobody Lives Forever* (Random House, 1990). She tells the stories of three police officers, all of whose lives have been deeply affected by a serial killer. As with all of her books, Buchanan provides a gritty, tough Miami background for her riveting story.

With *Contents Under Pressure* (Hyperion, 1992), Buchanan begins a series of mysteries featuring crime reporter Britt Montero. Elizabeth Montgomery played her in a television movie made from the book. Britt is relentlessly curious and ready to drop anything (including her personal life) to go after a story. She loves the crime beat, although many others, especially her mother, think it's no place for a woman. Britt always wants to prove them wrong. The Edgar-nominated *Miami, It's Murder* (Hyperion, 1994) tells the story of the Downtown Rapist, who is terrorizing Miamians, along with a mysterious series of events that appear to be revenge crimes. In *Suitable for Framing* (Hyperion, 1995), Buchanan tells two interwoven stories: one about a group of teenagers who steal cars and shoot the drivers, the other about a woman reporter who becomes a protégée to Britt.

Buchanan's stories of criminal events often focus on the people involved, and her characters come sharply alive for the reader. She is particularly notable for her skill in depicting how devastating violent crime is for the families of victims.

Authors of Other Hispanic Detectives

M. J. Adamson; Lucha Corpi; Earlene Fowler; Carolina Garcia-Aguilera; Wendy Hornsby (the Teague/Tejeda series); Mercedes Lambert; Janet LaPierre; Marcia Muller (the Elena Oliverez series); Michael Nava; Manuel Ramos; Dell Shannon; Richard Martin Stern (the Johnny Ortiz series); Paco Ignacio Taibo II; Marilyn Wallace (the Cruz/Goldstein series); Sherryl Woods (the Molly DeWitt series).

Burke, Jan • Irene Kelly, Jan Burke's heroine, knows about violence firsthand. In an excellent series of mysteries, Irene confronts violence, hate crimes, serial killers, and other madnesses of modern life as part of her job as a reporter in Southern California. Irene also has a strong and interesting relationship with Frank Harriman, a local homicide detective. In *Sweet Dreams, Irene* (Simon & Schuster, 1994), she is working on stories about political campaigns when she hears a rumor about a vicious smear campaign against a local candidate. Irene begins to investigate, and the story quickly escalates into brutal murder and intimidation. Unfortunately she isn't allowed to work on crime stories anymore in case she leaks information to Frank Harriman, and he is under constant suspicion of leaking items to her as well. Burke provides a masterly depiction of the professional and personal difficulties of such a relationship. In *Dear Irene,* (Simon & Schuster, 1995), Irene is still recovering from the physical and emotional injuries suffered in her previous case. She begins to get letters from a serial killer who is obsessed with Greek mythology and signs himself Thanatos (Death). The killer may also be obsessed with her, and she is back in danger again. Burke's use of the history of women defense workers in World War II as part of her plot, and her vivid Southern California setting give a particularly strong backdrop to this novel.

Goodnight, Irene was nominated for both an Agatha and an Anthony Award for Best First Mystery. *Sweet Dreams, Irene* was nominated for an Agatha Award for Best Mystery.

Conant, Susan • All those dog-lovers tired of seeing cats get all the cover art in pet-centered mysteries found a welcome canine advocate in Conant. Her series detective is Holly Winter, columnist for the magazine *Dog's Life* and malamute enthusiast. Between writing her column and training her malamute Rowdy, Holly stumbles on crimes, usually involving dogs in some way, in and around Cambridge, Massachusetts.

Sparked by a sense of humor with a strong streak of irony, Holly has a pithy narrative voice and little patience for those who fail to treat animals with respect. In addition to giving man's and woman's best friend a share of the spotlight, Conant also manages to raise the consciousness of her readers with her plots, which often involve issues relating to animal welfare. These issues sometimes make the books perhaps less cozy than some readers might prefer, but Conant, like Nancy Pickard, has the knack of blending trenchant social comment with an entertaining story. The series begins with *A New Leash on Death* (Berkley, 1990).

Readers looking for other mysteries with dogs playing a role should try the work of Rita Mae Brown, Melissa Cleary, Virginia Lanier, Carol Lea Benjamin, and Laurien Berenson.

Cooper, Susan Rogers • For Cooper's series of mysteries featuring romance-writer-turned-sleuth E. J. Pugh, see the section "Nancy, Frank, and Joe Grow Up."

D'Amato, Barbara • D'Amato began writing crime fiction with classic puzzle mysteries such as *The Hands of Healing Murder* (Charter, 1980). She also wrote the true crime story *The Doctor, the Murder, the Mystery* (Noble Press, 1992), which won an Agatha Award.

D'Amato switched to writing a series with a memorable female protagonist in 1990. Journalist and occasional sleuth Cat Marsala does great research in preparation for writing her stories. Cat is also feisty, observant, and fun; she's a good counterpoint to the serious social issues and crimes that she investigates.

In each of the novels in the series, Cat's research for her current assignment eventually leads her into a murderous situation. D'Amato obviously enjoys researching each topic extensively herself. *Hard Tack* (Scribner, 1991) tells us about what it's like to sail on the Great Lakes, while *Hard Women* (Scribner, 1993) explores the everyday lives of hookers and high-priced call girls. Cat investigates the crimes she encounters as carefully as she does her basic research; her interviewing techniques help get the story plus solve the murder.

D'Amato came up with a winner in a recent departure from the Cat Marsala series. *Killer.app* (Forge, 1996) is a combination of fast-paced techno-thriller and tough police procedural, and it takes place in D'Amato's customary Chicago setting.

Handler, David • A journalist and screenwriter, Handler makes extensive use of his experiences with publishing and Hollywood in a series of satirical mysteries featuring writer Stewart "Hoagy" Hoag. First in the series is *The Man Who Died Laughing* (Bantam, 1988). Once upon a time, Stewart Hoag was the toast of the publishing world, thanks to his brilliant first novel. He won the hand of the actress Merrilee Nash, and they settled down to live happily ever after with their basset hound, Lulu. But the second novel just wouldn't come. Inspiration dried up, along with Hoagy's marriage. Merrilee got everything but Lulu and Hoagy's typewriter. Now, to make a living, Hoagy ghostwrites celebrity biographies. Somehow murder takes a hand in all these stories, and Hoagy and Lulu are on hand to sniff out the truth. Handler has an acerbic wit, and the characters and story lines are reminiscent of the types of Hollywood excesses that make the tabloids fly off the newsstands. *The Man Who Cancelled Himself* (Doubleday, 1995), tells the story of a popular television star who may have torpedoed his own career by being caught doing something naughty in a porno theater. *The Man Who Would Be F. Scott Fitzgerald* (Bantam, 1991), which won the Edgar for Best Paperback Original, recounts the tale of New York's latest literary wunderkind, Cam Noyes, who's having trouble writing his second novel. Enter Hoagy to the rescue. Wickedly funny, David Handler is inimitable, one of the most original voices in contemporary mystery fiction. Readers will need to look for some of these books in libraries and used bookstores.

Hart, Carolyn G. • For Hart's series of mysteries about older reporter sleuth Henrie O, see the section "Murder, She Wrote."

Hayter, Sparkle • Though it might seem improbable, "Sparkle Hayter" is not a pseudonym. Born in Canada, Hayter is a former television newswoman who has worked for CNN in Atlanta, WABC in New York, and Global Television in Canada. She has also been a freelance reporter, during which time she covered the Afghan War, and she has performed stand-up comedy. Utilizing her own experience as a network reporter and as a comedian, Hayter has created a hip and funny sleuth in Robin Hudson, who works for the All News Network in New York. In her debut, *What's a Girl Gotta Do?* (SoHo, 1994), Robin is having trouble all over the place. She's being blackmailed, her ex-husband has a young, pretty, and pregnant girlfriend, and her boss wants her to investigate a sperm bank. The final insult is being accused of murder; thus Robin turns gumshoe to save her own skin. Not worried in *Nice Girls Finish Last* (Viking, 1996), Robin is trying to improve her outlook despite her nasty boss, her failed marriage, and her murdered gynecologist. With a new personal defense weapon at hand—her trusty hot-glue gun—Robin plunges once more into murder and mayhem at the All News Network. The pace is fast, and the humor is nonstop in this sparkling series. *What's a Girl Gotta Do?* won the Arthur Ellis Award for Best First Novel.

Hornsby, **Wendy** • Hornsby has been earning a name for herself as a rising star of police procedurals. Critics and readers rave about her talent for telling great stories about what it's like to be an LAPD cop, especially after the Rodney King incident changed the public perception of Los Angeles and its police force. Her series begins with *Telling Lies* (Dutton, 1992). Maggie MacGowen, a documentary filmmaker from San Francisco, is the hero. As she investigates the shooting of her sister, Maggie meets and becomes involved with homicide detective Mike Flynn. She returns to L.A. and Mike in the gripping *Midnight Baby* (Dutton, 1993), a story about the murder of a young girl who runs away from home. Hornsby creates realistically detailed crime scenes and ethical dilemmas in her tales of police officers and their families. She is especially good at building suspense and describing the dark underside of Los Angeles, and her plot twists keep the reader engrossed until the very end.

The first two mysteries written by Hornsby featured Southern California policeman Roger Tejeda and professor Kate Teague. These are hard-boiled police procedurals, with a fair amount of violence and good descriptions of the Southern California coast. Tejeda comes from a middle-class Latino background, while Teague is an Anglo heiress from an old money family, so they are an interesting study in contrasts. Readers may need to look for the Teague and Tejeda books in libraries and used bookstores.

McDermid, Val • Journalist McDermid has created two separate series of mysteries, one of which features journalist Lindsay Gordon, who, in her own words, is "a cynical socialist lesbian feminist." In her debut, *Report for Murder* (St. Martin's Press, 1990), Lindsay finds herself embroiled in a murder in just the type of setting she despises, a girls' school, a bastion of privilege that Lindsay dislikes. But Lindsay needs the work of writing a feature article about the school, so she goes for a weekend. Murder occurs, an old friend of Lindsay's is arrested, and Lindsay solves the crime. Lindsay reappears in *Open and Shut* (St. Martin's Press, 1991), which is set in Glasgow. Lindsay is much as she describes herself, and McDermid weaves the politics of feminism and alternative lifestyles into her novels compellingly. McDermid invests her characters with energy, wit, and intelligence.

For McDermid's series of private eye novels see the section "The Maltese Falcon."

McDonald, Gregory • Former newspaperman McDonald is best known for his groundbreaking and best-selling "Fletch" series, but he has also written the Flynn series and other novels. Fletch is Irwin Maurice Fletcher, an investigative reporter who is also the ultimate wisecracking cutup, always right in the face of any bad guys he encounters (and he meets plenty of them in this long-running series). A master of the one-liner, Fletch is also pretty good at donning oddball disguises and making up fake names to get the information he needs from people. However eccentric his investigative techniques may be, he remains dogged in his pursuit of a good story and a sardonic remark. Readers might take note that the chronology of the Fletch novels does not match the order in which they were published. McDonald has written his fast-paced crime novels in a smart, hip style, with pared-down, dialogue-driven, and highly cinematic prose. Fletch manages to find crime (and good stories) in many an exotic setting, such as Rio de Janeiro in *Carioca Fletch* (Warner, 1984).

The books in McDonald's Flynn series may be more conventional mysteries, but they are still funny and eccentric. Francis Xavier Flynn is a spy between jobs who apparently is working as a police inspector in Boston. His sidekick is retired detective "Cocky" Concannon, who is partially disabled after a stroke. Flynn is called in to solve unusual cases involving important people.

McDonald has a new series with Skylar Whitfield, a sexy young rascal from Tennessee who gets himself into all kinds of strange fixes.

McDonald won Edgar Awards for the first two Fletch books, *Fletch* (Bobbs, Merrill, 1974) and *Confess, Fletch* (Avon, 1976). The movies *Fletch* and *Fletch Lives*, with Chevy Chase as the smart-mouthed reporter, were based on McDonald's books.

Riggs, John R. • Riggs writes rural mysteries set in the town of Oakalla, Wisconsin. The town newspaper owner and editor,

Killer Books

Garth Ryland, not only investigates stories for his paper but is an amateur sleuth, too. Garth loves the countryside deeply, even in the depths of bone-chilling Wisconsin winters. He lives on an old farm with his housekeeper, Ruth, who is crusty and stubborn but who possesses a heart of gold. She has a great memory for all the secrets of the local folk, and he draws on that in his sleuthing. Indeed, many of the mysteries he finds seem to arise from old crimes and rivalries among the towns-people. In *The Haunt of the Nightingale* (Dembner, 1988) Garth finds a mute woman living in his barn in the middle of the winter. He gives her food and blankets, then hears her singing beautifully. One of his closest friends is killed, and he suspects a past link to the mysterious woman. Garth slowly makes friends with her and gains her trust so he can discover her identity and find out who has hurt her and perhaps com-mitted murder. *The Last Laugh* (Dembner, 1984) is about the death of the town practical joker. It's a very black comedy, with dark, prophetic musings on the long-term repercussions of teenage cruelty. As Riggs tells his weird, macabre story, the reader discovers that he knows all about the disturbing impor-tance of gossip and extended family relationships in a small town. Readers will need to look for most of these books in libraries and used bookstores.

R owlands, Betty • Rowlands is one of the current generation of English writers who is ably continuing the traditions of the Golden Age of classic English mysteries. Her series heroine, Melissa Craig, is a famous crime writer herself. Melissa decides to retire to the countryside to concentrate on her writ-ing, and she buys a semidetached cottage in the Cotswolds.

Luckily she becomes fast friends with her next-door neighbor, Iris Ash, an artist and textile designer. In the first book in the series, *A Little Gentle Sleuthing* (Walker, 1990), Melissa is just learning to live independently, after many years surrounded by family. Iris finds a body in the woods, and Melissa's curiosity impels her to investigate. By the time of *Over the Edge* (Walker, 1993), Melissa has gained confidence as an amateur sleuth, and she is ready to investigate a crime she encounters in the South of France. A German visitor is found at the bottom of a cliff at the beginning of the novel. Was he pushed by a disturbed former member of the French Resistance who hates Germans, or by an unknown enemy with contemporary problems? Rowlands evokes the fascinating medieval and World War II history of the area as an essential element of her plot. Rowlands's charming mysteries are peopled with eccentric characters, and she strews her red herrings adroitly. Readers will need to look for some of these books in libraries and used bookstores.

Shankman, Sarah • She began her life in crime as **Alice Storey**, to separate the criminous Storey from the mainstream fiction-writing Shankman, at an editor's insistence. Thus the first two novels in her Samantha Adams series, *First Kill All the Lawyers* (Pocket Books, 1988) and *Then Hang All the Liars* (Pocket Books, 1989), were published under the Storey name. Sam Adams is a journalist, born and bred in Atlanta. After the death of her policeman lover in San Francisco, the formerly hard-drinking Sam has returned to her native Atlanta, where she now works for the *Constitution*. The two Storey novels are thoroughly enjoyable stories with a nicely realized setting and interesting characters. But with the switch back to her real name with the third novel of the series, *Now Let's Talk of Graves* (Pocket Books, 1990), Shankman's full voice unleashed itself, and the result was a wickedly funny novel. Set in New Orleans during Mardi Gras, *Graves* is a veritable feast of eccentric characters, pitch-perfect southern dialogue, and a rollicking plot that keeps the reader gasping with laughter and guessing till the end. The fourth novel, *She Walks in Beauty* (Pocket Books, 1991), peeks behind the scenes at the Miss America pageant, and Atlantic City will never be the same. Shankman gives the reader an unusual combination of unsparingly satiric humor and a keen eye for the often absurd contradictions of the contemporary South. Her work is evolving into her own unique style of crime novel.

Walker, **Mary Willis** • Texas writer Walker has quickly become well known, for her first two novels each won prestigious awards in the mystery world. Her first book, *Zero at the Bone* (St. Martin's Press, 1991), won the Agatha, tied for the Macavity, and was nominated for the Edgar for Best First Novel. Her second novel, *The Red Scream* (Doubleday, 1994), won the Edgar for Best Novel. *Zero at the Bone* features dog trainer Katherine Driscoll in a novel surrounding mysterious doings at the mythical Austin, Texas, zoo. Austin is also the chief setting for Walker's series about true crime reporter Molly Cates. In *The Red Scream* Molly is excited about the publication of her first true crime book, on a notorious Texas murder, when the case grabs her attention again. The murderer, Louie Bronk, is slated for execution soon, and Molly wants to do follow-up interviews with the family of one of Bronk's victims. The family happens to be headed, however, by a wealthy and powerful Austin businessman who doesn't want Molly to stir up the case any further. When someone starts carrying out copycat-style murders, Molly can't help but become involved, no matter the threats to her personal safety. In *Under the Beetle's Cellar* (Doubleday, 1995) Molly tries to discover everything she can about the leader of a religious cult holding a group of eleven schoolchildren and their busdriver hostage. Molly is stubborn and dogged on the trail of a crime; she's haunted by the memories of her own father's unsolved murder years before. Walker knows how to kick the suspense into high gear, and Molly Cates is a tough and memorable heroine.

Zimmerman, R. D. • Hailing from Minnesota, Zimmerman is the author of two series of mysteries with amateur sleuths. In the more recent series, Zimmerman began with *Closet* (Dell, 1995), which was nominated for an Anthony for Best Paperback Original. This novel introduces Minneapolis television journalist Todd Mills. Agonizing over an ultimatum from his lover, Todd arrives home to find that Michael has been brutally murdered. The secret that Todd has been so desperate to keep has now been forced into the open, whether he likes it or not. *Closet* is a powerful story, as Todd struggles to comprehend all he has lost and what there yet may be to gain from acknowledging the truth about his sexuality. Zimmerman writes with compassion and integrity about a difficult subject. The second in the series, *Tribe* (Dell, 1996), was nominated for the Edgar for Best Paperback Original. The third, *Hostage* (Delacorte, 1997), finds Todd in a showdown with AIDS activists who have kidnapped a high-profile congressman. Zimmerman combines highly emotional political issues and their effects on private lives in an uncompromising and illuminating tale.

In his first series, Zimmerman introduced a very unusual duo of detectives, Maddy and Alex Phillips, who are sister and brother. Horribly injured in an accident, Maddy is both blind and paraplegic. The settlement she won in the ensuing lawsuit, however, has enabled her to rebuild her life, for she has moved to a remote island in Lake Michigan. A distinguished psychologist specializing in forensic hypnosis, Maddy solves mysteries by talking with her brother, Alex, and hypnotizing him when necessary, so she can extract every possible clue from him. Alex, of course, serves as Maddy's legs, ears, and eyes. Their first case is *Death Trance* (Morrow, 1992). Alex is grieving over the murder of his lover, and Maddy helps him solve the murder with her own unique talents.

Besides these two series, Zimmerman is the author of several suspense novels, including the Edgar-nominated *Deadfall in Berlin* (Fine, 1990).

For Further Reading • Carol Cail; Mary Daheim (the Alpine series); Tony Fennelly; Antonia Fraser; Mickey Friedman; Alison Gordon; Lesley Grant-Adamson; Patricia Hall; Lucille Kallen; Susan Kelly; Kathryn Lasky Knight; Michael Mewshaw; Meg O'Brien (the Jesse James series); Gary Provost; Robert Richardson; Lora Roberts; Annette Roome; Diane K. Shah (the Paris Chandler series); Barbara Burnett Smith; Polly Whitney.

Films to look for include • *Absence of Malice*; *All the President's Men*; *And Justice for All?*; *The Big Clock*; *Deadline-U.S.A.*; *Fletch*; *Fletch Lives*; *The Front Page*; *Front Page Woman*; *His Girl Friday*; *The Mean Season*; *Peeping Tom*; *The Verdict*.

Amateur Sleuths

Nancy, Frank, and Joe Grow Up: American Mysteries

Many readers probably got their start with mysteries in the same way, through discovering either Nancy Drew or the Hardy Boys. There have been many other popular series of mysteries for young readers throughout the twentieth century, but probably no others have the immediate name recognition of Nancy, Frank, and Joe.

Bright, determined, eager for adventure, Nancy and the Hardy brothers represent something that all of us as young readers probably wanted to be: adventurous, fearless, and capable. These characters provided role models for millions of youngsters, and for many of us they no doubt whet a taste for mysteries that has continued from childhood through adolescence to adulthood.

Nancy, Frank, and Joe were essentially amateur detectives. They didn't get paid for what they did, though they might receive a trophy or some other token from the grateful people they helped with their efforts. (It was up to their fathers, Carson Drew the attorney and Fenton Hardy the private detective, to collect the big fees!) It's amazing what these teenagers were able to accomplish (when did they go to school, for Pete's sake?). Just imagine what they could do after they were all grown up…

Abbott, Jeff • One of a rapidly growing number of mystery writers hailing from the state of Texas, Abbott infuses his series with a down-home type of charm. In the first novel, *Do Unto Others* (Ballantine, 1994), series sleuth Jordan Poteet has given up his job with a Boston-based publisher to return home to Mirabeau, Texas, to help his sister care for their mother, stricken with Alzheimer's. Tiny Mirabeau doesn't have much to offer in the way of employment for a publishing executive, so Jordan (Jordy to his friends) takes the job of librarian at the public library. The job turns out to be more challenging than Jordy expected, when one of his patrons is murdered—not long after a very public argument with him. Jordy turns sleuth to save his own skin, despite the fact that Mirabeau's chief of police, Junebug Moncrief, is a childhood friend. Along the way to the solution of the crime, Jordy also falls in love, discovers more about his family than he really wanted to know, and demonstrates that he's a very capable amateur sleuth. *Do Unto Others* won both the Agatha and the Macavity Awards for Best First Novel. Further novels in the series find Jordy and his family and friends confronting murder and long-buried emotional issues in the best amateur detective fashion.

Adams, Deborah • Small southern towns seem to be full of interesting, often eccentric, characters—at least, that is, in mystery fiction. Adams, unlike many of her peers, uses the setting of Jesus Creek, Tennessee, as the link in her series of mysteries.

Many of the same characters appear in each book, but most of them are narrated by different characters each time, with the setting offering the connection from one book to the next. In the first book in the series, *All the Great Pretenders* (Ballantine, 1992), a rich young woman disappears, and a psychic tries to find her, while Jesus Creek is in the midst of its sesquicentennial celebrations. Various denizens of the town relate the stories: the chief of police in *All the Deadly Beloved* (Ballantine, 1996) and a rookie police officer in *All the Blood Relations* (Ballantine, 1997). Adams writes lovingly but with mordant wit about her cast of characters, and she makes Jesus Creek a fun place to visit—though you might not want to live there!

Albert, Susan Wittig • Once a professor of medieval literature and a university administrator, Albert now writes full-time from her home in the Texas hill country. China Bayles, the heroine of Albert's series, is a former corporate lawyer who grew tired of the rat race and left it behind in Houston. She has moved to the Texas hill country and opened a shop that specializes in herbs. Despite the slower pace of life in Pecan Springs, Texas, though, China still manages to run across her share of murders. Her first appearance is *Thyme of Death* (Scribner, 1992). Through the series she is building her relationship with Mike McQuaid, a former cop turned professor of criminal justice at a nearby university. Herb lore mixes with crime-solving as China tries her best to balance personal and professional lives. *Thyme of Death* was nominated for both the Agatha and the Anthony Awards for Best First Novel. Along with her husband, William, Albert writes a series of historical mysteries as **Robin Paige** (see the section "Once Upon a Crime").

Authors of Gardening and Botanical Mysteries

Susan Wittig Albert; Alisa Craig; Joan Hadley (a.k.a. Joan Hess); Ann Ripley; Marion Rippon; Rebecca Rothenberg; John Sherwood; Rex Stout.

Barr, Nevada • Barr is a park ranger who sets her mysteries in national parks such as Mesa Verde, the Natchez Trace, and Isle Royal. The heroine in this series is Anna Pigeon, a National Park Service ranger. Anna lived in New York City until her husband died, and then she started over again and learned in the park service to be both a gutsy outdoorswoman and an officer of the law. She loves the wilderness now, where people can't get too close to her and where she can gain strength from observing nature and wildlife. Barr's skill in describing the elusive beauty of wild places makes her first mystery, *Track of the Cat* (Putnam, 1993), an unusual and memorable novel. This mystery set in West Texas won both the Agatha and the Anthony Awards for Best First Mystery Novel. In *A Superior Death* (Putnam, 1994), Anna is working in Isle Royal National Park in northern Michigan, on Lake Superior. She has learned to deal with a cold climate and with the deep dives she must make into the frigid lake to investigate crimes in the park. Barr's skill at writing about natural history brings the cold and remote splendor of the park's attractions alive for readers.

Bowen, Gail • Canadian mystery writers aren't very well known in the United States, and so readers miss out on some unusual books by good writers. Gail Bowen is one such author; she is an

English professor in Saskatchewan who writes a series about Joanne Kilbourn, a political writer, commentator, and professor. Joanne's husband, a rising young political figure, has been murdered as the series of novels begins with *Deadly Appearances* (Douglas & McIntyre, 1990). As the series develops, Bowen creates an effective backdrop for murder on the vast, rolling prairies of Saskatchewan. The recurring characters are mainly politicians, artists, and journalists as well as Joanne's children and friends. Joanne has a big, comfortable house, and she is a busy, smart woman who cares deeply about her family. She is an amateur sleuth who stumbles on murder in the time-honored tradition of classic mysteries. *A Colder Kind of Death* (St. Martin's Press, 1995), which won the Alfred Ellis Award for Best Novel from the Canadian Crime Writers' Assocation, begins at Halloween. The man who killed Joanne's husband is killed in prison, and his wife returns to taunt and insult Joanne. The stage for murder is set, and for Joanne's inevitable status as a prime suspect. Joanne slowly discovers the real story about what happened when her husband died, and she finds that she must even investigate her oldest friends if she wants to know the full truth. Bowen provides a vivid and intelligent backdrop of Canadian politics and culture in all of her novels, and they are well worth searching out.

Braun, Lilian Jackson • Cats and mysteries seem to be a winning combination. Perhaps the first mystery writer to discern this was journalist Lilian Jackson Braun, who began writing about two talented Siamese cats in 1966. She wrote *The Cat Who Could Read Backwards* (Dutton, 1966) and two more novels, then took a break from writing novels for eighteen years. In the earlier books in the series, Jim Qwilleran, known to all as Qwill, lives in a large midwestern city and works as a journalist at the *Daily Fluxion*. The extravagantly mustachioed Qwill is a grumpy, confirmed bachelor. In *The Cat Who Played Brahms* (Jove, 1987) he inherits a fortune but must go to live in rural Pickax City. Qwill retires and moves North, but he continues to write for a local newspaper, and the cats get him involved in snooping around local crimes. The cats are Koko and Yum Yum, who have extraordinary powers of perception and strong personalities: Koko is psychic, intelligent, and curious, while Yum Yum is coy, playful, and affectionate. The cats nose out evidence and clues, and in each book they are likely to send Qwill feline hints about a crime that has been committed. Their curious and sympathetic owner eventually understands what the cats are trying to communicate to him and thus is able to solve the mystery.

Churchill, Jill • Jill Churchill is a pseudonym used by Janice Young Brooks, who also writes historical novels. The titles of her mysteries featuring amateur sleuth Jane Jeffry all have clever puns on the titles of literary works: *War and Peas*, *From Here to Paternity*, *A Quiche Before Dying*, and so on. Jane Jeffry, a widowed homemaker and mother, lives in the suburbs of Chicago. Jane has three kids, nosy neighbors (especially her best friend, Shelley), and a network of friends who do volunteer work for charities and help each other out when trouble strikes. Jane, Shelley, and their friends also help solve local murders, in the classic way of amateur sleuths, by deduction and the application of common sense. Jane's particular friend, homicide detective Mel VanDyne, is amazed by how the women can draw valuable conclusions from their everyday knowledge of housework and neighborhood customs. In the Agatha Award-winning *Grime* *and Punishment* (Bantam, 1989), for example, Jane makes a crucial deduction by knowing how women typically vacuum a room. Churchill uses the traditional format: The murders occur in a small town among a closed circle of suspects, and the puzzle is solved by the use of well-hidden clues and logical deductions made by the amateur sleuth. Aside from the mystery plot, the books are brimful of wry comments on motherhood, living in suburbia, raising teenagers, and other conditions of modern life.

Coben, Harlan • Wisecracking sports agent Myron Bolitar is the hero of Coben's Edgar, Anthony, and Shamus Award-winning series. Myron once had a promising future as a professional basketball player, but an on-court injury put an end to that dream. Then Myron went off to law school, worked for the FBI awhile, then decided to become a sports agent. With the help of his best friend, Windsor Lockwood IV (known as "Win"), who is a financial whiz, Myron is a fairly successful agent when the series opens with *Deal Breaker* (Dell, 1995). His biggest client, football star Christian Steele, is in big trouble. His fiancée has disappeared, and it looks like Steele could be responsible. Myron investigates, with the aid of his assistant, Esperanza Díaz, a former professional wrestler, and Win, who thinks nothing of blowing away any bad guys who get in Myron's way. Complicating matters is the fact that the missing girl's older sister is Myron's old flame Jessica, who burned him badly once before. Can Myron solve this case with his heart intact?

As the series continues, Coben develops the relationship between Myron and his rather frightening best friend, Win, giving the reader a better understanding of Win's somewhat obsessive care for Myron. Coben uses the convention of the sociopathic sidekick with some interesting twists, and at the ending of *Fade Away* (Dell, 1996), Win more than lives up to the expectations of his character.

Coben has a breezy, humorous style. Myron Bolitar has considerable appeal, and the plots are fast-paced and well constructed. *Deal Breaker* was nominated for the Edgar Award for Best Paperback Original, and it won the Anthony Award in that category. *Fade Away* won the Edgar for Best Paperback Original.

Cooper, Susan Rogers • Cooper writes two series of mysteries with amateur detectives. The first of these is E. J. (Eloise Janine) Pugh, a housewife and romance novelist in Black Cat Ridge, Texas. E. J., her husband, Willis, and their children become involved in the horrific murders of their next-door neighbors in the first of the series, *One, Two, What Did Daddy Do?* (St. Martin's Press, 1992). Could Roy Lester really have killed almost his entire family before killing himself? E. J. and Willis refuse to believe it, and thus begins a nightmarish situation that puts them all in danger. They appear again in *Hickory Dickory Stalk* (Avon, 1996). E. J. is being harassed by someone, and when her prime suspect turns up dead, E. J. once again has to protect her family by turning sleuth.

Cooper's second amateur sleuth is stand-up comic Kimmey Kruse, who first appears in *Funny as a Dead Comic* (St. Martin's Press, 1993). Kimmey looks like a good suspect when another comic, a former lover, is murdered. Kimmey fights an attraction to the Chicago homicide cop, Sal Pucci, who is assigned to the case. He even seems to dog her steps when she encounters murder among her Cajun relatives in Port Arthur, Texas, in *Funny as a Dead Relative* (St. Martin's Press, 1994). Kimmey is funny, vulnerable, and very appealing. Readers will need to check libraries and used bookstores for these two titles.

For Cooper's police detective series see the "Hill Street Blues" section.

Craig, Alisa • See **MacLeod, Charlotte**.

Crider, Bill • Himself a professor of English literature at Alvin Community College in Alvin, Texas, Crider has shared that profession with one of his series characters, Carl Burns. Burns is a professor at Hartley Gorman College in Pecan City, Texas, who sometimes finds himself a bit at odds with the college administration. When someone murders a difficult administrator in the first book in the series, *One Dead Dean* (Walker, 1988), Carl Burns turns sleuth, and in so doing, runs afoul of the sheriff. Crider, as always, writes with adroit humor in this series, and his gentle lampooning of academic politics and the denizens of the ivory tower make for very enjoyable reading. Readers will need to check libraries and used bookstores for some of these titles.

Besides the Carl Burns series, Crider also writes the Sheriff Dan Rhodes books (see the "Hill Street Blues" section) and the Truman Smith books (see "The Maltese Falcon" section).

Cross, Amanda • Perhaps the spiritual heir to the late Dorothy L. Sayers, Cross is the author of a series of academic mysteries that are completely distinctive. Her series character is English professor Kate Fansler, who comes from a wealthy and socially prominent New York family. Kate often finds her values at odds with those of the rest of her family, because she is a staunch and, at times, outspoken feminist. In a career that has spanned more than three decades, Kate has solved numerous crimes with a literary bent, including *The James Joyce Murder* (Macmillan, 1967) and *The Players Come Again* (Random House, 1990). Acclaimed by her fans and critics alike for the richness of her dialogue, Amanda Cross always provides a veritable feast for the lover of the English language. Kate first appeared in the novel *In the Last Analysis* (Macmillan, 1964). Perhaps her most interesting case is recounted in *Death in a Tenured Position* (Dutton, 1981), when she investigates the death of the only woman to have received tenure in the Harvard English Department.

Daheim, Mary • Once upon a time a writer of historical romances, in recent years Daheim has given her attention to two series of mysteries, both with amateur sleuths. The first of these sleuths is Judith McMonigle, who has turned her family home into a bed-and-breakfast named Hillside Manor Inn. The city that serves as the setting in this series is never named but is otherwise a thinly veiled Seattle. Judith, a widow with one college-age son, operates the bed-and-breakfast despite the ill-natured and often hateful interference of her mother, Gertrude, who lives with her. Aided by her cousin Renie, Judith solves the crimes that come her way, to the aggravation of her old flame, a policeman, Joe Flynn. First in the series is *Just Desserts* (Avon, 1991).

Daheim's second series features Emma Lord, journalist turned newspaper owner, in the small town of Alpine, Washington, in the foothills of the Cascade Mountains. Like Judith McMonigle, Emma Lord is a single mother, with troubled relationships in her past. The first book in this series is *The Alpine Advocate* (Ballantine, 1992). Although one series is written in the third person (Judith) and the other in the first person

(Emma), Daheim's voice in both series is wry, occasionally ribald, and often sarcastic. Both series have a pleasant, cozy feel.

Davidson, Diane Mott • Readers who like to tempt their taste buds while they tease their brains will have fun with Davidson's series. The heroine is Gertrude "Goldy" Bear, a caterer who has a knack for running into murders. In the first of the series, *Catering to Nobody* (St. Martin's Press, 1990), Goldy is catering a wake for her eleven-year-old son's favorite teacher, and her ex-father-in-law almost dies from something he ate at the wake. Goldy has to work hard to figure out what's going on, both to save her business and to save herself from going to jail for attempted murder. Complicating her life is her abusive former husband, a prominent doctor in their Aspen Meadow, Colorado, hometown. Davidson writes convincingly about a strong woman dealing with a very difficult situation, trying to run a business and steer clear of her nasty ex, while rearing a son. In addition to the entertaining stories and characters, Davidson offers mouth-watering descriptions of food—recipes included!

Authors of Mysteries with Cooking Themes

Claudia Bishop; Camilla Crespi; Mary Daheim; Diane Mott Davidson; Ellen Hart; Peter King; Janet Laurence; Valerie S. Malmont; G. A. McKevett; Amy Myers; Tamar Myers (the Magdalena Yoder series); Katherine Hall Page; Joanne Pence; Virginia Rich; Phyllis Richman; Rex Stout.

Dominic, R. B. • See **Lathen, Emma**.

Douglas, Carole Nelson • Along with her acclaimed series of Victorian mysteries, Douglas writes a series of mystery novels featuring the sleuthing partnership of Temple Barr, a Las Vegas publicist, and Midnight Louie, a large and sardonic black cat. Louie loves to wander about Vegas at night looking for trouble, and he certainly finds it and brings it home to his human companion. Louie narrates the books in his own inimitable style, and his world-weary musings may remind the reader of a smart feline version of such classic hard-boiled PIs as Philip Marlowe and Sam Spade. These amusing mysteries are tailor-made for those readers looking for a sleuth with a difference. The series begins with *Catnap* (Tor, 1992), a diverting romp through a city that never sleeps.

For Douglas's series of historical mysteries see the section "Once Upon a Crime."

Authors of More Animal-Related Mysteries

Lydia Adamson; Garrison Allen; Marian Babson; Carolyn Banks; Carol Lea Benjamin; Laurien Berenson; Barbara Block; Lilian Jackson Braun; Rita Mae Brown; Melissa Cleary; Susan Conant; Carole Nelson Douglas; Patricia M. Guiver; David Handler; Jody Jaffe; Barbara Moore; Lillian Roberts; Karen Ann Wilson.

Elkins, Aaron • After spending time in several professions, among them that of forensic anthropologist, Elkins turned to writing mystery novels. He endowed his series sleuth, Gideon

Oliver, with one of his professions. Gideon, known in the media as "the Skeleton Detective," gets called in as an expert witness around the world on cases involving unusual remains. In his first appearance, *Fellowship of Fear* (Walker, 1982), Gideon is in Europe and finds himself involved in the middle of a James Bond-type scenario. Later books in the series follow a more traditional mystery format. Perhaps the best of the series is *Old Bones* (Mysterious Press, 1987), which won the Edgar for Best Novel. Here Gideon is in Brittany, attending a conference, and he gets entangled with a mystery surrounding a local family. Other stories have taken Gideon to various exotic parts of the globe: Egypt in *Dead Men's Hearts* (Mysterious Press, 1994), Tahiti in *Twenty Blue Devils* (Mysterious Press, 1997), and Alaska in *Icy Clutches* (Mysterious Press, 1990).

In addition to the Gideon Oliver books, Elkins writes a series about Chris Norgren, an art curator. The first of these is *A Deceptive Clarity* (Walker, 1987). Readers who like mysteries about art will enjoy these tales. With his wife, Charlotte Elkins, Aaron Elkins has written a series about professional golfer Lee Ofsted, the first of which is *A Wicked Slice* (St. Martin's Press, 1989).

Fowler, Earlene • Fowler's mysteries in the Benni Harper series all have a quilting theme, and each has cover art that shows the quilt pattern for which the book is named. In the first book, *Fool's Puzzle* (Berkley, 1994), Benni is a rancher's widow and the curator of a folk art museum on the central California coast. Benni stumbles over a murder victim one night at the museum, but she is so offended by the local police chief's arrogant attitude toward her that she withholds important evidence from him. So begins a lively, contentious relationship between two strong-willed people. Benni noses around her town, looking for clues to the murder, and Chief Gabe Ortiz keeps trying to stop her. Fowler's vivid settings remind the reader that ranches and cowgirls like Benni still exist in California. *Fool's Puzzle* was nominated for an Agatha Award for Best First Novel. In later books Benni and Gabe continue to argue despite their growing relationship. Benni has a smart mouth, Gabe is stubborn and reserved, and sparks fly as their personalities clash and they continue to investigate crimes.

Haddam, Jane/Papazoglou, Orania • The popular series of "holiday" mysteries published under the name of Jane Haddam are really written by Connecticut author Orania Papazoglou. Her likable and intelligent hero is Gregor Demarkian, a retired FBI agent, and each book is set during an American holiday. Demarkian is often called the Armenian-American Hercule Poirot in the books, and many of his cases are solved against a backdrop of Armenian culture, especially in the tightly-knit Armenian community in Philadelphia. The series begins with a Christmas mystery, *Not a Creature Was Stirring* (Bantam, 1990). Gregor is often assisted in his cases by his great friend Bennis Hannaford, a rich and intelligent writer of fantasy novels, and by Father Tibor Kasparian, an Armenian Orthodox priest. Demarkian is an expert in poisons and the behavioral analysis of serial killers, and the crimes he solves are traditional puzzle mysteries.

Under her own name, Papazoglou has written several cozy mysteries featuring writer Patience (Pay) Campbell McKenna. Pay writes everything from respectable articles in national magazines to formula romance novels (under a pseudonym, of course), but she is best at writing true crime and even solving crimes herself along with her loyal friend Phoebe.

Hager, Jean • Mysteries with a backdrop of Cherokee culture and history are Jean Hager's specialty. One of her memorable series centers around Molly Bearpaw, an investigator for the Native American Advocacy League. Molly works out of Tahlequah, Oklahoma, and deals with cases in which members of the Cherokee tribe may have been denied their civil rights. In *Seven Black Stones* (Mysterious Press, 1995), Molly investigates two mysterious deaths that seem to have no link except for the presence of seven black stones found near each of the bodies.

Hager also writes a series of traditional cozy mysteries. In a small town in Missouri, Tess Darcy has inherited a lovely Victorian house and its iris gardens from an aunt and has turned her new home into a thriving bed-and-breakfast business. Unfortunately, murder comes to stay on a regular basis at Iris House, and Tess must cope with sleuthing as well as cooking. In the first entry in the series, *Blooming Murder* (Avon, 1994), murder even occurs during the annual iris growers' convention. Members of the local garden club are all suspects, and the story is well embellished with gardening lore.

Harris, Charlaine • For the setting of her first mystery novel, *Sweet and Deadly* (Houghton Mifflin, 1981), Harris used her native Mississippi delta and the fictional town of Lowfield. The heroine of this novel, Catherine Linton, has the characteristics that are hallmarks of Harris's creations. Catherine, like Nickie Callahan of *A Secret Rage* (Houghton Mifflin, 1984), is intelligent, independent, and attractive. Catherine Linton is delving into the mysterious deaths of her parents while working as a society editor for the Lowfield *Gazette*. Nickie is a former New York model who has tired of the "glamorous" life and has returned to the South for a college education. The small town of Knolls, Tennessee, is being terrorized by a rapist, and Nickie falls prey to him. Writing with sensitivity and compassion, Harris handles a difficult subject well. Lately Harris has begun a series starring Aurora "Roe" Teagarden, a diminutive librarian with a sassy tongue and an affinity for true crime. In the Agatha-nominated *Real Murders* (Walker, 1990), Roe finds herself investigating the murders of fellow members of her "real murders" club. All the victims have died in a way reminiscent of some famous true crime. Roe's adventures continue in *A Bone to Pick* (Walker, 1992). In the recent *Shakespeare's Landlord* (St. Martin's Press, 1996), Harris introduced Lily Bard. Lily is a woman with a dark secret in her past, and she has moved to tiny Shakespeare, Arkansas, to start a new life. The murder of her landlord disturbs Lily's calm, however, and she proves to be a determined, clever sleuth who is well able to defend herself physically when necessary. In all Harris's novels, wit, humor, intelligence, and southern settings are her hallmarks.

Hart, Carolyn G. • Hart has been acclaimed as one of the foremost contemporary writers of traditional mysteries. She is now producing two ongoing series of tightly plotted novels in the classic mode. Hart has won Agatha, Anthony, and Macavity Awards for Best Novel for several of her novels.

Hart's first series stars Annie Laurance, who owns Death on Demand, a mystery bookstore on Broward's Rock Island off the coast of South Carolina. Annie is the very model of a curious and enthusiastic amateur sleuth, and she is ably assisted in her sleuthing by her husband, Max Darling. There's a whole group of unforgettable characters, too, including Annie's batty mother-in-law and a demanding bookstore customer, who like to think they are helping Annie and Max out with their detection, but are just as liable to get in the way or muddle about making things worse. Hart often pays tribute in her novels to other honored mystery writers, especially those from the Golden Age of crime fiction, and she builds on the traditional styles of mysteries to create her own unique designs. First in the series is *Death on Demand* (Bantam, 1987).

For Hart's series about older sleuth Henrie O, see the section "Murder, She Wrote."

Hart, Ellen • Lesbian restaurant owner Jane Lawless is the sleuth in Hart's first series of amateur detective novels. In her mid-thirties, Jane is recovering from the death of her longtime lover a few years before the series begins. Her restaurant, The Lyme House, reflects part of her heritage; her mother was English, and Jane spent most of her childhood and adolescence there. Her father, Raymond Lawless, is a well-known criminal lawyer in Minneapolis, where the books are set, and Jane has a difficult relationship with him, which begins to improve over the course of the series. Jane is often assisted in her investigations by her flamboyant friend Cordelia Thorn, an actress and theater director in St. Paul. Cordelia is as theatrical as Jane is quiet, and the two make an effective and engaging detective duo. First in the series is *Hallowed Murder* (Seal Press, 1989).

Hart has a second series sleuth in Sophie Greenway, a food

critic. Sophie's husband, Bram Baldric, is a radio talk show host in Minneapolis. The two often find themselves involved in murder; the first occasion is *This Little Piggy Went to Murder* (Ballantine, 1994). A professional chef for many years, Hart writes with authority and charm about food in both series.

Hess, Joan • Hess is a master of the comedy-mystery. Currently she is producing two series of books. One series is set in the small town of Maggody, Arkansas, and it features Police Chief Arly Hanks. Arly has returned to her childhood hometown reluctantly, after a bitter divorce in New York City. Maybe her smart mouth helps to keep her sane in Maggody, which must be the mother of all eccentric, rural communities. Unfortunately, Arly's mother, Rubella Belinda, who runs Ruby Bee's Bar & Grill, and her best buddy, beautician Estelle Oppers, are always trying to help Arly solve crimes. Other occasionally upright citizens include Brother Verber, the pastor of the Voice of the Almighty Lord Assembly Hall and a busy reader of pornography, dimwitted janitor Kevin Buchanon and his mountainous bride, Dahlia, and Hizzoner Mayor Jim Bob Buchanon and his smarmy and mean wife, Mrs. Jim Bob. It's always a joy to meet the peculiar denizens of Maggody again and see how Hess turns each book into a hilarious take on contemporary American life: the widespread belief in UFOs, the weirder end of the country music industry, faith healing, and so on. This is one of those unforgettable series of novels that just keep on getting better with each book.

Hess's other series is set in a college town in Arkansas, and its tales are very much in the classic mode of amateur detection. Bookstore owner Claire Malloy is a persistent and curious sleuth despite the hindrance of her whiny teenage daughter Caron, Caron's ever-present sidekick Inez, and the irregular attentions of attractive local cop Peter Rosen. The first book in this amusing series is *Strangled Prose* (St. Martin's Press, 1986).

Isaacs, Susan • Best-selling novelist Isaacs has penned several mystery and suspense novels, a number of which have been turned into successful movies. Her first novel, *Compromising Positions* (Times Books, 1978), became a hit starring Susan Sarandon and the late Raul Julia. This book tells the story of suburban Long Island housewife Judith Singer, who becomes fascinated with the murder of a local orthodontist, Dr. Bruce Fleckstein. Isaacs uses the frame of the mystery plot to satirize the oddities of upper-middle-class families, and her wit is never better than in *After All These Years* (HarperCollins, 1993). Returning to Shorehaven, the setting for her first novel, Isaacs tells the story of Rosie Meyers, who gets a very unpleasant suprise on her twenty-fifth wedding anniversary. Her husband wants a divorce. Sometime later, Richie Meyers winds up dead, and Rosie is the chief suspect. Suburbia was never so deadly—or so funny—than in the hands of this consummate storyteller.

Kemelman, Harry • The hero in a long series of religious mysteries, mostly named after the days of the week, is David Small. He is the rabbi of a suburban congregation in Barnard's Crossing, Massachusetts. Rabbi Small uses logic, in the Talmudic tradition, to help the local police solve crimes in the community. As a scholarly man who is not much of a rabbinical politician, Rabbi Small is constantly fighting ethical battles with his board and his congregation, usually over attempts to water down the ethics and observances of Judaism. The rabbi's success at sleuthing helps not only the community and the victims of crime but also helps to silence the critics at both ends of the religious spectrum who think he should approach worship in a more or less strict fashion. The late Harry Kemelman was always interested in the politics of how a temple is run, and particularly in the relationship of the rabbi to his employers, who are the board of directors of the synagogue. Kemelman not only entertained his readers but also taught them gently about Judaism in general, and about the differences among Orthodox, Conservative, and Reform temples. His popular novels have been much valued over the years for their contribution to a better understanding of Judaism by Americans of other religions.

Lake, M. D. • Lake is the pseudonym of Allen Simpson, who retired from his job as a Scandinavian literature professor at the University of Minnesota and began to write mysteries set at a large midwestern university. His books are traditional puzzle mysteries, and the protagonist is Peggy O'Neill, a police officer at the university. Peggy is curious and persistent, and as a campus cop she has access to all of the university's buildings at any hour. She likes to work the "dog shift," and she runs into some strange and terrible doings on her nightly rounds. Her sense of curiosity draws her inevitably into solving crimes. Peggy is a lively and strongly independent character, with useful contacts and friends on the city police force and among the other campus cops. With a personality that tends toward the practical, Peggy knows from experience how to cut through the lies and rationalizations she hears so often from suspects. Although Peggy is the main character, her coworkers on the campus police force—Ginny, Lawrence, and Paula—appear regularly in the books. In *Poisoned Ivy* (Avon, 1992) Peggy can't resist finding out all about the accidental victim of a messed-up homicide attempt; she calls it doing a psychological autopsy. She is sneered at by some of the snootier and more suspicious elements on campus because she's not a town police officer, just a campus cop. But Peggy is certainly a real sleuth, with a decided aptitude for investigating murders.

Langton, Jane • Langton is a New England writer of mysteries and young adult books. She is noted for her dazzling flights of imagination, her lyrical prose, and the witty pen-and-ink drawings with which she illustrates her novels. Her mysteries are decidedly unusual ones, for she concentrates more on devising unusual characters and describing her setting than on strewing clues or mystifying the reader. Retribution for her villains is sometimes achieved through the vast impersonal workings of the universe rather than in the courtroom. Langton's series characters are Homer and Mary Kelly. Homer is a Thoreau scholar and former lawyer and policeman who worships at the shrine of New England transcendentalism, and his admiration is mirrored in many of the books. Most of these poetic and delightful novels are set in historic Concord and Boston, and the ideas of such nineteenth-century giants as Thoreau, Emerson, and Dickinson are very much present in their plots. Langton's books also make excursions into the worlds of natural history, art, and music. In recent books Langton has increasingly concentrated on presenting environmental concerns, and her descriptions of the natural world are graceful and memorable, especially in *Natural Enemy* (Ticknor & Fields, 1982) and *God in Concord* (Viking, 1992).

Authors of Environmentally-Oriented Mysteries

Nevada Barr; James W. Hall; Carl Hiaasen; Jane Langton; Janet LaPierre; John D. MacDonald; Kirk Mitchell; Judith Van Gieson; Randy Wayne White.

Lathen, Emma/Dominic, R. B. • Since 1961, Mary Latsis and Martha Henissart have been doing a nearly impossible task: writing wonderful novels that turn the esoteric worlds of banking, accounting, and finance into the stuff of exciting mysteries. Latsis and Henissart are an economist and a lawyer, respectively, but throngs of devoted readers know them by the *nom de plume* of Emma Lathen.

The hero of these novels is John Putnam Thatcher, senior vice president of Sloan Guaranty Trust in New York. Over the course of many books, Thatcher has become a legendary sleuth, with a lively team of characters to assist him: Miss Corsa, his loyal secretary, and fellow bankers Everett Gabler and Charlie Trinkham. In each book Thatcher becomes involved in a financial matter that not only affects his bank but also sets the scene for murder. The authors have a distinctive talent for writing clearly and entertainingly about complicated financial intrigues, for combining these business matters with current events, and for creating tightly plotted mysteries that produce fascinating and civilized novels. The first Lathen novel was *Banking on Death* (Macmillan, 1961).

The two authors also have written a few political mysteries under the name **R. B. Dominic**. They feature Ben Safford, a Democratic congressman from Ohio. As in the Lathen novels, the authors have created detailed and realistic backdrops for each book and have surrounded Safford with a spirited group of professional colleagues and crime-solvers.

MacLeod, Charlotte/Craig, Alisa • MacLeod's novels are humorous, often gently satirical, and imaginative. Under her own name, she writes two series of novels. One features husband-and-wife sleuths Sarah Kelling and Max Bittersohn, who are often helped by some of the more eccentric Boston Brahmins of the Kelling clan. MacLeod also writes the Peter Shandy series, set in rural Balaclava County, Massachusetts, in which some very odd academics at Balaclava Agricultural College, along with Professor Peter Shandy and his wife, Helen, manage to solve dastardly crimes. MacLeod has a great fondness for the stranger byways of the English language, and her unusual mysteries are delightfully daffy.

MacLeod also writes two series of Canadian mysteries under the pseudonym **Alisa Craig**. The Grub-and-Stakers series recounts the dizzy adventures of the Grub-and-Stake Gardening and Roving Club, in Lobelia Falls, Ontario. Another series focuses on Royal Canadian Mounted Police officer Madoc Rhys; his wife Janet; and the unconventional and musical Rhys family.

McCrumb, Sharyn • McCrumb has written three series of books, two of which are fairly typical mystery series, while the most recent series of novels merges mysterious elements with an emphasis on regional background and local history in a most pleasing way.

The books featuring forensic anthropologist Elizabeth MacPherson are light, frothy novels at the outset of this first series. Although Elizabeth solves murders with her forensic knowledge, she also concerns herself with British royalty in *The Windsor Knot* (Ballantine, 1990) and participates in a hilarious mystery tour in *Missing Susan* (Ballantine, 1991). The later MacPherson novels, including the Agatha Award-winning *If I'd Killed Him When I Met Him...* (Ballantine, 1995), are darker and more intense.

McCrumb also wrote a pair of mystery-science fiction novels featuring professor and writer Jay Omega and his feisty sidekick Marion Farley. The Edgar Award-winning *Bimbos of the Death Sun* (TSR, 1988) is a sharply satirical view of a science fiction convention, with an attendant murder.

With *If Ever I Return, Pretty Peggy-O* (Scribner, 1990) McCrumb began publishing increasingly mainstream novels that tell mesmerising stories set in Appalachian Mountains communities. These are often called "the Ballad series," as each book's title comes from a traditional ballad of the region. The hauntingly lovely *She Walks These Hills* (Scribner, 1994), which won the Agatha, Macavity, and Anthony Awards for Best Novel, certainly shows how talented and imaginative a writer McCrumb has become over the years. Her books are not to be missed.

Meyers, Annette • Corporate shenanigans, murder, and theatrical intrigues combine to make lively entertainment in Annette Meyers's mysteries. The Wall Street partnership of headhunters Xenia Smith and Leslie Wetzon not only finds jobs for stockbrokers but also solutions to baffling crimes in the business world. Smith is a shallow, greedy, manipulative yuppie; Wetzon is a former chorus dancer who is warm, caring, and loyal. Wetzon is an amateur sleuth and the real star of the stories, and everybody, including Wetzon herself, continually wonders why she puts up with her difficult partner. As well as creating memorable characters in her mismatched duo, Meyers has devised vibrant New York settings for her mysteries. Some of the best novels in this series are the ones with theatrical backdrops, such as *Murder: the Musical* (Doubleday, 1993), in which Meyers draws upon her own experience in the theater to tell a story of murder on Broadway. Readers will need to check libraries and used bookstores for most of these works.

For an entry on **Maan Meyers**, the pseudonym of Annette and Martin Mcyers, see the section "Once Upon a Crime."

Oliphant, B. J./Orde, A. J. • Oliphant is a pseudonym for science fiction writer Sheri S. Tepper, who writes a second mystery series under the pseudonym A. J. Orde. Oliphant's series character is crusty and intrepid Colorado rancher Shirley McClintock, who debuted in *Dead in the Scrub* (Fawcett, 1990), which was an Edgar nominee for Best Paperback Original. After spending a number of years in Washington, D.C., in an influential position, the fifty-something, six-foot-two Shirley has returned to the ranch her parents left her. Intolerant of fools, with a razor-sharp mind, Shirley is a natural when it comes to ferreting out the truth behind mysterious deaths. Shirley also has strong opinions on many subjects, and she gives these opinions free reign in each book. Oliphant/Orde's other series character, Jason Lynx, is much the same in this regard. Writing as Orde, the author has created another complex and intriguing character. Mysteriously orphaned, Lynx was taken in as an adolescent by a well-to-do Jewish businessman, who has turned his interior design business over to Jason when the series begins, with *A Little Neighborhood Murder* (Doubleday, 1990). In the third book of the series, *Death for Old Times' Sake* (Doubleday, 1992), Orde finally reveals the secret of Lynx's past. Literate and thought-provoking, both these series offer rewarding reading.

Page, Katherine Hall • Winner of the Agatha for Best First Novel for *The Body in the Belfry* (St. Martin's Press, 1990), Page has quickly become a favorite with readers of the traditional mystery. Page's series character is Faith Sibley Fairchild, the daughter of a minister and now married to a minister and living in the small Massachusetts town of Aleford. Before her marriage, Faith had been an exclusive caterer in Manhattan ("Have Faith"). She's making an adjustment to life in a small town with her husband, Tom, and their small son Ben. Something of a food snob, Faith is nevertheless a charming character as she comments inwardly on the food habits of her fellow townspeople and other amusing information about small-town life. Page handles the conventions of the traditional mystery novel, with its enclosed setting and relatively small cast of characters, very well. The atmosphere of the small town is an effective backdrop for the series, though Page often takes her characters farther afield: to Maine in *The Body in the Kelp* (St. Martin's Press, 1991) and to France in *The Body in the Vestibule* (St. Martin's Press, 1992).

Papazoglou, Orania • See **Haddam, Jane**.

Peters, Elizabeth • The celebrated novelist and Egyptologist Barbara Mertz uses two pseudonyms for her best-selling mysteries and suspense novels: Elizabeth Peters and Barbara Michaels.

Under the Peters name, Mertz writes books about Vicky

Bliss, an art historian; Jacqueline Kirby, a librarian and romance novelist; and Amelia Peabody Emerson, a Victorian archaeologist and adventurer (for the last series, see the section "Once Upon a Crime"). Although each heroine is very much her own woman, they share some common attributes: They are lively, smart, and adventuresome women who solve mysteries in exotic locations.

The first Vicky Bliss novel is *Borrower of the Night* (Dodd, Mead, 1973). Vicky works in a German museum with her rotund and ebullient boss, Herr Schmidt, and they both like nothing better than an adventure with the mysterious Sir John Smythe, a charming rogue and art forger. Vicky appears for an Egyptian adventure in the Agatha Award-nominated *Night Train to Memphis* (Warner, 1994).

The first Jacqueline Kirby book is *The Seventh Sinner* (Dodd Mead, 1972). Not at all the stereotypical librarian, Kirby is a middle-aged woman who thoroughly enjoys her forays into adventure and mystery. In *Die for Love* (Congdon & Weed, 1984), for example, she decides to make money by writing a swashbuckling romance novel and does her research (as well as finding murder) at a hilariously described convention of romance fans. *Naked Once More* (Warner, 1989), the fourth Kirby novel, won the Agatha Award for Best Novel.

Some of Peters's best nonseries mysteries are *Summer of the Dragon* (Dodd, Mead, 1979); *Devil-May-Care* (Dodd, Mead, 1977), a wicked spoof of her own Barbara Michaels novels; and *Legend in Green Velvet* (Dodd, Mead, 1976).

For the romantic suspense novels written under the name Barbara Michaels see the section "The Road to Manderley." For the Amelia Peabody Emerson books consult the section "Once Upon a Crime."

Pickard, Nancy • Jenny Cain is the lively, thoughtful protagonist created by Pickard in her series of mysteries. Jenny is the director of a local philanthropic foundation in Port Frederick, Massachusetts (a town known locally as Poor Fred), and many of the crimes she becomes involved with are linked to her work. Her dysfunctional family haunts her, especially her mentally ill mother and her irresponsible father. Jenny marries a policeman, Geof Bushfield, and he tries with little success to protect her from the grim realities of life and crime. The mysteries are generally set in the fictional New England seaport of Port Frederick, although Jenny occasionally goes on the road. In the Agatha and Anthony Award-winning *I.O.U.* (Pocket Books, 1991), one of Pickard's most acclaimed works, Jenny tries to come to grips with the death of her mother and with the cause of her mother's long-term mental illness.

Pickard also has written *The 27 Ingredient Chili con Carne Murders* (Delacorte, 1993), which is based on a manuscript left by Virginia Rich at the time of her death. It is a noteworthy blending of the writing styles of Pickard and Rich, with Rich's series protagonist, 'Genia Potter, finding murder on her Arizona ranch.

Rice, Craig • Craig Rice was a pen name used by Georgiana Ann Randolph. She also wrote a few books under the names Daphne Sanders and Michael Venning, and she was the ghostwriter of mysteries published under the names of celebrities Gypsy Rose Lee and George Sanders. At one time Craig Rice was one of the most famous mystery writers in America, with her picture on the cover of *Time* magazine in 1946. Her books continue to be reprinted, and many contemporary readers enjoy the humorous crime capers and outlandish exploits of Chicago lawyer John J. Malone and his sidekicks Jake and Helene Justus. Malone, a short, cigar-chomping lawyer, is always ready to help beautiful women or old friends in trouble, especially if he can get enough money from them to pay off his bar tab. His friend Jake owns a nightclub and is married to the beautiful heiress Helene. Jake and Helene love to play the sleuth and are capable of almost any amount of drunken mischief while helping out Malone with his cases. The books are set mostly in Chicago, with strongly realized settings, such as Joe the Angel's City Hall Bar, where many of the characters hang out. Rice's writing is sharp and crisp, and the stories are fast-moving and furiously funny. The mysteries have close parallels to the screwball comedies that were so popular in 1930s and '40s movies such as *Bringing Up Baby* and *His Girl Friday*.

Rice also wrote several mysteries about the adventures of Bingo Riggs and Handsome Kusak, street photographers and con men. Readers will need to check libraries and used bookstores for most of these works.

Rinehart, Mary Roberts • See her entry in the section "The Road to Manderley."

Sanders, Lawrence • For a series of lighthearted crime novels, Sanders created a new hero, Archy McNally, who first appears in *McNally's Secret* (Putnam, 1992). Archy McNally is a thirtysomething playboy-turned-sleuth in Palm Beach, Florida. He works as an "investigator" for his father, a staid and respectable attorney; Archy is the chief and sole member of the Discreet Inquiries Department of McNally and Son.

Charming, attractive, rich, and occasionally a bit feckless, Archy dashes his way through each case with considerable aplomb. He has quite a way with the ladies, though he has his heart bruised sometimes. After an affair turns sour in *McNally's Secret*, he later picks up with an old flame, Connie Garcia, who's more than a match for him. Archy's cases involve mystery and mayhem, and often murder, among the wealthy and famous of Palm Beach society, and Sanders offers the reader glimpses of a lifestyle that many of us can only dream about. Frothy, funny, and fast-paced, the adventures of Archy McNally make splendid escape reading.

Taylor, Phoebe Atwood/Tilton, Alice • Creator of two distinctive series of mysteries with a definite New England flavor, Taylor produced thirty-three novels in the space of her twenty years as a full-time writer. The first of these series featured Asey Mayo, the "Codfish Sherlock," as he was dubbed. Asey Mayo hails from Wellfleet, on Cape Cod, and he is every inch a native of the Cape. Tough, clever, and independent, Asey makes a formidable foe for the murderers who commit crimes anywhere around. There is considerable humor in this series as well, for Taylor delights in creating colorful and unusual characters, and the dialogue is as witty as the pace is fast in the stories. As a whole the Asey Mayo books are a treasure trove of humor and local culture of the Cape in the 1930s and '40s. Asey debuts in *The Cape Cod Mystery* (Bobbs Merrill, 1931).

Under the name **Alice Tilton**, Taylor wrote eight novels about Leonidas Witherall, a look-alike for William Shakespeare; hence he is often called "Bill" by his friends. This series is even more fast-paced and farcical than the Asey Mayo books; they are truly screwball comedy brought to the printed page. First in the series is the appropriately titled *Beginning with a Bash* (Collins, 1937; Norton, 1972).

Tilton, Alice • See **Taylor, Phoebe Atwood**.

Truman, Margaret • The daughter of President Harry S. Truman knows her Washington well, and she has written interesting mysteries set in and around the nation's capital. Famous Washington landmarks such as the White House and the Supreme Court building make good sites for murder in her classic puzzle mysteries. Some of Truman's novels feature the sleuthing partnership of Mac Smith and Annabel Reed. Mac is a professor of law and Annabel is a former attorney who now owns an art gallery. Even in the nonseries books, Truman often adds a dash of romance to accompany the detective work. Of course, political intrigue is always in the air in Washington and it is ever-present in these stories as well. Truman has an insider's knowledge of political processes, and she shows her intimate acquaintance with the details and minutiae of White House life, for example, in *Murder in the White House* (Arbor, 1980).

Zubro, Mark Richard • A schoolteacher in Illinois, Zubro is the author of two series of mysteries that feature gay men as the protagonists. Zubro's first novel, *A Simple Suburban Murder* (St. Martin's Press, 1989), introduced schoolteacher Tom Mason and his lover, Scott Carpenter, who live in suburban Chicago. Tom is fairly open about his sexuality, but Scott, a professional baseball player, is afraid to come out of the closet, early in the series. In their first adventure in sleuthing, Tom and Scott work on the puzzle of who murdered one of Tom's fellow teachers. Was it the man's missing son? The duo uncover some unsavory doings before they finally reach the answers they were seeking. Many of the books in this series feature troubled teens, with Tom and Scott doing their best to help set things right, all the while working through their own domestic problems. Zubro presents an entertaining twist on the conventional detective duo with Tom and Scott.

For Zubro's series of police procedurals, see the section "Hill Street Blues."

For Further Reading • Sarah Andrews; J. S. Borthwick; Rita Mae Brown; P. M. Carlson (the Maggie Ryan series); Frances Crane; Camilla Crespi; Elizabeth Daly; William DeAndrea; Jane Dentinger; Doris Miles Disney; Carole Epstein; Jay Finkelstein; Jacqueline Girdner; Tim Hemlin; Jonnie Jacobs; Toni L. P. Kelner; William X. Kienzle; Virginia Lanier; Frances and Richard Lockridge; Marlys Millhiser; Donna Huston Murray; Tamar Myers; BarbaraNeely; Hugh Pentecost; Ellery Queen; Lev Raphael; Gillian Roberts; Alan Russell (the Hotel Detective series); Barbara Burnett Smith; Aaron Marc Stein; Karen Hanson Stuyck; Lee Thayer; S. S. Van Dine; Carolyn Wells; Polly Whitney; Barbara Wilson.

Movies • the Ellery Queen movies; *Having Wonderful Crime*; *Home, Sweet Homicide*; *Lady of Burlesque*; *The Mad Miss Manton*; *Manhattan Murder Mystery*; the *Mr. and Mrs. North* movies; the *Philo Vance* movies; *Shadow of a Doubt*; the *Thin Man* series.

TV series • *Diagnosis, Murder*; *Ellery Queen*; *The Hardy Boys*; *Hart* *to Hart; Mr. and Mrs. North; Mrs. Columbo (Kate Loves a Mystery); Murder, She Wrote; Nancy Drew; Scarecrow and Mrs. King.*

Murder, She Wrote: Older Detectives

Just because a detective is an older man or woman (that is, a senior citizen) doesn't mean that he or she doesn't have the necessary brainpower with which to solve a puzzling murder case. Agatha Christie's Miss Marple, that clever spinster detective, demonstrated that her knowledge of human behavior equaled that of any professional detective, and she could solve any puzzle put before her. Many of the older detectives in mystery fiction have been women, perhaps as a result of the popularity of Christie and Miss Marple. One of the most enduring is Jessica Fletcher, portrayed with grace and style for more than a decade by Angela Lansbury. Though the presence of Jessica Fletcher undeniably meant that someone would soon die, nevertheless Mrs. Fletcher was there to nose out the truth and help bring the villain to justice. "Older" doesn't mean less clever, as the detectives in this section demonstrate with great ease!

Arnold, Margot • Far-flung locales, a duo of highly educated—and highly opinionated—sleuths, and stories full of anthropological and archaeological detail are the specialty of the pseudonymous Arnold. Her series detectives, Penny Spring and Toby Glendower, longtime friends and colleagues, offer interesting contrasts. Penny, an American long resident in England, is a world-famous anthropologist. Toby (actually Sir Tobias) is

Welsh and equally renowned as an archaeologist. The best of friends, they quibble and squabble with each other as each new adventure presents itself, and between them they bring the culprits to justice. Their first case, *Exit Actors, Dying* (Playboy, 1979; Foul Play/Countryman, 1988), took them to Greece. Subsequent tales took them to Scotland, Hawaii, Cape Cod, Brittany, and New Orleans, among other places. The armchair-traveling mystery reader will find much to enjoy in the company of Spring and Glendower, courtesy of Margot Arnold.

Beaton, M. C. • For Beaton's mysteries featuring Agatha Raisin, check the entry in the section "Calling Scotland Yard."

Borton, D. B. • Borton is a *nom de plume* used by Lynette Carpenter, a young woman author who has managed to get into the head of an older woman character and portray her with warmth and affection. Cat Caliban is the amusing, lively heroine of a series of light mysteries that nonetheless deal intelligently with topical issues, such as the plight of the homeless in America's cities.

Cat is a middle-class widow in the suburbs of Cincinnati who is looking for a way to get meaning and excitement back into her life after many dull years of marriage and motherhood. Like most mothers and wives, Cat always has been good at investigating unusual events, so she decides to adopt the life of a private investigator. She buys a small apartment house in the inner city, and researches her new job at the public library. She is still learning her trade in *One for the Money* (Berkley, 1993) when she finds the body of a bag lady in the next apartment. In this and her next few cases, she acquires an eccentric band of assistants who are her friends, tenants, local homeless people, and the neighborhood kids. Cat Caliban is not the typical old-lady sleuth, unless the old lady is likely to be a member of the Gray Panthers and the local karate club.

Carvic, Heron • The late Heron Carvic created one of the most endearingly dotty sleuths in mystery fiction. Before his death in 1980 Carvic penned five novels about the English spinster Emily Dorothea Seeton, retired teacher of art and slightly unworldly catalyst of crime-solving. Miss Seeton is a true "innocent." She doesn't see the evil in anyone or anything, going blithely on her way but somehow managing to foil the dastardly criminals despite her ignorance of their true intentions. The first of Carvic's five novels about Miss Seeton is *Picture Miss Seeton* (Harper, 1968). Since Carvic's death, the series has been continued, with the permission of his estate. **Hampton Charles** penned three novels, and since then the series has been continued by **Hamilton Crane**, a pen name for **Sarah J. Mason**. The small village of Plummergen, with its eccentricities and gossipmongering, much of it revolving around poor Miss Seeton, lives on, and Miss Seeton continues to be involved in humorous criminous escapades. With her umbrella firmly in hand, the "Battling Brolly" crosses paths with criminals, never quite realizing just how lethal a secret weapon she continues to be in the unorthodox arsenal of Chief Superintendent Delphick of Scotland Yard. Mason's sprightly style, with its attention to the oddities and quirks of the language, is well suited to the unusual Miss Seeton. Under her own name, Mason wrote *Let's Talk of Wills* (St. Martin's Press, 1985), a mystery in the traditional English vein. Beginning with *Murder in the Maze* (Berkley,

1993), Mason begins a second series featuring Detective Superintendent Trewley and Sergeant Stone of the Allingham constabulary. Many of the same qualities that are present in the Seeton books are present in this new series as well. Those with a taste for the eccentric English mystery novel will find Mason/Crane just their cup of tea.

Charles, Hampton • See **Carvic, Heron**.

Christie, Agatha • See the section "The Butler Did It."

Christmas, Joyce • After writing several novels, some nonfiction books, and children's plays, Christmas turned to the mystery novel. Her series detective is Lady Margaret Priam, a genteel Englishwoman living in New York City. In her first appearance, *Suddenly in Her Sorbet* (Fawcett, 1988), Lady Margaret is attending a charity fundraiser when someone poisons the organizer, a *grande dame* of New York society. Aided by her young friend and fellow socialite, Prince Paul Castrocani, Lady Margaret dives into the case. Along the way she becomes interested in the investigating police officer, detective Sam de Vere, and in subsequent novels the two pursue a romantic relationship. Christmas handles the intriguing social world of New York City with deft skill, her slightly ironic eye yielding the reader quiet amusement at the foibles of the rich and often tasteless. Though much of the action in the series takes place in New York and its environs, Lady Margaret occasionally investigates farther afield. In one novel, *Friend or Faux* (Fawcett, 1991), she returns to England to help her brother, the Earl of Brayfield, solve the murder of one of his guests.

Recently Christmas has begun a second series, starring retired businesswoman Betty Trenka. In her debut, *This Business Is Murder* (Fawcett, 1993), Betty moves to Connecticut to start her retirement, but quickly bored, she takes a temporary job at a local business and turns sleuth when someone starts murdering the employees. Nosy, competent, and worldly, Betty demonstrates that older women make excellent detectives.

Crane, Hamilton • See **Carvic, Heron**.

George, Anne • A former Alabama State Poet and a Pulitzer Prize nominee for poetry, George is currently spinning humorous tales of murder set in Birmingham, Alabama. The narrator of the stories is Patricia Anne Hollowell, a recently retired English teacher who is sixty years old and happily married to her businessman husband, Fred. Patricia Anne's sister, Mary Alice Crane, is as tall and outspoken as Patricia Anne is compact and quiet. Between the two of them they manage to get themselves involved in various murderous goings-on. In their debut, *Murder on a Girls' Night Out* (Avon, 1996), which won the Agatha Award for Best First Novel, Mary Alice buys a country and western bar, the Skoot 'n Boot. Nobody expects a body to turn up, but when it does, the sisters dig in and solve the crime. In *Murder Runs in the Family* (Avon, 1997), the sisters discover after a family wedding that genealogy is a deadly business, and you never know who might kill to keep shameful ancestors a dark secret. The interaction between the sisters and the lively, realistic dialogue make this series enormously appealing to readers who like their mysteries humorous and on the cozy side. Patricia Anne and Mary Alice prove that life past sixty is fun and full of adventure.

Gilman, Dorothy • Who would ever suspect that a lovely little old grandmother was really a spy for the CIA? That is the premise behind Gilman's long-running and enormously popular series of novels about Emily Pollifax. Bored with widowhood and retirement, Mrs. Pollifax decided one day to apply at the CIA to be a spy. At first they scoffed at her, but upon rethinking the situation, they decided she might just work. After all, who would ever imagine she was a spy? Thus the redoubtable Mrs. Pollifax was off on her first adventure, *The Unexpected Mrs. Pollifax* (Doubleday, 1966). Thanks to the CIA, Mrs. Pollifax (and her fans) have trotted around the globe over the past three decades, having many adventures, in places such as Albania, Mexico, Switzerland, Africa, China, Morocco, and Italy.

In addition to her series of Pollifax novels, Gilman has written other popular stories of mystery and adventure, like *Incident at Badamya* (Doubleday, 1989) and *Caravan* (Doubleday, 1992). Other popular nonseries books include the suspense novel *The Tightrope Walker* (Doubleday, 1979) and the humorous *A Nun in the Closet* (Doubleday, 1975).

Gray, Gallagher • The morning after he has retired as personnel manager of a prestigious Wall Street bank, T. S. Hubbert receives a telephone call seeking his help in solving the murder of one of the bank's partners. With the people skills honed from thirty years in personnel selection and management, T. S. wades into the fray, assisted by his octogenarian aunt, Lillian Hubbert. "Auntie Lil," as she is affectionately called, spent more than sixty years in the fashion industry, and she has a flair for the dramatic that Bette Davis would have envied. Together, T. S. and Auntie Lil make a formidable detective duo. As the series progresses, they gain assistance from secondary characters such as Herbert Wong, a retired messenger for T. S.'s old firm, and Lilah Cheswick, the widow of the murder victim in the first book. The pseudonymous Gray, who is in reality Katy Munger, has created vivid and interesting characters for her series. Readers will enjoy the books as much for keeping up with the exploits of Auntie Lil as they will for solving the intricately designed puzzles of "whodunit" that Gray has created. The first book in the series is *Hubbert & Lil: Partners in Crime* (Fine, 1991).

Hart, Carolyn G. • After winning numerous awards for her first series featuring amateur sleuth Annie Laurance Darling, Hart created a new series, starring a feisty older woman, Henrietta (Henrie O) O'Dwyer Collins. Henrie O is a clever journalist from Oklahoma (Hart, too, worked as a journalist in Oklahoma), and she follows her inquiring nose into some complex and puzzling situations. The first novel in the series is *Dead Man's Island* (Bantam, 1993), which won an Agatha Award for Best Novel and aired as a television movie with Barbara Eden and William Shatner. Henrie O is called in by an old flame to investigate a series of mysterious happenings at his estate on an island off the coast of South Carolina. When the inevitable happens, Henrie O solves the murder, despite the ever-present threat of a hurricane. In *Scandal at Fair Haven* (Bantam, 1994) Henrie gets mixed up in murders in an exclusive Nashville suburb. Hart demonstrates that murder in suburbia can be just as nasty as murder on the mean streets any day. Henrie O is a forceful, intelligent, and effective sleuth, putting her years of experience in journalism to good use. She can be tough and uncompromising, just the sort of ally one needs in a tight corner.

For Hart's first series of amateur detective novels see the section "Nancy, Frank, and Joe Grow Up."

Haywood, Gar Anthony • Besides creating a series of hard-boiled private eye novels, Haywood also writes humorous mysteries starring Joe and Dottie Loudermilk, an elderly African-American couple who are traveling the country in their classic Airstream trailer. But their five adult children are still capable of getting into serious trouble, so Joe and Dottie must, of course, help them out. The stories are told, engagingly enough, from the point of view of Dottie, and Haywood does a great job of getting into the head of an older woman, a wife and mother who worries about her kids and loves her sometimes overbearing and impulsive husband, and who knows all their faults but loves them anyway. The Loudermilk books are funny, warm, and appealing traditional mysteries. First in the series is *Going Nowhere Fast* (Putnam, 1994).

Lewis, Sherry • Fred Vickery is over seventy, and his doctor has warned him to take better care of himself. Fred's daughter Margaret fusses over him, and Fred tries not to annoy her. But things just keep happening, and Fred can't help himself, as when, out for a morning stroll, Fred finds a dead body in the lake. The dead woman, Joan Cavanaugh, may have committed suicide, but Fred doesn't believe it, and he's determined that the murderer won't go free, despite the cost to his own health and well-being. So he starts nosing around his small town of Cutler, Colorado. Despite warnings from his good friend the sheriff, Fred persists in his investigation in *No Place for Secrets* (Berkley, 1995). Lewis draws her small town with warmth, knowing full well that such a venue can be a hotbed for the types of secrets that can lead to murder. Inquisitive and tenacious, Fred Vickery demonstrates that brainpower doesn't diminish with age, even though he can't do some things as quickly as he once could. But then, if the doctor would only let him have caffeine! A charming series, the Fred Vickery stories will please those who have enjoyed the adventures of Jessica Fletcher and other older sleuths.

Matteson, Stefanie • Matteson's heroine is Charlotte Graham, an Oscar-winning film and stage actress who lives in New York City. Charlotte is a lively character who might remind readers of Katharine Hepburn or Bette Davis. As well as being an intelligent and observant sleuth, Charlotte is a movie star of the old school: elegant, aristocratic, and strong-willed. The first book in Matteson's series, *Murder at the Spa* (Charter/Diamond, 1990), takes place at a chic spa in upstate New York, where a client is murdered during treatment. Matteson provides a detailed background of the operations of a health spa, and she recounts the history of American spas as part of her scene-setting. *Murder at Teatime* (Diamond, 1991) is set on a secluded island off the coast of Maine; this novel includes plenty of herbal lore and information on rare books, especially early herbals. *Murder on the Cliff* (Diamond, 1991) takes place in Newport, Rhode Island, and *Murder on the Silk Road* (Diamond, 1992), one of the best in the series, takes Charlotte to China for further adventures. These novels are notable for the research Matteson has done to provide detailed backgrounds for each, and her skill in weaving her research into vivid, interesting backdrops for her stories.

McInerny, Ralph/Quill, Monica • For many years a professor of philosophy at the University of Notre Dame, McInerny has also written two series of mysteries about older sleuths, Father Dowling and Sister Mary Teresa "M. T." Dempsey, the latter under the pseudonym Monica Quill. Father Roger Dowling is a parish priest in the fictional town of Fox River, somewhere to the west of Chicago. A strong sense of Catholicism pervades the series. Father Dowling is a mostly conservative Catholic, and while he is interested in seeing justice done when he turns sleuth, he is also interested in the spiritual welfare of those he is trying to help. First in the series is *Her Death of Cold* (Vanguard, 1977). Veteran actor Tom Bosley portrayed Father Dowling in the television series.

The irascible Sister M. T. Dempsey, elderly and cantankerous, is known as Attila the Nun. She, like Father Dowling, is a traditionalist and devoted to the ways of the old church. She lives in her defunct order's house in Chicago with a couple of her younger associates from the order. One of them, Sister Kim, acts Archie Goodwin to her Nero Wolfe, bringing her information so she may cogitate and solve the crimes. First in the series is *Not a Blessed Thing!* (Vanguard, 1981).

In addition to these two series, McInerny has written a number of books about lawyer Andrew Broom, the first of which is *Cause and Effect* (Atheneum, 1987).

O'Marie, Sister Carol Anne • Perhaps the only nun actively publishing crime fiction, Sister Carol Anne has created a popular character in her nun detective, Sister Mary Helen. At seventy-five, Sister Mary Helen is nominally retired, but in her first appearance, in *A Novena for Murder* (Scribner, 1984), the good sister is anything but retired as she pokes her nose into the murder of a history professor at Mount St. Francis College for Women in San Francisco. With the wisdom—and the wit—that have come from fifty years' service to her order, Sister Mary Helen and her cohorts, the other nuns and San Francisco homicide detectives Kate Murphy and Dennis Gallagher, solve the murder. Sister Mary Helen, who loves murder mysteries and disguises them with her prayerbook cover, is a charming character. Like other older women sleuths, the good sister proves that age does not necessarily diminish one's capacities, and in this case, certainly, age has provided a thorough understanding of human nature and its many foibles and follies.

Authors of Clerical Sleuths

Veronica Black; G. K. Chesterton; Margaret Frazer; Kate Gallison (the Mother Lavinia Grey series); Andrew Greeley; D. M. Greenwood; Lee Harris; Isabelle Holland; Harry Kemelman; William X. Kienzle; Ralph McInerny; Sister Carol Anne O'Marie; Ellis Peters; Monica Quill; Father Brad Reynolds; Joseph Telushkin; Peter Tremayne; Barbara Whitehead.

Quill, Monica • See McInerny, Ralph.

Roosevelt, Elliott • The late Elliott Roosevelt wrote a series of mysteries with his mother, first lady Eleanor Roosevelt, as the amateur sleuth. The mysteries are replete with political infighting and insider details of life at the White House. Roosevelt depicts his parents in their dignified, public roles as president and first lady, but he also tells us small details about their lives and personalities. We learn about FDR's daily routines as president, and even more about Eleanor's love for people and her compassionate spirit. Roosevelt gives us a very affectionate look at his famous parents and at the great political and historical events of the 1930s and '40s. The heroine is always called "Mrs. Roosevelt," everyone treats her with respect, and an atmosphere of great intelligence and dignity clings to her. President Roosevelt is depicted more tangentially as remote, idiosyncratic, and ferociously busy. Mrs. Roosevelt's well-known concern for the average person and her role as FDR's conscience in matters such as racial discrimination are part of the backdrop in each of the criminal cases she helps to solve. She always wants to get to the bottom of the problem in order to help someone. Historic personages such as Churchill, Truman, Nelson Rockefeller, Molotov, and the British royal family wander in and out of the stories and sometimes are even suspects. Roosevelt creates works in the time-honored tradition of puzzle mysteries, with classic elements like charts, lists of characters, maps, and the inevitable gathering of suspects at the end of the story. These are cozy, well-researched, and interesting mysteries.

Sawyer, Corinne Holt • Little old lady detectives have been a staple of mystery fiction almost from the beginning, and Sawyer has taken a stock character and added an enjoyable spin. Her series, set in a posh retirement community in Southern California, features not one but two "little old ladies" who are nothing like stereotypes. One of the main characters is the peppery and often irritating Angela Benbow, widow of an admiral. Though she might look like a small, delicate blossom, Angela is just about as tough as old boots. Her boon companion is Caledonia Wingate, also the widow of an admiral, but physically the opposite of Angela. Tall, imposing, and never afraid to throw her considerable weight around, Caledonia serves as an effective damper on Angela's sometimes ill-conceived plans. When murder strikes their exclusive retirement community in *The J. Alfred Prufrock Murders* (Fine, 1988), Angela, Caledonia, and a small circle of their friends decide to investigate. Eventually the officer in charge of the case, suave and attractive—but young—Lieutenant Martinez, allows them to "help." Sawyer writes with clear eyes and no false sentimentality about the elderly. Her characters are engaging and believable, her plots solidly constructed, and her humor restrained but effectively employed. The first novel in the series was an Agatha nominee for Best First Malice Domestic Mystery Novel. Readers will need to look for some of these works in libraries and used bookstores.

Squire, **Elizabeth Daniels** • Squire is a newspaperwoman from North Carolina who now writes amusing, light mysteries. Her first novel, *Kill the Messenger* (St. Martin's Press, 1990), is set at a small newspaper where the owner-editor has been poisoned just as a major conglomerate makes a buyout bid. In the traditional mode, everyone around the victim is a suspect and has a secret to hide.

With *Who Killed What's-Her-Name?* (Berkley, 1994), Squire began a series of mysteries with Peaches Dann, who manages to be a successful amateur sleuth in spite of having a terrible memory. Aside from her investigative activities,

Peaches is collecting all the coping mechanisms she's learned over the years to write a book called *How to Survive Without a Memory*. Her feisty eighty-three-year-old father is forgetful, too, and on some of his bad days he's convinced there are burglars on his roof. His fears may be all too accurate when his sister is killed and left in his backyard. In this first case and in subsequent ones, Peaches finds that she actually can use some of her memory tricks to help solve murders. Aided and abetted by her close friend Ted, a semiretired history teacher, Peaches uses computer databases and solves crimes with aplomb. These charming cozies have interesting settings in the mountains of North Carolina, and fun advice on how to improve a wayward memory. Squire's plots are always well constructed, and she provides thought-provoking commentaries on modern superstition and regional customs as well.

For Further Reading • Irene Allen; Marian Babson (Evangeline Sinclair and Trixie Dolan series); Richard Barth; Eleanor Boylan; Simon Brett (Mrs. Pargeter series); Emily Brightwell; Pat Burden; W. J. Burley; John Dickson Carr; G. K. Chesterton; Ann Cleeves; V. C. Clinton-Baddeley; Leslie Ford; Jane Haddam; Mary Bowen Hall; Kathleen Moore Knight; Graham Landrum; Nancy Livingston; Gladys Mitchell; Gwen Moffat; Kate Morgan; Haughton Murphy; Robert Nordan; D. B. Olsen; Stuart Palmer; Virginia Rich; Serita Stevens and Rayanne Moore; Patricia Wentworth; James Yaffe.

Movies • *Miss Pinkerton*; *Mrs. Pollifax—Spy*; *Murder at the Gallop*; *Murder Most Foul*; *Murder, She Said*; *The Penguin Pool Murder* (the first of six Hildegarde Withers movies, followed by *Murder on the Blackboard*, *Murder on a Honeymoon*, *Murder on a Bridle Path*, *The Plot Thickens*, and *Forty Naughty Girls*).

TV shows • *Diagnosis: Murder, Fatal Confession: A Father Dowling Mystery, Father Dowling Mysteries, Hetty Wainthropp Investigates,* the Miss Marple series; *Murder, She Wrote, The Snoop Sisters.*

The Butler Did It: English Mysteries

There is something about England—part of that small island of Great Britain that once ruled the world's largest empire—that continues to fascinate mystery readers. Ever since Sherlock Holmes operated out of 221B Baker Street in London, eager readers have devoured countless volumes of mysteries set in England. Ah, England—that placid country where murder seems such a shocking crime! England—that world of small villages and elegant country houses, where the aristocrats and the wealthy happily live their lives, with murder appearing as an uninvited guest to disturb the calm and order.

England has changed much over the past century, when Sherlock Holmes solved his first crime. But readers continue to be fascinated by murder with an English accent. The authors in this section, both classic and contemporary, demonstrate why.

Allingham, Margery • Born into a family of writers in 1904, Margery Allingham entered the only profession that seemed sensible to her. She published her first novel when she was only sixteen, and she went on to have a career as one of the most distinguished crime writers of the twentieth century. Her enduring creation is Albert Campion, who first appeared in *The Black Dudley Murder* (Doubleday, 1929; published in England as *The Crime at Black Dudley*). Something of a minor hood on his first appearance, Campion metamorphoses into a more respectable guise by his second appearance, in *Mystery Mile* (Doubleday, 1930). Campion is actually a member of a very distinguished—and straitlaced—English family, and his antics necessitate the use of the "Campion" pseudonym. Helped (or hindered, as the case may be) by his manservant, Lugg, Campion becomes involved in many an entertaining adventure. *Police at the Funeral* (Doubleday, 1932) finds him solving the mysterious murders of an eccentric family in Cambridge, while in *Kingdom of Death* (Doubleday, 1933; also published as *Sweet Danger* and *The Fear Sign*), Campion meets the young woman, Amanda Fitton, who eventually becomes his wife.

Campion was never as eccentric as Dorothy L. Sayers's creation Lord Peter Wimsey, nor so colorful as Agatha Christie's Hercule Poirot, but he was always a solidly reassuring presence in each and every adventure he undertook. Also, unlike the others of his ilk, he aged in real-time fashion, so that the latter books in the series show him as a man in later middle age. Throughout the books, Allingham's sense of humor is an important element. As the series progressed, however, that sense of humor turned blacker, culminating in what many consider Allingham's masterpiece, *The Tiger in the Smoke* (Doubleday, 1952). After Allingham's death from cancer in 1966, her husband, Philip Youngman Carter, who collaborated with her in working out plots for her books, completed one novel, *Cargo of Eagles* (Morrow, 1968), and penned two further adventures for Albert Campion. The actor Peter Davison portrayed Campion for a number of Allingham novels and stories filmed and shown on PBS's *Mystery!*. He was ably seconded by Brian Glover as Lugg. Readers will need to look for some of these works in libraries and used bookstores.

Babson, Marian • Babson is an American author living in England. She writes traditional English mysteries that have a fascinating blend of psychological nuance and unconventional characters. Earlier novels sometimes feature Douglas Perkins, a partner in the London public relations firm of Perkins & Tate, as a series character. The Perkins series begins with *Cover-up Story* (St. Martin's Press, 1988). Recently Babson has concentrated on producing a series of humorous mysteries about Trixie Dolan and Evangeline Sinclair, who were movie stars in the Golden Age of Hollywood. The two actors, who are still lively and acerbic, may be looking for work that will revive their careers, but they never can resist snooping about in some enticing murder cases. The series begins with *Reel Murder* (St. Martin's Press, 1986). Babson is also well known for writing smart, charming tales that feature cats, such as *Nine Lives to Murder* (St. Martin's Press, 1994), an amusing mixture of theatrical and feline mystery. Readers will need to look for some of these works in libraries and used bookstores.

Barnard, Robert • Barnard writes mysteries in the classic English style, but he adds to the traditional mix his own distinctive flourishes of humor, ranging from farce to satire. His first novel, *Death of an Old Goat* (Walker, 1977), is a savage satire of Australian academia. Barnard lampoons pretension in every form. A favorite target is the English class system. What would happen if a lower-class branch of the family inherited a noble title and the wealth and estate to go with it? Barnard answers that question with mordant wit in *Corpse in a Gilded Cage* (Scribner, 1984). Barnard has written several novels about Scotland Yard detective Perry Trethowan, beginning with *Death by Sheer Torture* (Scribner, 1982), when Perry has to investigate the murder in his own family, a notorious group of eccentrics. More recently Barnard has written about black police constable Charlie Peace, who first appeared as a second fiddle to Perry Trethowan. In *Death and the Chaste Apprentice* (Scribner, 1989) Charlie is the chief investigator. Later he works in the West Yorkshire area with Superintendent Mike Oddie in *A Fatal Attachment* (Scribner, 1992). Barnard combines wit, style, and psychological acuity in a mix that makes him a truly special vintage. Readers will need to look for some of these works in libraries and used bookstores.

For the historical mysteries Barnard writes as **Bernard Bastable** see the section "Once Upon a Crime."

Bentley, E. C. • One of the seminal figures in the mystery genre, E. C. Bentley is little known today to the general reader, but fans of the classic English mystery novel and even of many of today's amateur sleuths have seen the results of Bentley's influence at work. Bentley was the creator of Philip Trent, who first appeared in *Trent's Last Case* (Century, 1913, first published as *The Woman in Black*). Bentley intended Philip Trent as something of an antidote to the prevailing models of the scientific sleuth and the "great detectives" who were so popular during the first decades of the twentieth century. Trent is a young artist and man about town. He is intelligent but not always as discerning of character as he might be. In *Trent's Last Case* he is hired by a leading London newspaper to aid the police in the murder of one of the world's most powerful businessmen, Sigsbee Manderson. Trent in many ways set the mold for the young-man-about-town type of sleuth, and Dorothy L. Sayers's Lord Peter Wimsey is perhaps the most famous example of Bentley's influence. Trent appeared twice more: in the novel *Trent's Own Case* (Knopf, 1936) and in the short story collection *Trent Intervenes* (Knopf, 1938). Readers will need to look for some of these works in libraries and used bookstores.

Brett, Simon • The creator of two witty, amusing series of mysteries, Brett is also a successful playwright and radio and television producer in his native England. His first series detective is the actor Charles Paris. When he first appears, in *Cast, in Order of Disappearance* (Scribner, 1976), Charles Paris is a moderately successful actor with an established reputation. Not exactly one of the big names in the English theater, he is nevertheless working steadily. As the series progresses, however, Charles's career turns onto a slow downhill slide. With his fondness for Bell's whiskey and his ineptitude when it comes to his personal relationships, Charles seems destined to fail at just about everything. He proves, however, to be an able sleuth, and Brett has kept him employed for more than twenty years now. As a series, the Charles Paris books provide an insider's view of the English theater and television communities, and Brett's mordant, often acid, wit is one of the appeals.

Brett's second series character is the widowed Mrs. Melita Pargeter, whose late husband was a gentlemanly crook. Aided by various shady associates of her husband, Mrs. Pargeter, a sexy and engagingly updated version of Miss Marple, finds herself involved in various mysterious escapades. The first of them is *A Nice Class of Corpse* (Scribner, 1987), a tribute to the classic Golden Age mystery. Mrs. Pargeter's subsequent adventures have departed increasingly from the conventional English mystery, but they remain as entertaining as ever. Readers will need to look for most of Brett's books in libraries and used bookstores.

One of Brett's nonseries novels, *A Shock to the System* (Scribner, 1985), was filmed with Michael Caine in the lead role. Brett himself wrote the screenplay for this excellent movie.

Authors of Actors in Mysteries

Linda Barnes (the Michael Spraggue series); Carol Brennan; P. M. Carlson (the Maggie Ryan series); Jane Dentinger; Ellen Hart (the Jane Lawless series); Ngaio Marsh; Edward Marston (the Elizabethan series); Stefanie Matteson; Annette Meyers; Anne Morice; Barbara Paul; Les Roberts; Dorian Yeager (the Vic Bowering series).

Cannell, Dorothy • Sly, gentle comedy is what Dorothy Cannell does best in her charming mysteries. Most of her books chronicle the life and adventures of Ellie Simons Haskell, amateur sleuth. The first in the series (and Cannell's first novel), *The Thin Woman* (St. Martin's Press, 1984), has been a cult favorite with mystery readers for years. In this eccentric comedy-mystery, Ellie Simons is an overweight interior decorator who somehow falls into a romantic situation straight out of her dreams. The problem is that she has to lose quite a bit of weight and find a hidden treasure in six months to inherit a castle and win her true love. Later in the series, Ellie marries and becomes the harried mother of twins. But she's still a sleuth at heart, even though her family and the rather peculiar members of her unconventional household at Merlin's Court sometimes hinder her efforts just a bit (and sometimes more than that). Cannell's characters are endearingly dotty in the best tradition of English literary eccentrics.

God Save the Queen! (Bantam, 1997) is an irresistibly light and airy confection, with a plot involving a murdered butler, a medieval toilet, an innocent young girl, a set of peculiar aristocrats, and some missing family silver.

Carr, John Dickson/Dickson, Carter • Though American by birth, Carr lived for many years in England, and he chose to set many of his mysteries there. His two chief series characters were both English, and his books fit well into the mold of the classic English mystery novel. Writing as John Dickson Carr, he created Dr. Gideon Fell, who was based, to a great extent, on the author G. K. Chesterton. Big and bibulous, Dr. Fell is an extravagant character, as befits the "great detective" often found in the classic English mystery. He first appears in *Hag's Nook* (Harper, 1933). Carr delighted in constructing complex plots, and he was particularly adept at the specialty known as the "locked room" or "impossible crime" story, wherein the body was found in circumstances in which it is impossible for any human agency to have committed the crime. Carr's most famous novel in this vein is *The Three Coffins* (Harper, 1935; published in England as *The Hollow*

Man). In addition to the Dr. Fell novels, Carr wrote several books about a French sleuth, Henri Bencolin, who debuted in Carr's first novel, *It Walks by Night* (Harper, 1930).

Under the name **Carter Dickson** chiefly, Carr wrote about the cases of Sir Henry Merrivale, or "H. M." as he is known. Like Gideon Fell, H. M. is a bit larger than life, a Character with a capital "C." He first appears in *The Plague Court Murders* (Morrow, 1934). There is considerable humor in the Dickson books, for H. M. is so broadly drawn as to be almost a caricature, but the combination of bombast and complex plots still makes for entertaining reading. Readers will need to look for some of these works in libraries and used bookstores.

For the historical mysteries that Carr penned, see the section "Once Upon a Crime."

Charles, Kate • Though she is an American, Charles has set her series of mysteries in England, where she has lived for more than a decade. Charles infuses her series with her own love of English ecclesiastical history and architecture and makes use of her background as a parish administrator to add conviction to her portrayal of the inner workings of the contemporary church. The main character in the series is solicitor David Middletown-Brown, who is a self-taught expert on church architecture and history, and in this role he often finds himself drawn into nefarious doings of an ecclesiastical nature. In the first book of the series, *A Drink of Deadly Wine* (Mysterious Press, 1992), David must confront difficult secrets from his own past when he is called on for help by a charismatic priest, Gabriel Neville. In the course of this investigation, David meets the artist Lucy Kingsley, with whom he develops an unusual relationship. In later books David and Lucy work together in the unraveling of mysteries. Full of church politics and intriguing characters, this series has much to offer the fan of the traditional English mystery.

Christie, Agatha • According to the publishing world, only the Bible and William Shakespeare have outsold Agatha Christie. Her name is immediately recognized all over the world, across boundaries of language and culture, synonymous with "murder mystery." Christie gave the world of the mystery two of its most memorable characters, Hercule Poirot and Miss Jane Marple. Poirot, he of the "little grey cells," is a former Belgian police detective, retired to England, where he takes on cases as a private detective. He is often assisted by the bumbling Captain Arthur Hastings. Miss Marple is the quintessential English spinster, who lives quietly in her village of St. Mary Mead but who knows more about human nature than any psychologist with a string of university credentials. In the more than five decades in which she wrote, Christie was enormously productive, sometimes penning two novels a year. Having worked in the English equivalent of a pharmacy during World War I, she gained an impressive knowledge of poisons, which she put to good use in her work. Christie played sleight of hand better than anyone, and her puzzles are among the most neatly constructed in the entire genre. She excelled at waving an important clue right in the reader's face, then deflecting attention away from it so that the reader followed a "red herring" instead.

Poirot first appeared in *The Mysterious Affair at Styles* (Lane, 1920; Dodd, Mead, 1927), though one of his most famous cases was *The Murder of Roger Ackroyd* (Dodd, Mead, 1926), in which

Christie used an audacious idea to great effect. Miss Marple made her debut in *The Murder at the Vicarage* (Dodd, Mead, 1930), then appeared in twelve more novels and numerous short stories. During the past decade both characters have been immortalized on the small screen, with the actor David Suchet portraying Poirot and Joan Hickson portraying Miss Marple. Albert Finney and Peter Ustinov have portrayed Poirot on the big screen, while the late Margaret Rutherford and Angela Lansbury offered interesting interpretations of Miss Marple for the movies. Christie's other series characters, Tommy and Tuppence Beresford, were brought to life on the small screen as well, with James Warwick and Francesca Annis in the roles.

Crispin, Edmund • Crispin was the pseudonym used by Robert Bruce Montgomery. Under the name Bruce Montgomery he also composed music, especially music for films (he wrote the scores for some of the slapstick British *Carry on...* movies). Crispin's detective hero is Gervase Fen, an eccentric Oxford don and professor of English language and literature. These are utterly delightful comedy mysteries, with a sharp edge of satire. Crispin's chase scenes are especially hilarious and notable. Fen has a red convertible roadster named *Lily Christine*, which he drives atrociously and at great risk to pedestrians all over Oxford. Probably the most famous of Crispin's detective stories is the much-beloved *The Moving Toyshop* (Lippincott, 1946), a charmingly complicated tale of a toyshop that mysteriously moves in the middle of the night, a missing body, a series of odd legacies, a very frightened elderly woman, and the frenetic amateur investigations of Professor Fen. Unfortunately, Crispin wrote only nine mystery novels and two collections of short stories.

It can be hard to find these in the United States, but they are well worth searching out, especially for fans of classic British mysteries. The first book in this engaging series was *The Case of the Gilded Fly* (Gollancz, 1944; first published in the U. S. as *Obsequies at Oxford* by Lippincott, 1945), a locked-room mystery set in the midst of a turbulent theatrical company where one of the actresses is murdered.

Dickinson, Peter • Peter Dickinson has created some of the most eccentric and memorable worlds in mystery fiction. These are not unearthly worlds, just distinct communities of oddly self-absorbed people who might inhabit the house next door in a quiet London neighborhood. Each household is furnished in marvelous detail and portrayed with loving attention, and every one comes fully alive for the reader. Dickinson's writing is civilized and elegant, very much in the grand tradition of classic British mysteries. His early books often feature an aging Scotland Yard inspector, Jimmy Pibble. Dickinson's first novel was *Skin Deep* (Hodder & Stoughton, 1968), published in the United States as *The Glass-Sided Ant's Nest* (Harper, 1968), a fascinating story about the last survivors of a Stone Age tribe from New Guinea. Pibble is called in when the chief of the tribe is killed, and he finds that the Kus have been living quietly in London for twenty years, trying to keep their customs and taboos alive far away from their jungle home. The story of the tribe and its brush with murder is wild and highly unlikely, but it's also completely absorbing. *A Pride of Heroes* (Hodder & Stoughton, 1969), published in the United States under the title *The Old English Peep Show* (Harper, 1969), finds Pibble dealing with a family of dotty English eccentrics. Two elderly brothers, both famous war heroes, have retired and turned their ancestral acres into a stately home-and-zoo theme park. When Jimmy Pibble arrives to investigate a suspicious death, he has no great reverence for the upper classes, and his sleuthing makes the aristocrats and their hungry lions very nervous. These books are the epitome of English eccentricity, and both won the Gold Dagger Award for Best Novel. *The Yellow Room Conspiracy* (Mysterious Press, 1994) is the story of an old murder that is finally being told thirty years after its occurrence. On the surface it may be a murder mystery, but it's really a story of what life was like for the English upper classes during the war and afterward. Readers will need to look for most of these works in libraries and used bookstores.

Dickinson now is perhaps as well known for writing critically acclaimed children's books as he is for his lively and whimsical mystery novels.

Dickson, Carter • See **Carr, John Dickson**.

Ferrars, E. X. • One of the *grande dames* of the classic English detective story, the late Miss Ferrars produced a novel or two a year from 1940 until her death in 1995. Known in England as "Elizabeth Ferrars," she began writing with a series detective, Toby Dyke, who first appears in *Give a Corpse a Bad Name* (Hodder & Stoughton, 1940). These books are adequate representations of the genteel English mystery, but it was not until Ferrars abandoned Dyke that she found a better and fresher voice. Ferrars writes convincingly about civilized people faced with that most uncivilized of crimes, and each novel unfolds like a small but elegantly presented movie.

In recent years Ferrars adopted two sets of series characters. One series features Virginia Freer and her estranged but not-quite-divorced husband, Felix, who has a gift for staying on the right side of the law—just barely. They appear first in *Last Will and Testament* (Doubleday, 1978). The other series features Andrew Basnett, retired professor of botany (supposedly modeled on Ferrars's husband). Basnett, who debuts in *Something Wicked* (Doubleday, 1984), serves as an effective tool for Ferrars to write simply and affectingly about life in old age. Ferrars is of a special vintage, one that connoisseurs of the English mystery will always enjoy. Readers will need to look for most of these works in libraries and used bookstores.

Gash, Jonathan • Gash gave to the mystery world one of its truly original characters, the raffish antiques dealer Lovejoy. Though Lovejoy definitely has an eye for the women, and more than a way with them, his first love is, and always will be, antiques. He is a "divvie," someone who has special feelings for divining antiques, and his love for them leads him into all sorts of misadventures. The first in the series is *The Judas Pair* (Harper, 1977). The action in the books can be manic, often violent, as Lovejoy dashes about trying to outfox the villains, but the lore of antiques provides fascinating background for the reader. The books have been brought successfully to the small screen, with Ian McShane playing a slightly cleaned-up version of the original in the books.

Heyer, Georgette • The late Georgette Heyer (pronounced more like "Hare" rather than "Higher") is best known for her sparkling and witty historical novels. But she wrote an even dozen mystery novels. While a number of Heyer's mysteries featured the Scotland Yard men Superintendent Hannasyde or Inspector Hemingway, these detectives are generally minor characters in the novels. They solve the crimes, but the focus of the stories is on the characters directly involved in the crime. Heyer's favorite setting was the country house party, and she uses the enclosed setting to great effect. She peoples her books with amusingly eccentric characters; strong undercurrents of jealousy, spite, and hatred; and at least one pair of star-crossed lovers. Among the best of Heyer's mysteries is *Envious Casca* (Doubleday, 1941), with a group of characters for whom "house party from hell" might be an apt description. Heyer excels at creating wickedly funny and entertainingly obnoxious characters. Atypical among Heyer's mysteries is *Penhallow* (Doubleday, 1943), a darker, more brooding work. Readers will need to look for most of these works in libraries and used bookstores.

Moody, Susan • British writer Susan Moody has created a series of mysteries featuring Cassandra Swann, a professional bridge instructor and amateur sleuth. The series begins with *Death Takes a Hand* (Otto Penzler, 1994). Cassandra is a witty and humorous detective, and the books provide plenty of scenes at the bridge tables. Playing a cutthroat game of cards, after all, can set the stage for murder.

Earlier, Moody produced a series of mysteries starring Penny Wanawake, a black amateur investigator. Penny is the daughter of an African ambassador and a titled Englishwoman; she is six feet tall, outspoken, and a talented photographer. She and her jewel-thief lover have set up a scam in which he steals jewels from the rich, and they give the proceeds to feed famine victims in Africa. Penny is beautiful and flippant, with an active sex life in these novels. The Penny Wanawake books are tongue in cheek and lively, with a distinctly wry wit. Readers will need to look for most of the Penny books in libraries and used bookstores.

Roe, C. F. • Behind the initials lurks Francis Roe, a vascular surgeon from Scotland who has retired from medicine to write full-time. He is the author of a series of mysteries featuring Dr. Jean Montrose, a general practitioner, in Perth, Scotland. Known affectionately as the "wee Doc" to her patients, Jean Montrose is a conscientious and compassionate doctor. She is also an enterprising amateur sleuth. While she juggles her medical practice and her sleuthing activities, she also has to deal with a fractious husband and two lively daughters. Her first case is recounted in *A Nasty Bit of Murder* (Signet, 1992; published in England under the title *The Lumsden Baby*). Dr. Jean is called to a stately home to examine the lifeless body of the heir to a noble family. The immediate suspect is the child's dissolute father, but Dr. Jean thinks the mysterious death bears further investigation The policeman assigned to the case, Douglas Niven, finds Dr. Jean a useful ally, and they work together in subsequent cases. Roe writes with a cozy style, Dr. Jean Montrose is an attractive character, and the setting is distinctive.

Rowe, Jennifer • Editor of *The Australian Women's Weekly*, Rowe has made murder "down under" increasingly popular with her series of clever mysteries set in Australia. Despite their setting, the books in this series have very much in common with the classic English mystery. The first novel in the series, *Grim Pickings* (Bantam, 1991), which has already been a miniseries in Australia, is cast in the traditional mold. There is a good-sized cast of characters in an enclosed setting—in this case, an apple farm. The Tender family, along with various friends, has gathered to help elderly Aunt Alice harvest her crop, and immediately the tensions begin to surface. On the scene is Verity Birdwood, known as "Birdie," researcher for one of the television networks, and her nimble mind makes her a natural as an amateur detective. Birdie is a prickly, difficult character. She hides her feelings, even from her best friend, Kate Delaney, who also appears, along with her husband and daughter, in several of the books. The Australian setting is a pleasing change from the usual venue of the traditional mystery, and Rowe's skill in devising intricate plots makes her work delightfully reminiscent of the best of the Golden Age detective story. *Murder by the Book* (Bantam, 1992) offers murder in a publishing house, and the recent *Lamb to the Slaughter* (Bantam, 1996) finds Birdie coming to the aid of an old friend, a lawyer with a high-profile client just asking to be murdered. Readers will need to look for most of these works in libraries and used bookstores.

Sayers, Dorothy L. • Sayers is one of the great names of crime fiction. She is famous for her series of classic novels featuring Lord Peter Wimsey and for her astute essays on the form of the mystery novel. Sayers's mysteries were written during the Golden Age of crime fiction and are very much representative of their time. Critics tend to be divided on her fiction: Some consider her mysteries to be of the highest quality; others think they are steeped in British snobbery and reflect Sayers's love of the aristocracy and the Church of England. But many readers love the novels, and a recent poll of mystery writers in England voted Sayers's novel *The Nine Tailors* (Harcourt, 1934) the best mystery of the 1930s.

As the series begins, Lord Peter Wimsey, Sayers's memorable amateur detective, seems to be an amiable upper-class fool with a set of overly refined tastes. But he matures during the series and is much changed by the influence of Harriet Vane, the woman he loves (although to the very end he still "talks piffle" supremely well). Peter collects rare books and vintage wines, he plays the piano, he speaks many languages, and he does odd bits of work for the Foreign Office in times of international crisis. He is a scholar and a gentleman, but he loves to potter about sticking his aristocratic nose into mysterious crimes. Sayers created many memorable secondary characters, such as Lord Peter's valet Bunter, the curious and intelligent Miss Climpson, the fluttery Dowager Duchess of Denver, and Chief Inspector Charles Parker. Sayers's settings are often beautifully drawn as well; especially noteworthy is her depiction of the fens of East Anglia in *The Nine Tailors*. Sayers's mysteries remain very popular today, and readers still argue about her characters, the ethical issues she raises, and her complicated and exact plotmaking. The two sets of television miniseries based on her novels also have proved to be quite popular. *Gaudy Night* (Harcourt, 1936) is much loved by women readers for its articulate discussions of the practical and theoretical issues that face modern women in their daily lives, and not least for its lively depiction of amateur sleuth and mystery writer Harriet Vane. Sayers wanted to move the detective novel away from pure puzzles and toward the mainstream of modern fiction, and in doing so she changed the form of mysteries in the twentieth century—and told some exceptionally good stories.

Sherwood, John • Sherwood is a retired BBC executive best known for a charming series of gardening mysteries. His heroine is Celia Grant, a practical, hardworking horticulturist with a nursery business she inherited from her husband. The plots of these traditional cozy mysteries revolve around gardening, and botanical clues and information abound. The first one in the series was *Green Trigger Fingers* (Scribner, 1985). Sherwood provides very civilized settings for Celia's adventures; her business may be in England, but gardening and sleuthing alike take her to Madeira, Italy, and Australia. Celia has a young, good-looking, and determinedly working-class assistant, Bill Wilkins, who helps her in the business and in her sleuthing as well. Sherwood also wrote *Death at the BBC* (Scribner, 1983), published in England with the title *A Shot in the Arm* (Gollancz, 1982), a devilishly satirical mystery about office back-stabbing at the BBC in the 1930s. He has written several detective novels in the classic English mode as well. Readers will need to look for most of these works in libraries and used bookstores.

Wentworth, Patricia • Governess-turned-inquiry-agent Miss Maud Silver is the heroine of Wentworth's long-running series of classic English detective stories. Miss Silver put aside ministering to the educational needs of her young charges to open her own discreet business as a private inquiry agent. Though she is a spinster like Agatha Christie's Miss Jane Marple, Maud Silver is a professional who gets paid for her work. She appears as a minor character in *Grey Mask* (Lippincott, 1929), and after a hiatus she reappears as the sleuth in *The Case Is Closed* (Lippincott, 1937) and thereafter in some twenty-nine cases. She often crosses paths with Scotland Yard's Inspector Lamb, who features as the sleuth in several of Wentworth's novels. Lamb's assistant is the attractive young Frank Abbott, for whom Miss Silver has a great fondness. Miss Silver is well known in the better circles of society, and she finds entrée to the troubled households of the upper classes with little difficulty. In most of Miss Silver's cases there is a young couple whose romance seems ill fated because of the murder to be solved, but in Miss Silver's competent hands the case is solved, the young couple are exonerated, and all is right in this very traditional world. Among Miss Silver's best cases are *The Brading Collection* (Lippincott, 1950), *Poison in the Pen* (Lippincott, 1955), and *The Fingerprint* (Lippincott, 1956). Readers will need to look for some of these works in libraries and used bookstores.

For Further Reading • H. C. Bailey; Josephine Bell; Anthony Berkeley/Francis Iles; Nicholas Blake; Leo Bruce; G. K. Chesterton; Anna Clarke; Ann Cleeves; Eileen Dewhurst; Dorothy Dunnett; R. Austin Freeman; Anthony Gilbert; Michael Gilbert; Gerald Hammond; Mollie Hardwick; Cyril Hare; Tim Heald; Janet Laurence; Roy Lewis; Nancy Livingston; Philip MacDonald; John Malcolm; Jessica Mann; Anne Morice; Roger Ormerod; Iain Pears; John Rhode/Miles Burton; Joan Smith; David Williams.

Look for traditional mystery films such as • *Appointment with Death*; the *Bulldog Drummond* series; *Clue*; *Death on the Nile*; *Evil Under the Sun*; *The Last of Sheila*; *The List of Adrian*

Messenger; *A Murder Is Announced*; *Murder on the Orient Express*; *Murder She Said*; *Sleuth*.

And for TV shows • especially PBS series, that feature Miss Marple, Hercule Poirot, Lord Peter Wimsey, Inspector Alleyn, Tommy and Tuppence Beresford, Hetty Wainthropp; and Lovejoy, on A&E.

Sci Fi/Horror/Fantasy Mysteries

The X-Files

Many of us no doubt remember those classic—and slightly campy—television series of the 1960s, *Dark Shadows* and *Star Trek*. Certainly *Star Trek* has proved to have a life far beyond its original air dates in the late '60s, with several spin-off series on television and a string of successful movies. There was even an attempt to update *Dark Shadows* in recent years, but it was unsuccessful, though plenty of fans of the original show are still around.

Horror and science fiction remain popular. But Barnabas Collins turned gumshoe? Captain Kirk and Mr. Spock playing Holmes and Watson?

You bet! A fast-growing trend in popular fiction is the blurring of genre lines between mystery and science fiction, fantasy, and horror. The popularity of the television series *The X-Files* has demonstrated that the viewing public has a taste for such genre-bending fare. Writers of fiction have been doing that for a while, and readers wanting more can find it on the shelves at the bookstore.

Asimov, Isaac • The late Asimov was one of the undisputed giants of the science fiction world. He wrote some "straight" mysteries, such as the stories about the "Black Widowers," a club whose members pose problems for the others to solve but that are actually solved by the waiter, Henry. Asimov's most famous mystery novels, though, are the ones that combine science fiction and mystery in an entertaining way. The first of these is *The Caves of Steel* (Doubleday, 1954), which introduced the detective duo of Elijah Baley, a human detective, and his robot "Watson," E. Daneel Olivaw. Set a millennium in the future, the "robot novels" feature a world where the Earth is overpopulated and the rest of the galaxy has been colonized. Baley is a detective in New York City, one of those who has been left behind on a moribund planet, while others, the "Spacers," have conquered the universe. When a prominent Spacer is murdered, however, it's up to Baley to find the murderer. He has been assigned a partner, one of the despised robots so prized by the Spacers. One might expect a robot to be a perfect detective, but Asimov demonstrates that human intellect can still be superior to robotic intelligence. Baley and Olivaw make an effective team, however, and Asimov gave them four entertaining cases to solve over the course of some three decades.

Chesbro, George C. • Chesbro writes a memorable and highly unusual series about Mongo, a.k.a. Dr. Robert Frederickson, a sleuth with a difference. Mongo may be a dwarf and a doctor of psychology, but that never prevents him from also being a PI with a Superman-like ability to get himself out of some very tough fixes. He is in the PI business in New York City with his average-sized brother, Garth, and they make a very good living of it once they've solved some near-impossible cases. There are always wild and outrageous doings as the Fredericksons cross the country in search of a killer, getting themselves into and out of trouble in every chapter. Like a Saturday-morning serial, the action never stops, and the reader easily suspends disbelief and has a rousing good time. Most of these rattling good yarns have a fair amount of the supernatural or the fantastic about them. Typically enough, the recent *Dream of a Falling Eagle* (Simon & Schuster, 1996) is a hilarious tale of voodoo, a right-wing Republican Speaker of the House (a thinly disguised Newt Gingrich), stolen poems, grisly killings, and assorted mayhem. Readers will need to look for most of these works in libraries and used bookstores.

Cook, Glen • A popular author of fantasy and science fiction, Cook has penned a series of genre-blended mystery/fantasy novels starring a private eye named Garrett. Garrett operates in the city of TunFaire, which is an interesting mix of the city of fantasy novels and the seedy, crime-ridden burg so beloved of hard-boiled detective writers. Garrett is like many of his more conventional private eye peers. He has his troubles with women, he is often short of the ready, and he has connections in the underworld who help him on his cases. Connections like the half elf Morley Dotes, a kingpin in the world of crime, give Garrett some extra muscle and protection when he needs backup. Cook's work contains echoes of classic private eye fiction. For example, *Old Tin Sorrows* (Signet, 1989) takes some of its theme from Chandler's classic *The Big Sleep*, but Cook adds a twist by turning the story into a combination locked-room and English manor house mystery.

The first in the series is *Sweet Silver Blues* (Signet, 1987). Readers looking for a twist with their private eye stories will find Glen Cook's Garrett series amusing and entertaining, but they'll need to look for some of the books in libraries and used bookstores.

Elrod, P. N. • Not many detectives get the chance to solve their own murders, but in *Bloodlist* (Ace, 1990), reporter Jack Fleming does just that. Fleming wakes up one night to discover that he has been murdered and is now a vampire. Putting his investigative skills to work and trying to cope with his initiation into the world of the living dead, Jack sets out to discover who killed him. Patricia Elrod has set her series of vampire detective novels in the Depression era, and the 1930s background helps give the books a suitably hard-boiled feel. Fleming finds a friend in actor Charles Escott, who becomes his Watson. In the course of the series, Fleming also makes the acquaintance of one Jonathan Barrett, also a vampire. Elrod is writing a series of historical novels, with some mysterious twists, starring Barrett. The first of these is *Red Death* (Ace, 1993), set during the Revolutionary War period. Readers will need to look for some of these works in libraries and used bookstores.

Hamilton, Laurell K. • The heroine of Hamilton's genre-bending horror mystery series is Anita Blake, a self-styled "vampire hunter" who operates out of St. Louis. Blake's "real" job is that of animator—that is, she raises people from the dead. In the world Hamilton has created for this series, vampires, zombies, ghouls, werewolves, and other shapechangers are part of society, just like everyone else. There are laws on the books governing various aspects of nonhuman life, and there's even a vampire church, one that truly can promise eternal life. Anita Blake has a personal hatred of vampires, and she's well known for this. Thus, when a serial killer starts preying on the vampires of St. Louis, who better to track down the killer? This is the premise of the first book in the series, *Guilty Pleasures* (Ace, 1993). Subsequent books in the series build on relationships established in this book, and Anita finds her path continually crossing that of various denizens of the undead world. Hamilton has created a fascinating world where fabulous and frightening creatures roam, and one exceedingly tough woman, Anita Blake, tries to do her job and to stay alive.

Harris, **Deborah Turner** • See **Kurtz, Katherine**.

Hawke, **Simon** • Hawke blends mystery and fantasy into a unique blend with a number of "Wizard" novels, set in various cities around the world. Ancient evil is walking the Earth, in the form of some very nasty wizards who prey on the unsuspecting to sustain their energy. The only persons standing in their way are a collection of odd characters, including a Cockney punk, Billy Slade, possessed by the spirit of Merlin, the ancient magician; Wyrdrune, who shapechanges into Mordred; and Kira. Their fight against this hideous evil takes them to various places, such as Santa Fe in *The Wizard of Santa Fe* (Warner, 1991), Los Angeles in *The Wizard of Sunset Strip* (Warner, 1989), and London in *The Wizard of Whitechapel*

(Warner, 1988). Magic, murder, and mayhem make an entertaining combination in Hawke's work, and he spices the mix with an engaging sense of humor.

Hightower, Lynn S. • Born in Tennessee but currently hailing from Kentucky, Hightower began her career with a series of futuristic police procedurals somewhat reminiscent of the popular film *Alien Nation*. The first of the series is *Alien Blues* (Ace, 1992), and the setting is Saigo City about half a century in the future. The main character is homicide detective David Silver, who works with his partner and brother-in-law, Mel Burnett, to track down murderers in this dark and disturbing future world. A group of slightly superior aliens, the Elaki, have come to Earth to help the Earthlings sort out some of their serious problems, but the mix of Elaki and Earthling is an uneasy one. The Elaki resemble extremely large manta rays, and David and Mel are forced to work with an Elaki with the Earth name of String on their investigations. Hightower offers a compelling picture of a world of the future in which the old problems of prejudice and violence have not been solved, they have merely mutated into slightly new forms.

For Hightower's series of contemporary police procedurals see the "Hill Street Blues" section.

Hughart, Barry • An interest in Far Eastern cultures led Hughart to create a fantasy mystery series set in an ancient China that never was. The first of the series, *Bridge of Birds* (St. Martin's Press, 1984), introduced a scholar and wise man, Master Li Kao, and his hulking assistant, Number Ten Ox. A mysterious illness has struck the children of his village, and

Number Ten Ox seeks someone to solve the problem. His choice is Master Li, and together they set out to find the Great Root of Power, discovering crime and adventure along the way. *Bridge of Birds* won the World Fantasy Award for Best Novel. In *The Story of the Stone* (Doubleday, 1988), Master Li and Number Ten Ox investigate the murder of a harmless monk, seemingly done in for a worthless manuscript. In *Eight Skilled Gentlemen* (Doubleday, 1991), the tireless duo are on the trail of the killer of mandarins in the Forbidden City. The only suspects are eight bloodthirsty demons from Chinese legend. If Master Li and Number Ten Ox don't solve this one, the fate of China is sealed.

Hughart offers an entertaining mix of fantasy, detection, sly wit, and intriguing setting for readers looking for something inimitably different. Readers will most likely need to look for these works in libraries and used bookstores.

Kurtz, Katherine, and Harris, Deborah Turner • Two bestselling fantasy novelists have collaborated for this series of fantasy mysteries that offer a blend of mystery, adventure, the occult, and the grand saga of the eternal battle of good against evil. The stories are set in the present day, but the legends, sites, heroes, and villains of the past reach forward to shape the present. Set mainly in Scotland, the novels mix Judeo-Christian mythology with such Eastern ideas as reincarnation. Talismans, places of power, rituals, psychic powers, and studies of the occult supplement the standard detective tools. The main character in the series is Sir Adam Sinclair, the "Adept." The "Master of the Hunt" in the eternal struggle against the forces of evil, Sinclair has considerable gifts at his disposal, and his qualifications as a physician and psychiatrist open many doors. He is accompanied by two seconds: Detective Chief Inspector Noel MacLeod—whose high rank in the police gives the team access to police cooperation, forensics, surveillance, and so on—and Peregrine Lovat, an exceptional young artist whose psychic powers enable him to see the images of reincarnated souls and other spectral phenomena. Lovat's sketches of his psychic visions provide valuable clues to the team as they scour the countryside in search of villains and powerful talismans.

First in the series is *The Adept* (Ace, 1991), in which Scots artifacts associated with legends of occult power are stolen by the forces of evil. The Adept's team must fight to recover them, and the denouement takes place on the shores of Loch Ness. As the series continues, the battle against evil escalates. Good triumphs, but the danger and the difficulty grow with each installment in the series.

Lackey, Mercedes • Well-known fantasy writer Lackey also has written several entertaining novels that blend aspects of the detective novel with the fantasy genre. In *Sacred Ground* (Tor, 1994) Jennifer Talldeer is a private detective of Osage and Cherokee heritage who successfully combines her gifts as a shaman with her skills as a detective. Her grandfather Mooncrow, a revered shaman, is her teacher and guide to the matters of the spirit. In this case Jennifer is trying to figure out just who is behind the mysterious events at a construction site in Tulsa, when fragments from an ancient Native American burial site are unearthed. In a series of three novels to date, practicing witch and psychic Diana Tregarde solves mysteries that involve some otherworldly criminals. *Burning Water* (Tor, 1989), the first published of the series, finds Diana in Dallas, helping an old friend who is now a cop try to stop a series of increasingly savage ritual murders. In *Children of the Night* (Tor, 1990), chronologically the first of the series, set in New York City in the early 1970s, Diana helps track down a mysterious group of vampire like creatures who feed off violent human emotion rather than human blood. Lackey's inimitable blend of spiritualism, fantasy, and detective fiction can provide great entertainment for the adventurous mystery reader.

Pratchett, Terry • Pratchett is the creator of "Discworld," an alternate universe that is so alternate it's not quite like anything else in contemporary fiction. An inimitable blend of fantasy and humor, Pratchett's works have become international best-sellers, with his tales of the folk of Discworld. A number of the recent novels in the Discworld series have elements of mystery and detection, though readers might be laughing too hard to notice. In *Guards! Guards!* (Gollancz, 1989) a young dwarf named Carrot makes his way to the city of Ankh-Morpork, oldest and grubbiest and most important of cities on Discworld. Carrot is a dwarf only because he was adopted and reared by dwarfs; in actuality, he's more than six feet tall. (This should tell you something about Pratchett's sense of humor.) Carrot has decided to join the Watch in Ankh-Morpork and help keep the city on the straight and narrow. (Little does he know....) Some wicked person has begun awakening long-dormant dragons, who have a penchant for breathing fire and destroying things—and persons. So it's up to the highly inept Watch to figure out who's doing it and put a stop to it. All the while the endearingly innocent and naive Carrot gets his introduction to life in the Big City.

In *Men at Arms* (HarperPrism, 1996) the Captain of the Watch is retiring to marry a very wealthy woman, and Corporal Carrot has been tapped to succeed him. Someone has discovered a new and evil weapon, which may be used to kill, and Corporal Carrot must muster his inept forces to seek out the murderer. Pratchett combines hilarious fantasy and a bit of social commentary in a dazzlingly funny novel. The novels are loaded with quirky characters, outlandish situations, and footnotes—footnotes that are as fun to read as the rest of the books. For a reading experience quite unlike any other, give Discworld a try! (Readers will need to look for some of these works in libraries and used bookstores.)

Robb, J. D. • Robb is a pseudonym for best-selling romance and suspense writer **Nora Roberts**. In this series of futuristic police procedurals set in the year 2058, the main character is Lieutenant Eve Dallas of the New York police. A homicide specialist, Eve is a driven and committed professional who will let nothing stand in the way of bringing murderers to justice. In the first of the series, *Naked in Death* (Berkley, 1995), Eve encounters an enigmatic Irish billionaire named Roarke, who is a suspect in the investigation. Against her will, Eve is drawn to this man, and as the series develops he becomes vitally important to her as he helps her overcome the dark secrets of her past. Robb's careful exploration of the character of Eve Dallas and her relationships with those around her make this series compelling reading. The complex plots, filled with interesting details about future developments in computers and other technology, make the narratives as entertaining as the characters. Several of the books involve crimes against women, and through Eve Dallas, Robb makes her passionate interest in the subject powerful but not preachy. There are usually a couple of steamy and entertaining sex scenes per book.

Shatner, William • Former *Star Trek* commander William Shatner has published a very successful set of science fiction mysteries, the *Tek Wars* series. Tek is a kind of druglike virtual reality chip that enables the Tek addict to put on a headset and visualize all kinds of pleasant (or terrible) fantasies. Tek has become a scourge of the twenty-second century in these crossover novels. In the first book in the series, *TekWar* (Phantasia, 1989), former policeman Jake Cardigan has been rejuvenated from his suspended animation on a prison space station. Jake had been unjustly convicted of selling Tek; he is convinced that he was framed in order to get him put away in prison. He returns to Earth to take a job for the Cosmos private eye agency, and is assigned the job of finding a scientist and his beautiful daughter, missing since their plane went down in Mexico. Meanwhile, Cardigan's wife has divorced him while he's been asleep and imprisoned, and he can't locate her or his son. He was a Tek addict; now he is fighting his addiction. In succeeding books Jake finds more adventures while fighting the dreaded Teklords and protecting his family. The Tek novels are fun to read, with plenty of in-jokes about current events and Shatner's acting roles.

For Further Reading • Randall Garrett; Barbara Hambly; Lee Killough; William F. Nolan; J. Michael Reaves; Fred Saberhagen.

Films to look for • *Alien Nation; Alphaville; Big Trouble in Little China; Blade Runner; Brazil; Cat People; A Clockwork Orange; Dead Again; Demolition Man; Don't Look Now; Dune; Farenheit 451; The Fifth Element; Forbidden Planet; Gattaca; Ghost; The Hidden; Highlander; House of Wax; Judge Dredd; The Last Action Hero; Mad Max; Radioactive Dreams; Repo Man; Robocop; Slipstream; Time After Time; Total Recall; Twelve Monkeys; Westworld; The Wraith.*

TV shows • *Alien Nation; The Bionic Woman; Buffy the Vampire Killer; Early Edition; Forever Knight; Hercules: the Legendary Journeys; Highlander; The Lazarus Man; Millenium; Pretender; Roar; The Six Million Dollar Man; TekWar; Twin Peaks; The Wild, Wild West; The X-Files; Xena: Warrior Princess.*

Indexes

Index by Character

Marlowe, Philip...Chandler, Raymond
Marple, Miss Jane.....................................Christie, Agatha
Marsala, Cat..D'Amato, Barbara
Martinelli, Kate..King, Laurie R.
Mary Helen, Sister....................................O'Marie, Sr. Carol
Mason, Perry...Gardner, Erle S.
Mason, Tom...Zubro, Mark Richard
Master Li...Hughart, Barry
Matthews, Daphne.....................................Pearson, Ridley
Mayo, Asey...Taylor, Phoebe A.
Mayo, Gil..Eccles, Marjorie
McClintock, Shirley....................................Oliphant, B. J.
McCone, Sharon..Muller, Marcia
McCorkle, Cyril..Thomas, Ross
McDonald, Paul..Smith, Julie
McEvoy, Jack...Connelly, Michael
McGarr, Noreen..Gill, Bartholomew
McGarr, Peter...Gill, Bartholomew
McGee, Travis..MacDonald, John D.
McKenna, Patience Campbell..................Papazoglou, Orania
McKeon, Bernie..Gill, Bartholomew
McLeish, John..Neel, Janet
McLeod, Noel..Kurtz & Harris
McMonigle, Judith.....................................Daheim, Mary
McMorrow, Jack...Boyle, Gerry
McNally, Archy...Sanders, Lawrence
Mega, James Owen...................................McCrumb, Sharyn
Meiklejohn, Charlie....................................Wilhelm, Kate
Mendoza, Luis...Shannon, Dell
Meren, Lord...Robinson, Lynda S.
Merrivale, Henry..Dickson, Carter
Meyer, Meyer...McBain, Ed
Middleton-Brown, David.........................Charles, Kate
Midnight Louie...Douglas, Carole N.
Millhone, Kinsey..Grafton, Sue
Mills, Todd...Zimmerman, R. D.
Milodragovitch, Milo..................................Crumley, James
Mitchell, Cassandra...................................Wright, L. R.
Mitchell, Meredith......................................Granger, Ann
Mondragon, Rita..Satterthwait, Walter
Mongo (Robert Frederickson)..................Chesbro, George C.
Monk, Dittany Henbit..............................Craig, Alisa
Monk, Osbert...Craig, Alisa

Spenser.. Parker, Robert B.

Spraggue, Michael...................................Barnes, Linda

Spring, Penelope.....................................Arnold, Margot

Stark, Joanna.. Muller, Marcia

Staziak, Pete.. Engel, Howard

Stern, Alejandro....................................... Turow, Scott

Stock, Joan...Tourney, Leonard

Stock, Matthew... Tourney, Leonard

Stokes, "Dipper".......................................Ross, Kate

Stoner, Harry...Valin, Jonathan

Strachey, Donald...................................... Stevenson, Richard

Stryker, Jack..Gosling, Paula

Sturgis, Milo..Kellerman, J.

Sughrue, C. W. "Sonny"...........................Crumley, James

Surgelato, Don.. Matera, Lia

Sussock, Ray..Turnbull, Peter

Swann, Cassandra.....................................Moody, Susan

Swinbrooke, Kathryn............................... Grace, C. L.

Tamar, Hilary...Caudwell, Sarah

Tanner, Evan.. Block, Lawrence

Tanner, John Marshall..............................Greenleaf, S.

Teagarden, Aurora "Roe"..........................Harris, Charlaine

Teague, Kate.. Hornsby, Wendy

Tejeda, Roger...Hornsby, Wendy

Thanet, Luke..Simpson, Dorothy

Thatcher, John Putnam............................Lathen, Emma

Thorn..Hall, James W.

Thorne, Cordelia.......................................Hart, Ellen

Tibbett, Emmy... Moyes, Patricia

Tibbett, Henry...Moyes, Patricia

Tkach, Sasha..Kaminsky, Stuart M.

Tomlinson.. White, Randy W.

Tonneman family.......................................Meyers, Maan

Tramwell, Hyacinth...................................Cannell, Dorothy

Tramwell, Primrose...................................Cannell, Dorothy

Tregarde, Diana...Lackey, Mercedes

Trenka, Betty...Christmas, Joyce

Trent, Philip...Bentley, E. C.

Trethowan, Perry.......................................Barnard, Robert

Trevorne, Kate...Gosling, Paula

Trimble, Lucy...Wright, Eric

Trinkham, Charlie......................................Lathen, Emma

Tryon, Glynis...Monfredo, Miriam G.

Geographic
Index

UNITED STATES, BY STATE

Alabama
George, Anne

Alaska
Stabenow, Dana

Arkansas
Harris, Charlaine
Hess, Joan

Arizona
Jance, J. A. (Joanna Brady series)

California
Baxt, George
Burke, Jan
Chandler, Raymond
Connelly, Michael
Crais, Robert
Dawson, Janet
Dunlap, Susan
Egan, Lesley
Forrest, Katherine V.
Fowler, Earlene
Gardner, Erle Stanley
Gores, Joe
Grafton, Sue
Greenleaf, Stephen
Hammett, Dashiell
Hansen, Joseph
Haywood, Gar Anthony
   (Aaron Gunner series)
Hornsby, Wendy
Kaminsky, Stuart
   (Toby Peters series)
Kellerman, Faye
Kellerman, Jonathan

Kijewski, Karen
King, Laurie R.
   (Kate Martinelli series)
Leonard, Elmore
Lescroart, John T.
Linington, Elizabeth
Macdonald, Ross
Martini, Steve
Matera, Lia
Maxwell, A. E.
Millar, Margaret
Mosley, Walter
Muller, Marcia
Nava, Michael
O'Marie, Sr. Carol A.
O'Shaughnessy, Perri
Padgett, Abigail
Patterson, Richard North
Pronzini, Bill
Roberts, Les (Saxon series)
Rosenberg, Nancy Taylor
Sawyer, Corinne Holt
Shannon, Dell
Simon, Roger L.
Smith, Julie (Paul MacDonald,
   Rebecca Schwartz series)
Wallace, Marilyn
   (Cruz & Goldstein series)
Wambaugh, Joseph
Wings, Mary

Colorado
Davidson, Diane Mott
Dunning, John
Lewis, Sherry
Oliphant, B.J./Orde, A.J.
Ramos, Manuel
White, Stephen

Connecticut
Katz, Jon
Kelman, Judith
Papazoglou, Orania

Florida
Buchanan, Edna
Hall, James W.
Hiaasen, Carl
Leonard, Elmore
MacDonald, John D.
Parker, Barbara
Sanders, Lawrence (McNally series)
White, Randy Wayne
Willeford, Charles
Woods, Sherryl (Molly DeWitt series)
Woods, Stuart

Georgia
Harris, Charlaine
Shankman, Sarah
Trocheck, Kathy Hogan
Woods, Sherryl
  (Amanda Roberts series)

Illinois
Bland, Eleanor Taylor
Campbell, Robert
Churchill, Jill
D'Amato, Barbara
Elrod, P. N.
Kahn, Michael A.
Kaminsky, Stuart
  (Abe Lieberman series)
McInerny, Ralph
Paretsky, Sara
Quill, Monica
Rice, Craig
Zubro, Mark Richard

Louisiana
Burke, James Lee
Grisham, John
Smith, Julie (Skip Langdon series)
Womack, Steven (Jack Lynch series)

Maine
Boyle, Gerry

Massachusetts
Barnes, Linda

Boyer, Rick
Clark, Mary Higgins
Conant, Susan
Craig, Philip
Doolittle, Jerome
Healy, Jeremiah
Higgins, George V.
Kemelman, Harry
Langton, Jane
MacLeod, Charlotte
Mathews, Francine
McDonald, Gregory (Flynn series)
Page, Katherine Hall
Parker, Robert B.
Pickard, Nancy
Tapply, William
Taylor, Phoebe Atwood

Michigan
Gosling, Paula
Estleman, Loren
Leonard, Elmore

Minnesota
Hart, Ellen
Lake, M. D.
Zimmerman, R. D.

Mississippi
Grisham, John

Missouri
Dreyer, Eileen
Hager, Jean (the Iris House series)
Hamilton, Laurell K.
Hart, Carolyn G.
Kahn, Michael A.

Montana
Crumley, James

Nevada
Douglas, Carole Nelson
  (Temple Barr-Midnight
  Louie series)

New Jersey
Bruno, Anthony
Clark, Mary Higgins
Coben, Harlan
Evanovich, Janet
Wesley, Valerie Wilson

New Mexico
Hillerman, Tony
Satterthwait, Walter
    (Joshua Croft series)
Van Gieson, Judith

New York
Adcock, Thomas
Block, Lawrence
Christmas, Joyce
Clark, Mary Higgins
Cross, Amanda
Davis, Dorothy Salisbury
Deaver, Jeffery W. (Rune series)
Friedman, Kinky
Friedman, Philip
Gray, Gallagher
Hall, Parnell
Handler, David
Hayter, Sparkle
Himes, Chester
Isaacs, Susan
Lathen, Emma
Maron, Margaret
    (Sigrid Harald series)
McBain, Ed
Meyers, Annette
Monfredo, Miriam Grace
O'Connell, Carol
O'Donnell, Lillian
Paul, Barbara (Marian Larch series)
Sanders, Lawrence (Delaney series)
Scoppettone, Sandra
Spillane, Mickey
Stevenson, Richard
Stout, Rex
Vachss, Andrew

Wallace, Marilyn
Wheat, Carolyn

North Carolina
Maron, Margaret (Deb Knott series)
Squire, Elizabeth Daniels

Ohio
Borton, D. B.
Hightower, Lynn (Sonora Blair series)
Roberts, Les (Milan Jacovich series)
Valin, Jonathan

Oklahoma
Cooper, Susan Rogers
    (Milt Kovac series)
Hager, Jean

Oregon
Wilhelm, Kate
    (Barbara Holloway series)

Pennsylvania
Constantine, K. C.
Haddam, Jane
Scottoline, Lisa

South Carolina
Hart, Carolyn G.
    (Annie Laurance series)

Tennessee
Adams, Deborah
Grisham, John
McCrumb, Sharyn
McDonald, Gregory (Skylar series)
Womack, Steven
    (Harry Denton series)

Texas
Abbott, Jeff
Albert, Susan W.
Brandon, Jay
Cooper, Susan Rogers
    (E.J. Pugh series)
Crider, Bill
Crumley, James

Friedman, Kinky
Herndon, Nancy
Lindsey, David
Swanson, Doug J.
Walker, Mary Willis

Vermont
Mayor, Archer

Virginia
Cornwell, Patricia
McCrumb, Sharyn
Michaels, Barbara

Washington
Daheim, Mary
Emerson, Earl
Jance, J. A. (J. P. Beaumont series)
Krentz, Jayne Ann
Pearson, Ridley (Lou Boldt series)

Washington, D.C.
Clark, Mary Higgins
Dominic, R. B.
Michaels, Barbara
Patterson, James
Roosevelt, Elliott
Truman, Margaret

Wisconsin
Riggs, John

CANADA

Bowen, Gail
Craig, Alisa
Engel, Howard
Millar, Margaret
Sale, Medora
Wright, Eric
Wright, L. R.

UNITED KINGDOM

Allingham, Margery
Arnold, Margot
Babson, Marian

Bannister, Jo
Barnard, Robert
Beaton, M. C.
Bentley, E. C.
Brett, Simon
Burley, W. J.
Butler, Gwendoline
Cannell, Dorothy
Carr, John Dickson
Carvic, Heron
Caudwell, Sarah
Charles, Hampton
Charles, Kate
Christie, Agatha
Cody, Liza
Crane, Hamilton
Crispin, Edmund
Crombie, Deborah
Curzon, Clare
Dexter, Colin
Dickinson, Peter
Dickson, Carter
Douglas, Carole N.
   (Irene Adler series)
Du Maurier, Daphne
Dunant, Sarah
Eccles, Marjorie
Ferrars, E. X.
Francis, Dick
Fraser, Anthea
Fyfield, Frances
Gash, Jonathan
George, Elizabeth
Graham, Caroline
Granger, Ann
Grimes, Martha
Harrod-Eagles, Cynthia
Harvey, John
Heyer, Georgette
Hill, Reginald
Holt, Victoria
Innes, Michael
James, Bill

James, P. D.
King, Laurie R. (Mary Russell series)
Kurtz, Katherine &
   Deborah Turner Harris
Llewellyn, Caroline
Lovesey, Peter
Marsh, Ngaio
McDermid, Val
McGown, Jill
McIlvanney, William
Meek, M. R. D.
Melville, Jennie
Moody, Susan
   (Cassandra Swann series)
Mortimer, John
Moyes, Patricia
Neel, Janet
Perry, Anne
Peters, Elizabeth
Peters, Ellis
Porter, Joyce
Radley, Sheila
Rankin, Ian
Rendell, Ruth
Robb, Candace
Robinson, Peter
Roe, C. F.
Ross, Kate
Rowlands, Betty
Sayers, Dorothy L.
Sherwood, John
Simpson, Dorothy
Stacey, Susannah
Stewart, Mary
Tey, Josephine
Thomson, June
Turnbull, Peter
Walters, Minette
Wentworth, Patricia
Wingfield, R. D.
Woods, Sara
Yorke, Margaret

AUSTRALIA

Cleary, Jon
Corris, Peter
Day, Marele
Holt, Victoria
Rowe, Jennifer

REST OF WORLD

Arnold, Margot
Dibdin, Michael
Freeling, Nicholas
Gill, Bartholomew
Gilman, Dorothy
Gur, Batya
Highsmith, Patricia
Holt, Victoria
Kaminsky, Stuart M.
   (Rostnikov series)
Keating, H. R. F.
Leon, Donna
Llewellyn, Caroline
Mann, Paul
Marshall, William
McClure, James
Moyes, Patricia
Nabb, Magdalen
Peters, Elizabeth
Simenon, Georges
Sjowall, Maj & Wahloo, Per
Stewart, Mary
Upfield, Arthur W.
Van De Wetering, J.
Whitney, Phyllis A.

HISTORICAL SETTINGS

Alexander, Bruce
Barron, Stephanie
Bastable, Bernard
Baxt, George
Brightwell, Emily
Carr, John Dickson

Author Index